"Who knew that a novel about a faltering company's HR department could be so gripping and compassionate? . . . Medoff does a great job of making the reader care about each and every character."
—Susan Taylor, Book House of Stuyvesant Plaza, Albany, New York

"Shrewd and deeply affecting. . . . Sharply drawn intimate details about the lives of each character add even greater depth and broaden the timeless appeal of this very smart, thoroughly absorbing story."
—*Shelf Awareness*

"A sweet, sharp funny tale."
—*Parade*

"Jillian Medoff unfolds these characters' daily lives, the hours spent at the office, with precision and a strong dose of humanity."
—*Southern Living*

"An engrossing narrative. . . . A sharp-eyed novel of corporate manners."
—*Kirkus Reviews*

"An ultimately hopeful, completely inventive tale."
—*Library Journal* (starred review)

"Incisive. . . . Medoff's scenarios will be familiar to everyone employed everywhere."
—*Booklist*

"A sharp and moving novel."
—*Publishers Weekly*

"A wonderful novel about the most boring place in the world: the HR department at a dreary, failing company. Medoff digs deep into the lives of five exceptionally ordinary people, and turns their trivial work dramas into humane comedy. . . . Brilliant." —*Atlas Obscura*

"The darkness and anxiety surrounding jobs and money is palpable in this book, and Medoff forces readers to experience these feelings through her powerful prose." —*Daily Nebraskan*

"If you've ever worked in a corporate environment, you'll appreciate the satire of this dysfunctional office and its cast of characters. While you're at it, pick up a copy for your work wife too." —Yahoo Lifestyle

"[A] thoroughly enjoyable exploration of what it means to run an office in the twenty-first century. Through the lens of five members of an HR team, we see all the highest highs—and lowest lows—of what it takes to keep a company afloat." —MSN Lifestyle

"In Jillian Medoff's hands, this is much more than a workplace satire. It is a sharp, engaging, and smart look at the people we work with and the deep inner lives we all lead."
—*Popsugar*, Best Winter Books of 2018

"If there is a silver lining within the financial crisis, *This Could Hurt* might be it." —*Free Lance-Star*

"Hilarious as it is heartfelt, this smart novel has everything you've been missing since your favorite shows went off air: love, loss, living life."
—*Bustle*

"Bitingly relatable and unexpectedly touching." —*Daily Break*

"A wickedly-accurate account of life in a small and struggling company during the dark years of the 2008 economic crisis. . . . Unput-downable." —*Relentless Economics*

"Corporate America has been trying to stamp out individuality for decades, but Jillian Medoff brings it back to fresh, sexy, sharply funny life again. *This Could Hurt* is a missive to everyone who feels stranded in an office: You are not alone."
—Katherine Heiny, author of *Standard Deviation*

"The workplace novel has long been the territory of male novelists—well, no more. Medoff's provocative, comic portrait of modern American office life not only upends female stereotypes like a cheap desk, but it also earns Medoff a place at the table. And all for seventy cents on the male dollar."
—Elissa Schappell, author of *Blueprints for Building Better Girls*

"Funny, painful, and ultimately redemptive, *This Could Hurt* is a beautifully drawn canvas of corporate America in all its lunacy."
—John Kenney, Thurber award–winning
author of *Truth in Advertising*

"You wouldn't expect a corporate HR department to house a thrill-ride of a novel, but Jillian Medoff pulls off the impossible here. . . . Medoff knocks this one out of the park."

—Darin Strauss, National Book Critics Circle
award-winning author of *Half a Life*

"Clear your Outlook calendar and have tissues at the ready for this huge-hearted page turner that reaffirms the healing power of plain old kindness."     —Courtney Maum, bestselling author of *Touch*

"Tender and compelling, Jillian Medoff's *This Could Hurt* reveals what happens when the ties that bind us start to fray and we are called upon to care for each other."

—George Hodgman, *New York Times* bestselling
author of *Bettyville*

"Searing, sexy, and surprisingly funny, Jillian Medoff's *This Could Hurt* burns through the pages. No one is safe in this cruel but compassionate take on corporate America. I loved it."

—Marcy Dermansky, author of *The Red Car*

# THIS
# COULD
# HURT

# THIS
# COULD
# HURT

*a novel*

## JILLIAN
## MEDOFF

HARPER

NEW YORK · LONDON · TORONTO · SYDNEY

# HARPER

A hardcover edition of this book was published in 2018 by HarperCollins Publishers.

P.S.™ is a trademark of HarperCollins Publishers.

This is a work of fiction. Names, characters, places, and incidents are products of the author's imagination or are used fictitiously and are not to be construed as real. Any resemblance to actual events, locales, organizations, or persons, living or dead, is entirely coincidental.

HarperCollins books may be purchased for educational, business, or sales promotional use. For information, please email the Special Markets Department at SPsales@harpercollins.com.

FIRST HARPER PAPERBACKS EDITION PUBLISHED 2018.

*Designed by Fritz Metsch*

Library of Congress Cataloging-in-Publication Data has been applied for.

ISBN 978-0-06-266077-0 (pbk.)

18 19 20 21 22   LSC   10 9 8 7 6 5 4 3 2 1

*For Jen Gates and Emily Griffin:*
*without you there is no me*

*This book, being about work, is, by its very nature, about violence—to the spirit as well as to the body. . . . To survive the day is triumph enough for the walking wounded among the great many of us.*

—From the Introduction to *Working*, Studs Terkel, 1972

*Employees are not to be treated the same as family.*

—Miss Manners

## Part I

# PUNCHING IN

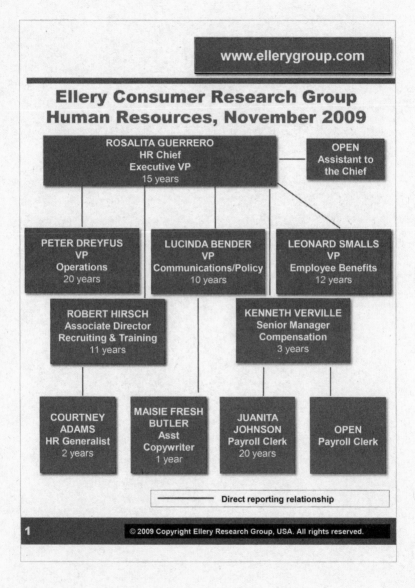

www.ellerygroup.com

# Ellery Consumer Research Group
# Human Resources, November 2009

**ROSALITA GUERRERO**
HR Chief
Executive VP
15 years

**OPEN**
Assistant to
the Chief

**PETER DREYFUS**
VP
Operations
20 years

**LUCINDA BENDER**
VP
Communications/Policy
10 years

**LEONARD SMALLS**
VP
Employee Benefits
12 years

**ROBERT HIRSCH**
Associate Director
Recruiting & Training
11 years

**KENNETH VERVILLE**
Senior Manager
Compensation
3 years

**COURTNEY
ADAMS**
HR Generalist
2 years

**MAISIE FRESH
BUTLER**
Asst
Copywriter
1 year

**JUANITA
JOHNSON**
Payroll Clerk
20 years

**OPEN**
Payroll Clerk

———— **Direct reporting relationship**

ROSALITA GUERRERO,
CHIEF OF HUMAN RESOURCES,
EXECUTIVE VICE PRESIDENT

NOVEMBER 2009

HR had hit bottom. Ever since last year's crash, when Rosa's department shrank from twenty-two to sixteen to thirteen, her people had been terrified. Briefly, manic laughter punctuated their fears (*This cannot go on!*), but resentment followed, then bitterness. Now the group was down to eleven, and despair had set in. Still, Rosa was optimistic. Business is cyclical, she told her husband. Everything rises, eventually. "In a year, we'll be on our way back up." She paused. "Or am I deluding myself?"

Howard didn't reply, so Rosa answered for him. "Sure you are, Rosie. But what are you gonna do? Retire? Can't see that happening, kiddo; not yet, anyway."

The apartment was quiet. Rosa's home was her sanctuary in the sky, a co-op on the forty-fourth floor, with sweeping city views. Unfortunately, she rarely had time to enjoy them. This morning, for instance, she was rushing to a conference at the Hilton.

Her phone rang. Seeing it was Leo, she sighed. Still, she said "Good morning, Leo" with warmth and affection.

Leo jumped right in. "Sorry to call so early, but since you'll be out of pocket all day with Rob—"

"I'll be in after lunch. I have a meeting with Rutherford at four."

"Oh? It's not on your calendar." He paused, awaiting details, but none were forthcoming. After a beat, he exhaled. "Well, okay . . . the new large claims report came in. Have you seen it?"

"Not yet. Read me the highlights."

Every three weeks, Cigna, their health benefits administrator, sent over a list of employee medical claims that exceeded twenty-five grand. Rosa and Leo, her VP of benefits, scrutinized the claims for anomalies before e-mailing the list to Rutherford Beaumont (the CEO, her boss), along with ideas for future benefit cuts. As Leo started to tick off the list, he gasped. "Holy shit, Rosa. Check this out: 'Charges related to bariatric procedure'—that's gotta be Doug LaSalle's gastric bypass, right?—ninety-six thousand dollars!"

"Stop, Leo! That's confidential." Still, she couldn't help picturing the fastidious CPA, who over the past decade had quietly ballooned up to 488.5 pounds (46.6-inch waist, 47 BMI). Knowing Doug's biometrics down to the decimal was Rosa's job; last year, when Cigna declined his surgery, he'd come to her, the HR chief, to help him submit an appeal. "It's also unkind."

"It's just us," Leo said defensively. "And I'm not judging him—*I* don't like being fat either—but that's what Rutherford will say when he sees this claim. From a cost-benefit standpoint, Doug should've joined Weight Watchers for a small weekly fee—or learned to find joy as a large man—instead of having a six-figure surgery on Ellery's dime."

Instead of replying, Rosa opened her bag and took inventory: wallet, sunglasses—she touched her face, regular glasses—flip phone, company BlackBerry, mints, business cards, Advil, the works. She tossed in a Valium (just in case) and then turned to the mirror, applied another coat of Chanel Rouge Noir, and adjusted her St. John knit suit.

As chief, Rosa's appearance was critical. She was a Warm Autumn, so her signature colors were tomato red and blood orange ("vivid" and "commanding," per the makeup girl at Bloomingdale's). Rosa's biggest priority was her honey-gold hair, which she had blown out every third day, highlighted once a month, and deep-conditioned every six weeks. She also had an abiding faith in facials, which left her olive skin smooth and dewy. So despite the featherweight lines at her temple and soft folds around her neck, most people believed she was still in her fifties.

"You know what, Rosa?" Leo was saying. "You should give Rutherford a heads-up about this report before he sees it, just to soften the blow. Also? You need to call Greg in—"

Rosa cut him off. "Fetch the car, James," she said using her drollest, driest uptown accent. "I have a board meeting at noon."

"What does that mean?"

"It means stop bossing me around. *I'm* chief, remember? I know how to do my job."

"I apologize." Leo sounded contrite. "Just making sure nothing slips through the cracks." His voice softened. "It's November tenth, Rosa; I figured you had other things on your mind."

This choked her up. Not only the reminder of the anniversary, but the fact that Leo had remembered. "Excuse me, Leo." Rosa's voice broke. "I should go." As she hung up, tears stung her eyes. "Hear that, Howard?" she said aloud. "It's November tenth."

Howard had been dead five years—to the day—but Rosa still talked to him. Not all the time, not like a nutty person talking to walls, just a playful, bereaved wife who felt the need to say "I haven't forgotten you, kiddo" every once in a while.

Rosa missed her husband terribly. When they met, she was forty-seven and had long given up on love. Then Howard Rothman appeared: older, wiser, and married before; a thickset, bearded man who favored bespoke suits; spoke in low, measured tones; and always knew what he wanted. "Life is more than just punching a time clock," he told her after only a handful of dates. "Marry me." Rosa was skeptical, but as a woman in business, she was used to long odds. Plus, she'd forgotten how delicious it felt to have fun, to look forward to the workday ending. Howard was a corporate attorney, so he understood the demands of a big job, but he took himself less seriously. He found Rosa's bossiness endearing, but only up to a point. When she went too far—shouting at him to set the table, it's almost eight!—he reined her right in. "Fetch the car, James," he'd mutter as he pulled plates off shelves, forks from drawers. "I have a board meeting at noon." As far as he was concerned, Rosa Guerrero could be chief all day, but she wasn't chief here, in their home; rather, she wasn't *his* chief. Here, she was Rosie Rothman, a good-natured kid from the hard side of town who loved soft pretzels, fat franks, the Yankees—and him.

"One thing's for sure," Rosa mused aloud. "Morale won't improve until we restore confidence." With Howard gone, Rosa didn't have many people to talk to, not executive-to-executive, not about issues that made her churn at three in the morning. She knew he wouldn't respond (don't be ridiculous), but voicing her concerns helped her tease out a strategy.

*Rosie*, Howard would've said, *stop winding yourself up. It's just a job.*

This used to infuriate her. HR chief wasn't "just a job." Not at a self-insured midsize company, not in a goddamn recession. Being chief at Ellery in 2009 was like running air traffic control during a typhoon. It was up to Rosa not only to guide each pilot to safety but also to protect the people on the ground *and* maintain the airport's profitability. How could anyone call this "just a job"?

Ellery Consumer Research was among a glut of boutique research firms that had flourished during the tech boom and were now fighting for market share. Using cutting-edge technology and enormous data sets, Ellery provided clients like Walmart and GM with insights into customer purchasing preferences. Theirs was numbers-driven soft-science work, the projects so brainy (cross-media tracking, digital optimization) that only the researchers and (some of) the salesmen grasped the nuances. For Rosa, though, the details of Ellery's work product were critical. As HR chief, she oversaw the entire employee experience from recruiting through separation, along with comp, training, benefits, communications, and policy. She didn't just order printer paper and track service anniversaries; she made sure obese CPAs didn't develop type 2 diabetes, go blind, and lose their jobs. (Leo's cost-benefit analysis was wrong, by the way. Shelling out six figures for gastric bypass now would save Ellery half a million in disability payments later.) As chief, Rosa kept the whole fucking enterprise afloat.

Last night, Rutherford had caught her off guard. He'd stopped by her office, ostensibly to talk about revenue and head count. Instead, he asked, "How's Rob Hirsch doing?"

Rosa glanced up. Twenty-five years before, she and Rutherford had worked together at Sony USA. She was North America division head of HR; he was a cocky young buck on the rise. As part of his executive training, she was assigned as his mentor. Now they were both at Ellery, but the young buck was CEO, and she reported to him. Funny, but when Rosa looked at his face, instead of a craggy, middle-aged man with a graying buzz cut, she often saw a shaggy southern boy, hair too long, drawl too thick, with a lot yet to learn. While she found much of their reversal wonderful, miraculous even, she wondered how it had happened so quickly.

"What about Rob?" she wanted to know.

"Just curious how he's faring. Seems to have a lot on his plate."

"Everyone does, Rutherford. But Rob's just fine; thanks for your concern."

The CEO had paused. "You can't save them all, Rosa," he warned.

Watch me, Rosa thought now, twisting her scarf. Eleven years before, she'd hired Rob to ramp up Ellery's internal training programs. He had a warm, easygoing personality, and though she sensed he was aimless and (possibly) (very) lazy, she had a lot of experience helping immature men find direction. Besides, as a family man, Rob wasn't a bad bet. But the ensuing years were rough, for Rob and for Ellery. When the economy dipped in 2002, and they had to cut staff, she asked him to add recruiting to his training duties and oversee both disciplines. Of course he complained—they all did—but he stepped up, impressing her and, for a time, the CEO. Recently, though, Rosa had noticed a marked shift in Rob's attitude. Could be messiness at home, could be boredom, burnout, could be a lot of things, but he came in late, skipped out early, left his assignments half-finished and wanting. As his supervisor, it was up to her to keep him on task, so she'd asked him to accompany her to today's conference, where she planned to sit him down and set him straight.

*This could hurt*, she'll say, point-blank. *So brace yourself. Rob, people are talking.*

Rosa didn't blame Rutherford for his concerns, especially about head count. They both got the same reports; she knew business was lousy, despite all the corrective measures they'd put in place last year. The market collapsed in September; by November, the executive committee had suspended capital expenditures, frozen raises, gouged budgets, and vetoed all discretionary spending. Two hundred people were let go, and those left behind were shell-shocked. But the following June, when the board nudged Rosa to announce the end of layoffs, she balked. "It's never over, Rutherford," she reminded him, "not even when it's over." Now look—another downsizing was headed their way like an out-of-control train; and this time, the numbers were so bad that anyone could be pushed onto the tracks, not just erratic performers like Rob but hotshots with long tenures and rich salaries—like herself. Ellery itself was a target, too. The company could be spun off, sold for parts, gobbled up by a behemoth like Nielsen. No one knew what was next, which was why she preferred to mete out information strategically, rather than offer hollow reassurances only to contradict herself six months later, blindside the troops, and lose any credibility.

As an HR executive, Rosa had to model smart behavior for other managers to follow. Her primary challenge was keeping her group engaged while simultaneously assessing each one's value as a performer, team member, and long-term investment. A business unit was not a family—period. Yet what fueled an employee's success, and in turn, the company's, were the very qualities that bound a family: loyalty, diligence, humor, grace. As chief, Rosa knew who among her staff she could depend on, as well as who'd love to stab her in the back. But during times of uncertainty, people stepped out of character (usually to their detriment), which is why, once word got out that more cuts were coming, she had to be the voice of clarity and calm. Her team had to know that if the layoff train was en route, she would derail it—even if that meant leaping in front of it.

Down on the street, Rosa signaled a taxi. Sliding into the backseat, she ran through her ever-growing to-dos: Rob, head count, engagement survey, large claims. (Christ, *a hundred grand* for bypass surgery; how could she spin that? ) On top of everything else, it was November 10. *Oh, Howard, I miss you, kiddo.*

"You say something?" the cabbie asked, turning around.

Rosa rolled down her window. The fall air was crisp. She smelled burning leaves, the earthy tang of a policeman's horse. From somewhere far off, she heard the fading howl of a siren. "The Hilton, please." She fished out her phone and speed-dialed Leo. "Leo?" Competing with the wind, Rosa was forced to shout. "*Leo!* You there?"

## 2

ROBERT HIRSCH,
ASSOCIATE DIRECTOR,
RECRUITING & TRAINING

For once, Rob was eager to go to work. Grabbing his keys, coins, and wallet, he pocketed his BlackBerry and hustled down the hall. When he stepped into the kitchen, Maddy smiled. "Look who's up early," she said before returning to the paper.

"Not so early." The table was littered with signs of their daughters, Alison (thirteen) and Jessie (nine): half-eaten waffles, sticky forks, frayed yarn bracelets, two copies of *The Hunger Games*. "Girls gone?" Rob swiped at a puddle of syrup, then sucked on his pinkie. "They didn't say good-bye."

"You were in the shower." Maddy studied his face. "You're in a good mood today."

"I am, yes." Why was that such a surprise? Turning to the cabinet, Rob found his OBER mug and poured himself coffee. (A gift from Allie one long-ago Father's Day, the mug was badly chipped, and the *R* and *T* had since flaked off, but Rob would sooner sever his thumbs than throw it out.) "Big day, Maddy."

Maddy put down the paper. "At work?" Her voice sang of worry: *What now?*

That her husband was unhappy at Ellery was no secret. (Recently,

Rob had learned Ellery was unhappy with him, too, though he had yet to disclose this to Maddy. These days, mention your job and your wife gets the shakes. If 2008 was a rollicking roller coaster of pink-slip parties and ex-banker bacchanals, then 2009 was the head-splitting hangover, the global economy splayed on the couch, wired, tired, too broken to move.)

"Yes, big day at work—but it's all good." Rob shook out a bowl-ful of Fiber One twigs, which he ate over the sink. "So remember last month," he said between mouthfuls, "when Rosa took me to lunch? We went to that conference at the Hilton? Today we have a follow-up."

"Well, that explains the coat and tie. You look great, by the way."

"Actually, I dressed up for you, so you'll think I'm a *play-uh*." Pivoting on his heel, Rob stumbled, but his disco move made Maddy laugh, and he glowed in triumph. If he could do nothing else, if this whole loan idea fell through, at least he and Maddy had fun together, which, given all the hard-luck stories they'd heard about middle-age marriages, was saying something. Still, his wife was right about the sport coat and tie: he had dressed up for Rosa, his boss.

Two more bites of Fiber One, a final swallow of coffee, and then Rob set his milky bowl in the sink and bent to kiss Maddy's neck. "You smell delicious." Fourteen years of marriage, and it still thrilled him to look at her. Padded in all the right places—ass, thighs, tits, belly—Maddy was generous in body as well as in spirit. Her hair was thick and black, her eyes smoky, her skin silky. To Rob, Maddy was magnificent, even as she faced forty-two, with silver strands woven through her curls and a bit of sag and wobble beneath her chin. As for himself, a forty-three-year-old slacker in baggy Dockers and brown sweater-vest, he harbored no such illusions. Rob had been balding and soft as far back as his teens, and even though his face had gained character and he could fill out a jacket, he'd forever feel like a runty sidekick, grateful for any girl's attention.

"Speaking of work . . ." The lenses of Maddy's gold-rimmed

reading glasses winked in the light, making it difficult to see her eyes. "How's Lucy these days?"

"Great," Rob replied, his tone noncommittal.

Lucy Bender was Rob's office wife, but Maddy was convinced she had a crush on him—a crush she felt he encouraged. The first time she said this, Rob had been incredulous. For one thing, he was far too needy for a tough nut like Lucy, a word nerd who once broke up with a guy because he didn't bring any books on vacation. ("Who doesn't *read*? Plus, he kept wanting to *talk*. So *selfish*, right?") For another, Rob craved physical affection, and was forever pawing at Maddy like a sex-starved adolescent. Unlike his real wife, Lucy would never stand for his bullshit.

Rob didn't think Maddy was jealous, but he felt flattered all the same. For this reason and others—because his wife was a knock-out, because she could've married someone with ambition and more hair but instead chose him—he was secretly plotting to buy her an apartment. Lured by Brooklyn's public schools, he and Maddy had been renting a third-floor walk-up in Park Slope for years. Their place was too small, and the neighborhood far too expensive, but a down payment in a less desirable area still required cash they didn't have. Even so, Rob's father had drummed it into his head that only suckers and losers pay rent ("May as well set hundred-dollar bills on fire"); and now, for the first time in his life, Rob might have a chance to stop. He hadn't told Maddy this—he hadn't told anyone, not even Lucy—but the month before, when he and Rosa were at lunch, she'd offered to help him financially. Twenty grand, thirty, it didn't matter; the money (within reason) was his. Rob had reported to Rosa for over a decade, so while they weren't friends per se, they did share a certain closeness, or rather, familiarity. And despite her demands as a manager, she happened to be a very generous person. Three years back, when Lucy's mother needed chemo, Rosa had given Lucy six weeks off with pay to take care of her. Occasionally, too, she offered her guest room to Peter Dreyfus, sparing him a long commute to Jersey. Thirty grand was more than a few extra sick days, however; that kind of money could change Rob's life. But it could also further strain his and Rosa's relationship, which was already suffering a crisis of confidence. This is why he was heading in early today; he wanted to discuss the situation with Rosa, candidly, before saying yes.

Maddy was loading his bowl into the dishwasher. An art historian, she ran a small, upscale gallery in Soho. Today she wore a form-fitting skirt, high-heeled boots, and sheer tights. To Rob, a guy lit up by visuals, she looked sophisticated but sexy, especially her silky red shirt, which was a half size too small and emphasized her big tits. Seeing him stare, Maddy tugged at the buttons. "I overdid it at Thanksgiving," she said, sheepishly. "I have to lose weight, Robby."

"You look amazing." Rob slipped his fingers inside the blouse and stroked the rise of her breast in a circular motion. Watching her face soften, he rubbed her nipple until it became a hard nut. His erection strained the seams of his khakis.

"Don't you have to meet Rosa?" Maddy glanced behind her, even though the apartment was empty. "You don't want to be late."

"Rosa can wait," he said, willing his wife to strip off her boots and her tights, hike up her skirt, and then fall back with her legs spread so he could lick her and lick her until she exploded.

Maddy's eyes were closed, her back arched, but just when Rob was sure he had her, she pushed him away. "Robby, stop. We can pick this up tonight."

A tiny dart of rejection pierced his chest, but he remained undaunted. "I have a surprise for you," he said brightly, arranging himself inside his pants. "So when I come home with something great, don't say you weren't warned."

Maddy handed him the newspaper. "Better not be a dog." She gestured to his head. "Where's your hat? It's freezing today."

Rob moved to the foyer, where he shrugged on his puffy coat

and lifted his bag. "I don't need a hat," he announced, stepping out of his home and into the world. "I'm a warrior."

They both laughed as the door slammed behind him.

DOWN IN THE subway station, Rob stomped his feet to get warm. As usual, Maddy had been right about the hat. It was the first week of December and unseasonably cold. He thought of the warm bed he'd left behind. "*Fuck*," he said aloud.

Peering into the tunnel, Rob spied a bogey in his peripheral vision. Cappy Cuomo! He jerked his head back, but felt exposed, a small animal of prey with nowhere to hide.

Gus "Cappy" Cuomo, formerly EVP of sales, had been axed nine months before. Though they lived only a few blocks apart, Rob hadn't seen Cappy since he stormed out of the office last March, threatening to sue. As head of recruiting, Rob had bookended Cappy's tenure at Ellery, poaching him from Nielsen when the economy was solid, then conducting his exit interview a few years later after everything went to shit. Normally these two events— onboarding and separation—would be their only points of extended contact, but in a stunning act of idiocy, after making the offer, Rob had invited Cappy *into his home*, a rare breach of the work/life fire- wall he regretted once the words left his mouth ("You're so close, Gus. Bring the wife for dinner"). During the strained meal, Cappy zeroed in on Rob's weak spots, questioning his ability to provide for his family ("You're *renting*?") and career decisions ("Jesus, *eleven* years at Ellery?"). Then, apparently interpreting Rob's overture as subservience, once they were back in the office, Cappy began calling him with problems—his computer didn't boot up fast enough, he needed staples, a toilet was clogged—as if Rob were the concierge of a luxury hotel and Cappy its sole occupant. Rob came to despise Cappy, who liked to peacock down the halls wearing European-cut suits and a tasseled beret (hence Cappy). Even more than Cappy's colossal entitlement, Rob hated the guy's stupid fucking hat.

Cappy, who'd spotted Rob and was lumbering over, still wore a stupid hat, this one a woolly trapper deal with enormous flaps that hung like tongues over his ears. "Hey, Rob! Hey!"

Seeing the train approach, Rob pretended not to hear. When it stopped, he elbowed his way inside and then ignored Cappy, who snagged a seat in the corner. At Fulton Street, the doors opened and more people got on. The crowd pushed Rob to the right, and he stopped directly in front of his ex-colleague, who was now tapping out e-mails.

Cappy looked up; Rob forced a smile. "You okay, Gus?" Being in the dominant position, i.e., gainfully employed, Rob infused his question with chords of feeling. *Rough out there, isn't it, buddy-boy? Times are tough, son.* "You're looking good."

"I'll tell you one thing," Cappy boomed. The guy didn't talk, he yelled. "I'm happy as fuck to be done with Ellery. That bitch Rosa tried to screw me out of vacation pay!"

Rob nodded, though this wasn't true; in fact Rosa had managed to get Cappy, who'd been a few months shy of his vesting anniversary, more money than he was due by lobbying Rutherford to credit him for the full five years. (Rob had also benefited from Rosa's largesse: when she found out he'd told Cappy about the layoff a few days prior, she could've canned him too but didn't. "He lives near me," Rob explained. "I see him all the time." Having facilitated hundreds of separations, he understood that so much of the humiliation resided not in the job loss but in the sudden awareness that everyone but you knew what was coming.)

"Listen, Rob," Cappy was saying. "I need a favor. My kid needs a job next summer. He's still in school, but maybe he can work in consumer research—not at Ellery, obviously, but somewhere."

"Grad school? Most researchers have doctorates or are working toward them."

"High school. Kid's a senior. What about HR? Can you call

someone at Nielsen? I'd call myself, but I didn't leave on such great terms—as you know."

"*High school?* What could he possibly do in HR?"

"Whatever you do. Google people, make calls, fill out forms, file shit."

Feeling stung, Rob was about to point out the lunacy of this statement when he realized that this was exactly what he did. He sourced and interviewed potential employees, processed in the ones they hired, and processed out the ones who left. As training manager, he also did other things, but interviewing and processing were his primary activities. So a high school senior could do his job. In fact, a gung ho kid might be a hell of a lot better at it. Even so—he glanced down at Cappy—*fuck you, fucker.* "Sorry, Gus, can't help."

Cappy replied with a grunt, and the two men settled into a tense, resentful silence. Fuck you, Rob thought again. Fuck this job, fuck this life.

When had he started feeling so miserable? Rob couldn't say. But judging from the thousands of résumés clogging his in-box (for Ellery! A company in *free fall*), he'd likely be trapped for a while. This is why buying a home now made sense. First, the timing: prices were still at market lows. Second, his credit was decent (for the moment). Third, he'd build equity he could tap later for the girls' college funds. Finally, he needed a positive diversion. Rob's hope was to find a short sale or foreclosure. Not that he wanted to benefit from some poor schmuck's misfortune, but who was he if not some poor schmuck, too?

The train was packed, and the collective body heat made Rob sweat inside his big coat. Standing over Cappy, he inched closer until their knees touched. When Cappy shifted, Rob pressed harder. The urge to hurt Cappy was unbearable: a kick in the balls, a charley horse, even hocking a loogie on the guy's trapper hat would suffice. Although Rob was by nature a live-and-let-live kind of guy, the past twelve months had ripped something open inside. His salary was just on the wrong side of six figures, which meant raising two kids in New York wasn't merely a slog, it was a testament to all his lousy life choices. Even so, before the downturn, Rob had begrudged no man his prosperity. To his mind, rich guys possessed a knack for making money, a specialized skill akin to woodworking or rewiring a home, one that, owing to the genetic lottery, he simply happened to lack. Indeed, because his own talents were limited to high scoring at Brick Breaker, Rob could appreciate the genius required to turn arcane concepts into cash, cash into wealth. But then the market crashed, and as one banker after another was revealed to be no more gifted than a career criminal who raped the weak and less fortunate, Rob suddenly found himself thirsting for blood.

Fourteenth Street was Rob's stop. It also turned out to be Cappy's, and as Rob disembarked, Cappy's voice rang out behind him. "Hey, Rob. Hold up! I've been meaning to ask: You and Bender still a thing?"

Rob whirled around. "What about Lucy?"

"Just curious how it's going." Cappy's grin was oily. His voice dropped. "Everyone knows about you two."

Mortified, Rob opened his mouth to deny this, but the express train across the platform clattered into the station and cut off any sound.

llery Consumer Research was located on the ninth floor of a renovated building on Tenth Avenue that had once housed a commercial printer. The cavernous space had cathedral ceilings, enormous windows, and thin walls, so every sound was amplified. Ellery employed six hundred people; two-thirds were in New York and the rest divided between sister companies in Raleigh and Atlanta. The staff had expanded and contracted multiple times in the past decade, but today's was the leanest yet. After the last bloodletting, Rosa had assured them HR was safe, which Rob opted to believe despite rumors to the contrary. Really, what choice did he have? When he considered his vulnerability, his thoughts spiraled. In some scenarios, Maddy (whose career, while rich in intellectual rewards, was lousy in earnings) left him for a well-dressed banker with good posture and a diversified portfolio. In others, he harvested his own organs to sell on the black market or cashed out his battered 401(k) and moved to a windswept prairie town. In all of them, his life came to the same bitter end: losing his wife and daughters and sharing his nephew's bunk bed in his wealthy sister's Park Avenue co-op.

It was ten after eight when Rob stepped off the elevator. He walked quickly through the empty reception area and down the long halls. It felt like a graveyard. There used to be an early crew here every morning: long-haired Max from Legal, shaved-head Max from IT, Yvonne with the scarves from Marketing, Drake, the mail guy from Soweto. They were all gone now, along with so many others. Christmas was only three weeks away, but you wouldn't know it from the ninth floor. Rows of cubicles sat unoccupied, with orphaned computer parts and picked-over supplies scattered on desks. A doorless office served as a storage area for chairs, which were stacked haphazardly like a multicar pileup. Months before, a space heater caught fire, and while it was unrelated to the layoffs, the seared swath of floor and sooty streaks on the wall gave the place a dystopian, scorched-earth feeling. The holidays used to be the best time of year for HR. Rob recalled many an afternoon spent drinking martinis and wrapping presents. People brought in home-made banana bread while vendors like Cigna sent gift baskets loaded with expensive cheese and salami. But these days, no one was celebrating. Instead of a twinkling tree and festive poinsettias, there was an anemic cactus with a few strands of tinsel, a wax-encrusted menorah, and a Kwanzaa-inspired fruit bowl. Rob missed the days when he and Lucy would indulge in boozy lunches and then hike to Barneys to see the windows. Now he ate brown-bagged turkey sandwiches at his desk while googling old friends and swallowing his envy.

HR was in the rear of the building, along with Finance, Legal, and the other non-revenue-generating departments. Managers' offices lined up according to length of service, with Peter Dreyfus beside Rosa's large corner spot; Leo Smalls, Rob, and Lucy in the middle; and Kenny Verville, the new kid on the block, tacked on at the far end. A row of cubicles sat outside the offices; most were vacant. With only three assistants, most managers did their own grunt work, but Rob still had Courtney, who was already bent over her desk, typing away. He raised a gloved hand, but she didn't look up, so he kept moving. Lucy had therapy on Wednesdays and wasn't in yet; still, Rob rushed past her closed office door. Rosa's loan was his private business, but it had come about so unexpectedly, he feared if he saw Lucy he might blurt out the story, and that was the last thing he needed: Lucy with her laser focus, drilling him for details.

THREE WEEKS BACK, Rob and Rosa had attended a corporate talent symposium at the Hilton. The networking breakfast was poorly attended, so they decided to stay for the keynote luncheon, but after taking note of the small crowd and dry chicken, Rosa offered to treat him to Mia Dona, her favorite restaurant. As they sat down, she observed that it had been a rough quarter and suggested wine— but only one glass, as she was needed in the office. (Rob, who had no such restrictions, planned to get ripped and skip out.) They ended up ordering a bottle of merlot, over which Rob shared his ideas for restaffing the Travel and Tourism unit, a problem she'd asked him to solve a few weeks before. When he paused—which was her cue to say *Yes, yes, great plan*—she quietly sipped her wine. "Of course," he clarified, "this is just a first pass."

Rosa's head was tilted against the banquette, her eyes half-closed. In repose, her face appeared elastic, as though the skin had slid down and resettled into flimsy folds under her chin. She rarely relaxed, so seeing this pleased Rob. Of course, it would've pleased him more had she praised his ideas, but once he stopped talking, they lounged together in a collegial silence.

"Howard loved Mia Dona," Rosa said eventually. "I like it too, but knowing how he felt makes this place extra special. We were newlyweds when I came to Ellery. Peter helped me settle in, and he and Howard hit it off, which I found so strange. Peter was just a facilities guy; Howard was a big muckety-muck attorney. Funny how that happens, right? Oddball pairs."

Rob had heard the story of Peter and Howard many times. Still, he had an enormous reservoir of patience for women of a certain age, which included his late mother, whom he missed deeply, especially now, as the wine began to loosen him up.

"Howard passed away in November, so this is a tough month for me. But"—she opened a compact and blotted her face—"no need to dwell." She clicked the compact closed. "I'd love another drop," she said, sliding her glass across the table. •

Rob marveled at her composure. If Maddy died, he wouldn't be able to function, even five years later. As other diners passed by, he saw an older man, then another, glance in Rosa's direction. Was she attractive? Lucy believed so, but Rob was on the fence. He preferred a softer look, and Rosa was buttoned-up tight. Her fancy St. John knitwear and nude pantyhose belonged to a bygone era, when HR was called Personnel and run by women with beehives and big bosoms. Over the years, she'd grown heavier around the middle, but her clothing was perfectly tailored and she leveraged accessories to dramatic effect, favoring chunky gold jewelry, sensible pumps, and leather handle bags. "So, Robert," she said. "The year is almost over. How do you feel? Anything you might have done differently?"

"I feel very good." Rob took another gulp of wine. Truth be told, he was feeling very buzzed, having drunk most of the bottle himself. "It was a successful year."

"Rob, have I told you about my mentor, Al? Alfred Moscowitz?"

"You may have mentioned him once or twice." Rob settled in; a story was coming.

Rosa sipped her wine. "Where I grew up, no one went to college; most people didn't finish high school. The boys got jobs, girls had babies. But not me. I wanted a fancy career in advertising; I wanted to work in a skyscraper and make TV commercials. I learned how to type, and became a secretary at an insurance company. Not my dream job—far from it—but my mother was sick and we needed money. Anyway, I was a go-getter, right from the start. Came in early, stayed late, went above and beyond. My boss noticed, and after a year—maybe two, I don't remember—he offered to pay for college. At first, I refused. I was just a kid, but boy, I had pride. 'Thank you,' I said, 'but I don't accept charity.' Al was adamant. 'Don't be crazy, Rosie'—that's what he called me, Rosie—'It's not a gift, it's a loan. Consider it a down payment on your future.' I had no idea what to do. In those days, we talked to our priest, but this was bigger than Father Joe, this went beyond the neighborhood. So I rode the subway—which I liked to do, even though it was dangerous—and had a good long think. In the end, I took the loan and went to night school. I got straight As, went to grad school, and now look at me. I'm chief. That's the power of mentorship, Rob. A great one can change your life." She paused. "I hope you consider me a mentor."

"Of course I consider you a mentor, Rosa." Afloat on the wine, Rob felt sentimental and expansive. "So does Lucy. We all do. We know you're the only one looking out for us."

She nodded. "I'm doing my best to protect you—all of you—but you have to meet me halfway. Rob, don't misunderstand. I know you've been busy with recruiting. Still, training is just as important, and I fear our lack of attention is starting to show." Rosa lowered her voice. "What's going on? Everything okay at home? I'm hearing about unreturned calls, incomplete projects. We need to right the ship before it sails off course. I can help you." She paused to enunciate. "I want to help you."

Rob's heart raced. Was his job at risk? The room suddenly shrank and grew dark. He wanted to bolt; he had to call Lucy. "Everything's great at home," he said, a true statement. "Nothing's changed." Another true statement, but also the source of his woes: every day was another day was another day. When did it end? When he died? He drifted awhile, reflecting.

"It's a wonderful quality," he heard Rosa say. "I'd like to see you capitalize on it."

Was she talking about him? He had a wonderful quality? "Sorry, Rosa. I missed that."

"I said you have a terrific way with people. You're understanding, and you encourage without pushing. Which is why I think you're the ideal manager to create a formal mentorship program. Overseeing such a highly visible initiative will satisfy your training goals and enhance your value to the organization. I spoke with Rutherford, and he agreed."

That she'd discussed him with the CEO made Rob feel better. I *am* understanding, he thought. *And* good with people. Last week he'd successfully guided Courtney through a complex web-based recruiting tool. (Well, she'd guided herself, but he'd printed out the manual for her.)

"So is it possible to get a proposal by the end of the month?" Rosa asked.

"How about next week?" he said magnanimously. And because he was heady with his own *value*, because he decided, right then and there, to buck up and fly right, Rob told Rosa his hopes for the future. "Look," he said. "We both know I didn't plan to work in HR, that I fell into this business and ended up with a twenty-year career."

"That's how a lot of people end up here," Rosa said. "But you've done well."

"'Well' is a bit of a stretch. I've done 'okay.' I do have goals, though."

"Which are?"

Rob considered the question, but nothing came up, jobwise. "I'd like to own an apartment. Lots of New Yorkers rent—we have for years—but I need to build equity."

"So make it happen. Borrow the money from your 401(k). Or better yet, your father."

"Our relationship is complicated." Rob tried to imagine that conversation, him asking his asshole father for money. "He'd lord it over me for the rest of my life."

"If you want it that badly, you'll suck it up, Rob. Besides, it would be a loan, not a gift. If you borrow thirty grand and pay it back over, say, ten years—that's less than two hundred a month. That's practically *nothing*. Look"—she paused to drain her glass—"I'm here to help. I'll do whatever I can. As I said, *I want to help you.* Thirty grand sounds like a lot, but it's really just moving assets between funds. Of course, you have to consider taxes, but that's why we pay accountants." Rosa glanced at her watch. "Oh, Rob! It's so late!" She dug in her purse for her wallet. "Also, Rob? Your Travel and Tourism ideas won't work, but you're on the right track."

It took Rob a few beats to realize what she was offering. "Wait . . ." He coughed into his hand, tried to straighten up. "Rosa, that is very generous." A lump formed in his throat. He felt a sweeping sense of relief. "Thank you; really—*thank you.*"

She looked at him blankly.

"You said you could help." For a second, Rob was afraid he'd misheard, but then Rosa flashed a smile. Her teeth, like her lips, had a purplish cast from the wine, making her look girlish. Yes, she was his boss, but she was also his mentor, maybe even his friend.

"Of course," she said grandly, signing the bill. "I'd be thrilled to help you."

"YOU'RE IN EARLY, Rob," Rosa said now.

Rob stood at her door, still wearing his coat and gloves. Barely 8:20, and already a small crowd had formed outside her office. "One at a time," she told them. "I'll get to everyone. Except you." She pointed to Hal Foster, from Finance. "Unless you're approving another hundred grand in my budget, you're banned from this hallway."

"That's cold, Rosa," Hal said, laughing. The rest of the crowd joined in.

Rob rarely arrived at this hour, so he'd forgotten that Rosa was in highest demand before nine. "I can see you're busy," he told her. "Let's just talk later."

"Later will be worse." Ushering Rob in, she shut the door and sat down at her desk. Facing her computer, she typed as she talked. "Please excuse my back; I'm on deadline. So, I've been noodling over your Travel and Tourism ideas. Let's forget hiring an outsider—it's too expensive. But what if we have Kelly Ray oversee the unit? Crazy, I know, but if we promote from within, there's investment on both sides. Plus, we put a woman in a senior spot. Everyone wins, right?"

Rob was impressed. "Yes, actually." He never could've come up with that, which was why she was chief and he was what he was. "So . . ." For a second, he felt tongue-tied. "Um . . . so, remember the talent symposium? You told me about your mentor? He helped you pay for college?"

"Al Moscowitz." Rosa's face softened at the name. "Great man, changed my life."

"Exactly! Which is why I appreciated *your* offer to help *me*. At first I didn't think I should accept a loan from you—because you're my manager, I mean—but then you didn't mention it again, so I wasn't sure where we stood."

Rosa swiveled around. "Oh?" Her face was immobile, her eyes fixed on his, but Rob could see from her rapid blink-blink-blinks that she was startled. "A loan?"

Rob was stumped. During all his agonizing over whether or not to take Rosa's money, he never considered she might've forgotten offering it. "I had a bit to drink"—he chuckled weakly—"but you did mention a loan, nothing extravagant, just something I could put toward a home."

"How much are we talking about?"

"Twenty . . . maybe thirty?"

"*Thousand?*" She went white. "Rob, there's been a terrible misunderstanding." She shook her head. "I'm . . . well, I'm not sure what to say, except I'm sorry." Her sympathetic smile only made it worse. She looked like a teacher dealing with a subpar student who couldn't grasp a vital lesson. "I believe I was talking about your father offering you a loan, not me."

Rob bit his lip. He was a moron. A moron! What HR chief in this universe would offer her employee a loan? Clearly, he'd had more to drink that day than he realized. "It's okay," he assured her. "No big deal." No new apartment, his surprise a bust. "Sorry to bother you, Rosa."

"No bother, Rob," Rosa said, feigning cheer. "My door is always open."

ALONE IN HIS office, Rob couldn't shake off his shame. Not only had he been criminally off base, but he'd looked like an ass in front of his boss. Ignoring his phone's message light, he launched Brick Breaker on his BlackBerry. Laser-bombing chunks of wall had a soothing effect, and after ten minutes of intense battle, he felt ready to face the day. This meant reading Gawker, making coffee, and hitting the men's room—whatever it took to avoid his work. To-day his plan was to Google-stalk his ex-best friend and send him an e-mail, because why not? Why. The. Fuck. Not. Nothing—not even Evan's probable success—could make Rob feel smaller than he already did. Besides, Evan might respond with encouraging words; maybe he'd take Rob under his wing again. Thirty years before, Evan Graham had saved Rob's life—well, his social life. His first day at Dartmouth, a nerdy Jew among the golden goyim, Rob felt so out of place, he was ready to repack his suitcase and return home to Long Island when his roommate sauntered in.

"Bobby Hirsch!" Evan had extended his hand. "Great to meet you." Wealthy, magnetic, a popular scholar-athlete (with an un-ending supply of the most potent weed Rob ever smoked), Evan instantly boosted Rob's status.

Rob hit compose. ~~Hey Evan! Dear Evan. Dude!~~

From their first day at Dartmouth and for fourteen years after, Evan had been Rob's best friend. Maddy liked Evan too—at first. Amused by his flirting, she chatted with his girlfriends; she even signed off on his and Rob's crazy scheme to quit their jobs and start a business. Evan, for his part, turned up the charm, kept his hands off her, and stayed out of their marriage. When the business tanked, though, the two men's relationship splintered. They tried to stay friends after Rob went to Ellery, but soon drifted apart, then slowly, inevitably, lost touch.

Evan, Rob started again. How long has it been since we've seen each other?

Nine years, he thought.

If you want to get a drink sometime, I'm around. Miss you, buddy. Give a call.

He double-checked his work signature at the bottom, making sure his BlackBerry number was correct. (Rob only had one device, business and personal; Ellery paid, why use two?) Then he sat for a moment, and considered his next move. Hope you're doing great, he added. All good on my end.

He pressed send.

Ten minutes later, Rob was strolling to the conference room for Rosa's weekly senior staff meeting, BlackBerry in hand, a new game of Brick Breaker on the screen.

"Quickly," Lucy said, grabbing his arm. "Can you review my deck? Before Oswald gets here." Oswald was Lucy's nickname for Rosa, along with the Wizard, the Wiz, Oz, Ozzy, Ozzy Osbourne, Ozymandias, Ozzy Gosling, Ryan Gosling, Gooseberry, and other variations reflecting equal parts affection and irritation.

"Do I have to?" Studying his device, Rob launched bombs, then rockets.

She waved a sheath of papers in his face. "Be a pal, Rob."

His game over, Rob flipped through her PowerPoint, entitled *Harnessing Social Media to Promote Policy, Enhance Engagement, and Drive ROI.* "Jesus, Luce. Is all this really necessary?" Each week, Rosa had one of her managers research a timely issue and prepare a case study for the group. Today, apparently, was Lucy's turn. "Handouts, too?"

"Just a few." Lucy's foot jiggled. She had restless legs syndrome (self-diagnosed) and never stopped twitching. "It's mostly filler." Lucy liked to downplay her efforts, but Rob knew better. A veteran of Wall Street, she'd spent her formative years satisfying C-suite HR executives. Now, as VP of communications, Lucy's drive and intensity put the rest of them (well, him) to shame.

Sighing, Rob fished a pen out of his pocket. He traveled light, always had—pencil, pad, company BlackBerry—unlike Leo Smalls (Benefits) and Kenny Verville (Comp), who sat across the table, hunched over their devices, gear lined up like weaponry: laptops, pens, pencils, highlighters, keycards, water, coffee, company Black-Berries, personal iPhones (a novelty, but both men had one), banana (Leo), muffin (Leo), trail mix (Leo), mocha Frappuccino with extra whip (Leo).

"So?" Lucy was waiting.

"Very impressive," Rob said. "The charts really pull it together."

"Please, Rob. You barely read it!" This was from Leo, who continued to tap out e-mails. Beside him, Kenny did the same. Leo was white and very fat, Kenny was black and very tall, and both were overdressed for Ellery's business-casual environment. Sitting side by side in their funereal suits, lips pursed in similarly sour expressions, the two of them looked like a late-night comedy duo performing a skit about kooky employees.

"Lighten up, Leo," Lucy said, blowing her bangs off her forehead. She tucked a rogue strand behind her ear. Over the past decade, Lucy's appearance had changed. Back when she was nearing thirty, with her wide-set blue eyes, unruly hair, and heart-stopping body, she was striking enough to shift the tenor of a room; now, nearing forty, she was still attractive, though pleasing in the way of a once-grand house that has fallen into disrepair. Her looks not-withstanding, Lucy was more than just a colleague to Rob. She was his better half, serving as his conscience at Ellery. She was certainly a harder worker, putting in long hours, gunning for extra assign-ments, mentoring the junior staff. Lucy was the type of employee Rob would've aspired to be if he'd had any aspirations.

Leo kept watching the door. "So where is Her Highness?" He extricated the phone console from a tangle of Ethernet cords and punched in Rosa's number. "Hey," he said to her voice mail. "It's twenty till. Everyone's here except Peter, who's on the road." Sign-ing off, Leo turned to Lucy. "Weird, right? When was the last time Rosa Guerrero was late to a meeting?"

"Nineteen seventy-six," Lucy mumbled. Head bent, she was using a red Sharpie to mark up her PowerPoint. "Maybe Ozzy's talking to Rutherford?"

"No, she would've told me." Leo chewed on a pen cap. "Should we be concerned?"

Rob found Leo tiresome, particularly his sycophantic obsession with Rosa. (On the other hand, this obsession wasn't without its advantages. Case in point: Leo had arrived at Ellery only six months before Rob, but since then, he'd been promoted four times, Rob only twice.) Not that Rob's irritation with Leo was anything new; they'd known each other since 1988, when they both worked at Revlon—Rob on staff, Leo temping. In those days, he went by Leonard and had a full head of hair, which he dyed jet-black, along with his eyebrows. Rob's most distinct memory of Leo was the time he broke down outside their supervisor's office after being denied a permanent position. Crying! In the hall! Over a job! As soon as Leo left, Rob forgot all about him. So a decade later, when Leo called (on Rosa's behalf) out of the blue, inviting him to interview at Ellery, it took Rob a minute to place the name.

"You're quiet," Lucy said, turning to Kenny. "Do you know where Oswald is?"

Shaking his head, Kenny continued to stare moodily at his computer.

What's his problem today? Rob wondered. Our forecasting process too slow? Our software out of date? Though Kenny Verville ("V-as-in-Victory-E-R-V-as-in-Victory-I-L-L-E") was the least experienced of all five managers, his MBA was from Wharton, so he looked down on the rest of them, even Lucy. He was also the best looking. Tall with long legs and broad shoulders, Kenny had a lean torso and massive chest, all of which he accentuated with body-conscious suits. Rob knew he was Kenny's physical inferior, though that didn't bother him. (Given his smallish stature, Rob was always inferior to someone.) What Rob envied was the younger man's future, which, unlike his own, had yet to be written.

Leo's BlackBerry rang. "Oh!" His voice, rising three octaves, made him sound like a cartoon mouse. "It's her, it's Rosa! Hey, where are you? It's late, and we're worried."

"Is she coming in?" Lucy asked, gathering up her folders. "Rather, can we leave?"

"Sure thing, Rosa." Leo kept rubbing his scalp. His now-graying hair was styled in a pompadour to hide his thinning crown. When he got excited, he patted it down as if calming a willful animal. He covered the phone. "Guys, Rosa apologizes for missing our meeting, but she had to step out. She'll be working remotely—"

"*Remotely?*" Lucy balked. "The woman who claims telecommuting killed the economy?"

"So the meeting's canceled?" Rob rose from his seat, resuming Brick Breaker.

"Wait, Rob! We're not done." Attempting privacy, Leo hunched over. "Sure, Rosa. I'll swing by with the files. No, I don't mind; I can also pick up lunch. Turkey on rye? No mustard?"

Hearing this, Rob wanted to knock Leo's head against the wall.

Swiveling back around, Leo clicked off his phone. "Again, Rosa sends her apologies. There was a last-minute crisis."

"What happened?" Lucy asked.

Leo pulled an imaginary thread off his sweater-vest. "She didn't say."

"Of course she did, Leo. What's the crisis, and which files did she ask for?"

Leo sighed. "Vendor invoices going back *ten years*. Records of *everything* we spent—cleaning costs, supplies, water delivery." He stood up and sat back down. "Lucy, she mentioned Dave Darnell."

"In Legal? Okay, that's odd." She grabbed Rob's arm. "Don't you think it's odd?"

Rob shrugged; he couldn't think straight. A patch of fog had rolled in and settled above his eyes, clouding his vision. This loan business was a big blow. Bigger still was realizing Rosa had invited him to lunch last month to criticize his shitty work. She'd offered to help because he was, in fact, at risk. "Very odd," he agreed, hiding his growing panic. "Strange times, Luce."

# 4

"Evan and I had a rare relationship," Rob said the next day. "Most men go their whole lives without admitting they love other men. Not sexually, Lucy. *Intimately*."

"Christ, Rob; that sounds *so* gay. Not that I'm judging," she added quickly. "Be whatever you feel."

It was raining, and their flimsy umbrellas kept flipping up against the wind, providing little protection. The ground was slushy: dirty snow and wet detritus combined to form a gray sidewalk soup. More snow was in the forecast, if not for Friday, then definitely the weekend.

Grabbing Rob's hand, Lucy pulled him up Ninth Avenue. "Let's go. I'm freezing."

Several times a week, Rob and Lucy took a short midday walk. When it was warm out, they strolled along the West Side Highway; on cold days, they roamed the aisles of the Associated Supermarket on Fourteenth Street. A relic from when the meatpacking industry dominated the neighborhood, Associated had a seedy, down-at-the-heels quality, but it was heated, well lit, and offered a destination.

Standing outside the store, Rob waited for the doors to swing open. Lucy was still holding his gloved hand. He considered letting go, but didn't want to make a big deal of it, particularly if she was merely being sociable. "Come on, Rob!" she said. "You do this *every time*. It's *not* electronic; you have to *push*." Using her shoulder to shove the door open, Lucy marched inside. "I'm just teasing you about Evan. Clearly, you were *intimate*."

While it was true Rob and Evan never said "I love you," they had been very physical together. They wrestled like eight-year-olds, clutching each other in choke holds, rolling over chairs, crashing into coffee tables. A natural athlete, Evan had played lacrosse since middle school, whereas Rob, a former smoker, couldn't climb a flight of stairs without getting winded. But when it came to killer instinct they were equally matched. Still, Rob believed their brutality was rooted in affection—and yes, even love.

"It's good you reached out to him," Lucy said. "I hope he'll want to get together."

Rob was insulted. Why wouldn't the best man from his wedding want to see him? "Just because we haven't spoken in a while doesn't mean we stopped caring about each other."

"Actually, Rob, that's exactly what it means." Lucy took off her hat, and the static electricity made her hair fly. "It's warm in here, no?" She unzipped her puffy coat and then leaned forward to unzip Rob's but he jerked away.

"Lucy, I'm not a *toddler*." Startled by her breach of his personal space, he kept his coat zipped, even though he was already sweating.

Under her cardigan, Lucy's blouse had a coffee stain, but Rob didn't point it out. Once upon a time she had been an impeccable dresser, but now she wore the same basic outfit every day: black slacks, white shirt, scuffed loafers. (Leo liked to mock her "uniform" when she was out of earshot. "Since when did this place become the fucking Red Lobster?" were his exact words.) Raising daughters had taught Rob that strict rules governed what he could—and, more important, could not—say about a woman's wardrobe choices; he also knew that Lucy, thirty-eight and divorced, was more sensitive than she let on.

Lucy was still talking about Evan. "I get why you're curious, Rob. That guy could charm *anyone* out of her underwear. How many women do you think he's racked up since 1999?"

"Come on, Lucy." Rob regretted telling her about Evan's conquests. So what if he'd slept with a lot of women? He'd also been a good friend, and had brought out a hidden side of Rob, made him more open with people, more willing to take risks.

In the produce section, Lucy inspected the bananas. "So if you guys were such good buddies, why did you wait so long to contact him? And why e-mail him now?"

"I miss him." The people Rob was closest to—his wife, his daughters, Lucy—he loved deeply, but they were women and thus shared few of his interests. In truth, they overwhelmed him with their moods. Why must they always feel so much, so often? To maintain his sanity, he kicked aside his daughters' pink tulle and nail polish, hunkered down with his music and TV, and shrank the world until it became manageable. (Same with work: unable to keep pace, he parked in a warm spot and dog-paddled.) But now Rob was in a rut; plus, he was aging—and fast. His knees hurt, his back ached, he couldn't fuck as long or as hard as he used to. Worse, he had no one to share this with, no one to say, *Hey buddy, me too.* The guys at Ellery—Leo, Kenny, Peter—were coworkers, not friends, not men to hash out his worries with over beers. Bereft of male camaraderie, Rob felt cold and vulnerable as the second half of his life tunneled before him like a black hole, and while he knew he'd never be eighteen again, Evan's male perspective might shore him up, help him go the distance. For Rob, getting his best friend back felt like a second shot at survival.

Holding a box of half-price Cheerios, Lucy steered him toward the checkout line. "This morning, Oswald left the office *again* for some top-secret offsite. No one knows where she is, not even Leo. It's all very high drama. You have no intel, I take it?"

In the checkout aisle, an elderly man leafed through *People*. His back was turned, but Rob recognized the coat, a black Burberry trench with leather elbow patches. That's Peter Dreyfus's coat, he thought. He leaned forward to say hello, but upon closer inspection, he saw the coat was shabby—frayed collar, torn patches, belt hanging loose. Peter was too fastidious to ever look that sloppy. He was also younger than this guy, whose shoulders slumped in defeat. But when the man turned around, Lucy yelped. "Peter! Oh my God! What are you doing here?" Seeing his face, Rob felt a little foolish. It *was* Peter.

"Hey, Lucy." Peter Dreyfus, VP of operations, flashed a strained smile. As he ran his hand through his silver hair, he craned his neck to peer behind them. "Leo here too?"

Rob shook his head. "Nah. Just us. You coming or going?" He gestured to the old-fashioned garment bag in Peter's arms. "I thought you were on the road all week."

"I am." He sounded tired. "Flew out yesterday, spent the day in Atlanta, then flew back this morning to meet with Rosa. Tonight I'm flying *back* to Atlanta, if you can believe that."

"Did you meet with Rosa in the office?" Lucy asked, but Peter didn't respond. They all watched the checkout girl scan his purchases: a Diet Coke, two oranges, a bag of Snyder's Bavarian pretzels, travel-size Tums. After helping bag the groceries, Peter rested a hand on Rob's shoulder. "I'm off," he said. "Have a good week."

"Wait for us," Lucy said. "We'll walk back with you."

Though the older man nodded, Rob caught his split-second hesitation. Peter was a reserved, quiet man; with his soft leather loafers and dignified air, he acted as the team's elder statesman. Rob could see he didn't want to wait, but was too much of a gentleman to say. Rob waved him on. "Go ahead." He pointed to Peter's belt, which was dragging on the floor.

Smiling gratefully, Peter ambled away, holding the belt in his hand like a tail. Outside the store, when he bent his body against the weather, he seemed to shrink three inches.

"Well, that was strange," Lucy said as she put her cereal on the conveyor belt.

"What was?" Rob peered out the window, wishing he had a stronger umbrella.

"Why did Ozzy blow off our staff meeting yesterday? Why did Peter fly back from Atlanta for just one day? Ozzy was out *all morning*, apparently with Peter, so why didn't they meet in the office? Plus he's shopping *here*, which means he walked an *entire* avenue in this weather for an *orange*. It's like he doesn't want anyone to know he's in town."

"Maybe it's personal, Miss Marple." Despite Peter's twenty-year tenure at Ellery, only Rosa knew him well. He had an ex-girlfriend and an ex-wife, but Rob had never met either one.

"Maybe," Lucy said, but she didn't sound convinced. After paying for her cereal, she swung the bag forward and hit Rob's backside. "Let's motor."

Out on the street, Rob opened his umbrella, which Lucy chose to share instead of opening her own. It was clumsy at first, but she linked their arms and pressed her body close so they could move in unison. To Rob, this felt weird—why was she constantly touching him?—though he said nothing.

"My hands are like ice," she said, clenching and unclenching her right fist, as if trying to leach warmth from the air. "I should've worn gloves." She paused. "I hope you hear from Evan."

"Why does it matter so much to you?"

Suddenly Lucy stopped, right in the middle of the busy sidewalk. "You're my friend; I want you to be happy." She tilted her head up, expectantly. A raindrop ran down her neck. "Rob, can I ask a question?" Her lips were parted, her breath visible in the cold air.

Rob's own breath caught. What was going on? Did she want him to kiss her? Here? Now? "It's freezing, Luce," he said brusquely, extricating himself. "Let's move." He picked up the pace, not caring that she would get drenched.

Lucy trotted to catch up. "Did something happen yesterday? You seemed miserable during the managers' meeting."

"No, nothing." Frustrated, Rob slowed down. Again, he covered their heads with his umbrella; again, she held his arm so they could match strides and stay dry. *Please, Lucy*, he wanted to say. *Please stop touching me. I'm happily married.* Let's say Rob didn't have Maddy, and Lucy wasn't his coworker. Then he might not mind. (She looked pretty right now, too; her cheeks were flushed, her eyes shone.) In fact, if he didn't have Maddy and Lucy wasn't Lucy, Rob would definitely kiss her; he'd probably take her to bed. But he *did* have Maddy, and she *was* Lucy. Feeling her shivering, he fumbled for his gloves. "Take these," he said gently. But instead of putting them on, Lucy clutched his arm tighter, tried to draw him in closer.

THAT NIGHT, ROB couldn't stay hard. He lay on his back under Maddy, who was straddling him and moaning "Robby, Robby." His wife's body usually made him stiffen on sight, but now, as she loomed above him, ample and wanting, he felt dwarfed by her size.

Maddy moaned again. Or did she sigh? Was she bored? Rob couldn't tell, nor could he concentrate. His BlackBerry rang, startling him.

"You gonna get that?" Maddy asked, breathlessly.

"Nah. Who could it be?"

"Lucy?" She smiled playfully. "You should answer. If it's Lucy, it could be important."

Maddy started to roll off, but Rob repositioned her and thrust forward. "Hey, get back here." Thrust again. "It's not Lucy. Who-ever it is will leave a message." He focused his attention back on Maddy, who, he reminded himself, was the best thing that had ever happened to him. They met in a bar when he was twenty-eight. Luckily, Evan wasn't with him that night. So spying Maddy across the room inspired Rob on many levels, the top two being her sex-iness (big curls, big boobs) and that Evan wouldn't get in his way. Rob elbowed his way through the crowd. "Buy you a drink?" he asked casually, hedging his bets. Wonder of wonders, Maddy said yes. Yes to a drink, yes to a date, yes, eventually, to marriage. Even more miraculous: two kids and fourteen years later, they were still hot for each other. (That their small apartment often required them to fool around in hushed tones so as not to wake the kids only helped to jack up the excitement.)

"Robby?" Maddy looked down at his face, into his eyes. "You okay? You with me?"

"I'm good." Lifting his hips, Rob struggled to find their usual rhythm, but his penis was a limp, clammy nub, and the faster he rubbed, the smaller he got. He became hyperaware of his every move: the in-and-out of his breathing, his fingers pressed against Maddy's skin, the way he frogged his legs beneath her as he worked to gain leverage.

A minute later, he nudged her off. "I'm sorry. It's not gonna hap-pen." He moved to position his mouth between her legs so she could finish, but she shook her head.

"It's fine, Rob. I'm okay." Maddy rolled onto her back, her hair fanning out on the pillow. "So why are you sorry?"

"Just am." He reached for his phone. "I should check. It could be important."

"Lucy Bender." Maddy grinned. "That woman is in love with you, Robby. And if I didn't know you were crazy about me, I might be inclined to get very jealous."

Rob started to disagree and then stopped as he heard the voice mail. It wasn't Lucy who'd called—*it was Evan*. Evan called him back! "Bobby Hirsch," he heard for the first time in years and years. His best friend's gravelly laugh hummed in his ear. "Bobby Hirsch. Long time, right? How are you, man?"

Rob's heart soared.

## 5

LUCINDA BENDER,
VICE PRESIDENT,
COMMUNICATIONS & POLICY

DECEMBER 2009

t wasn't love, Lucy knew that. It was a schoolgirl crush, lustful long-
ing to spice up her life. But it was realistic, and therefore unique.
No more mooning over men like the delicious yet unavailable Jamie
Dimon.[1] She was ready to meet someone, to embrace this, this . . .

"This *feeling*," she continued. "Evan and I had a *connection*, a similar *sensibility*. So what if I haven't seen him in nine years? You said
yourself that strange things happen every day."

The therapist nodded.

"Evan is forty-three, so he's the *perfect* age. He went to Dartmouth,
so he's *smart*. He's wealthy, but rather than sponge off his parents,
he became an EMT, so he has *values*. He *cares* about people. He's
also *freaking hot*, which sounds shallow but whatever. Oh! This is
the best part: his first marriage failed. Isn't that great?" Dr. Ahmet's
skeptical look reminded Lucy of a face her mother, Valerie, might
make. "Because we have that in common," she explained. Lucy had

---

[1] The endless media coverage of Wall Street's wicked ways bored Lucy senseless—
except for stories about Jamie Dimon. JD was Lucy's all-time favorite dirty banker.
What a marvel, that man! From his great Hellenistic head and smug, satisfied grin
to his billion-dollar assets and rumored illicit trysts (hel-*lo*, Money Honey!). That
Lucy had once worked in corporate communications for J.P.Morgan & Co. was
their only link; still, his presence (male, older, aggressive) loomed large.

also been married once, right after college. She was twenty-two and (to her mind) wise beyond her years; he was thirty-five, barely divorced, and her comp lit professor; the whole thing lasted nine months—another inappropriate relationship better left forgotten.

"Is this man, this Evan—is he in a relationship now?"

Lucy didn't appreciate the way Dr. Ahmet said "this Evan." It made him feel removed and unlikely, and smacked of disapproval, which again reminded her of Valerie. Funny thing about therapy: Lucy could stifle thoughts of her mother all week, but as soon as she sat down on Dr. Ahmet's bamboo chair, the old bird ran roughshod. "They're in the country this week*end*," her mom had said last night, referring to Lucy's sister, Willa, and brother-in-law, Donald. "Looking at country homes." Her tone was solemn and reverential, as if her younger daughter were viewing burial plots instead of overpriced real estate.

"Where in the country?" Lucy hated herself for asking.

"*Some*where *bey*-ond *Bed*-ford. They want enough *lund* to board horses."

*Lund?* Lucy winced. The bizarre British inflection was a recent development, but no topic thrilled her mother more than the various ways Willa and Donald spent Don's money. All the Bender women were obsessed with money. Lucy's father, a jazz musician, had bailed on them when Lucy was six and Willa three,[2] forcing mother and daughters to live hand-to-mouth. In response, Lucy had excelled in school and became a solid corporate citizen, while Willa succeeded at marrying well, Don being her third rich husband. Lucy loved her work life; all of it—the fixed schedules, the flurry of deadlines; even her keycard (which sometimes stopped working for no reason at all) delighted her. Still, she resented her sister for having it so easy—not that she dwelled on Willa, who like Valerie, was only an issue during

---

[2] Percy Bender (aka Deadbeat Dad, Dirtbag, Percival, Walker Percy, Walkman) left behind no farewell kisses or apologies, just two hundred bucks, a few ratty shirts, and a copy of *On the Road*.

the fifty-minute hour Lucy spent with Dr. Ahmet every Wednesday morning. Then again, Lucy had been seeing Dr. Ahmet for five years (another questionable relationship she had yet to sever), which meant her mother and sister had already gotten way more airtime than either deserved. "According to Google," Lucy continued, "Evan hasn't remarried. Rob will learn more when they get together. They were supposed to meet last Friday, but it snowed."

The snow! The snow! New York had been unprepared for the first snowfall, and the freezing storm paralyzed the city for days. Christmas was next week—New Year's the following—and Lucy wanted Rob and Evan to reschedule soon, on the off chance Evan needed a date for any holiday parties.

"'Tis the season," Dr. Ahmet said, adjusting his tie.

Craving Jamie Dimon was not Lucy Bender's only bad habit. She also stayed in lousy situations too long, believing she could change them despite evidence to the contrary. After graduating from the isolated, suicide-haunted Cornell, she took a job in HR communications at what was then J.P.Morgan & Co. (now JPMorgan Chase). A loyal foot soldier, she toiled in silence for seven years, passing up lucrative offers from competitors along the way. Eminently capable but reluctant to self-promote, Lucy wrongly believed her hard work would speak for itself. Indeed, had the less self-effacing Sally Rakoff[3,4] not leapfrogged over her, she'd still be at the bank today. Instead, she'd spent the past decade at Ellery. Make no mistake: reporting to Rosa Guerrero aka Ozzy Oswald had been a worthwhile learning experience. But time does march on, and Lucy found herself, once again, at a professional dead end, facing the dreaded question *Now what?*

According to Dr. Ahmet, Lucy's inertia and indecisiveness

---

[3] Sally, now HR division head, reported to one of Lucy's former bosses, Walter Grant, aka the Stone Cold Fox. That Lucy had once had a fling with the Fox could be advantageous when (if?) she started looking for a new job.

[4] Everyone complains about men's underhanded, backdoor business deals, but you know what? Women are worse.

reflected her discomfort with adulthood. This had appalled her. "I'm an old soul, a fucking *redwood*. How can you say that?"

"The destructive choices we make as grown-ups are responses to pains we suffered as wee tots," he'd said in his thick Pakistani accent. "You do not assume responsibility and pro-gress, you roost in the nest like a baby bird."

"*Of course* I assume responsibility! I make my own decisions. I support myself."

"You assume responsibility, but not *re-spon-si-bility*. You say, 'Deadbeat Dad abandoned me. I have no life partner. My Wizard boss no longer brings me inspiration. Worst of all, I dwell in Queens. I stay where I am because this is my life.' Better to say, 'I am angry, I am tired, I am uninspired. This is my life because I stay where I am.' There is a difference in the two perspectives, no? It is the goat on the mountaintop yet again."

"Why is living in Queens the worst of everything?"

Dr. Ahmet raised an eyebrow. He was a trim and meticulous man with dark features and long, elegant fingers. "While I do not like that borough myself, I am only repeating what you have told me."

This, Lucy had realized, was the most personal detail Dr. Ahmet had ever revealed. She also realized her life wouldn't change until she entrusted her psyche to a doctor whose therapeutic paradigm transcended Aesop's fables. Still, she adored Dr. Ahmet, who did occasionally produce a well-turned metaphor.[5] Plus he was in-network, so her co-pay was only forty bucks.[6]

"So what do you think about Evan?" she asked Dr. Ahmet now. "For me, I mean?"

---

[5] "We all have a blind spot," he said once. "Yours, perhaps, is love." To which Lucy retorted, "A bit broad, no?" Dr. Ahmet sighed. "Lucinda, such is our challenge. Together, we shall whittle down this vast, wild world until it is a diamond we can hold in our palms."

[6] Dr. Ahmet's eloquence notwithstanding, like her mother, Lucy was a proud penny-pincher.

Two weeks before, when Rob told Lucy he'd e-mailed Evan, she'd said nothing about wanting to meet Evan herself (remeet him, rather). But the very next day, apropos of nothing, Rob blurted out, "Maddy is the love of my life, Luce. I know someone will feel the same about you." His sentiment was so kind, Lucy forgave him for pointing out, again, that he was happily married and she was tragically alone. But then he added, "Evan called last night!" and this segue (however clumsy) did suggest he was thinking along the same lines: *Evan and Lucy would be great together!*

"Your thoughts, Dr. Ahmet?" Lucy repeated. "About Evan? Perfect, right?"

"As I have said: the blind fruited bat sees the sky only when the barn has burned down."

"Which means what? Am I the bat or the barn?"

"You must think it through to its natural destination."

As far as Lucy was concerned, Evan could very well be her destiny. They met right when she started at Ellery. At the time, he and Rob were trying to salvage their friendship after a failed business venture, and every few days, Evan stopped by the office. He was a relentless flirt, and the attention was intoxicating. Once he invited Lucy to get a beer, but Rob went too, and the evening proved awkward. The men were clearly on the outs, and she felt caught in the middle: so drawn to Evan she could barely speak yet aware Rob was a new coworker and friend. Finally Rob went to the bathroom, and Evan grabbed her hand. "Your mouth . . . ," he murmured drunkenly into her ear. "Your mouth is magnificent, Lucy Bender. Christ Almighty, I'd love to . . ." Pressed against his chest, Lucy felt warmth spread between her legs. "What?" she whispered back, imagining Evan's long fingers sliding inside her, the wetness. "Tell me what you want to do." But just as she leaned forward, Rob returned to the table. Red-faced, Lucy sat up. "It's late," she said. "I should go." Very soon after, the two men stopped talking, and the ineffable Evan faded to black.

"Evan feels inevitable," Lucy told Dr. Ahmet. "Like the universe wants us together."

"So you must be open but protective, Lucinda. You do not know the man."

No, she didn't *know* Evan, but she *knew all about* Evan.[7] It was perfect, right? A long-lost flirtation, a resurrected love triangle—these scenarios played out every day for other people. Why not her?

"Dr. Ahmet, does meeting Evan sound"—Lucy didn't want to say plausible, which could raise more questions in the therapist's mind—"healthy?"

"How can I know, Lucinda?" Dr. Ahmet's laugh had the same rich melody as his speech.

Lucy was losing patience. He was the *doctor*. He should have *answers*. Years before, Leo from work had started dating a guy in IT named Horatio. It was only supposed to be a frivolous affair, but when it ended, Leo became so distraught he found a therapist named Dr. Saul. At first glance, Dr. Saul was a loon. Instead of using a chair, he would park himself on the floor and contort his body into complex yoga positions. Once Leo went to the guy's house in Yonkers, where they baked a pie. But Dr. Saul did have great advice. He told Leo to move to Brooklyn, cut out grains, and stop texting Horatio *ASAP*. This was the kind of therapist Lucy wanted—someone decisive like Dr. Saul, someone who'd say, *That Evan sounds dreamy. Go get him, girl.*

"I know you think I'm deluding myself," she blurted out, angry at this sinful waste of time. "But I'm still *trying*; I'm still getting *out*

---

[7] Full disclosure: Lucy went out with Evan a second time, but never told Rob. (She never even told Rob she was attracted to Evan. Why borrow trouble, she figured.) Evan took her to a members-only drinking club in the East Village where, over tequila shots, he told her how crazy-sexy she was and how hard she made him. Later, when they were making out in the cab, he confessed he had a girlfriend. *Of course* he did. Timing is everything, right?

*there.* You know, Dr. Ahmet, I'm not sure this is working." Although she preferred not to get emotional in therapy, there it was. She stood up; her ass hurt from the chair. "I think we're done here." She meant for good.

"So we will pick this up again next week," Dr. Ahmet said, with finality.

## 6

Lucy was stuck. She'd left Dr. Ahmet's office and arrived at her own, but now her keycard wasn't working—again—and she couldn't pass through the turnstiles. The Asian guy at reception offered to buzz her in, but she declined. She needed an ID card that functioned *every day*, and this was *bullshit*. Frustrated, she headed downstairs—again—to see Sanchez.

Lucy's building had two security guards—the Asian guy and Sanchez. Sanchez used to man the reception desk, but then reception became the Asian guy's domain and Sanchez moved down to the basement. Lucy and Sanchez started on the same day ten years back, and since then had exchanged polite nods in the morning and muffled good-byes in the evening. He never asked Lucy to present ID, and when she forgot her keycard, he buzzed her through the turnstiles and then rode with her up to nine and buzzed her in there. If, like today, her keycard malfunctioned, he'd fix it up, one-two-three. All this routine, such familiarity, and yet Lucy wasn't sure what to call him. Sanchez was the name embroidered on his jacket, but she didn't know if this was his first or last name, or, come to think of it, the name of the building. Consequently, Lucy never addressed him directly. Getting around his name took work, but to ask at this point would embarrass them both. "Can I help you, miss?" Sanchez asked when Lucy knocked on his door.

"My keycard," she said, handing it over. "It's not working again."

Sanchez nodded solemnly. Lucy wondered how old he was. His eyes were bright and he had a full head of thick black hair, but his rugged face and weathered skin gave him the wise, weary look of an old-timey cowboy. It took only a minute to log in her number and re-program the settings. Under the lights, his dark hair shone like patent leather. He presented the card with a flourish. "For you," he said, so softly Lucy was forced to lean in. "Have a good day, miss."

"Thank you . . ." The normal beat of conversation dictated she say "Thank you, *Sanchez*." Instead she repeated, "Thank you." She was rarely so thick tongued, but Sanchez's reserve, which hinted at a sensitive inner life (or conversely, a deep dried-up well) made her bashful.

"You're welcome, miss."

"Well, have a good day."

"You too, miss."

Fearing their good-byes would go on indefinitely, Lucy broke eye contact. Sanchez saddened Lucy—no degree; some trade school; an *esposa*, *niños*, and an *abuela* to support; the drudgery of a minimum-wage job. This was only speculation; all she knew for sure was that he had coffee and a bagel for breakfast and, on occasion, subbed in a croissant. Once she mentioned Sanchez to Rob, but he had no idea whom she meant. "He's worked here ten years!" she exclaimed. But when she pointed him out, Rob had shrugged. "I only know the Asian guy," he said defensively. Lucy couldn't believe it. "Rob, that's so *racist*."

With a working keycard, Lucy was up on nine in a flash. As she strode through the halls, she got a text from Maisie Fresh Butler, the empty-headed, untamed assistant she supervised: U HERE YET? At twenty-three, Maisie Fresh spoke in Facebook posts: Malia Obama's poise (*Like!*), cheese enchiladas (*Like!*), or yeast infections (*Dislike!*).

Tapping keys as she walked, Lucy quickened her pace. Yes. I have arrived. Are you here as well?[8] Rather than swing by her office, she headed to the conference room for Rosa's senior staff meeting. But when her phone rang and she saw it was Valerie, Lucy stopped short. Her mother, seventy-six, lived alone in Redding, Connecticut, the rural town where Lucy grew up. She was a cancer survivor; her eyesight was failing. At her age, a phone call could mean anything—embolism, stroke, a fall down a flight of stairs. "Mom? What's wrong?"

Valerie kicked off mid-sentence. ". . . so remember those waxy things on my face? Dr. Hineman . . ." Her voice was lost in static. ". . . biopsy . . ."

"*Biopsy*? Mom? I can't hear you. What *waxy* things? Are they *serious*?"

". . . *surgery* . . . wouldn't say . . . *serious* . . ."

The connection died. "Mom!" Dialing her mother back, she stepped into the conference room and flicked on the lights. "Where are you? Are you at the doctor now?"

"I'm in Costco," Valerie said, their connection restored. "And they have the *cutest* shearling vests. Calvin Klein! Twenty bucks! You need one? Should I send one to Willa?"

"Seriously, what's up with your face?"

"They're cysts!" Valerie's voice boomed. "Dr. Hineman took them off, one, two, three. *Lucy*, these Costco vests are *luxurious*. Why are they so cheap?"

She hung up.

Lucy knew the closeness she shared with her mother bordered on unhealthy, but that's what she got for not having a husband and children to absorb all her downtime. Three years before, when the

---

[8] Lucy hated texting and refused to communicate using LOL and IMHO and other god-awful abbreviations. Having worked hard to acquire a brilliant command of the English language, she could not—would not—butcher it.

old bird got cancer, Willa and her second husband were content to throw cash in Valerie's direction while Lucy waded knee-deep into the suck. Truth be told, when brought to her knees, their mother preferred Lucy, not Willa, holding her hand. But according to Dr. Ahmet, this is what Lucy wanted, too. "You are full of resources, Lucinda," the therapist liked to remind her, "full of hustle. If you wanted a family, you'd have one." Lucy wasn't sure if she wanted a family or not, although the idea of molding a child's mind intrigued her. Mostly, she wanted to create something of her own, something enduring she could be proud of. Marriage and raising kids would satisfy this, but Lucy suspected she could be just as satisfied renovating a country home. She wanted to be in charge, but of what, specifically, was where it got murky. Having no choices, no agency, was a killer, but having too many was equally crippling.

Five minutes later, Rosa strolled into the conference room with a cheery "Hello, Lucy." Lucy greeted her with a pleasant "Good morning," which she repeated to Leo, and then Kenny, as they stepped through the door. Rob shuffled in last, eyes downcast. *You okay?* she mouthed, but he didn't look up. God, he looked depressed. Not about Evan, she hoped.

Rosa settled into her seat at the head, shuffled her papers, and looked up. "Before we get going," she said, glancing around the table, "I have an important announcement."

In the past two weeks—since Rosa skipped their meeting with no explanation—tensions in the office had heightened. While Rosa's calm demeanor gave nothing away, Lucy was sure more layoffs were coming. Or a merger. Or a sale. Coming from banking, she knew all the signs: strange men in dark suits wandering the halls, long-term projects (i.e., the engagement survey) put on indefinite hold, the boss having hush-hush talks behind closed doors and refusing to share details. In this way, Lucy wished she were more like Rosa—strong willed but levelheaded, focused, restrained. Look at her now, the perfect chief-in-charge with her St. John ensemble, polished pumps, and fresh lipstick. While HR was considered a soft spot in many companies, Rosa managed her staff with the highest rigor, pushing them to act as thought leaders and take on projects beyond their comfort zones.[9]

"This news will be made public in a few days, but I felt you should hear it from me first."

"Hold on, Rosa." Lucy looked around. "Shouldn't we wait for Peter?"

"That's what I have to tell you." Rosa paused. "Peter is no longer employed at Ellery."

Leo's mouth fell open. "Why?"

"He's no longer up to the job. Recently, there've been incidents where he failed to think through the consequences. I can't tell you anything more. Peter is our coworker and he's also an employee who deserves our discretion." She cleared her throat. "Moving along . . . you each have a spreadsheet detailing your 2010 initiatives. Rutherford is cutting another ten percent of our budget, so I need to know which projects are mandatory and which can wait."

*Peter Dreyfus?* While Lucy felt vindicated—she *knew* something was up when she saw him at Associated—she couldn't believe it. Peter was a good man and a hard worker. As VP of operations, he single-handedly kept three facilities up and running. Of all Rosa's senior managers, Peter was the only one who'd trekked into the office during last week's blizzard. The guy wasn't perfect, but his spotty memory and lousy communication skills were eclipsed by a herculean work ethic. Besides, he was only sixty-three. Certainly Rosa could have kept him on a little longer. What were a couple of years when weighed against a man's self-respect?

Concerned, she texted Leo from under the table. Did you know

---

[9] Thanks to Ozzy, Lucy worked closely with Rutherford Beaumont, Ellery's CEO. In fact, owing to her years on Wall Street, he sometimes consulted her on strategy issues, which was exhilarating. At the bank, she was more likely to spot a unicorn than her elusive but all-knowing spirit sensei Jamie Dimon.

about Peter? Across the table, his BlackBerry blinked, and she saw him glance down. Leo liked to pretend he knew everything, but this time he shook his head. *No.*

"Rosa, this is a big shock," Lucy said. "Can't you tell us anything else?"

Rosa considered this. "What I don't understand is, who *drives* into Manhattan from central Jersey in the middle of a snowstorm? I had to pay for *two nights* at a hotel because he couldn't get home." She looked at Lucy. "Does he have *no* common sense?"

Lucy was stunned. Despite Rosa's promises of discretion, not only had she just disparaged their favorite colleague but she had intimated he was too addled to do his job. "When is Peter's last day?" Lucy asked bitterly. Business or not, Peter Dreyfus had been an Ellery employee for twenty years; he deserved better.

Rosa's tone was curt. "That's all being worked out." Leftover gift baskets sat on the table; after examining their contents, she held up a box of stoned wheat crackers. "Anyone?" No takers. Next she found a tin of Godiva chocolates, and, after what looked like a silent debate over whether or not to indulge (she didn't), passed it around. This time everyone else dug in. "So." She pointed to Lucy. "Where's my engagement survey?" As Lucy opened her mouth to remind her it was on hold, Rosa shook her head. "No excuses, get it done." She turned to Kenny. "Salary projections?"

Kenny bit into his chocolate. "I gave them to Henley."

Rosa's jaw tightened. "I told you to give them to *me.* Let's get one thing straight, guys"—she eyeballed her managers—"we are under major scrutiny. Not just HR, every business unit at Ellery. Your projects have to be completed flawlessly, and on time. I am trying to protect you, but my reach has limits." She rummaged through a second basket. "Send me those projections, Kenny. Lucy, I need that survey. Please. I don't want to ask again."

Rosa's BlackBerry rang, which was strange. She was a stickler for the house rules, which dictated that devices must be switched to vibrate—no rings, pings, or jingles. Stranger still was her distress. "They're here *now*? Yes, I can join you." She stood up to leave but didn't move. "Excuse me," she said absently, as if disoriented. "I'm sorry." Then, snapping to attention, she walked out.

FIFTEEN MINUTES LATER, Rosa hadn't returned.

"You really don't know what happened with Peter?" Lucy asked.

"How would I?" Leo said.

"Rosa tells you everything, Leo."

Empty Godiva tins littered the table. The crackers were gone, too, along with the mini salami packets, cheese spreads, and nuts. Lucy, Rob, and Leo were alone—Kenny had hit the road as soon as Rosa turned the corner. "This is the first I heard about the hotel," Leo told her, wadding up a ball of salami wrappers. "I also have no idea where she went just now, though I assume it has to do with Peter."

Lucy couldn't remember ever seeing Oswald so rattled. Usually nothing fazed her. The phone rang all day. People showed up, unannounced. But she was the master of triage: Roger is at Lenox Hill with chest pains. *Call Maureen at Cigna; our group number is 07042.* Lindsey wants to lodge a second complaint about Sid. *Tell Lindsey to stop by at two, but ask Dave Darnell from Legal to sit in.* There's mold in the supply closet. Should Peter call OSHA? *Are you insane? Peter should go to the hardware store and buy bleach.* Jeremy Flynn gave himself an insulin injection during a client meeting again. *Oy vey.* Once Lucy asked Rosa if she minded the chaos. "Mind?" Rosa had laughed. "I love it! I'm like the Wizard of Oz, handing out hearts, brains, and courage to people in need."[10]

Ten years before, Lucy had been the one in bad shape. Kicked to the curb after seven years of exemplary service at JPMorgan, she came to Ellery for an interview feeling beaten up and unwanted.

---

[10] And lo, Ozzy Oswald was born.

Rosa crowed over her education and experience and then hired her on the spot. As a result, Lucy devoted herself to her new boss. Along with Leo, Rob, and Peter, they built an HR infrastructure, improved benefits, and implemented a competitive pay structure; they also developed performance metrics, revamped training, revitalized recruiting, and spruced up the office with artwork and greenery. Their days were long and intense, and Lucy relished coming to work. After a few years, however, she began to feel antsy, though this had nothing to do with Rosa, and everything to do with Lucy.

"Leo," she asked again, "you really have no idea why Peter is leaving?"

"Maybe he drained the minibar at the hotel," Rob interjected.

"That's crazy." Lucy changed the subject. "Did you and Evan make a plan?"

"Why are you bringing Evan up?" Rob cut his eyes at Leo, as if to say, *Don't discuss my private life in front of him!*

"Why shouldn't she?" Leo asked, scanning his phone. "We're all friends here."

Rob turned to Lucy. "You told him about Evan?"

Leo sighed. "*Of course* she told me, Rob. She wants *you* to go out with Evan so *she* can go out with Evan. Isn't that obvious?"

"You want to meet Evan?" Rob looked shocked, which in turn shocked Lucy. How could he be so obtuse?

"*Re*meet," she corrected. "I already met him, remember? We had drinks, all three of us. But sure, I'm curious."

"It seems kind of weird to reintroduce you when I haven't seen him in years myself." Rob slumped in his chair. "As you know," he added.

Lucy told him to forget it. "Dumb idea." But in her mind, she was screaming. *What the fuck, Rob? Don't be selfish!* Couldn't he see she was desperate for a passion project, a new career, a new man— *something*? At work, she went through the motions (she was an A-plus student, after all), but until Rosa retired, Lucy would have to chug,

chug along, with no *heat*, no *energy*, no *va-va-voom*. For the past decade, at least once a year, she got sick of all the bullshit and went on
interviews, only to wind up more conflicted: How could she leave
Rosa, the only person who'd offered her a job when she needed it
most? Who gave her time off to care for her mother? No matter how
high the pay or impressive the position, Lucy wouldn't take it. Then
the market crashed, and now she couldn't leave even if she wanted
to. Why pay Lucy one-sixty a year, when two younger, hotter eager
beavers[11],[12] cost only fifty apiece?

The door opened and Kenny strolled in.[13]

"Did you see Rosa?" Leo asked.

"En route." Kenny sat down and hunched over his phone, so
when Rosa showed up a moment later, it looked like he'd never left.
This pissed Lucy off even more.

Revived, Rosa dove in with no preliminaries: "Ellery is in a
slump—that's not news—but we have a plan to revitalize. Rutherford
wants me to take a more strategic role for the next few months, which
of course I'm happy to do. However, it means I have to appoint someone to run our day-to-day business. Rob and I have discussed what
I need in a number two, but I'd also like to hear from each of you."

Whoa, Lucy thought. Hold on a second. Rosa had spoken to
Rob *already*? When was this? Was she thinking of promoting *him*?

---

[11] Lucy would never forget the time a former boss told her he wished she was
"younger and hotter," as in, "I'd be a lot more excited to come to work if my
staff"—aka Lucy, his entire "staff"—"was younger and hotter." To which Lucy
replied, "That was rude and disrespectful. If you ever say anything like that to
me again, I'll report you."

[12] Oh wait, she never said that. She never said anything. This was in the early
1990s; people were still reeling from Anita Hill's testimony. No one knew what
to say or how to say it. Instead Lucy mumbled *Shut up, shut up, shut up* under her
breath and vowed to one day tell the world and change the system.

[13] Where did Kenny get off? He was so disrespectful—ignoring Rosa's requests,
working from home whenever he pleased. Lucy would *never* treat her boss like
that, nor would she put up with it, if she were in charge. Sadly, Rosa was far
too impressed by Kenny's Wharton pedigree to fire, or even reprimand, him.

Lucy *loved* Rob, but he wasn't qualified to be Rosa's number two.[14,15] Maybe Lucy wasn't either, but she'd like to be considered, at the very least. She *could not* end up like Peter Dreyfus: middle management until she got old and fuzzy and then pushed out to sea on an iceberg.

As Rosa's words sank in, the energy in the room shifted. Phones were abandoned, spines straightened. Revitalizing meant restructuring, which meant more layoffs. The news about Peter Dreyfus only compounded the situation—if they could get rid of a respected colleague like him, they could do the same to any of them.

Lucy was imagining someone, Kenny probably, bundling her up in a ragged coat and shoving her into the open water. "Actually, Rosa," she blurted out, surprising herself. "I'd like to toss my hat into the ring."

Rosa raised her eyebrows. "Thank you, Lucy. I'll take that under advisement."

Her heart fluttered. That was proactive, right?[16] Feeling cocky, she took a stab in the dark. "Rosa, can you please tell us what happened to Peter?"

"I told you all I can. Peter used company funds without prior authorization. He violated policy." Shaking her head, she appealed to the group. "I've tried to intervene, but business is worse than they're letting on. I'll tell you something else: I was set to make Peter my number two, and now I have to replace him. How do you think that reflects on my judgment?"

Rosa was clearly distraught—she'd never reveal this kind of weakness otherwise—yet something about her story didn't add up

---

[14] Exhibit A, Rob's recent case study: "Acceptable Office Attire," which he illustrated using pictures his daughters cut out of *Glamour* magazine.

[15] And why hadn't Rob said something to her? They were *best friends*—she'd never keep news like this from him.

[16] This is *exactly* what Jamie Dimon would do: seize life by the big brass cojones.

for Lucy. Why fire Peter for one hotel bill? Couldn't he just pay the money back? But her confusion curdled into panic as she recalled all the cab rides home she'd charged to Ellery. Across the table, Rob seemed to be panicking too. They locked eyes. *Fuck.*

"Guys." Rosa sighed. "This is neither the time nor the place to discuss Peter. However, I will talk to Rutherford again. I don't want to talk out of school—or give you false hope—but there have been situations in the past where he reversed a decision. It's a long shot, but I'll see what I can do. In the meantime, we must concentrate on our work."

Lucy felt better. See? Rosa was reasonable. Plus, if anyone could persuade Rutherford to keep a valued employee, it was her. And Lucy liked Peter. He wasn't her first choice for a boss, but so what? "Rosa, thanks for being such a good advocate. Not just for Peter, for all of us."

Rosa took it in stride. "That's my job, Lucy."

A few days before Christmas, Lucy drafted the all-staff memo herself: *After twenty years of service. . . . We wish him well on all his future endeavors. . . .*

Peter Dreyfus was gone.

## 7

Lucy was tipsy. It was five o'clock on Thursday and the office had closed early for New Year's Eve. Due to a flurry of year-end deadlines, she was in Rosa's living room, helping her finalize some business correspondence. (And, as usual, a few personal letters.) This wasn't the first time Rosa had invited Lucy over for an afternoon of booze and business, but in honor of the holiday, she'd opened two bottles of pricey champagne. So now, in addition to being drunk, Lucy was horny and aching to flirt. This was unfortunate. She was due to meet up with her (single) (female) friends at the Four Seasons before ten, but at this rate, she'd be asleep by eight thirty.

"Hey, Rosa." Lucy was seated at her boss's rolltop desk in the living room, staring at the computer screen. "Did Rob ever say anything to you about his friend Evan?"[17]

---

[17] Lucy and Rob no longer discussed Evan. Upon hearing Lucy wanted to meet him ("remeet," she insisted), Rob closed down like a beach house shuttered for the season. "Jesus," he repeated. "Why does every woman go for Evan?" Lucy felt like a terrible friend. No one likes to be an afterthought—even if he is happily married with two great kids—so she ceased all Evan-related conversation. While this improved her and Rob's relationship, it cut off her pipeline, forcing her to pump anyone, even Ozzy Oswald, for info.

Peering over Lucy's shoulder, Rosa shrugged. "Why would Rob talk to me about his friend?"

Lucy didn't have an answer for that—he wouldn't—so she changed the subject to Peter. "One day, he's your new number two, and the next, he's out the door." She was slurring her words: *he's* came out *heesh*. Sit up, she commanded. Clear your fat head! You cannot get stuck here!

Playfully, Rosa smacked her shoulder. "Nosy girl. Focus on my letter, not on gossip."

The apartment was warm. Rosa held a champagne flute, and the glass was sweating, so cold water dripped on Lucy's head. "Did we say 'This year has been our best ever'?"

Lucy nodded. "Three times."

"What about 'We are poised for unprecedented growth'?"

"That too."

"I don't want to discuss Peter," Rosa blurted out, clearly wanting to discuss Peter. "But people shouldn't say I fired him. He resigned. Second, I did everything in my power to keep him—as I would for anyone on my staff, including you—but he felt it was time. That's business. People come and go. You can't get emotional, which is advice you should heed. You let your feelings get in the way of your job. To be a good chief, you have to separate church and state. Third, the hotel bill pissed me off; I won't deny it. But let's be clear: none of this is your concern. We need to finish my Christmas letter, which is late. Your engagement survey and policy review are also late, but it's New Year's Eve. I don't want to dwell on unpleasantness." Rosa was slurring too.

"Instead of 'Christmas Catch-up,' let's call this your 'New Year's Note.'" Lucy refused to address the survey, which was *not* late. Lucy was never, ever late; Rosa simply kept changing the rules.

"Fine." Rosa poured them more champagne, then tipped her head and drained her glass.

Seeing this, Lucy decided to slow down on the drinking, which didn't enhance their work product; nor were they well suited as col-laborators, even when sober, being bossy, opinionated women who would fight to the death to have the last word.

"Let's see what we've got." Bending forward, Rosa swayed. "Whoa! That sip went right to my head." She nudged Lucy off the chair and donned her glasses. "Happy holidays to la Guerrero *familia* . . ." Rosa skimmed the rest. "Lucy! This is all you have? Where is everything I said about hitting our targets and unprecedented growth?"

Lucy cracked up. "This is the letter to your *family*, Rosa. They don't care about revenue targets. They love *Kung Fu Panda*. Why don't we write about that?"

"How do you know about *Kung Fu Panda*?"

Lucy sighed. "I edited Michael's college application essay. Remember?"[18]

Rosa was studying a grainy black-and-white photo hanging over the desk. In it, a young couple wearing evening clothes stood on a beach, ankle-deep in the surf. Lucy moved beside her. She pointed. "Is this you?" She was referring to the woman, whose head was back, long hair aloft in the wind. It could've been Rosa—they both had the same wide mouth and heavy-lidded eyes. The man gazed at the woman adoringly, his left arm circling her tiny waist.

"Peter is a good man," Rosa said absently.

Lucy agreed. "Of course he is. No one would ever say other-wise." In fact, she noticed how Rosa always softened when he was around, and her face took on a girlish glow; but then, as if catching herself, she'd suddenly stiffen up and act overly formal. "You haven't heard from him?"

---

[18] Rosa didn't write nearly as well as Lucy—or that's what Rosa claimed when she asked Lucy to take over the bulk of her correspondence. (Lucy knew she was being played, but flattery was an effective motivational tool.) Rosa laid it on even thicker when she wanted Lucy to edit something personal. "No one has your magic touch, Lucy girl!" she said, handing Lucy her nephew's essay for Baruch. (Michael got in. Natch.)

"I have not. But as I said, it's business. You can't get attached."
Rosa stood up. "I'm hungry." Her hand brushed the photo. "These
are my parents in Spain years ago. They had true love. When I was a
kid, I used to look at this picture and imagine it was me. I had three
goals in my life: to get out of the South Bronx, land a good job, and
find true love."

"You succeeded. You live in Manhattan, you're chief. *And* you
found true love."[19,20]

"My father loved my mother," Rosa said, still gazing at the picture. "Still he left. She said he was prideful, but I think we kids
came along and got in the way. He loved her, not us."

"But you have a wonderful life," Lucy said, anxious to lighten
the mood, which had suddenly turned dark. "All your dreams came
true."

Rosa considered this. "When you put it like that, I guess they
did. Are you hungry?"

Lucy was ravenous, but if she said yes, Ozzy would make her stay
for dinner, and that could not happen, the two of them, alone on
New Year's Eve, bemoaning the absence of men.

Rosa lived on the East Side. She'd bought her apartment in the
late 1980s while at Sony; when she left, she used her severance to
renovate the kitchen and bathrooms. Now (according to Leo), it was
worth almost seven times what she'd paid. Lucy thought the place

---

[19] Though Rosa's marriage ended with her husband's tragic heart attack, the
fact that she found love after forty made Lucy's own situation seem less dire.
Lucy especially enjoyed hearing Rosa say she was satisfied with her choices.
Childless women in business are constantly asked to explain themselves, so
when Rosa said, "I didn't want to be a mother, I wanted to be an executive,"
Lucy felt hopeful. Honestly, Lucy never saw thirty-eight coming. To her
mind, she had lots of time even as the walls were closing in and the windows
slamming shut.

[20] To clarify: Lucy wasn't ruling out a baby, per se, but until the right man, or *a*
man, came along (and Evan was looking less promising every day) or she did
it herself (equally unlikely), motherhood was a back-burner project.

was gorgeous: off-white walls, sleek leather couches, un-fucking-believable views, built-in bookcases. Lucy's own co-op, further down on the economic scale, was less well appointed. She read once that Forest Hills was becoming hip, so while she was at JPMorgan, she used a big chunk of her savings to buy a stupid one-bedroom. Then she sat back and waited for the influx of youngish, like-minded go-getters. Twelve years later, she was still waiting.

Relaxing on the couch, Lucy listened to Frank Sinatra booming over the speakers. "Since when do you like Sinatra?" she asked Rosa, who'd returned from the kitchen.

Smiling, Rosa set down a tray loaded with nuts, olives, chips, and cheese. "We have a special guest joining us." As she said this, the intercom buzzed.

Lucy imagined it was Evan on his way up; that somehow Rosa and Rob had conspired to arrange a blind date for New Year's. The idea was lunacy, but for a second her spirits lifted.

Rosa was bustling around, plumping up pillows. After double-checking her lipstick, she pulled open the door. "Hel-*lo*," she called into the hall.

"*Hello*," a man called back. "*Hello. Hello. Hello.*"

Leo (Leo?) stepped inside holding champagne and roses, his cheeks and nose red from the cold. On his head, he wore a knit cap with reindeer horns; tinsel hung from both horns.

Spotting her, Leo's eyes widened. "Lucy? Oh my God! How funny. I thought you'd be . . . well, I don't know where, but definitely not here."

A beaming Rosa clapped her hands. "I did it! I surprised you both! I knew neither of you had a date, and figured we could have our own party."

Disappointment set in. While Lucy liked Leo, a little of him went a long way—which is why they were coworkers, not friends. With coworkers, you could spend time, confide secrets, even sleep together, but no matter how intimate the experience, you could always say "This will end, thank God" and go home. The one time she and Leo had ventured into a nonbusiness setting (2004, Saturday matinee, *Million Dollar Baby*), they both cried so hard, they couldn't look at each other. For her to be here, tonight, with these people, was to put her carefully constructed silo system at risk.

Oh no, Lucy thought. No, no, no way. But Leo had already draped himself around their boss's shoulder. "Thank you, Rosa," he said. "This is *so sweet*." He turned to hug Lucy, who immediately gagged—he stank of booze.

"What happened to jetting off to San Juan?" she asked, holding her breath.

"Horatio, the little shit, backed out," Rosa answered for him.

"You were going with *Horatio*?" Horrified, Lucy exhaled. "What would Dr. Saul say?"

Leo looked sheepish. "It was a brief holiday jaunt—we're *not* dating again—but flights were so *outrageous* we passed." He poured a glass of champagne, which he downed in three gulps, and then poured a second and drank that too. "Got any vodka, Rosalita?" Plopping down on the couch, he took off his winter gear—gloves, coat, scarf—everything but the hat. He shook his head in Lucy's direction. "Don't you just *love* the antlers?"

"*Love* them." Lucy turned to Rosa. "You're so generous." She was touched but concerned. Was this normal for a boss to do? Arrange a party for her direct reports? Invite them to her home under false pretenses?

Rosa's eyes shone. "So, this is what we'll do. After we have nibbles and more bubbly—if you're nice, I'll open the *really* good stuff—we'll get appetizers from Mia Dona. Then we'll each order dinner from our favorite place—my treat. We'll have a Hit Parade Buffet!"

Looking around, Lucy had a sudden, shattering vision of herself at forty-five and then fifty-five and then sixty-five, hosting her own orphan New Year's Eve out in Queens. Maisie Fresh, Courtney, and the payroll clerks would sit around her cheap coffee table, eating pigs-in-blankets and Velveeta nachos. "Rosa, this is lovely, but I really should get going."

Shushing her, Rosa pointed to the ceiling. "Listen, Leo. Listen to the music. It's for you."

Leo nodded his approval. Closing his eyes, he sang along to "Summer Wind" as he swayed drunkenly from side to side. Meanwhile, Rosa was handing out menus. "The charred octopus and lobster *fra diavolo* are divine. Screw Weight Watchers." She looked Lucy in the eye. "Stay, Lucy girl, enjoy yourself. You can meet your friends later."

At ten minutes to twelve, the three colleagues were molded to the couch cushions, surveying the wreckage. Between them they'd consumed two more bottles of champagne, several types of cheese, nuts, olives, hot wings, chips and dip, crudités, beef carpaccio, garlic bread, ricotta pansotti, and some unusual but delicious bacon balls. For dinner, they each ordered an entrée: cheese fondue for Leo, pasta with Dungeness crab for Rosa, and Ray's pizza for Lucy. Now, drunk, stuffed, and wiped out, they stared at the TV.

Lucy's stomach ached. The night had turned out to be fun; better, she decided, than being out on the prowl with all the other sluts. She was reminded of Christmas two years back. Rosa had invited her managers and their partners on a booze cruise around New York Harbor. Lucy went solo, figuring she'd hang out with Leo, but he glommed on to Rob's wife. At first Lucy felt trapped (out at sea! with work people!), but Kenny was also alone, and they ended up getting wasted on martinis. That night was fun, too, in a bizarre way. Recalling how a drunken Kenny had climbed to the edge of the boat, lifted his arms, and shouted, "I'm king of the world!" Lucy felt a glow of fondness for all her colleagues, even Leo, who was now zoned in on the TV as if Ryan Seacrest were sending him private messages through the screen. Unfortunately, Rosa ruined the moment. "Lucy?" she asked. "Why haven't you finished the engagement survey yet?"

"Come on, Rosa," Leo interrupted. "It's New Year's Eve!"

"I also want the policy review." No longer woozy, Rosa sat up. "Our policies are not current, including vacation accrual. The new guy in Marketing? Edward Fuchs? He just took a week off. News flash: people have to work more than a week before they're eligible for vacation. At Sony, I had an *entire staff* devoted to policy. But at Ellery, we don't do formal policy reviews, so one day Edward Fuchs is hired, and the next, he's taking vacation."

Yes, Lucy realized, a surprise New Year's party with your co-workers *is* weird. And no, she wasn't being ungrateful. Jamie Dimon would neither hold nor attend a gathering like this. "I'll do the policy review, but just so you know, Edward Fuchs had a personal issue—"

"*I* know about his issue, but why do *you*? We're supposed to be HIPAA-compliant."

"The ball is about to drop!" Leo yelped. Then, catching Lucy's eye, he winked. *Hang on*, he seemed to be telling her. *It's almost over.*

Seeing this, Lucy felt a surge of affection for him. "Leo's right; let's watch the ball." It calmed her, knowing they were in this to-gether. A few more minutes wouldn't kill her.

"Edward Fuchs's wife was diagnosed with a rare blood disease," Rosa continued. "He can take time off to care for her, but people are calling it 'vacation,' and it's not. It's 'family leave,' and when she dies it will be 'bereavement.' It's important to use precise termi-nology."

"Rosa, I said I'd look at the policies."

"Lucy, you want to be chief. You threw your hat in the ring. *Lucy, to be chief, you have to think everything through.* It's all connected—our *policies* and *people*, our corporate *personality*, how we're *perceived*—and it all flows through HR. That's the first thing my mentor taught me. HR is the warm, beating heart that pumps blood into the organi-zation. HR gives the company life, and as chief, everything flows through you. But to be successful, you must consider the whole organ; if you only focus on one artery, you kill off the patient. The larger concern is liability: one day someone will sue us because they weren't allowed to take vacation two days after they were hired. Edward Fuchs was allowed, so that's discriminatory. Sounds nutty, but they'll win. Why? *Because we don't have standardized policies.* You think I was so revered at Sony because I stayed under budget?" She scoffed. "It's because we never got sued."

"Stop it!" This time Leo shouted.

"Fine." Rosa was silent for a few minutes, and then she asked, "Did you know Peter was my first friend when I started at Ellery?" Lucy nodded, but she wasn't thinking about Peter. She was thinking about Evan. One way or another, she would see him again, and then maybe next year she'd have a different set of holiday plans.

Leo's eye caught the TV. "Oh my God! *We missed it.* We missed the countdown."

Rosa and Lucy turned. On the screen, confetti was flying and everyone was kissing. "Is this a bad omen?" Lucy asked, distressed. Closing her eyes, she bowed her head. *Please, God*, she begged even though she wasn't a religious person, and in fact believed blind faith to be symptomatic of an uncurious mind. *Please, God, I promise not to ask for anything else if I can be with a man next New Year's.* She looked up. *A man who isn't Leo, I mean.*

"We can do our own countdown." Rosa raised her hands. "Come on, together now—Ten, nine, eight . . ." But no one was in the mood, so the numbers were muttered, resentfully, under their breath. "Seven . . . six . . . five . . ."

## 8

## ROSALITA GUERRERO,
## CHIEF OF HUMAN RESOURCES,
## EXECUTIVE VICE PRESIDENT

Rosa was churning. This executive committee was a waste of time, energy, and resources. How many "mission-critical" lunches had she endured over the years? And how many of them had actually accomplished anything? Right now, it seemed like her entire career had been one long fifty-year meeting focused on a single theme: profits were imperative, people were expendable.

"We've been over this," she snapped, cutting off Charles Mayfield (EVP Finance). No one interrupted Charles, but life was too goddamn short. "To build a world-class research firm, you can't keep cutting staff. You do the opposite: recruit top talent with competitive salaries."

Charles lifted his turkey wrap and took a bite. From this angle, he looked like a jowly reptile unhinging its jaw. A narrow, skinny twist with a jutting Adam's apple, Charles was a man of enormous appetites. Rosa once saw him polish off six doughnuts in six bites, like a magic trick. He reminded her of her brother Nando, another man with an interior hole he could not fill up. Knowing this, she felt a twinge of compassion for Charles, even though he, like her brother, was selfish, egomaniacal, and mean-spirited.

"We're not hiring more staff," said Landry Eliot, Charles's chubby sidekick (EVP R&D).

"No way," Heather Gilmore (EVP Legal) chimed in. Heather, another skinny twist and the only other woman on the committee, had forged her career by echoing any man seated to her right. "If anything," Heather added now, "we should be picking off senior staff. Most of them are overpaid, anyway."

Landry cracked a smile. "Twenty-two, twenty-two, twenty-two, Rosa," he added, referring to the practice of hiring twenty-two-year-olds to work twenty-two hours a day for twenty-two grand a year.

"Then we're all out of a job." Rosa scanned the room. "No one here is under forty."

"It was a joke, Rosa," Landry said. "Where's your sense of humor?"

"That was funny," Heather said, like a puppet.

Rosa ignored them. "People are burned out," she told Rutherford, who sat across the table, where she couldn't nudge him. "We can't cut any deeper." As head of HR, it was her duty to advocate for employees—the actual people doing the actual work—although this way of thinking was anachronistic. No one at this level cared about the work; these people hadn't done any real work in years. To the executive committee, staff was merely a number that moved from one side of the ledger to the other. In fact, if they could find a way to run Ellery without employees—just get rid of them for good—they'd jump all over it.

The meeting dragged on for another thirty minutes, thirty-five, forty. Points were argued, tabled until next month, then revisited. They turned to slide 50 and then 51 and then jumped back to 10. Landry asked for clarification on footnote 7. Heather agreed: How could they vote without context?

Exhausted and fed up, Rosa sipped her Diet Coke. At her age, too much liquid meant too many trips to the ladies' room, but she needed the caffeine. Lately, the churning continued long after she got home, so she slept poorly. She had her niece Ariana on her mind, along with her own team. She was still short a number two, a payroll clerk, and an operations guy to replace Peter. She was hungry, and wouldn't mind another turkey wrap, even though the first one had too much . . . too much . . . she couldn't think of the word. Too much white shit. Rosa was trying to remember what the white shit was called when she noticed Charles eyeballing her and snapped to attention.

"Interesting." Charles smiled. Rather, his lips turned up, but there was no light in his eyes.

He was moving in for the kill, Rosa could feel it. "What's interesting?" she asked.

"You pushing for more staff." He crushed his bag of SunChips— pulverized it—and shook the crumbs into his mouth. "Why should we hire more people"—he continued to chew—"when you can't manage the ones you already have?" Charles was calling her out publicly for Peter Dreyfus's misdeeds; questioning her judgment in front of her peers. He muttered something under his breath, something that sounded like "old lady."

Rosa wasn't paranoid. She and Charles had never cared for each other, for no particular reason. And so what if she was an *older* lady? She ran rings around everyone here, especially Charles. Look at him, Mr. Big Shot. Pissed off at her for interrupting him at the beginning of the meeting, the man had bided his time for almost an hour, waiting to pounce.

"We're cutting another six percent," he said with the resolve of a judge striking a gavel.

Rosa saw red. Pain shot through her temple. Fifteen years before, Rutherford and Charles had begged her, *begged her*, to come to Ellery. "We can't build this business without you," they said. She knew this was true, so despite her newlywed status and Howard's entreaties to downshift, Rosa accepted their offer. Her assignment was to elevate the HR function from expense-driven administrator to strategic partner, and make Ellery the best of the best; basically, to replicate her success at Sony. In bull markets, this meant recruiting high-performing talent, investing in top rewards, and offering opportunities for growth. In downturns, when research—like marketing, like advertising—was the first line slashed, this meant layoffs, cutbacks, and triaging staff. In both cases, as HR chief, Rosa became one of Ellery's most powerful leaders; she was certainly the most experienced, having survived two energy crises, three recessions, Black Monday, the S&L debacle, the dot-com and housing bubbles, and last year, subprime mortgages. But now, after many years and many, many wins, they were telling her, their esteemed colleague, to sit down and shut up.

Anticipating her next move, Charles used his smug silence as bait.

Rosa was worked up, which was a mistake. In business, she knew, a marked lack of concern is a more effective negotiating tactic. Tip your hand, lose your leverage, that's what her own mentor used to say. Stay calm, she warned herself. "*Chuck.*" She said his name with disgust, looking not at Charles but Rutherford. She said it a second time, and Rutherford flinched. "Chuck, for God's sake; clean yourself up. You have mayonnaise all over your face."

*Mayonnaise!* Funny how words always pop up when you stop searching for them.

THAT NIGHT, ROSA soaked in the tub, poring over her favorite celebrities. A glass of merlot paired with *People* was how she sloughed off the workday grit. Oscar nominations hadn't been announced yet, but her money was on *The Hurt Locker*, Sandy Bullock, and George Clooney. She'd loved *Up in the Air*, although the downsizing scenes had cut a bit too close.

She tried to call Marcy, but no one answered. Rosa rarely saw her sister and brother, who had both left the Bronx years back and moved up to Rochester. Frankly, she liked her nieces and nephews more than her siblings, but the kids were grown now, with kids of their own, so she didn't see much of them either anymore. Still, she was a proud aunt and prouder great-aunt. She scattered all their photos on her shelves and hung their artwork—collages, finger paintings, watercolors—on her walls.

At sixty-four, Rosa was the eldest sibling, Marcy the youngest. Between them were six years and two brothers, one obnoxious, the other dead. Rosa headed up the family—the privilege and curse of being the firstborn and the favorite of their mother, Anita. "Don't depend on a man," Anita used to tell her. "Be a person first, then get married." Unlike Rosa, Marcy was pregnant at sixteen, divorced at twenty—the privilege and curse of being Anita's baby. But not unlike most girls in their old neighborhood.

Grunting, Rosa shifted her weight. In retrospect, she should've sprung for the oversize tub, the one with the jets. Although it seemed too fancy at the time, now she felt large and ungainly in this tight space. Rosa was not fat, but as she moved into middle age, her stocky frame, heavy bosom, and round belly became first a nuisance, then a health risk. Two months before, when her beloved St. Johns started to hang wrong, she agreed to try Weight Watchers with Leo. She also began walking to the office twice a week—an hour-long trek and excellent exercise. At the moment, her biggest issue was those few extra pounds; her reflux, cataracts, and tension headaches were manageable. However, three months after Howard died, she did have a TIA, a mini stroke-like attack, and that was scary, mostly because she'd had no idea what was happening. It started as a throbbing headache, so she'd taken two Advil and hoped it would pass. But her fingers tingled with pins and needles and then stiffened so tightly she couldn't bend them. She thought it was muscle spasms until her phone rang and instead of saying "Hello," she blurted out gibberish. Her neurologist said the TIA, while frightening, was largely a warning, that in fact she was lucky.

"You're at risk for a stroke, Rosa," Dr. Brady told her. "So let's take precautions."

Slow down, be careful, take it easy. Lately Rosa heard this more often than she liked. After today's meeting, Rutherford took her aside, reminded her to ignore Charles. She braced herself, waiting for him to add, "It's just a job," but Rutherford knew better. "The guy's an asshole" was all he said. Of course Charles was an asshole, but he wasn't wrong about Peter, who'd been Rosa's make-it-go-away guy from her first days at Ellery. Peter was hardworking, dependable, and utterly loyal. In the end, though, he screwed up. True, only the executive committee and the board knew what had really happened; everyone else was given the cover story about the hotel bill. Still, how could Rosa have missed it? Was it stress? Too much on her mind? At the moment, her head was pounding; so was her neck and jaw. This worried her because she knew it was job-related tension. But what should she do instead? Retire? Knit? Become a throwaway person? Rosa didn't just *like* to work, she *needed* to work. She'd said this once to her sister, Marcy, who balked. "Bullshit, Rosalita. You *need* to worry. You *need* to feel important. You should let things go, enjoy life more."

"What if I said that about Ariana?" Rosa had retorted. Marcy constantly fretted over her eldest daughter, who couldn't hold down a job. "What if I said 'Let her go, live your life'?"

"It's not the same. Ariana is my *child*. You're obsessing about your *employees*."

"I *know* it's not the same," Rosa said, like always, but she was miffed. "I know."

# 9

Employees stole. Rosa often forgot this, inclined as she was to see the best in people, but they did—and how. If it wasn't Post-it notes and pens, it was tissues and Sweet'N Low, coffee cups and toilet paper; it was toner cartridges and printer paper, whiteboard markers and erasers. She once heard about a kid who worked in IT at an Internet start-up. Supposedly, he rolled ten ergonomic chairs, each stacked with a few boxes' worth of new iMacs, down the elevator, across the lobby, and out of a Brooklyn office building. A single chair cost a thousand bucks, and this kid rolled ten of them into a waiting van, at high noon, with the security guards offering to help. "Oh, that's okay," he'd said politely. "I've got it." Maybe this was just another HR legend, but Rosa believed it. She could picture it, too: skinny boy in an oversize hoodie, thousands of dollars in unrecoverable assets, insurance paying only ten cents on the dollar because the guards were contractors, not building employees.

Employees stole, even the good ones.

The next day, Rosa was in her office. Squinting at her computer, she crafted an e-mail, speaking aloud as she typed. "No, Kenny, you cannot work from home next Friday. You worked from home

last Friday." She shook her head, dismayed by Kenny's audacity.
The kid was so bright, but he was channeling his gifts in the wrong
direction. If he gave to the business as much as he took, he could be
her finest employee—and he was still in his thirties! The first time
she met him, Rosa had been on the fence, but he followed up their
interview with a handwritten note on monogrammed stationery.
Who wouldn't be persuaded by such lovely manners? And despite
his ego, Rosa happened to like Kenny, or at least, the man she believed he could someday be. And let's be honest: Kenny Verville
wasn't such a risk. He came with big ideas but a lousy track record,
so he flew in like a bird—cheap, cheap, cheap. Recently, though,
he'd started to play her for a fool, and this aggravated her. "As you
know, I do not believe in, quote, working from home, unquote.
Period. Return—Enter, rather. Enter." Even after three years, he
pretended not to know she wanted him in the office, at his desk.
Workers should work where they work. Was this so much to ask?

Rosa believed in face time, in relationships built across desks,
in the elevators, and over tuna fish sandwiches—relationships that
couldn't happen if you never left your house. She believed in equality and fair play, and to work remotely was to be disadvantaged
because you weren't in her line of sight. Nor did Rosa agree with
studies claiming that work/life balance benefited the organization.
Work/life balance benefited the employee. Period. No organization
benefited from people making calls from the dentist's chair. Sometimes Kenny sent her links to these studies, but she deleted them.
Most of these so-called studies were written by freelancers, so of
course they advocated for flextime. Did he think she was that naive?
Besides, Kenny was out of the office too much as it was, and her
money was on him looking for another job. She feared he was just
like other young people who expected a quick return on a meager
investment. These kids demanded work/life balance, fancy titles,
six-figure salaries—*Oh, by the way, I'm headed to Nepal to build huts for
poor people, so I need a month off starting next week*—and if they didn't

get what they wanted the minute they asked, they put down their tools and walked off the job. These kids didn't realize that a career was a living, breathing entity. It required forethought and care, especially when first taking root. A career needed time to flourish; it had to be nurtured so that it gave back and a new generation could rise up and take over. This was how businesses cycled, how economies thrived, how civilizations endured. You wouldn't raise a child part-time, would you? You wouldn't expect him to grow up without discipline and direction, with no thought given to his education and character. Why would you expect that of your life's work?

"No," Rosa repeated, annoyed now. "No. No. No."

She typed quickly. When she was a teenager, her mother had forced her to take a secretarial course. "You want to scrub floors for a living?" Anita had asked, as if her mother knew from cleaning houses. Anita managed the books for a law firm near Penn Station—she barely scrubbed her own floor. But she was right about Katie Gibbs. Rosalita still typed 120 words a minute, rarely making a single error. Years before, to entertain her nieces and nephews, she used to tell them to shut off the lights and stand behind her while she typed: Now is the time for all good men to come to the aid of their party. The quick brown fox jumps over the sleeping dog. My name is Rosalita Luz Esperanza Guerrero and I am the smartest person you will ever meet. Now get me some cake. The kids laughed but did as she asked, all five sprinting toward the kitchen, fighting over whose turn it was to hold the plate.

"What do I care?" Rosa decided, drafting a second e-mail to Kenny. "Work from home. Work from the dentist's chair. Just give me my salary projections." She hit send ("Send," she said) and then swiveled around to face the papers piled on her desk. "Leo!" she shouted. "Could you come in here?" She waited a beat. "Please."

Her phone rang. It was Leo. "I'm on the other line, Rosa. Give me two minutes."

Employees stole time, too. Once it was only a few drunken

lunches, but now with the Internet, they gossiped and shopped, read the newspaper, even watched TV, all while at their desks. How many times had she spotted Facebook on Kenny's computer screen? Or seen Lucy trolling bargain shoe sites? Did they think she didn't know? Normally, this would make Rosa furious. But not anymore. Now that one of her *own* employees had accepted kickbacks on *her* watch, what did she care if Lucy bought a pair of discount loafers at ten thirty on a Tuesday morning?

Rosa was still stumped about Peter. She thought she knew each of her managers inside out, but in fact she was as oblivious as the security guard who stood on the street, watching some kid wheel a conga line of chairs into a van. "How did I miss it, Howard?" she asked aloud. "Peter and I were so close." He was one of her favorites, too. When she arrived at Ellery, Peter had immediately programmed her keycard, hooked up her computer, and had someone draft a company-wide memo announcing her arrival. Back then these simple tasks could have taken weeks, but he understood she was an executive and treated her accordingly. In return, Rosa showed him respect, and over the years, he became the perfect consigliere. Together, they elevated HR from a ragtag bunch of clueless clerks into a team of professionals. Leo and Lucy helped, Rob too in his own way. But Peter she could trust with the jobs no one else wanted, the real heavy lifting. When she needed two hundred copies before dawn, or someone to fly to Atlanta and back the same day, she asked, and boom, he did it. Which is why, when he showed such initiative by replacing their longtime custodial service with the newer, sleeker Spring Cleaners and saved Ellery fifty grand in the process, Rosa knew he deserved another promotion. That was two months earlier, in November, and the timing was perfect. Recently, she and Rutherford had been debating the idea of her focusing on strategy and giving the day-to-day to someone else. Peter, she decided, would make an ideal number two, and she told him so over dinner at Mia Dona, right before Thanksgiving.

"We're restructuring again," she'd blurted out. "I need your assistance." At first she regretted her candor—merlot made her talky—but with Peter she was safe.

Peter hadn't been expecting a promotion, which pleased her. He wasn't an entitled person, so he was able to experience joy. (She saw the opposite in younger generations, the inability to feel happiness. Because kids expected so much—money, jobs, love—they were never satisfied, even when they got everything they wanted.) "But why me?" he'd asked. "What about Leo or Lucy? You always said Lucy's as smart as a whip."

"Leo is content where he is," she told him. "Lucy is smart, but she's not ready. You, Peter, are ready. You're like me—we both came from nothing." Peter Dreyfus was a scrappy kid; he came from a small town in Jersey; after high school, he'd worked on construction crews. He understood what it meant to leave home financially strapped and make your way in Manhattan. "While Ivy League degrees are nice, they're not everything. Grit, hard work, and loyalty matter just as much. Oh, you still have to do all your facilities work; you can't give that up yet."

"As I said, Rosa, I will do my best to meet the demands of the position."

Peter's courtly manner always tickled her. He was the consummate gentleman, divorced and childless, devoted to his family, with a wallet stuffed with their pictures as proof. They had fun together; they laughed at similar movies and TV shows. Plus, he was so stable, so diligent—so much like *her*—she wasn't concerned when she happened upon an invoice from Spring Cleaners for twenty-five grand. That's odd, was all she thought. Didn't Peter say the first payment was thirty-five? It seemed like a simple mistake, one easily explained, but when Rosa dug deeper, she realized it was neither simple nor a mistake. Although she was due in a senior staff meeting, the invoices took priority. Plus, she was too upset to face her people. So she left the office and went home, telling no one (a first), though she did call

Leo, who brought over four boxes of files. Then she spent the entire day alone, combing through Peter's contracts, invoices, and canceled checks. By tracking the paper trail, Rosa found that several vendor payments—cleaners, water delivery, travel agency—were each off by a few grand, going back at least eighteen months. All told, Peter had skimmed off close to a hundred thousand dollars—and God knows how much more when he renegotiated the lease in Raleigh.

Rosa knew Peter's malfeasance wasn't her fault, but she still felt responsible and she still felt duped. As colleagues, they'd shared many meals together (meals she enjoyed very much), during which she divulged more of her personal life than was probably appropriate. When Howard was still alive, she'd occasionally talk to Peter about him, not to disparage her husband but to get a man's point of view. Confident in his own brains and background, Howard didn't always grasp how challenging corporate life was for her, all the obstacles she'd overcome, why she had to keep fighting. ("It's a C-level company, Rosie," he'd say about Ellery. "Just give them C-level work.") While Rosa admired Howard, she could relate to Peter, who was like a lot of the men she'd grown up with: not formally educated, but good at listening and skilled with their hands. After Howard died and Peter became her rock, she also felt a sparkle of romance. (Knowing Peter felt it too, she sometimes indulged in fantasies where they retired together and grew old as a couple. These she kept to herself, of course. Maybe someday; for now, though, their boundaries were set.) Peter was one of the dearest friends Rosa ever had, and along with Howard and her mentor, Al, one of the best men she'd ever known. His theft was terrible, yes, but what galled her wasn't just the deception and betrayal; it was the inelegance of his scheme—so stupid, so easily detected. How could he could steal so brazenly? How could she be so blind, and for so long? How could he do this to the business they'd built? Was she really at risk, or was Chuck Mayfield taunting her?

These were the questions that kept Rosa churning long into the night.

"Oh, Howard," she said sadly, still at her computer but no longer typing. "Oh, Peter."

So instead of beginning the succession process, she had to call Peter on the road, and demand he fly back from Atlanta and meet her at Starbucks. When he showed up, disheveled and red-eyed, she gave him every opportunity to come clean; she even showed him the invoices she'd found. But Peter just shook his head. "I don't know anything about that," he kept saying, avoiding her eyes. In all the years Rosa had known Peter Dreyfus, he'd never given her any reason to doubt him, so she waited a few days, hoping he'd confess, or at least offer a plausible explanation. But at the same time, and despite how much it pained her, Rosa contacted Rutherford and then Ellery's attorneys, who immediately opened their own investigation. When it became clear that Rosa's instincts were correct, she called Peter into her office and fired him on the spot. Right before Christmas! She felt like a monster. As a first-time offender, Peter was able to bypass prison, but he had to return the money and was banned from the premises. The board and executive committee were both informed, and Rosa was forbidden from discussing it with anyone, including her staff, including Peter himself. So not only was he beyond her reach, she was forced to concoct a fake reason to explain his dismissal to her staff. Everyone knew how hard he worked, so she made up some story about a hotel room. As if she'd care about that! The whole situation broke her heart, particularly when she heard why Peter stole in the first place.

"My house," he said sadly. They were seated across from each other at her small conference table. Again, Peter wouldn't meet her gaze. "My brother's house, too. I cosigned for him; now I'm underwater times two. I've never been good with finances, Rosa."

"Why didn't you come to me?" Rosa had been so angry tears

stung her eyes. "You think I haven't loaned money before? Just last month, I offered to help Rob buy an apartment!" (In truth, she'd offered to help Rob get his act together and felt sick when he misinterpreted. Oh, the look on his face!) "I thought we were friends, Peter. When Howard died, you came to my house. You brought me soup. You fixed my sink. I trusted you."

"We are friends, which is why I didn't want to put the money between us."

"So instead you stole? Look at me, Peter." She lowered her voice. "Instead you stole?"

Peter had started to cry. He cried so hard his shoulders shook. Frankly, it wasn't manly, and it certainly wasn't professional. Peter was an adult who had to face the consequences of his actions. He was her friend, but he was also a criminal. "I don't want to turn you in, Peter. If it was just you, I wouldn't. But it's not just you. It's Lucy, Rob, Leo, and Kenny. It's the assistants and the payroll staff. It's everyone at Ellery, the other five hundred and ninety-nine employees. If I protect you, I betray them. It's five hundred and ninety-nine to one, Peter. I have no choice."

Startled by Lucy's voice outside her office, Rosa glanced up. Out in the hall, Lucy and Rob were standing side by side, heads bent, deep in conversation. Seeing Rob reminded her again of their loan misunderstanding. How could he be so foolish? He was in HR! Still, she wished she could help. Rosa was especially enamored of Maddy, Rob's wife; she'd never forget how kind Maddy was to Leo during one of their holiday outings. (Drinks at Rockefeller Center in '06 or booze cruise in '07? Rosa couldn't recall, but it had to be one or the other—in 2008, Rutherford put the kibosh on parties.) As usual, Leo had been distraught over Horatio, and Maddy spent the evening consoling him while Rob played with his BlackBerry. (Booze cruise—definitely. That same night, Lucy kept whining about being seasick to hide the fact that she and Kenny were drunk as skunks. The memory of Lucy and Kenny doubled over with laughter made Rosa smile.) Speaking of Kenny, it didn't escape her that his wife had yet to attend a single Ellery event.

Rosa's stomach growled. She checked her watch; it was after eleven. Where was Leo? She called his extension, but he didn't answer. "Leo!" What was he doing that was so important?

You know what was strange, though? The money Peter stole was irrelevant. Nor did she care about looking like a hard-ass; as chief, she was paid to be the bad guy. What upset her was that even though Peter was a thief and a liar, she'd miss him terribly. Which was the sad truth about being the boss; you can't always take people with you. Rosa had decades of best work friends, all of whom promised to stay in touch, meet her for lunch, see a movie. But how many of them did she actually speak to? Two, maybe three, every other year? That's what happens when you leave a company. You cease to exist. The hole you once filled knits together, or someone else takes your place. Soon the people who knew you go, and all that's left of your presence is your slanted signature on yellowing invoices. Then those get tossed, too.

Rosa shouldn't have called Peter weak. Stealing for his family didn't make him weak; it made him desperate, and a lot of people were desperate these days. Who didn't feel the ground shift underfoot while watching the news? If she could, she'd ring Peter up and apologize, tell him what he'd missed, air out all the feelings she'd packed away. But she knew it was a stupid move, legally, to try to make contact. Corporate America, Rosa always said, was so fucking unfair.

"Do you need something?" She looked up. Leo stood in her doorway. "When you called before? Did you need me?"

"I wouldn't mind a coffee," she replied tartly. "With milk. Which I know is three points, so don't say it." Why had she let Leo convince her to go on this stupid diet? He even hired a Weight Watchers person to lead meetings in the conference room, though Rosa refused to attend. "It doesn't look right," she told him, although, in truth, there was no way she'd ever discuss her body in public.

"Coffee from the kitchen?" Leo asked, turning to leave.

"I'd rather have Starbucks."

Leo looked at his watch. "I'm finishing up the wellness proposal—"

"Well, that's good, since I asked for it in October." She bit her tongue. "I'm sorry, Leo. I don't mean to be rude. I'm just so upset about . . . about everything."

Leo nodded. "I know, Rosa. It's okay. Just a reminder: we have Katie Reynolds coming in at five. As soon as I distribute her résumé, I can run out."

*Katie who?* Rosa searched his face.

"Katie Reynolds. We're interviewing her to replace Cassandra. You need an assistant."

"I know," Rosa said, but in truth she'd forgotten, probably because she'd written the girl off once she heard the name Katie. It bothered her that a grown woman, an aspiring career woman, would call herself Katie. Even an assistant would earn more respect as a Kate or a Katherine. It was like the old adage about dressing for success: your clothing should reflect the position you want, not the one you have. Katie was a kid, but Katherine was a comer. "Don't worry about Starbucks, Leo. I'll go myself." She smiled slyly. "I need a snack."

"Rosa, it's been two months! You're doing so well. Don't ruin all your progress."

Two months on this diet, two miserable months, deprived of her beloved treats. Was this what was bothering her? Or was she upset because Peter, her potential number two, had stolen when he could've come to her instead? Or because Lucy was still mad at Rosa for calling her sloppy? "What do you mean by *sloppy*?" Lucy had snapped, whipping around so fast Rosa felt a breeze. "What do you think I mean, Lucy?" Rosa genuinely wanted Lucy to look like the executive she could be, which meant putting on lipstick and dry-cleaning her clothes, the way she did when she first got here.

Why couldn't Lucy see that the higher she rose, the more harshly she'd be judged? That people would say things to her and about her they'd never say to a man: *Why don't you have kids? Do you not like children? Must be great to only care about yourself. When are you retiring? You're holding back the rest of us! Ha ha; kidding!* Dye your roots, Lucy, Rosa ached to say. Trim your bangs. Christ, what Rosa spent on her own hair could feed a developing nation, but it was a requirement of her job, part of her uniform. Okay, maybe *sloppy* was the wrong word, but the idea was right and her intentions were pure.

Despite what people might think of her, no one could say Rosa Guerrero didn't care about her employees, the hundreds of workers whose lives she administrated from nine to seven every day. She cared about their medical benefits and bonus calculations, their professional courage and PSA levels. Rosa cared about Lucy, and though she knew she rode Lucy hard (Lucy, who still owed her an engagement survey), Rosa cared less about the survey than knowing Lucy had her priorities straight. If Lucy stopped mooning over Rob, who clearly loved his family beyond all measure, she could be chief one day.

Rosa also cared about Rob, who, sadly, was going nowhere fast. Someone had to say it: Rob Hirsch was a lousy recruiter. He was conflict-avoidant, lacked negotiation skills, and did his job on the fly. He forgot he worked for Ellery, not the candidates, so he empathized too much on their behalf and then gave away the store. Good man, yes, no question, but shitty businessman. This was why Rosa was trying to shift Rob's focus away from recruiting and back to training; maybe by motivating people instead of rejecting them, he could motivate himself. Rob had to prove he was indispensible not to her or to Ellery but to Rutherford, who constantly pestered her, *Cut staff, cut them all, I don't care, just save money.* Back in November, when she asked Rob to create a mentoring program, she'd handed him a lifeline, but 2009 ended and 2010 began, and still no proposal.

Even so, did this mean she no longer cared about him? Of course not; if anything, she cared *more*. She'd fight harder, dig in deeper— whatever it took to save him.

If Rosa had one fatal flaw, it wasn't that she cared too much about her people but that she cared what they thought of her. This humiliated her even as she admitted it was true. Rosa was craving a cheeseburger—a big juicy burger with extra pickles. If I could just have a cheeseburger, Rosa thought, this job would be so much easier.

STANDING IN STARBUCKS, Rosa was baffled by the crowd. How can these people lounge here like this? Don't they work?

"Large coffee with milk, please," Rosa said when she reached the counter. A boy wearing a ball cap repeated her order, using words she neither heard nor understood. "Yes," she repeated politely. "Large coffee. Milk. Chocolate doughnut." She shuffled down the line for her coffee, which another ball-capper handed her. "This is *black*," she said impatiently. "I asked for milk."

"Milk is over there," the second ball-capper said, pointing to a far counter.

Since when did buying a cup of coffee become a three-act opera? Weaving through the crowd of customers, she ate her doughnut in two bites. At the milk counter, she tried to open a pitcher, but the lid was screwed on too tight. After a few unsuccessful attempts, Rosa got aggravated and smacked the pitcher against the counter, accidentally spilling someone else's coffee, along with her own. Both cups splashed against her wrist as they fell to the floor.

"I'm so sorry," Rosa said to the tall man whose coffee was all over his shoes. He bent down to wipe them. "Not to worry," he said. "It's fine. Life happens!" Hearing this, her eyes flooded with tears of embarrassment.

A hand, a woman's hand, suddenly materialized and pressed a wad of napkins against Rosa's wrist. Rosa wasn't used to being touched, but the woman moved so quickly, she didn't have a chance to protest. "Here," the woman murmured. "Let me help you."

Looking up, Rosa expected another ball-capper, so she was startled to see a girl in her twenties wearing a navy suit that didn't fit right. The girl's hair was cut short in a bob, and she wore a pearl necklace and matching earrings. Grabbing more napkins, the girl wiped off Rosa's knit jacket and requested another coffee from the barista. "She'd like milk," the girl said firmly.

"Please." Mortified, Rosa spoke softly. "I'm fine." Still, she was moved by the girl's kindness.

"It's okay," the girl said, continuing to blot Rosa's jacket. "Let me."

She was just a kid, Rosa realized, seeing the spray of freckles across her nose. And yet she was tending to Rosa the way a mother cared for a child. This moved her too, how gentle the girl was, how capable; it reminded her, in a roundabout way, of her own mother, Anita. Rosa was only in her twenties when Anita was diagnosed with cancer. As expected, her care fell to Rosa, the eldest daughter, though none of her siblings had the means to help, even if they'd wanted to. Rosa moved back to her childhood apartment near the Grand Concourse, where she got up early, tended to Anita, worked all day, and then came home at six to relieve the nurse. She fed her mother, bathed her, and held her hand through the long nights. "This can't happen yet, Mommy," she whispered as she cried. "It's too soon. Please don't leave me." One year later, almost to the day Rosa moved in, her mother passed, curled on the bed, as weightless as a shadow. But Rosa's responsibilities didn't end there. In the intervening forty years, a sister, a brother, two nephews, and three nieces were on her (then her and Howard's) payroll at any given time. It had been decades since anyone besides her husband took care of Rosa. Yet here she was in Starbucks allowing this girl, this stranger in pearls, to clean her up and fetch her coffee.

When Rosa bent down to retrieve a loose cup, she noticed the girl's pumps. They were Prada. "I have the same shoes! Prada, right?"

"I wish." The girl laughed. "They're knockoffs from T.J.Maxx."

Rosa liked her nonchalance about money. At that age, she had been far too self-conscious to joke about how little she had. "I enjoy T.J.Maxx," she said, lifting the napkins off her wrist. "Lots of bargains."

"Oh!" The girl looked closer. "Does that hurt?"

Rosa's wrist was red, which surprised her. While she felt the splatter of wet coffee, the pain had only lasted a second. But now that someone was asking, Rosa nodded because it did hurt; it hurt very much.

"Excuse me," the girl said to a ball-capper. "Do you have a first aid kit?"

The ball-capper scrambled to find the kit, likely inspired by the girl's pretty face. The girl thanked him and turned back to Rosa. I was pretty like that once, Rosa thought.

"You're still pretty," the girl replied, scaring Rosa, who didn't realize she'd said it aloud. Afraid it might happen again, she kept her mind blank and mouth shut as she watched the girl unscrew a tube of ointment and rub the soothing cream all over her reddened skin.

BACK IN THE office, Rosa was not happy. "What are you talking about, Lucy? You said you'd have another draft of the engagement survey *today*."

"Rosa, you explicitly told me to wait." Lucy pointed to Rosa's wrist, which was swaddled in surgical gauze. "Wow, that looks painful." She started to explain why the survey was delayed, but Rosa was preoccupied; her arm was killing her. "My keycard isn't working again," Lucy added.

"Don't change the subject." Rosa paused. "We wouldn't have these keycard problems if Peter were still here. You should see the people Rob's bringing in—very low quality, I'm afraid. You never realize how good someone is at their job until they leave."

"You'll find a new Peter, someone equally good. Rob will make it happen; he's an excellent recruiter. Speaking of hiring, have you made any other decisions?"

Lucy didn't care about operations, Rosa knew; she was angling for the number-two spot. Rosa was well versed in all her tricks. Not that the younger woman wasn't capable. She was smart; she was diligent; she could do the work. But there were other factors to consider when choosing a successor, and those had less to do with the work and more to do with the job. Could Lucy commit? Would she get bored and leave? Stay and grow resentful? On the other hand, Lucy was here, and she was willing. Most important, she'd hold up under Rutherford's scrutiny.

Rosa was studying a print on her wall, a serigraph of *Les Velours* by Matisse. "Peter bought that for me at MoMA. The next facilities guy should appreciate art." She knew she wasn't allowed to talk about Peter, but fuck the lawyers; he was her friend. "Lucy, has anyone heard from Peter?"

"Rob e-mailed him, but he never responded. It's as if he just . . . I don't know"—Lucy shrugged—"disappeared."

During Rosa's last dinner with Peter, she'd watched him cut his baked potato into small pieces and then butter each one individually. He ate slowly, savoring every bite, unlike most men—unlike her—who were used to solitary meals and gulped their food quickly without tasting it. Peter took care when he ate, the same way he once took care when he worked. He used to have respect for his employer; he'd taken pride in his job. How did he justify throwing all that away?

"Everyone is still stunned," Lucy said. "It happened so abruptly."

"Yeah, well. He was careless."

"I thought you said he was good at his job."

"People who are good at their jobs can still be careless." Rosa ached to spill her story. Lucy, she'd say, being chief isn't easy. It's not just the long hours, complicated work, and difficult decisions. Or that to protect your people, you often have to choose between them. It's because on occasion you'll be made to look insensitive on someone else's order, someone higher up. Can you do that, Lucy; can you act like an asshole because a situation demands it? Can you live with knowing people don't like you? What will you do about Rob? And where was Leo, by the way?

Her phone rang. It was Leo. "Are you ready?" he asked.

"Ready for what?" How many times had she told him to be specific when he called?

"For your interview with Katie Reynolds. She's with Kenny now. So far, everyone loves her."

"Yes, I'm ready." Rosa thanked him and hung up. "Lucy, did you talk to this Katie person?" She blanched again at the childish name. "What did you think?"

"She's very personable. Smart, mature, and dependable. But it came up that she never finished college."

"If she doesn't have a degree, why did we invite her to interview in the first place?"

"It wasn't clear from her résumé. Maybe Rob missed it?"

"Well," Rosa said, considering this. "You don't have to be a snob. I didn't have a degree when I started. I went to night school and worked during the day."

"How am I a snob? A college degree is a requirement of the job. It says so on our website."

"We should change that. We can't discriminate against people. This is America; long may she wave." Rosa was interrupted by a knock. "Come in!" When the door swung open, she was shocked to see a familiar woman—a freckle-faced girl—wearing a baggy suit, pearls, and what looked like Prada shoes standing next to Leo.

The two women exclaimed at the same time. *I can't believe it's you. Oh my gosh! What are you doing here? This is so funny!*

"How's your arm?" Katie asked.

Rosa raised her wounded wing, still wrapped up. "You're a miracle worker." Sending Leo and Lucy away, she ushered Katie into a chair and offered her water, chocolate, a handful of nuts. She couldn't believe Katie was here! In her office! Coincidences like this used to happen all the time when she was younger. It was how she met Howard, in fact. He flirted with her at a newsstand one morning and then showed up at her door as a blind date the same night. Rosa was so giddy that even when Howard confessed that their earlier meeting wasn't accidental, that he'd intentionally scouted her out, nothing took away from the thrill of his second appearance. In those days, the world seemed enchanted, as if everyone was connected and possibility abounded. Seeing Katie here, so unexpectedly, filled Rosa with similar joy. "I can't believe it!"

They talked for a while, and then Rosa gave Katie a tour of her office, pointing out all her treasures: her crystal paperweight (MOST IMPROVED DEPARTMENT, 2001), the Baccarat vase for her tenth year of service, champagne flutes for her fifteenth. Watching Katie pick a thread off her skirt, Rosa was reminded of how the girl had dabbed at the coffee spill on her St. John, mindful of the delicate knit.

"So far everyone who's met you has said wonderful things. We're a close group, so I want you to speak to the whole team. But you'll report directly to me."

The two women looked at each other. They laughed again.

Rosa opened her arms. "If you take the job, you'll sit outside my door. Being my assistant isn't easy, but I promise you'll learn a great deal, Katherine." She paused, looked the girl square in the eye. "Is it all right if I call you Katherine?"

## 10

## LEONARD SMALLS,
## VICE PRESIDENT,
## EMPLOYEE BENEFITS

FEBRUARY 2010

L eo wasn't an early riser by nature, but Rosa liked having an HR manager on site before business hours in case of emergency, so he'd trained himself to wake up by five. This gave him enough time to shower, ride the train in from Cobble Hill, and reach his desk by six thirty, where he could enjoy his favorite Kenyan roast and a muffin, along with a few minutes of solitude, before the office shifted into high gear.

It was twenty minutes after seven. Finished with his muffin (cranberry lemon crumble), Leo bemoaned his gluttony. Tomorrow, he promised, loosening his belt. His suits were so tight he'd taken to wearing slacks-and-sweater combos, a wardrobe story that spoke volumes about his lack of restraint. He'd eaten piggishly through the holidays, and now it was almost Valentine's Day and he was still off the wagon—not just *off* the wagon, he was being dragged *behind* the wagon; he was slipping *underneath* the wagon *wheels*; soon the wagon would *run him over.* But tomorrow he'd have Special K and skim milk—no muffins, Frappuccinos, or cheese bagels. On Facebook, when he posted his plan to lose forty pounds, he got twelve likes, one share, and nine people telling their own dieting strategies, so now he had to follow through lest he run into one of his two hundred and sixty-two "friends" in real life and have nothing to show for his efforts.

Outside his office Katie was making a racket: opening and closing drawers, dropping files, knocking over chairs. "Morning, early bird!" he called out. "You beat me in *again*."

She peeked around his door. "Only by fifteen minutes!"

Katie was lovely, with a sweet freckly complexion, big green eyes, and white-blond hair that was pulled into a loose knot at her neck. But her skirt was too big for her lean frame, her jacket was similarly baggy, and her pleather shoes had a broken buckle. She is too pretty, Leo thought, to dress like a Hooverville street urchin— not that he was one to talk.

"Why are you here so early?" he asked. "Every day, I mean? Too much work?"

"Oh no!" she said brightly. "Not at all. But getting in early helps me organize myself."

Peter Dreyfus's last day in the office had been December 14, Katie's first day, January 11. For a whole blessed month, Leo had been alone every morning. He could blast soul music, log on to Chatroulette, streak through the halls—not that he would. Instead, he sat at his desk, buttered his muffin, and did his work. But it was so deliciously quiet! The only sound was the whoosh of a jet taking off or landing when he sent or received e-mails. (Leo's ex-boyfriend Horatio had downloaded noises off the Internet for him, so he had the choice of jets, birds, honks, farts, monkeys, or *boing-boings*.) Then Katie was hired, and Leo's me-time came to an end. Katie, it turned out, *was* a naturally early riser—a *very* early riser. From what Leo could tell, her internal clock cock-a-doodle-dooed at 3:00 a.m., allowing her to run ten miles, plow the fields, feed the village, build a cabin, and climb up and down Mount Everest, all before heading into work.

To be clear: Leo adored Katie. She was smart, plucky, kind, and full of energy. And he knew it was selfish and bitchy to want to eat his muffins alone, but he was a fat man pretending to diet. What could he do? Tell her not to come to work until he was done eating breakfast? As an alternative, he took Rosa's advice and found his better self, using the early hours to give Katie the lay of the land. He showed her how to coordinate Rosa's calendar, explained whose calls took priority, and made sure she could access Rosa's desktop on her own computer. This last lesson was critical because it allowed her to skim Rosa's e-mails and weed out anything unessential. Leo also tried getting to know Katie, but even when he asked basic, nonthreatening questions (where she lived, where she grew up, her top-secret superpower), Katie offered only one-word answers (Queens, Queens, invisibility). This puzzled him. Why was she so private? If she were older, he would've admired her reserve, but because of her youth, it was, paradoxically, a strike against her. The young were supposed to cross the line, if only so the old could feel superior.

Outside his office, Leo heard a crash. "Sorry!" Katie shouted.

Luckily, he could escape. Thanks to Manny Flores, head of Sanchez Security, Leo had access to the eleventh floor, which once housed a Bear Stearns satellite office and was now vacant. Two years ago, Leo had asked Manny for a key to the bathroom on eleven ("digestive issues"), and Manny obliged ("Don't need the details"), in exchange for Knicks tickets Leo bought with his own money. With Manny's help, Leo had smuggled up a desk, a chair, and a lamp to create his own private refuge.

Katie was still out in the hall—doing what, Leo couldn't say. He just wanted to be alone. Quietly, like a jumbo-size ninja, Leo rose from his seat. Then, as soon her back was turned, he hustled upstairs to eleven, where he could eat his goddamn lemon muffin in peace.

THE NEXT DAY, Leo and Rob were alone in the conference room; both had laptops open, but neither was working. Rob was focused on

his BlackBerry, and Leo was trying—and failing—to speak. "So . . .
uh . . . Rob." Leo cleared this throat. "How's everything going?"

Silence.

"I saw the greatest movie last weekend!"

Rob looked up. "Are you talking to me?"

"My watch stopped." Leo lifted his wrist.

This had been going on for an hour—Leo trying to talk to Rob
and Rob oblivious to Leo's distress. Earlier that morning, they had
been exiled to this conference room while maintenance men re-
paired the ceiling above their offices. A large patch of tiling had
collapsed during the night, exposing pink insulation material and
raw wiring. Cracked plaster covered the floor, and portions of the
wall looked unstable. Rob had said they'd be fine at their desks, but
Leo refused. Look! His pants were covered in plaster! "Rob, these
walls are full of *toxins*."

"Don't you think you're overreacting?" Rob had asked.

"Maybe you're not reacting enough," Leo retorted.

"Can't stay here," the building guys said. "The area is unsafe."

It had taken all of Leo's restraint not to say *I told you so* as he and
Rob packed up their laptops and headed down the hall. Their winter boots left a trail of white plaster prints on the carpet.

"Too bad Peter's gone," Rob observed as they walked past reception. "He would've had that ceiling fixed in no time."

Leo nodded noncommittally. "Rosa said you can't find his replacement." I bet it's hard to find an aging operations expert who
stalks his coworkers and embezzles a hundred grand, he thought.

"Yep. Operations guys don't know much about business, and
business guys know even less about operations. You can't get men
like Peter anymore, guys who can manage three properties and
hold their own in a finance meeting—not for what Rosa will pay."
Rob talked as he walked, greeting colleagues with friendly hellos.
Passing reception, he stuck his hand into the glass bowl filled with
Valentine's candy and kept going.

"So maybe we need a younger guy." Leo scurried to keep up. "Someone green . . . we can . . . train." This is *madness*; I *have* to get to the gym, he thought.

"Someone green can't negotiate with vendors, and someone with experience won't want to be trained." Rob had shrugged. "You see what I'm up against."

It didn't occur to Leo that this brief conversation, which had taken place five hours ago, would be their only exchange of the day. Now, aware the clock was ticking, Leo tried again. "What's got you so occupied?"

Rob held up his BlackBerry. "Brick Breaker. I'm about to beat my high score."

Leo didn't know how to respond, though he bet Rob would have better luck finding a new Peter if he put down his BlackBerry. Not that Leo meant to be snide. He liked Rob. In fact, he was the one who'd spotted Rob's résumé a decade ago and forwarded it to Rosa. When Rob came in and Leo saw how he'd matured since his callow Revlon days, he thought they might become friends, but whenever he suggested an after-work drink, Rob claimed to be busy. So Leo stopped asking, and then he was forced to watch from the sidelines as Rob gravitated toward Lucy.

"Did you say something?" Rob asked.

"Just checking the time. We have a meeting with Rosa at three, right?"

"Right," Rob said, returning to his device. "In fifteen minutes."

No matter how hard Leo tried to forge a connection, Rob blew him off. In many ways, Leo understood why. The office was a complex ecosystem with prescribed rules for social interaction. For gay men, corporate life held even more hidden dangers. Leo double-checked himself all the time, stayed away from phrases like "Hard day at the office," "Getting it from both sides," and "Servicing a client," and rarely touched anyone, lest some asshole misconstrue an innocent atta-boy. But this made him lonely at work, and he was already lonely at home. Leo had always mixed and matched his work friends and life friends; but as the years passed, and everyone kept changing jobs, they stopped getting together. Now, too, his once-single gay friends were pairing up, having kids, and drifting away. Despite being the most romantic man he knew, it had been a long time since someone both cute and age-appropriate had loved him back. But if he couldn't have a life-altering affair, he'd be content with a first responder. Not an *actual* fireman or EMT, unless he was cute and age-appropriate, but someone to love him, someone whose call he could count on in the event of a cataclysmic event. When the Towers fell in 2001, he, Rob, Lucy, Rosa, and Peter had watched the destruction on TV, right in this conference room. Leo was sure they'd all spend the evening together, the shared experience binding them forever, like family. Instead, a half hour later, people rushed home to their real families. At the time, Leo was living in Chelsea, so he wove through the streets like a refugee, the foggy air filled with pieces of ash, or what he thought then was ash. He stopped at St. Vincent's to offer help, or blood, or whatever, but they didn't need volunteers and couldn't take his gay blood, anyway. At home, he ate leftover egg foo yung and watched TV until dawn, thinking about his late parents. His brothers both called from Miami, so despite the day's horrors, Leo could look back, knowing he wasn't alone. But he and the twins weren't close, so he often felt like an orphan, tethered to no one, belonging nowhere. Where could a middle-aged man find a first responder in this godforsaken concrete jungle? Work? (God, no.) Not the gym. Not at cooking classes for singles, *Sex and the City* walking tours, or day trips to see New England foliage. Lately even Facebook, once Leo's salvation, amplified his loneliness. When he first joined, he felt welcomed to a community culled from every stage of his life. He was a generous poster, timely (*Obama makes history!*), reverential (*RIP Paul Newman*), and ingratiating (*More pix of your pooch Poncho, please!*). At the outset, Leo's Facebook self was the self he adored, his cocktail-party self without the morning-after blues, but like everything else, he took it too far. He checked his page way too often. If no one liked his comments, he plunged into despair. He deleted his posts and then reposted later to draw a bigger crowd. At some point soon, he'd have to bar himself from the site altogether to protect his own mental health.

"So what do you think happened to Peter?" he asked Rob now.

"Are you *kidding*?" Rob swiveled around. "They caught Peter *stealing*."

Duh, Leo thought. He meant "Has Peter resurfaced?" But because he finally had Rob's attention, he feigned shock. "*Stealing*? *Really*? I thought it was an expense-account thing."

"You didn't hear?"

*Of course* Leo had heard; Rosa had told him *the day* she found out. She told Leo *everything*. How could Rob not know that? He shook his head. "Who caught him?"

As Rob launched into the story of Rosa's forensic accounting, Peter's debt, and the gag order, Leo's attention wandered. Rob got a few facts wrong along the way, but Leo didn't correct him, given how hard it had been to get the guy talking. Still, Leo longed to blurt out the truth: Peter Dreyfus was a sexually confused stalker who went too far, freaked out, and got himself fired. Not that he could ever say this to Rob or Rosa—or anyone else except Dr. Saul.

When his problems with Peter Dreyfus started, Leo pretended not to see them; it wasn't until things had gotten well out of hand that he realized he had to face the situation head-on. Leo's reluctance to act wasn't only because he dreaded confrontation; it was also because his relationship with Peter was rooted in Rosa, and he didn't want to cause any disruptions. When Rosa's husband died, she and Leo grew closer, and he was often thrown together with Peter, both in and outside the office. For a long time, they were cordial and professional, if distant. But about two years ago, something shifted. Peter had started to call Leo at night, fairly late, and talk about random topics, like his home renovations. At first, Leo indulged him. Although Peter's ramblings were odd, Leo had a deep well of sympathy for other people's feelings, and loneliness wafted off Peter like crusted mothballs. Also? The attention felt good. Nor was Peter unattractive, with that silky silver hair and trim build. Was he gay? Curious? Who cared? It was nice to be someone else's crush for a change. But then Peter's behavior shifted again—this time, in a threatening way. During meetings, he'd sit next to Leo and "accidentally" bump his leg under the table, or he'd follow Leo into the elevator and position himself way too close. One day he walked into Leo's office and tossed a picture of two naked men that he'd ripped out of some dirty magazine on his desk.

Leo snapped. "What the hell, Peter. You can't do this anymore!"

Peter raked his fingers through his hair. "Can't do what?" Although he appeared cool and calm, his hands were trembling.

Seeing this frightened Leo. He moved toward the door, but Peter lunged forward and tried to kiss him. "Get the fuck off me!" Leo shouted. He imagined Rosa, how this would devastate her. "Stop it, I'm serious." Peter was so close that Leo could make out the veins in his face. The old man smelled like aftershave, bleach, and locker-room sweat.

"Why should I stop?" Eyes blazing, Peter smacked Leo's chest, hard. "Why should I stop? There's nothing going on here." He sounded menacing, unhinged.

Leo grabbed the phone. "I'm calling Manny!" His heart was pounding. "I'm reporting you to security." But once Leo started to dial, Peter wheeled around and walked out.

From then on, Leo's early mornings were a misery. Every day, as he rode up alone in the elevator, he'd brace himself, hoping Peter would be late. But as soon as Leo stepped into reception, he'd hear the old man strolling through the halls, hands in his pockets, jangling his keys like the crowned king of the manor. Peter's presence on the otherwise empty floor had unnerved Leo. He liked to barge into Leo's office without knocking, or stand silently at his door, tracking Leo with his eyes like a haunted Mona Lisa.

As a consequence, Leo felt jumpy all the time; he also felt ashamed and responsible, as if he'd led the old man on. Though Dr. Saul assured him this wasn't true, the situation felt untenable, and Leo started sending out his résumé. At the same time, Dr. Saul was helping him become an Authentic Person and live an Authentic Life by dialing down the hyperbole, cutting through his false chatter, and being honest about who he was. Leo started working harder in therapy. He talked about Peter, but spent equal time focused on his loneliness, and the difficulties he faced as a middle-aged corporate man with no family of his own. "Look around," Dr. Saul suggested. "Lonely people are everywhere." (Often, when Leo was at work, he'd want to ask, *Who here is as lonely as I am? Can I please get a show of hands? Lonely losers, represent*.) It took months, but as Leo's shame waned, he began to feel stronger and more in control. Although he knew he couldn't tell Rosa about Peter's behavior, since she adored Peter but would be forced to get involved, in the end the issue became academic. While Leo was spending his days and nights constructing an Authentic Self, Peter was engineering his own self-destruction. Eventually, inevitably, the old man was found out.

"So that's what happened," Rob concluded. "No one's spoken to Peter since December."

"Wow. Stealing, huh? You never really know your coworkers, right?" Leo wished he could tell Rob the truth, how awful it was, how scared he'd felt. But Rob wasn't a real friend, and to pretend otherwise didn't adhere to the tenets of Authentic Living.

A moment later, Rosa swept into the conference room with Katie trailing behind. "Sorry we're late! Katherine wouldn't let me leave my office until I signed off on the budgets."

"It's okay," Rob and Leo said simultaneously, neither man looking at the other.

Rosa eyed Rob's BlackBerry. "What are you working on?" Her voice was sharp.

"The usual," Rob said, dropping the device. It clattered when it hit the table. "Leo and I were brainstorming ideas for recruiting a new Peter."

This seemed to aggravate her. "Rob, Rob, Rob. Peter's been gone for *months*. Why are you dragging your *heels*?" Her voice rose higher until she was practically shouting. "How many times do I have to remind you to take this assignment *seriously*?"

Rob's face reddened. "I've brought in several candidates. You didn't like any of them." He glanced at the door, as if desperate to escape. Leo noticed that Katie was doing the same thing.

"Which means you need to work harder to find higher-quality people!" She stopped, slowed herself down. "Rob." She straightened her suit jacket, started again. "Rob, I apologize for my tone. In addition to a new Peter, Rutherford gave me the go-ahead to hire a second payroll clerk, so we have to fill that spot, too. If we don't enter all that data, we'll fall behind."

Though Rosa had never said so explicitly, Leo gleaned that Rob was in the shit, workwise. He didn't know how far, but it must be pretty damn deep for her to go after him this way in front of his co-workers. "Rosa!" he jumped in. "Rob just said we're brainstorming. He'll find whatever candidates you need."

"When?" She looked at Rob. "Kenny can't process all those checks by himself."

"Friday morning," Rob retorted. "Leo and I have a working dinner Thursday night."

"Fine," Rosa said pointedly. "I'm holding you both to it."

Across the table, Leo stared at his computer. In his peripheral vision, he saw Rob staring, again, at the door; this time looking wounded and fearful. Leo's own face, he hoped, was devoid of expression. So what if it was only a working dinner? *He and Rob had plans.*

## 11

The following Tuesday, Leo stood on the sidewalk, looking up. It was chilly out, and he was anxious to go inside, but wasn't sure he was at the right building. Confused, he checked the street again. Yesterday was President's Day, but Rosa had left him a voice mail saying she'd be at an offsite meeting today, and would he mind joining her? Also, please bring her laptop. She sounded rushed, and her words were garbled, so when he scribbled down the address—"100 East Seventy-Seventh, Room 1504"—he must've gotten it wrong. This was Lenox Hill Hospital.

Leo headed inside. Was Lenox Hill a client? He didn't think so. Ellery's health-care unit serviced medical manufacturers, not hospitals, although maybe this was a new direction. But as he got off the elevator and made his way through an actual ward, he didn't see any conference rooms or small offices. What kind of meeting could Rosa possibly be having here?

When he stepped, tentatively, into Room 1504—"Hello? Rosa?"— he was taken aback. There was his boss, hooked up to an IV drip and an EEG monitor. Or EKG? He wasn't sure. But the woman dozing in that bed was definitely Rosa.

He stepped closer. "Rosa?" Should he wake her? "Rosa? It's Leo." Her eyes fluttered open. She looked disoriented, frightened. "Rosa? It's Leo, from work."

Her eyes snapped into focus. "For God's sake, Leo. I know who you are. I'm not—" She struggled to sit up, smooth her blanket. "This isn't how it looks."

"What happened? Are you sick?"

"Do I look sick?"

Leo looked at her closely. Rosa's mouth drooped, and her right cheek was sunken, as if the scaffolding underneath had collapsed. "You're in a hospital." Leo kept his eyes on her right arm, which was curled in her lap like a pampered pet, waiting to see if she'd lift it. She didn't. Couldn't? "What's going on?" He waved at the machines. Heart attack? Stroke?

She motioned to him: *Lean closer.* "If I tell you, you can't repeat it. Please, Leo." *Please* had a slight hiss at the end, and *Leo* came out *Eo*, as if her tongue couldn't form the *L*.

"Don't be ridiculous; who would I tell?" Flustered, Leo busied himself with finding a chair. There was an unseemly aspect to being in this room while Rosa lay in bed, wearing a hospital gown. He felt compelled to look away—not for his own sake but for hers. Years ago, Rosa had told him about a Sony executive who'd stepped out of a meeting to take a call. When he returned, his face was stony—clearly, the news was bad—but he rejoined the group and the discussion went on. Later, she learned it was the man's wife on the phone; their son had been killed in a head-on collision. "He barely flinched," Rosa recalled. "Just sat down and kept talking." Though her intention was to share a negative example of Sony's culture, Leo could hear awe in her voice: sure, the guy's behavior was grotesque, but there was something to be said for his professionalism and focus, regardless of the circumstances.

"I promise you, Rosa," Leo told her, meaning this. "I won't tell a soul."

"I had a brain . . . a brain . . . thing." Rosa cleared her throat. "A minor incident."

"A stroke?" He could hear it now: slurring. *Inshident.* An *inshident, L-L-L-L-eo.*

"*Minor* stroke"—*minor shtroke*—"but I'm fine." She chuckled. "Thank God it didn't happen at work. I would've just died!" *Jusht died!*

"Rosa, please; don't say that. So what happened?" He looked around as if to find answers. "Did you know it was a stroke?"

"I was in the supermarket"—*shupermarket*—"of all places, feeling sick"—*shick*—"like I might throw up . . ." Rosa licked her lips. "Suddenly I lost my words. I knew an apple was an apple but it came out 'tree.' 'Tree?' the girl behind the counter asked, like I was demented. 'What kind of tree?' I got scared, so I jumped in a cab and came here. Trust me, Leo"—*trusht me, L-L-L-Leo*—"you can't be too careful, not with your brain."

"Oh my God! Rosa, that sounds petrifying." Leo's heart was beating faster. "But it was smart to come to the hospital—"

"I knew what to do." She smiled weakly. "Had a TIA." Sunlight streaming through the window washed her face of color and high-lighted the age spots on her skin. "Few years ago."

"You had a stroke before?" Leo wasn't sure if he was asking the right questions, and still not sure if he should be here at all.

"Not stroke—TIA is an indicator." *Not a schtroke.* "A brain distur . . . bance."

But Leo wasn't listening; he was searching his memory for ev-idence. When was this? Two years ago? Three? "Recently?" He thought he recalled a hitch in her step, moments of confusion, memory gaps. Or was he imagining this? "I can't believe you didn't tell me!"

"Why would I?" This appeared to aggravate Rosa, as if she could tell he was scrutinizing her. "You're on my staff. It's my business!" *Bushinesh.*

"I'm *not* invading your privacy." He felt stung. "I'm concerned." How could she call him her *staff*? Maybe he wasn't part of her family, but he was certainly more than just her *employee*. The word was an insult, given how many off-hours they spent together, especially after Howard died. Back then, Leo was at her house almost every day. "I didn't realize you were having all these health problems."

"I'm *not* have . . . probs . . . leave . . .'morrow." She tapped his bag. "You . . . laptop?" Suddenly, her speech was incomprehensible. All that slurring and stammering, those dropped consonants and mushy vowels.

"You've been here since Friday?" He looked around. "Where's your family?"

"Rochester. Everyone's busy . . . work, school, whatever . . . Marcy will be here 'night." She waved her left hand; her right still rested awkwardly in her lap. "Head count, please." She continued to wave until he took out the computer and booted it up.

A nurse walked in. "Doing okay, Miss Rosa?" Stocky, with curly hair and dark moles, she wore cranberry-colored scrubs and white sneakers that squeaked when she walked.

Leo stood up. "I should go." He put Rosa's computer on the bed, along with a sheath of files from his bag. "I don't want to be in the way."

"You're not." Rosa pointed to the chair. Her voice deepened, as if they were back in the office and she wanted something NOW. "Sit down, Leo." *Shit down, L-l-leo.*

Leo sat.

"This your son, Miss Rosa?" asked the curly nurse.

"Nephew." She said this looking straight at Leo, as if daring him to contradict her.

"Well, Mr. Nephew . . ." The curly nurse shone a light in Rosa's eyes, then wrapped a blood pressure cuff around her upper arm and started to pump. "You probably know Miss Rosa's not my easiest patient." She eyed the computer. "Miss Rosa, this yours?"

"Not mine, no, Mr. Nephew's." Rosa pointed to Curly's scrubs. "I like that purple color."

Blood pressure checked, Curly studied the monitors and made notes in her chart. "You need the restroom? You've been in the bed all morning."

Rosa shook her head. "When can I go home?"

The nurse turned to Leo. "Falling is common after a stroke, so if she does need to urinate or move her bowels, she has to use the walker. As far as her discharge date, she can discuss it with her doctor. I have no say in that decision, but he already told her not before Friday and most likely after the weekend. Miss Rosa *should not* do any work," she added, glancing at the laptop.

"I'm right here," Rosa squawked, but Curly was looking at Leo.

"Sure," was the most he could muster. He was unable to take his eyes off Rosa's right arm, which still hadn't moved.

Rosa didn't speak again until the nurse left the room. "Leo, I wouldn't ask unless"—*unlesh*—"I had to. Leo, listen"—*L-L-Leo, lishen*—"I need your help."

OF COURSE HE would help her. Leo had never betrayed Rosa's confidence, not once in twelve years; why would he start now? She had already told Katie she was home with the flu, so that was the story. (Check.) She didn't want anyone to find out about her stroke, her TIA, or the hospital—no matter what. (Fine, check.) She'd like for him to review her revised 2010 budget with Rutherford (check), and for Lucy to attend her executive committee meeting on Thursday. (Check.) "Unless I'm back," Rosa added. "Then I'll go myself."

"The nurse said you'll be here through the weekend." Leo adjusted the laptop on the bed to offer a better view of the screen. He was reluctant to let her work, but she was adamant.

"Oh, please, I'll be out in two days."

"If you leave against medical advice, Cigna won't cover you if something happens. I know you know this."

"One, the nurse is a dope. 'Mish Rosa, Mish Rosa.' Like I'm a goddamn child. Two, they're just covering their asses. *Liability*, Leo: I walk out and drop dead, they get sued. *Shued*. Third, I'm ninety-nine-point-nine percent recovered."

While it was true Rosa had an unsteady gait, also true she was slurring, if Leo didn't look too closely, she seemed very much herself. She wasn't drooling or shuffling like stroke victims on TV; maybe Rosa was as healthy as she claimed. Still, there was a lot at stake. "When people hear 'stroke,' they see a brain-dead old lady," she said, as if reading his mind. "It's the perfect excuse to get rid of me—and once they get rid of me, Leo, they'll get rid of you, too."

LEO STAYED THE rest of the day. He worked on his monthly benefits brief, negotiated with the 401(k) vendor on the phone, and e-mailed Rutherford to let him know he was taking over the budgeting process. He acted surprised when Katie told him Rosa was out sick ("How funny! I am too!"), warned Lucy about a flu going around, and never let on that Rosa was lying beside him, listening to all of this. At lunchtime he ran to the deli and brought back two turkey clubs and chicken soup. Rosa only ate the soup. (She had trouble swallowing.) When she left for physical therapy, the curly nurse chastised him for not letting her rest, so when she got back, he shut down the computer and they watched a Lifetime movie called *Hunger Point* while Rosa dozed. An hour later, a new nurse took Rosa's vitals, and she didn't care how Rosa occupied her time, so they went through the Raleigh town hall deck, conferencing in Lucy, who said she'd be happy to meet with the CEO and executive committee while Rosa recovered from the flu. As the afternoon wore on, Rosa became sluggish. Her slurring got so bad Leo couldn't understand her. An orderly came to take her for tests, and now Leo was packing up and preparing to go home.

A female doctor, a cool blonde wearing a crisp white coat over a navy cashmere sweater and slim black pants, stepped into the room. "Hi," she said, glancing around. "Where's Rosa?"

"CT scan, I believe." Shouldering his bag, Leo took out his MetroCard.

"I'm Dr. Brady. Her neurologist."

"I'm Leo Smalls." He extended his hand. "Nephew."

"Nice to meet you, Leo; I'm glad you're here." She had a firm grip and a kind smile. All Rosa had told him about Dr. Brady was that she had "professional hair," which he saw was pulled into a sleek chignon. "I'm trying to reach Rosa's sister, but she hasn't returned my calls."

"Marcy? Rosa told me she was stopping by tonight."

"Rosa said the same thing last night and the night before." Dr. Brady flipped through a chart. "But according to the staff, none of the rest of your family has visited."

"They live upstate." It occurred to Leo that Rosa had been alone here all weekend, including Monday, the holiday. Three days in that bed with no one to talk to.

"Rosa gave me permission to call Marcy. I left messages, but I didn't hear back."

"Well, I'm here." Leo offered his most ingratiating smile.

"Do you live near Rosa?"

"I live in Brooklyn." He paused. "But I see her every day."

"Great, Leo, that's great. I'm not comfortable releasing her unless I know she has someone to help her around the house."

"I can pick up her groceries and dry cleaning, if that's what you mean."

"She'll also need you to stay."

"*Overnight?*" Leo blinked. "At her *apartment?*"

"She'll need help getting dressed, going to the bathroom, showering—at least for the first few nights. Otherwise, she'll have to go to a rehab facility until she's steady on her feet."

"Oh . . . I guess . . . I mean, I didn't realize she'd need so much help." Leo tried to picture himself lowering Rosa onto the toilet. "I mean, I know Rosa had a stroke, but she told me she's, like, ninety-nine percent recovered."

Dr. Brady raised her eyebrows. "Leo, your aunt had an ischemic stroke."

He had no idea what that meant, but judging from her tone, it couldn't be good.

"Basically, it's a clot that interrupted the flow of blood to her brain. Although we were able to bust the mass intravenously and open the artery, as you can see there were aftereffects."

"You mean her speech?" Leo was getting nervous. Dr. Brady was offering more details than Rosa probably wanted him to have; more, truthfully, than he wanted to know. "Her arm?"

"The entire right side of her body was compromised. To be fair, the palsy and mild paralysis is already resolving, so that doesn't concern me as much as the risk of another stroke or aneurysm. Rosa is a high-performing executive with a lot of stress, so she's an ideal candidate for both, and from what I've observed, she seems unlikely to follow prevention protocols."

For a second, Leo reflected on how happy it would make Rosa to be called a "high-performing executive." "But she can go back to work, right?"

"Sure, at some point. A lot can happen after a stroke—heart attack, depression, falls—so she has to reduce her stress, which means taking time off. The symptoms she presented last Friday—memory loss, aphasia, elevated blood pressure—were likely stroke-related, but I've seen these same symptoms in patients who develop vascular dementia. Rosa's medical history makes her particularly vulnerable to dementia, unfortunately." Leo must've looked terrified, because Dr. Brady touched his arm. "I'm getting ahead of myself. As soon as Rosa's symptoms began, she came right to the hospital, so we were able to intervene immediately, and get her started on antiplatelet therapy. At this point, her test results are inconclusive, but we'll continue to monitor her brain function and cognition. While I'm confident she'll recover—if not completely, at least significantly—we are dealing with the brain, so there's a lot we don't know." Dr. Brady checked her watch before heading toward the door. "When Rosa gets back, will you tell her I'll stop by again?"

Sure, whatever you need, Leo said. Or that's what he thought he said. All of a sudden, he was overwhelmed. What was he still doing here? It was only six, but the sky was dark, so he sat in the shadows and tried to make sense of the day. As the light filtered out of the room and faded to black, he felt like he was fading with it.

Ten minutes later Rosa rolled in, her lips pursed in a sour knot. She was crabby and cranky. No, she did *not* want to get into the *goddamn* bed; she could sit up just fine. "Not the . . . the . . . the thing," she snapped, when the orderly tried to move her into bed. "The . . . thing." Pointing at the bed, she looked like an invalid: elderly, fragile, and mentally deficient.

"Why don't you lie down?" Leo said, aware that he sounded patronizing, as if he were addressing a toddler or a dog. "You must be exhausted."

She muttered something, but he couldn't make out her words.

"I have to go," he said, not wanting to leave but not wanting to stay either.

Rosa asked if he could run down and get her a Starbucks; she was dying for a decent cup of coffee. Oh, and maybe a doughnut. "Do you mind?"

Did he mind? Well, now that she was asking, Leo wasn't sure. It had been a long day, and he should probably go home. After all, he was only her employee; he wasn't her nephew. Speaking of which, where was Marcy? Where was her fucking brother? Leo was appalled. Their older sister was in the hospital, partially paralyzed, unable to speak or use the bathroom. Where were her people? When her mother died, Rosa had become the matriarch of the Guerrero *familia*.

Over the years, she'd supported Marcy, Nando, and a litter of nieces and nephews. Rosa had paid for Marcy's breast implants, Nando's flat-screen TV, one niece's *quinceañera*, another's Honda Accord, and a nephew's college tuition. Yet when she needed help, none—*not one of them*—had stopped by with flowers or to keep her company. Rosa's parents were dead. Her husband was dead. She had no one nearby. *She's spent three days in this place by herself.* The thought killed Leo. But what could he do? What should he do? Another human being was debilitated and alone. That she was his boss was immaterial. What would any decent person do in this situation?

"No, Rosa," Leo said, easing her out of her wheelchair and into the bed, surprised by how light she was. "Of course I don't mind."

WHEN DAVE, LEO'S father, was diagnosed with cancer, Leo was twenty-three and living in New York. He was temping at the time, and money was tight, so he didn't go home to see him. "My prognosis is excellent," his dad said from Miami. "Let's hold off for now."

"We'll let you know when you should come," his mother, Doris, promised.

Though Leo was torn, his parents knew best, so he didn't make the trip. Nor did he fly down when his dad went into the hospital a few months later. By the time his mom told him to get on a plane, his dad was unconscious, so Leo's mad dash to the airport was for naught; two hours after he landed, his father was dead. Then, unbelievably, the same thing happened four months later. His mother had a fatal heart attack, and again, Leo wasn't there. While he wasn't close to his parents, he still felt like he'd failed them; he suspected his brothers did, too. "How can you take care of your *boss*," he imagined the twins saying, "when you didn't even take care of your *mom and dad*?"

His brothers had a point, but so what? Leo had made his decision. Now the question was how far he'd go. How far was too far?

To Leo's mind, it was sleeping at Rosa's house, sitting on her couch in his pajamas, lowering her into the tub. Then again, life was long; anything could happen. He once read about a predatory health-care worker who convinced her elderly patient to invest in a church. With no one to object, the old woman signed a wad of bank slips, and the aide withdrew a cool million. The police investigated, but the case was flimsy. Not only did the bank have valid signatures authorizing the withdrawals, but the aide was gone, back to Eastern Europe, most likely. The story had haunted Leo for years. How easily it could happen to him! He had no family nearby to oversee his accounts if he was incapacitated, no one to trust with his personal affairs. Poor Rosa was alone in a hospital—purse gaping open, wallet spilling out—and someday he might be, too.

A week later, Leo was all in.

Truth be told, it was easy to pretend Rosa had the flu. This month was New York's second snowiest February on record, so employees were out sick all the time. Meanwhile, Leo was on the move like an undercover agent, traveling on a series of different trains from the office on the west side to the hospital on the east side, then all the way down to his apartment in Brooklyn and then back into Manhattan in the morning to repeat the same routine. Or if not a spy, then like a hobo riding the rails, but a hobo with a Jack Spade messenger bag and saucy Gucci loafers, full of direction and purpose.

Full disclosure: it wasn't all smooth sailing. Though Leo's intentions were honorable, he turned out to be a colossally inept secret agent. The cloak-and-dagger life fucked with his digestion and aggravated his eczema. His quest for an Authentic Self had made him a reluctant liar, so while he tried to pretend life was normal, inside he was a mess. (Dr. Saul pointed out that as exhilarating as it might feel to be needed—oh yes, it *absolutely* did—Leo had to take care of himself. While Leo agreed, who had time for therapy?) To his credit, the moment he realized he was out of his depths (day two), he got Rosa's blessing to tell Katie, his fellow early bird. Like him,

Katie was a caretaker—of people, of pets, of the lost and forlorn—who also adored Rosa. Of course she would help! So while Katie coordinated Rosa's schedule and triaged her e-mails, Leo focused on (i) Rosa, (ii) his work, (iii) Rosa's work, (iv) facilities, (v) avoiding Rutherford, and (vi) evading Lucy, who kept badgering him. Leo managed to dodge and feint the first few days, but on Friday, when Lucy appeared at his door, demanding he tell her where Rosa was ("I know her apartment doesn't have a paging system"—no fool, that Lucy), he knew the jig was up.

Lucy didn't mince words. "Leo," she said. "I cannot understand her. Rosa's not just slurring her words, she doesn't make any sense." According to Dr. Brady, some people didn't do well as inpatients; a few, in fact, could suffer from what she called "hospital delirium" and mentally deteriorate. This seemed true of Rosa, who, after a week at Lenox Hill, was lucid in the morning, but grew loopier and more forgetful as the day wore on. Still, when Lucy said point-blank, "Rosa is in the hospital," Leo pretended to sputter. "That's absurd," he said, as if mortally offended. "You can't be serious."

"Leo, I can hear the drag in her voice. Was it another TIA or an actual stroke?"

"You knew about the TIA?"

She leaned on his desk. "Don't look so surprised. You're not the only one Rosa is close to. I've known about the TIA for years. She tells me lots of personal things she doesn't tell you."

"Except where she is right now. Guess you're not as close as you think."

"You can't hoard her, Leo. She's my boss too—and my friend."

Leo considered this. "It was a stroke," he admitted. "She's been in Lenox Hill all week."

"We have to tell Rutherford." Lucy reached for his phone, but he brushed her away.

"So he can put Rosa down like a broken mule? No way." Rutherford was only in his fifties, and to Leo's mind, immature for a CEO.

If he had no problem firing young, healthy employees, why would he retain a sixty-four-year-old stroke victim?

"He'll see the large claim report, Leo. It won't identify her, but he'll figure it out."

"Not if we 'forget' to send it. Lucy, Rosa built this place. She can't just get kicked out and stashed in some nursing home." Leo kept picturing the old woman, the one swindled by her aide. In his mind, he'd conflated her with his father. Her hair was coiled up in a turban like an aging movie star, but she had his father's face—enormous beak, shaggy eyebrows, too-tanned skin. "Think of all the secrets she kept over the years, Lucy, all the people she protected. Now we have to protect her." He sighed. "This job is her whole life."

"But the stroke is a sign that she's working too hard! Maybe she needs to retire, or at least reduce her hours. This happens all the time, Leo—surgeons lose their touch, cops lose their aim, lawyers lose their bite. Deceleration doesn't have to mean the end."

Lucy was right, of course, which pissed Leo off. "And then you can be chief?" he asked. "Is that what you're gunning for? She's out and you're in?"

Looking startled, Lucy widened her eyes. "Fuck you, Leo," she snapped. "If I wanted Rosa's job, I'd *take* it. I'm trying to figure out how to *help* her. Besides, Mr. Know-It-All, I've already been asked to step in as her number two. Rutherford plans to make an announcement, so I'm not *coveting* her job, because soon I'll be *doing* her job." She stomped out of his office.

"I'm sorry, Lucy. I didn't mean that. I know you care about her." He followed her into the hall. "Where are you going?"

"Where do you think? Lenox Hill. I want to *see* her." She stopped. "Will you come with me? Rosa is a rock star . . . she's . . . I can't imagine . . ."

A few hours later, Lucy was all in, too.

One visit was all it took. Lucy and Leo only stayed an hour, but Rosa barely acknowledged them. Listless and morose, she stared blankly at the TV. She looked awful, too. Her face was stripped of makeup, her hair matted and dirty. Out in the hall, Lucy was teary. "That could be me one day. She seems so lost and lonely. I won't tell Rutherford, Leo," she added. "I promise."

From that day forward, Lucy took over Rosa's projects, Leo masterminded her day-to-day, and Katie handled her scheduling. Instead of waiting for Rosa's go-ahead, the trio made decisions on her behalf. "Rule of thumb," Lucy reminded them, "it's easier to ask forgiveness than beg permission." By the following Tuesday, Rosa could walk with a cane, so Dr. Brady let her go home rather than to rehab. At noon, Leo was at Lenox Hill to sign her discharge papers and then back in the office by five. He slept in her guestroom all week, though Rosa was less than thrilled and said "No way, José" about the bathroom. ("Privacy, *please*, Leo, for God's sake.") She balked at every turn, but Leo held firm. He made sure she ate right, went to bed early, took her pills, and used her cane. He accompanied her to speech therapy, physical therapy, and Dr. Brady's office, as well as the hairdresser, colorist, and nail salon, where he worked on PowerPoint slides and drafted e-mails while entertaining the staff with his funny computer sounds. At the end of the week, he went back to Brooklyn but called her every morning and evening. Though her siblings did come to visit, they only stayed one night, so despite Rosa insisting he was doing too much, Leo knew she was relieved to have his help.

As soon as she left the hospital, Rosa got better. Within days, her face regained its color, her eyes brightened, her speech tightened. She wanted to go back to work. "It's too much sick time," she said. "People will notice." Leo shook his head. Not only did sick come out *shick*, she was hobbling around on a cane and her arm was still lame. In the end, they compromised: Rosa would stay at home and pretend to be in the office. So every morning Leo flipped on her lights, hung a jacket on her chair, booted up her computer, and voilà!

"She's here," he'd say when anyone asked. "She just stepped out for a moment."

Believe it or not, it actually worked. After a week, Rosa's gait improved and she didn't need the cane, so she started coming to the office a few hours each morning. Then, for the rest of the day, Leo, Katie, and Lucy answered her phone, dialed in to her meetings, and finished her projects while she rested at home; more often than not, one of them would go to her place and work alongside her. Luckily, Rutherford was on the road, so most days passed without incident. Still, Leo was concerned. Dr. Brady had recommended that Rosa take a full six weeks off, but Rosa refused to slow down. "If people don't see me, they'll talk, and once they talk, forget it."

"You're jeopardizing your recovery," Leo warned.

"Better my recovery than my job, kiddo."

Three weeks later (one month poststroke), Leo was at his desk when Lucy called him with a question about retention rates. "I have to go over them with Rosa. I'll pick them up on my way to her place. Say, five minutes?"

Leo checked a folder. "Yes, I have them. Listen, can you also stop by Duane Reade? Dr. Brady called in a new beta blocker. But Rosa has to eat something before she takes it."

"I know that, Leo. Not only did I speak to Dr. Brady, I already picked up the prescription. Why don't you focus on your job and facilities; I'll handle everything else."

Not only was Lucy all in, she was acting very, very bossy. But Leo figured it was better to have a bossy Lucy on Rosa's side than a bossy Lucy working against her.

"Guess what?" Lucy appeared at Leo's door. "My keycard stopped working again."

"Wow!" Leo exclaimed. "What a wardrobe story!" Recently, Lucy had started dressing like an executive, the way she'd looked when she first came to Ellery. Today she wore a plum-colored silk blouse, dark gray pencil skirt with pinstripes, and shiny black pumps. "No more Red Lobster uniform."

"Oh, stop it, Leo. I'm an old maid." Still, she smiled. "So listen, Norm Handel just gave notice. We should figure out how to replace him before Rosa freaks. I need to get my ID fixed, so come with me to security and we'll talk on the way."

Standing up, Leo saluted. "Forward, march!"

Lucy returned his salute. "God, I *love* being large and in charge." She waved him along. "Okay, pick it up, soldier. We have lots to do."

Down in Security, Manny Flores was in front of a computer, scrolling through videocam building images. "Hey, Manny," Leo said, shaking his hand. "How've you been?"

"Leo! What can I do for you?" Manny wore pressed trousers, shiny loafers, and a windbreaker with SANCHEZ embroidered over his heart.

"Actually, we're here for me." Lucy handed him her card. "It's not working—*again*."

"No problem, miss. Let me fix you up." Manny turned to his computer.

Lucy watched his fingers tap the keys. "You may not remember this, Manny—Manny, right?—but we started our jobs on the same day."

"That's right, miss." He chuckled softly. "Ten years ago. And we're both still here."

Lucy pointed to his chest. "Is Sanchez your last name?"

Manny shook his head. "It's Flores, miss. Manny Flores."

"Manny Flores. That's a nice name." She grinned; her face reddened. "It suits you."

Her tone surprised Leo. Was Lucy *flirting*? Sure seemed so. Her voice was pitched high. "Manny runs Sanchez Security," Leo offered. "He oversees this building and two others."

"Two? Really? I had no idea. So tell me, Mr. Flores, why doesn't my keycard ever work?"

"Ah." Manny raised his eyebrows. "The ways of the office key-card are quite mysterious. But I am a keycard magician." He motioned to the camera. "May I snap a picture, miss?"

"You have my picture, Manny. You have fifty pictures. We do this every other day."

Manny positioned the lens. "It's good to have a few extra on file."

Leo reached out to fix Lucy's hair, but Manny shooed him off. "She's perfect." He clicked the shutter and processed a new card, which he handed to Lucy with a slight bow. "For you, miss . . ."

"Lucy," she said shyly. "My name is Lucy . . . well, Lucinda, really."

"I know, Lucinda Bender," Manny said softly. "I've known you for ten years."

How about that, Leo thought, watching Lucy laugh.

## 12

Time passed. Rosa improved. By the end of March, she was back at work full-time. Her gait was steadier, her right arm had better range of motion, her speech was almost clear. But now she had other problems. Despite her physical advances, Rosa was declining in more worrisome ways. At seven weeks poststroke, she should've been sharper; instead, she was addled. Names and faces eluded her. A few days earlier, Leo had stepped into her office and found her staring at the wall. "Rosa!" She glanced up, a blank look on her face. "It's Leo." Recovering quickly, she lashed out. "I know!" Still, she searched his eyes, looking terribly confused, as if she'd never seen him before.

On Tuesday morning Leo was at his desk when she called from her cell, sounding lucid and happier than she had in a while. "Good morning, Leo," she sang out.

"Good morning, Rosa. What makes this morning so good?"

"Fake it till you feel it. My niece taught me that. It's one of those sayings that sounds dumb, but is actually smart. So listen, I'm cabbing today. It's freezing out, like polar ice—way too cold to walk. Hold, please." Leo heard a grunt as she climbed into a cab, a sigh as she settled into the seat, and then her voice directing the driver to Fifty-Ninth and Lex.

"Rosa, wait! You're coming to the office. Hand the phone to the driver, I'll tell him—"

"Don't be such a bossy boss! You and Lucy both need to back off. For your information, I have a dentist appointment this morning, but if I don't hang up, I might throw up." She laughed. "Hang up or throw up. Sounds like 'fake it till you feel it.'"

Leo wanted to relax but couldn't. Rosa, he knew, didn't have a dentist appointment; she was covering up her mistake. Lately, this happened with alarming frequency. Her mind was appearing to yield and unwind, along with her management style. Staff meetings, once tightly controlled, began to meander. Paperwork—reports, P&Ls, proposals—was tossed out, unread. She was even slipping on the easy stuff—budgets, salary negotiations, staffing—fundamentals she used to do in her sleep. Though he, Lucy, and Katie were still on the case, it was clear to all of them that Rosa wasn't the same Rosa anymore.

"Hey, Leo." Rob stood at his door. "Do you have a second?"

"You're in early," Leo said, barely looking up from the Atlanta office lease, which was up for renewal soon. *Call Massy*, he added to his mental list.

Rob glanced behind him. "I came in to talk to you."

"About?"

"Brainstorming? Facilities? We discussed this, like, I don't know, two months ago? I found the *ideal* guy to replace Peter, but Rosa kept canceling his interview, so he took another job. I can't get her on the phone at all, even to discuss options. Leo, she's really fed up with me."

"Rosa's been preoccupied." Leo didn't know whether to be thrilled that he and Lucy were succeeding at covering for Rosa or annoyed that Rob was so disturbingly unobservant.

"Yeah, Lucy said she was having health problems. I noticed she's been in and out."

"Well, it was a little more than health problems. Anyway, Rosa's much better now."

Rob nodded. "Like I was saying, I'm in the hole, projectwise, and need some new ideas for recruiting. You and I never did have the brainstorming dinner we talked about a while back—which I know was totally my fault; I had that last-minute parent-teacher thing—but if you have time . . ." He trailed off, clearly reluctant to ask for Leo's help. Funny how two months ago, Leo had been the one begging for his attention. Now their roles were reversed. Guess it's true that the less you think about someone, the more likely they'll come around.

"I'm happy to brainstorm, but I'm slammed myself. How about after work—a drink, dinner?" He glanced at his calendar. "You good for Thursday? Mexican?"

"Perfect; Thursday it is." Rob seemed relieved. "Thanks, Leo."

"How deep in the hole are you?" Leo asked, genuinely curious.

As Rob leaned forward, they heard Rosa's voice down the hall. "Yoo-hoo, Leo, I'm here!" When she reached his office, she looked surprised to see Rob. "Mr. Hirsch! You're in early." Rosa seemed to be in a great mood. Her cheeks were flushed, her hair shone, and except for the unblended foundation under her jawline, her makeup was expertly applied.

"Just getting a jump on the day, Rosa," Rob told her.

"Good to hear. Hopefully we'll have a new Peter soon."

"We will. By the way," he added, testing her, "how was the dentist this morning?"

"What dentist?" She gave him a quizzical look. "Who said anything about the dentist?"

A finger of panic ran up Leo's spine.

ON THURSDAY NIGHT, Leo slid into a booth at El Ranchero, opened his laptop, and connected to the free Wi-Fi. He'd forgotten the volume was cranked up, so when a bunch of e-mails came in, the whoosh of jet engines roared through his speakers loud enough to make other diners look around. "Whoa," he said, fumbling to turn it down. "Sorry, too loud."

"What was that?" Rob craned his neck, trying to see Leo's screen. "Was it a plane?"

"Yeah, it's this sound thing for my e-mails. My friend in IT downloaded it for me."

Rob's laptop was open, too, but he was studying the menu. "Want to eat first? I'm starving." A waiter stood over them, pen poised. "I'll have a margarita on the rocks. But no salt. And a steak burrito—oh, and nachos. Nachos okay, Leo?"

"Great. I'll have a margarita, too, but frozen. And a tossed salad with chicken, please." A bowl of chips sat on the table. Leo selected one—tumbling off the wagon—then nudged it toward Rob, who grabbed a handful and ate them quickly, one after the other.

"Excuse me," Rob called the waiter back. "Make mine frozen too." He grinned at Leo. "I always feel funny ordering frozen drinks—too girlie, maybe—but I love them."

"You should get what you like; in fact, I'm gonna get enchiladas instead of a salad." That Rob had changed his order felt meaningful, but Leo wasn't sure why. Dr. Saul would know, but Leo was too busy to see him these days. At another table, a woman started choking. Both Leo and Rob turned to see a man jump out of his chair. For a second everyone froze, but the woman caught her breath, and motioned for him to sit, she was fine. "Hey Rob," Leo said, turning back. "How funny would it be if that guy called nine-one-one and your buddy Evan showed up?"

"Not very." Rob grabbed more chips. "But it would be one way to see him again." He studied his screen as he chewed. "Leo, I appreciate your help. Christ, I have no idea how I fell so far behind. Actually, I do: I'm sick of my job and can't face my work."

Surprised by Rob's candor, Leo settled comfortably into the

booth. It was nice to be out, away from the office, not worrying about Rosa. "It's no problem, Rob. Happy to give you a hand."

Their drinks and nachos arrived; both men dug in. Tomorrow, Leo swore, Special K. Rob wasn't in the greatest shape, either—he had a middle-age-man belly—but next to him, Leo felt like a hungry, hungry hippo. "So it's good Lucy got over her obsession with Evan, right?"

"I wouldn't know. We haven't talked about Evan; to be honest, I barely see Lucy anymore."

This hadn't occurred to Leo, that Lucy spending more time with him and Rosa meant she spent less time with Rob. "She's been pretty busy, I guess. But you know who asked her out? Manny Flores, head of security."

"A security guard?" Rob looked doubtful.

"That's what I thought at first, but she was pretty responsive to him. You know that laugh she gets when she's nervous?" Mimicking her, Leo made dolphin sounds.

Rob snickered. "I know Lucy pretty well; no way she'd date a security guard."

"You seem jealous."

"I'm not—not at all. I just think it's unrealistic."

"People change as they get older. They become open to new things. I mean, look at us. We're both different than we were twenty years ago. At Revlon, I mean."

"Yeah." Draining his drink, Rob signaled for another and then glanced at Leo's empty glass and held up two fingers. "You used to be *weird as shit*. What was going on with you back then?"

"My father was dying. He had leukemia. I was in shock, depressed, insane—all of it."

Rob sucked in his breath. "Whoa. Jesus, Leo, I'm sorry. I didn't know."

"Also"—Leo waved, lightening up—"I was *weird as shit*."

Weird, faggy, pudgy, pale—Leo had always been a misfit. Unlike his ropy, athletic parents who worshipped the sun, he wasn't built for South Florida. With his terrible skin—acne and eczema—and fat body, he felt elephantine, particularly next to his kid brothers, who grew tall and lean. As an adult, Leo invested in microdermabrasion, dressed above his pay grade, and called in a salon SWAT team to deal with his hair. He wasn't ugly now, just unremarkable: brown hair and eyes, everyman features. And his weight still plagued him.

"I didn't have a close family," he told Rob. "My parents loved me, but loved my twin brothers more, both of whom are handsome and outgoing. I often felt like an interloper when we went out together."

Rob scoffed. "I'm sure they loved you all the same. My daughters like to complain that Maddy and I favor one or the other, but we don't; we love them equally, just differently."

"It's nice of you to say that." He hesitated. "But once we took a trip to Disney. On Space Mountain, my parents tried to sit with Scott and Stuart, but they couldn't all fit in one car. 'I want to ride with my twins,' my mom said. My dad got up, but instead of sitting with me, he sat by himself, so we both rode alone. I was only nine." Leo didn't expect to tell Rob this story, though it was a defining childhood moment. His parents did a lot for him, including paying a chunk of his tuition to the University of Florida. And God knows he hadn't been an easy kid. But being an Authentic Person meant saying "I was my parents' third choice" to himself, and sometimes to the world.

"That's fucked up," Rob said. He was about to say more, but their entrées appeared. "I mean," he added once the server left, "it seems thoughtless, and I can't imagine doing it, but did you ever ask why? Maybe your dad needed time to himself. Hell, I love my kids, but there are moments when I'd rather bash my head in than spend one more second with them. Maybe he needed to get away—not just from you, from everyone."

"Yeah, maybe. I try not to dwell on my parents." He gave Rob a woeful smile. "They're dead, so it's easier and harder. To answer your original question, my dad was sick, and I was conflicted—I didn't want him to die, but I was angry and couldn't tell him. It feels awful when someone discounts you, and you want more than they're willing, or able, to give."

"Like I said, Leo, I'm sorry for your loss. I'm also sorry I was so cavalier. But I know how you feel." He paused. "That's how I felt about Evan, I mean, as an example. He is—he was—my best friend, but he can be a real dick sometimes. I was anxious to see him, and the more he kept blowing me off, the more anxious I got. After a while, it felt really shitty."

Although Leo was a little bothered that Rob was comparing a dead father to a lost college friendship, he let it go. Rob clearly needed someone to talk to; Leo needed someone, too.

"You may not know this, Leo, but I'm a pretty passive person." Rob grinned. "That was a joke. Seriously, I don't push myself to meet people, so I don't have many friends—male friends—guys to have a beer with or . . . I don't know . . . do whatever. I wish I did." He looked pained, as if admitting this was costing him. "As far as Evan, I've thought a lot about why seeing him matters so much. It's been nine years since our last real conversation; when I e-mailed him, I wasn't sure he'd reply, so why does it even matter? I don't know; I can't come up with an answer. I just do—did, rather. At this point, I'm done caring."

Rob took a bite of his burrito, and Leo started on his enchiladas. The two men ate in silence, though not an uncomfortable one. "Hey," Rob said after a while. "Will you show me that e-mail thing—the plane sound? That was cool. Maybe I can set it up for my kids."

It was clear Rob was done talking about serious things, so Leo didn't push him for more. He was just glad he was able to be his Authentic Self with a man he'd like to consider a friend. Though he could be wrong, it felt like Rob was being his Authentic Self, too. Which, all things considered, didn't happen often. Turning to his computer, Leo tapped out a few e-mails, including one to Robert .Hirsch@ellery.com: Hey Rob, thanks for dinner. Your buddy, Leo. Then he increased the volume, pressed send, and the two men listened as the jets soared up, into the ether.

# 13

## KENNETH VERVILLE,
## SENIOR MANAGER,
## COMPENSATION

found a quote!" Kenny whooped. "It's exactly what I need to blow this guy's mind."

Janine sighed. "Baby, you need the basics: education, experience, five-year-plan. Don't borrow trouble by getting fancy. It's late," she added, nuzzling their sleeping mutt, Dog.

Yesterday, Easter Sunday, had exhausted them (church with Kenny's parents, dinner with Janine's). Tonight they would've preferred takeout sushi and sex, but Kenny had a job interview in the morning, so Janine was helping him prep. While Kenny could see his wife was tired, if he kept going she would too. He loved her for that—not just her stamina but also her willingness to stick by him, come hell or high water. At Wharton, their roles had been reversed. Kenny was the gifted academic, Janine the student who veered off course. But out in the real world, where practice trumped theory, Janine led the charge. Even so, in this case, Kenny disagreed with her approach. To wow Donald Lee Kwon, he had to do more than spout typical job blah-blah-blah; he had to slide into CFO shoes and see the world through CFO eyes. Tomorrow, Kenny had to showcase his ability to *think*.

"Listen to this, Jeannie: 'What a man can be, he must be.' It's by Maslow, the guy who did the pyramid of human development. Remember? From Management Theory?"

"I got a C in that class."

"No, wait. The pyramid illustrates how we evolve; basic needs at the bottom, higher needs at the peak. It has cross-discipline applications, which is why it's so genius—"

Janine held up her hand. "Baby, it's too much. Stick to the script. Otherwise you'll look like an egghead professor. There's a difference between being smart and being brainy. Smart gets you the job; brainy gets your lunch money stolen."

Kenny lunged across the cushions and wrapped her in his arms. "I *am* an egghead professor, Jeannie; that's what you love about me."

In fact, Kenny's professorial persona was what had brought them together. In B-school Janine was a party girl who'd come to him, the egghead TA. "I'm failing," she said, holding out her notebook. "Can you help?" Of course he'd help, that was his job, which was why, instead of noticing her tight jeans and sweet ass, Kenny had focused on her work. But after only a few sessions, thanks to Janine's expert maneuvering, he asked her out. Love soon followed.

"You know what, Kenny?" Pinned beneath him, Janine's voice was muffled. "It's your interview, handle it however you want. But I'm done for now, and so is Dog."

Kenny smiled. "Trust me"—he kissed his wife and then Dog—"this one's in the bag."

"TELL ME AGAIN where you are?" Donald Lee Kwon, CFO of SCA Capital Advisors, scanned Kenny's résumé, then shot his cuffs to check his watch.

Tag Heuer, Kenny noted. Fifty grand, easy. "Ellery," he repeated, rubbing the face of his own, lesser, Cartier tank. Although he was never a watch guy—or money guy, frankly—Janine's family had taught him the value of quality. "Ellery Consumer Research—"

"Bet you guys got decimated last year, right?" Fluttering his fingers, the CFO simulated an explosion. "Advertising, marketing, research—ka-boom." This appeared to amuse him.

Kenny didn't feel right in his clothes. His Hugo Boss jacket, which fit perfectly when he put it on a few hours before, felt too tight. His tie was nearly asphyxiating him. "Actually, our numbers are up ten percent." An unconvincing liar, he glanced at his hands. "We're set for a banner quarter."

"Still, crazy time to be job hunting, right?" Slender and tall, Donald Lee had surprisingly thick hair for a man in his sixties; shaggy bangs shaded his eyes. When he swiped at them with manicured fingers, Kenny noticed that the executive's pinkie nails were long and sharp. Like his bangs, this trait was a departure from SCA's reserve, and hinted at a rebellious streak. At first Kenny welcomed this—he fancied himself a bit of a rebel, too—but now the guy seemed like a psychopath. "I'd hate to be trolling for work," Donald Lee added, wrinkling his nose, as if offended by the stench of unemployment. "It's fucking chaos out there."

Kenny swallowed. According to Rory, the HR assistant, this meeting was only supposed to be a formality: one in-and-out with the Big Man, and the director's job was his. But fifteen minutes later, Kenny still couldn't pierce Donald Lee's cloud of negativity. (Kenny was lucky to be here at all. SCA Capital, a multibillion-dollar hedge fund, rarely interviewed anyone except Wall Street insiders, but Janine's former boss made a call on his behalf—which reminded him: *Send Les bottle of Johnnie Walker.*) On the phone, Rory had been enthusiastic. "Donald Lee will *love* you. Just be yourself." Janine had said the same thing last night. Kenny *was* being himself, so why was he tanking?

"Chaos?" he asked stupidly. "Why do you say that?"

Donald Lee smirked. "Markets are dead. Money's dried up. No one's hiring. But maybe you work in a different United States than I do." He swiveled his chair to peer out the window.

SCA Capital was up on the sixtieth floor. From his office, the CFO had a panoramic view of the city; through the window, Kenny saw a bright sun rising. How great would it be if Donald Lee threw an arm across his shoulders and said, "Work for me, kid, and all this could be yours"? Instead the CFO tossed Kenny's résumé, like a tissue, into the air. Weightless, the paper floated to the floor. "You're kinda fucked, right, Kenneth?"

Kenny wouldn't go that far. Yes, this job market was challenging. Yes, he'd jumped around over the years, so he looked flaky on paper. But it wasn't all bleak. He was only thirty-four. His GMAT scores were in the ninety-ninth percentile, which had earned him—a black kid from a military family—a free ride at Wharton, BS *and* MBA. After school, he worked for the big players—Procter & Gamble, Johnson & Johnson—and now oversaw pay and rewards at Ellery, a multimillion-dollar research consortium. He also had a smoking-hot wife, who used to make a shitload of money as a bond trader. So no, Donald Lee—"kinda fucked" was not how Kenny Verville would describe himself. "I prefer Kenny," he said, plucking his résumé off the floor. "Actually, it's not a bad time to be looking. Most places cut the deadwood a while ago, so they're left with skeleton crews. Staff is burned out, and employers are realizing they whittled too close. Hiring should ramp up any day now, right?"

He nodded at Donald Lee. According to Janine, Kenny should mirror the CFO's behavior. If, say, Donald Lee cleared his throat, Kenny should clear his throat too (nonverbal reinforcement); he should also parrot back select words and phrases (verbal reinforcement). The idea was to seed the interviewer's mind with his own tics, so that when decision time came, he'd think, Let's hire Verville. He's exactly like me.

"In fact," Kenny added, "I've spoken to several funds looking to add staff. Seems the downturn ran its course, right?"

"Hell no." Donald Lee dismissed Kenny with a wave, apparently not understanding the difference between a rhetorical flourish and an actual question. "You've seen unemployment numbers; the whole economy is in the shitter. So let's talk about . . . uh . . ." Donald Lee again scanned Kenny's résumé. "Ellery—never heard of it. But my buddy heads up Comp at J&J; claims it's a real cushy job. Why'd you leave J&J?" He wrinkled his nose a second time.

Kenny knew his spiel cold. "I was ready for more responsibility, Donald Lee"—another Janine tip: Men love to hear their own names—"At J&J, I was one of twenty comp guys; at Ellery, I run the department. I also advise our CEO on creative ways to restructure."

"Downsizing?"

"Complete gutting—several rounds."

"There's your ten percent uptick, right? More layoffs coming?"

Kenny nodded. "Yes, probably. We promised employees we were done, but . . ."

"The check's in the mail, right?" Donald Lee barked out a laugh, like a seal. "Got good communicators? Makes a difference. Ours sucks. She's Barry's niece, right? You met Barry Hardy yet? CEO? No personality, no sensitivity. That's the niece I'm referring to." Behind his bangs, Donald Lee's eyes widened in mock disbelief. "Barry tells me I have a big mouth, so don't mention I shit-talked his niece. She's a nice kid, just spoiled and an airhead like her mother, who, by the way, sits on our board." He seal-barked again. "It's a fucking family affair!"

Kenny exhaled. He was starting to like this guy. "I suspect you're only half kidding, Donald Lee, so I'm happy to introduce you to our VP of comms. Don't worry—I won't rat you out. Wharton was full of spoiled kids. I should know—I married one! But I'm not your average suburban prince." He stopped. According to Janine, Kenny had a terrible habit of overstepping with men in authority (CEOs, fathers-in-law, TSA agents). He misinterpreted social cues, closing down when emotion was required and mistaking polite banter as a call for confession.

"Oh? What kind of prince are you?"

Fuck it, he thought. "My dad was career military; he's retired now. I was at Wharton on scholarship—no money, no rich uncles, no nothing."

"No shit." Donald Lee leaned forward. "My pop is ex-military. Marines. One tough motherfucker. Made me tough, too. You gotta be tough in this business, right?"

Though Kenny could be thick, he wasn't stupid. Donald Lee must've had it rough coming up on Wall Street some thirty years back—scrawny Asian kid with a bad accent. Talk about balls of steel, this guy was the real deal.

The big man was checking his Tag. "Nice watch," Kenny said admiringly.

Donald Lee nodded, yes, it was. "Let's keep talking. I think I like you, but I'm not sure yet." Another seal bark. "You were telling me why you left J&J, right?"

Kenny sat up. "May I speak candidly, Donald Lee?"

"Meaning what?" Don brushed away his bangs. "You've been full of shit till now?"

"Ha!" Kenny seal-barked. "I always knew Ellery would be a transitional spot. My real interest is analyzing how performance was rewarded in select historical contexts, then applying those methods to current market cycles, like last year's correction." He paused, and Donald Lee nodded, not indifferently, Kenny noted. "Say, for example, you consider employee comp as the dominant factor in satisfaction—wait, let's back up. You know Maslow's hierarchy? The pyramid?" Kenny formed a triangle with his fingers. "As you satisfy your base needs, you ascend higher, first to safety, belonging, self-esteem all the way up to morality, creativity, problem solving. 'What a man can be, he must be.' Anyway, in the past, pay was a reflection of output, but over time . . ." What was he talking about? *Abort! Abort!* All Kenny wanted to say was that he had ideas for comp theory vis-à-vis infrastructure, but having wandered into the thicket of his own words, he couldn't find a clearing. Nor did he have a point.

Turning to his computer, Donald Lee began pecking at keys.

"So that's my blueprint," Kenny concluded, nonsensically. "I went to P&G and J&J for large corporate experience, then Ellery to see the other side. Now I'm ready to apply this expertise to financial services and make my name." This wasn't true, exactly. Kenny's career trajectory had been a frenetic scramble, with personality conflicts, professional counseling, and extended periods of unemployment along the way. At Wharton, his devotion to studying was legendary. If a subject intrigued him, he'd work seventy-two hours at a clip, with a laser focus that could bend the world's edges. School was a sanctuary where he chased ideas like rabbits down into whatever random, circuitous holes they traveled. In retrospect, he should've stayed for his PhD and become an academic, worn open-collared shirts, comfortable shoes. Instead, he listened to Janine and went high-ticket corporate, only to discover that he wasn't cut out for the real world. Out here, smart people were made to repeat the same simple tasks over and over until all their intelligence drained out. Out here, Kenny couldn't get traction. His attention wandered, his already poor listening skills deteriorated. He lost track of time. Missed deadlines. Job-hopped, racking up tenure at five companies in ten years. Usually he quit, once he was fired, but each time a job ended, his relief was palpable. An optimistic man, Kenny felt sure his next one would be different. That one would catapult him above the huddled masses slaving over their pivot tables into the highest echelons of thought leadership. But as soon as he started, boredom would set in, his confidence would peter out, and the cycle would resume: disillusionment, despair, departure.

"Good to have a plan." Leaning back, Donald Lee laced his soft hands behind his head. "So tell me about your pop. Army guy, right? Tough motherfucker?"

Kenny pictured Sarge, eighty years old, still burly and hard, with muscles that bulged when he flexed and cords of veins, like telephone wiring, under his skin. His dad looked like a brute, but was in fact a gentle giant. "Toughest motherfucker ever. Ooh-rah." Then Kenny laced his own soft hands behind his head, kicked back, and kept talking.

KENNY'S INTERVIEW WAS scheduled to be only thirty minutes, but he stayed with Donald Lee for over an hour. When they finally got around to discussing the position, both men agreed Kenny was a perfect fit. ("I could do well here," Kenny observed, to which Donald Lee said, "Army brats follow the rules; I like that.") After they shook hands, he caught the A train at Fulton Street, which he rode up to Ellery, elated.

Janine called just as he stepped off the elevator. "How did it go?" she asked.

"It's happening, baby!" Kenny pushed open the glass doors. "The guy *loved* me. Practically hired me on the spot! The job is mostly strategic—lots of analysis and modeling, along with application— and I'm sure the money is *unbelievable*."

"That's great, Kenny. Sounds like it's exactly what you want . . . come here, baby," she said, clearly talking to Dog. "Give me a kiss." Three years back, his wife had picked up the bleeding puppy from the side of the road and nursed her back to health. Now they were inseparable.

"You sound unconvinced."

"Concerned. You've only been at Ellery a few years, and this is a big—"

"—leap, I know. More visible, higher risk. I get it. But I'm ready. And guess what? The guy's father was ex-military. I think that's what sold him."

"Whatever it takes," Janine said, though without much conviction. She didn't have anything against the military, but she didn't have anything for it either.

"Gotta go," Kenny said, turning the corner. "Love you."

Inside his office (which wasn't a true office but a cubicle with

makeshift walls, no ceiling, and a flimsy door), he estimated how
long it would take him to pack up. His shelves were loaded with
vacation memorabilia—beer steins from Munich, Hawaiian leis, a
mini Big Ben—and books he'd been lugging from job to job—
finance textbooks, *The Art of War*, 500-page tomes on comp theory.
On his walls were diplomas, a Penn pennant, and framed photos of
him and Janine in cities the world over. He glanced at his favorite,
a candid shot taken on Christmas Day a year earlier in front of their
house. Janine's hair had been longer then and hung to her shoulders
in face-framing waves. Her skin, darker than his, was the color of
a ripened cherry. She favored flamboyant clothing: orange tunics
and flowing dresses paired with sky-high heels that showed off her
calves. They stood arm-in-arm on the steps, wearing his-and-her
versions of the same black cashmere coat—same cut, same maxi
length, same luxurious silk lining, Janine's in lavender, Kenny's dark
grey. The matching coats were gifts from Janine's parents for their
birthdays. "Christmas babies!" Mrs. Jamison had exclaimed so many
times during their courtship that it became a family joke. Janine was
born on December 19 and Kenny on the twentieth, so neither was a
true Christmas baby, but his in-laws waited until the holiday to be-
stow their birthday gifts, which were, invariably, his-and-hers and
extravagant: coats, cars, Cartier watches, Louis Vuitton luggage.

He heard a knock. "Kenny, it's Rosa. Do you have a minute?"
Without waiting for an answer, she stepped into his office, stopping
Katherine, who was behind her. "I need to speak with Kenny alone.
I'll only be a minute." Rosa tried to close the door, but loose on its
hinges, it swung wildly and slammed in Katherine's face. "Sorry
about that!"

"No problem" was the younger woman's muffled reply.

Lowering herself into a chair, Rosa sighed from the effort. "I
thought you and I might have a chat." She crossed her ankles and
smoothed her suit, every move slow and deliberate.

The first time Kenny met Rosa, he was impressed by her poise and polish, especially compared to the very fat Leo, who sat in on the entire interview, unspeaking, for reasons never explained. Then, once he was hired, he learned she was shrewd and a supportive boss. Honestly, Kenny liked Rosa very much as a person. He respected her as an elder; she'd fought the good fight and survived. But as a business leader, Rosa had critical limitations. She was plodding and unevolved, like most older managers who came of age without technology. What mattered in the twenty-first century was synergy, automation, and fast-moving systems rooted in solid org theory, not the slow putt-putt of outdated worker-centric business models. Rosa's Big Idea was to invest in employees, which was fine if you had a machine that could time-travel back to 1995. In current thinking, people were only as valuable as the underlying processes; intellectual capital could be outsourced, so systems should allow for interchangeable staff—cheap labor, quick turnover, that's what yielded profits. Rutherford understood this. Rosa did not, or rather, she understood but didn't care. Nor did she "believe" in telecommuting, and she required her group to show up every damn day. This drove Kenny mad. Why invent new business tools, like Citrix and teleconferencing, if you don't allow your employees to use them?

"Please tell Leo about that door, Kenny," Rosa said. "If we don't get it fixed, someone will get hurt. Most accidents happen in the workplace, you know."

"You mean the home," he corrected her, offering a bright smile.

"No, the workplace. When people get hurt at home, it's not my problem. In the office, it's my dime, otherwise known as workman's comp." She paused. "So how are things?"

"Good—great, actually. Janine is in talks with UBS for a new job." He chuckled. "My wife isn't exactly the happy homemaker, so she's thrilled." Unlike Kenny's, Janine's career as a trader had been a steady upward climb—until it wasn't. After school, she went to Citigroup and then Goldman and then Lehman, where she stayed until the summer of 2008. She was laid off in June, a few months before the big kaboom, when the appetite for asset-backed securities had already thinned and Lehman needed sacrificial lambs. That was an awful day: Janine out on the street, holding her box of family photos and mugs, sobbing into the phone to him. She wanted to dive right back in, but Kenny convinced her to take a few months off. By the time she began looking in earnest, Bear had been consumed by JPMorgan, Merrill by Bank of America, Lehman was gone, and everyone else was on the brink. Ordinarily she'd have no problem finding something, but now it was two years later, and she was still on the dole. (For which, in his darker moments, Kenny blamed himself.)

"Good for Janine." Rosa's voice was terse. "But when I asked how things are, I was referring to your job, here, at Ellery. Kenny, you missed our senior staff meeting this morning. You didn't get in until ten, nor did you call."

"I apologize." Booting up his computer, Kenny studied the screen. He preferred not to look directly at Rosa. She had been sick recently (bronchitis? sinus infection? SARS?), and her recovery was slow. Even now, she moved sluggishly, and drooped in her chair like a leaf-heavy tree. When she spoke, her speech was slow and dragged as though the words were being pulled from her mouth. It seemed like she'd had a stroke, but when Kenny suggested this, Lucy had rolled her eyes. Even so, Lucy didn't deny that something had shifted for Rosa, mentally, in the past few months. Maybe a guy like Hal Foster in Finance didn't notice—which Kenny knew because they'd discussed it—but Hal wasn't with Rosa every day; he didn't sit next to her in meetings, close enough to see where her lipstick bled into the micro-crevices of her skin. Kenny did, and there were times when Rosa would drift off mid-thought or raise an unrelated topic and derail the conversation. Yet no one acknowledged it! Lucy balked when he mentioned it, Leo ignored him, and Rob was in his own world. These were people whose livelihoods depended on Rosa's ability to reason! So Kenny's next step was to alert Rutherford, with whom he had a fairly close working relationship. If Rosa was impaired, her manager—who happened to be Ellery's CEO—should know.

"That was a question," Rosa said sharply. "Where were you this morning?"

"Oh, sorry, Rosa. I had an asthma attack! I ducked into a walk-in clinic." Kenny didn't know if she'd believe this, but he also didn't care. "Just allergies, thankfully. Scary, though."

"We waited fifteen minutes. We also tried calling—several times. I'm sorry you didn't feel well, but turning off your phone is disrespectful to your colleagues."

"Again, I apologize; it was an oversight. Hey, is Lucy here? I have a question for her."

"If you'd been at our meeting, you'd know Lucy's whereabouts."

As Rosa went on to catalog everything Kenny had missed, he worked out the start date for his new job. Donald Lee wanted him to meet a few more people, which would take until mid-April. An offer might not come until a day or two later, and of course he'd counter. Offer two would take a day or two more, and again, he'd counter. But assuming they could hammer out a deal, he'd give two weeks (or not—he wouldn't mind a vacation) and start in May.

Kenny realized Rosa was staring at him. "Sorry, Rosa. What about June?"

"Another restructuring. Rutherford wants a clean slate by Q3." She sighed. "We'll have a mutiny, just watch. We swore we were done with the layoffs. We promised."

Kenny was imagining beaches and blue water. Luckily, Janine might have a new job too, thanks to Les Hough, who had been her boss at Lehman and was now at UBS. If so, Bermuda could be a celebratory trip for both of them.

"Kenny?"

He looked up. "Yes?"

Rosa erupted. "Dammit, Kenny, you have to focus! The numbers are *terrible*; Rutherford is on the *warpath*. We ended 2009 down thirty percent; now we're down twenty, and we're not even halfway through the year."

"I know," he said calmly, but it was too late. Rosa had launched into a Rant. That. Would. Not. End. Tuning her out, he watched the turkey flesh flutter under her chin. She was so excited her glasses kept slipping, and she used her middle finger to push them up. Kenny was dying to whip out his phone, get a shot of her flipping the bird, and send it to Janine.

"He wants to cut another thirty employees, including people from HR. *HR!* I talked him out of this last November, but now it won't be so easy."

"Rosa, Rosa. Rosa. Relax. We've been through this before. It's no big deal—"

"Don't interrupt me! And don't patronize. It's a *very* big deal." A thin vein bulged at her temple like a worm pulsing under the skin.

If she hasn't had a stroke, Kenny thought, she's sure as shit about to have one now. "I'm just reminding you that Ellery always does right by our people. We're being forced to make hard decisions, but so is everyone else. Folks read the paper; they see what's happened to the economy. They know it's not your fault."

"I don't care about *myself*." Rosa glared at him. "I care about our *employees*. Peter asked to meet with us next Tuesday, so clear your schedule. He was impressed with your work on the last restructuring, and wants you to team up with Hal Foster again. This is a very important, very visible project, and Peter will be counting on you. You need to be here every day."

"You mean Rutherford? You said Peter."

"Yes, Rutherford." She bit her cuticle. "How is Katherine faring with the payroll data?"

Kenny had been promised another payroll assistant, but Rob was taking too long, so Rosa had asked the new girl to help out. He'd shown her the process back in March—a month before, give or take.

They hadn't spoken since, so he assumed Katherine was faring fine. "A bit slow at first, but she's on her way." He paused. He was skating on thin ice. Rosa was already annoyed, and he should keep his mouth shut, but their systems were so antiquated that if she dipped even a toe into new waters, they could be five times more efficient. "Rosa, if we implement employee self-service, we could save nine dollars a head per month. No more data entry, no more stubs, no second clerk. ESS is *such* an easy fix."

Rosa got up from her chair. "You're a brainy kid, Kenny. And you have all these fresh ideas, some of which make sense. But to implement them, I need your help, only I can't rely on you because you're never here. It's clear this job is not important—"

Kenny's iPhone lit up. Instead of answering, he watched it vibrate on the desk. Rosa was watching the phone too, and kept watching it even after it stopped ringing.

After a very long silence, she said "I'll call Peter" in an odd, high-pitched tone. "We'll set up a meeting. I'm sure he'll be thrilled to see us. It's been a long time." Her eyes were glazed and vacant, as if her cranial wiring had suddenly short-circuited.

What's wrong with her? Kenny wondered. "You mean Rutherford. You said Peter again."

Rosa ignored him. Leaving his office, she swung the door closed but was too forceful, and the flimsy particleboard wobbled back and forth and then cracked on its hinge. "Fix this!" she snapped as the door clattered to the floor. "Someone could get killed around here."

AT LUNCHTIME, KENNY went to the gym. He had a boxing class three days a week, and liked to stick around to spar with the trainer. Afterward, he showered and dressed and went back to his desk, where he worked on his thank-you note to Donald Lee Kwon. It took him two hours to compose two drafts, and he sent both to Janine. Her redlined edits were returned with a note:

*K*

*I like paragraph 1 of Draft A and paragraphs 2 and 3 of Draft B.*
*You didn't mention you implemented new salary bands in 2007. Do*
*you mind picking up the dry cleaning on your way home? Dinner, too:*
*Chinese, two entrées with brown rice. Nothing fried.*
  *Big smooch*
  *JJ-V*
  *PS—UBS called!*
  *PPS—Big smooch from Dog too.*

After six years of marriage, Kenny and Janine made a great team. They started dating as undergraduates and stayed together through business school. When they graduated, Janine got cold feet, so they separated for a few years but ran into each other at Homecoming in 2002. Penn demolished Harvard 44–9 (Ivy League champs!), which added a drunken wildness to the fun, so after the game they took the train to Janine's place in Manhattan and stayed in bed for three days. One year later, they celebrated their twenty-eighth birthdays while honeymooning in Tahiti. ("We're married Christmas babies lounging poolside," read Janine's postcard to her parents. "Miss you both a lot. Next year, we'll all come together! I am so happy.")

His phone rang. It was Janine. "Dog wants to say hello." She put the phone next to the dog's mouth; Kenny heard panting. "What happened with Donald Lee?" Janine asked.

"No word yet, but I'm not concerned. What about UBS?"

She made growling noises. The dog chimed in. "Les wants to make a deal."

"That's great! Why do you sound so blasé?"

"We're still debating terms. I don't want to get ahead of myself."

"Do you think I'm getting ahead of myself?" Kenny knew it worried (and annoyed) Janine that he couldn't settle down. But Ellery was the wrong place to do it. This place was so dinky, there was,

literally, nowhere for him to go. Plus, the pay was lousy and the people were losers, content to stay at a third-rate company for decades
and do the same shit, year after year. Lucy, for instance, used to work
at JPMorgan; she could go anywhere! Instead, she was still waiting
for Rosa to get put out to pasture. SCA Capital, by contrast, had
everything he wanted. While he'd never earn the way Janine did,
she had her own issues around money. Janine was a smart, ambitious
woman with a chip on her shoulder that sometimes got the best
of her. Her granddad had made a killing selling life insurance, but
his wife and daughters were too dark-skinned and poorly pedigreed
for elite black society. Growing up, Janine internalized her mother's
bitterness, but instead of coveting entrée to upper-class organizations like Jack and Jill and The Links, she became hell-bent on out-
earning everyone, black and white. Janine's parents, who'd inherited
the family business, paid full freight for Penn and sent her down
I-95 in a brand-new screaming red BMW, while Kenny showed up
with a single footlocker and a crate of used books. But they com-
plemented each other. Janine was an overly indulged, fun-loving
girl who skewed hotheaded; he cooled her off. Kenny was smart but
lacked social skills; she anchored him and filled in the gaps. Kenny
Verville and Janine Jamison-Verville were a perfect couple, everyone
said so. Kenny knew he was blessed; now that he'd been tapped by
SCA Capital, his good life was about to get better.

## 14

Kenny always enjoyed visiting with Rutherford, who was a rational and forward-thinking CEO. During last spring's layoffs, when a finance guy misplaced a decimal point and three people walked away with ten grand more than they should have, Rutherford didn't flinch; he merely let the thirty grand go, along with the finance guy. He was a busy man, so Kenny never lingered or spoke out of turn, conscious that like the military, corporations adhered to a strict chain of command. As he sat in Rutherford's office, Kenny longed to give him an earful about Rosa, but she was there, too, so he kept himself in check. Kenny was also preoccupied; his interview with SCA Capital had been six business days before. According to their in-house recruiter, who'd called that same afternoon, Donald Lee had been "quite impressed" with him. So Kenny's next step was to meet Barry Hardy, the CEO, and he'd been waiting for a confirmed date and time for more than week.

Rosa was complaining. "How could you approve these layoffs, Rutherford? The count is too high. We won't just lose credibility; no one will be left to do the goddamn work!"

"If you need me to answer phones, Rosa, I'm happy to oblige."

Glancing at Kenny, Rutherford winked. "This was the board's decision, you know that."

Last spring, Rutherford and Kenny had kicked around strategies for making Ellery more profitable. One was to sever the bottom 10 percent, based on metrics as yet undecided; another was to move a portion of salaried staff to contingency positions. A third was to sell off business units to competitors. During these conversations, Rutherford had given Kenny a better view into the executive hierarchy. So while the CEO might refer to "the board's approval," Kenny understood that most financial decisions—and ultimate responsibility—rested with him.

"It wasn't the board's decision, Rutherford." Rosa scowled. "Please don't shirk; it's so unbecoming. These cuts are *your* recommendation." Years before, Rutherford used to report to her—or something like that, Kenny couldn't recall—which may explain why he didn't react when Rosa admonished him.

"You're right, Rosa," Rutherford said. "I did recommend reducing staff. So what should I tell the board instead? That I was wrong? That we won't do it?"

"That it pisses me off."

"I'll take that under advisement." His smile was affectionate. "But for the moment, I'm trying to run a business." Rutherford was a tall, skinny grasshopper. Forever in motion, he fidgeted with his watch, riffled through papers, tugged on his tie. Born into old tobacco money, the CEO exaggerated his down-home roots with seersucker pants, suspenders, and creamy bucks. Kenny wondered if his good-ol'-boy look was intentionally overdone to soften his image, given that his job required slashing staff, carving up benefits, and denying bonuses. "I realize this is difficult. There will be individual losers, but let's consider the collective gain."

"Losers? These are our people. Don't call them losers."

Rutherford sighed. "Rosa, what would you have me do? I'm out of options here."

"There are *always* options. You have to be creative."

Kenny glanced at his phone. He had two missed calls: one from Janine and the other from an unknown number, which he hoped belonged to SCA.

Rutherford drummed his hands on the table. "Here's the deal. I've looked at the numbers up, down, and sideways. Wait, let me back-track. Thank you, Ken, for helping the finance guys with the data cuts. Your analysis was spot-on."

"My pleasure." While Kenny enjoyed hearing praise as much as anyone, it also embarrassed him. *A man doesn't court himself,* Sarge had drilled into him. "Happy to help."

"These separations will be the same as the others. Last week, business unit leaders were told how many employees need to go. They have two weeks to submit revised org charts, which you and I"—he nodded at Rosa—"will review to make sure job functions are transferred correctly, gaps are identified, etcetera. When we're finished, Kenny"—he pointed—"will put together severance pack-ages with input from Finance. Rosa and I will review and send to Legal. As soon as Legal signs off, everything goes to the board. Questions?"

"You watch," Rosa said. "Six months from now, we'll be short-staffed and scrambling for bodies. We go through this every down-turn. There has to be a better way."

"That's not a question, Rosa. But I hear you, so let's spend a minute discussing how to mitigate the fallout. Kenny, you had some good ideas for reorganizing, cutting costs, and—"

"Knock-knock." Rutherford's secretary, Priscilla, stuck her head in. "Sorry to interrupt, but William Arden needs to speak with you."

Rutherford picked up the phone. "I hate to do this, folks. You mind waiting in the other room . . ." He turned in his chair, using his back to dismiss them. "Billy Boy! What's cooking?"

Out in Rutherford's reception area, Rosa took a seat; Kenny stood and listened to his messages. One was Janine, the other was

Donald Lee (the Big Man himself [!]), asking Kenny to call him. "Sorry, Rosa," he said, turning to leave. "This is life or death." Hustling down the hall, he dialed the CFO.

Donald Lee picked up on the first ring. "Thanks for replying so quickly, Ken—shit, I have another call; mind holding?" He clicked off before Kenny could choke out a response.

Back at his desk, two minutes passed. Kenny sent Janine an e-mail from his computer: Guess who I'm on hold with right now? Then two more. He started to sweat, picturing Rutherford tapping his fingers, waiting for Kenny, annoyed. Two more minutes. Rutherford had asked for ideas, and Kenny was anxious to share. First, Ellery needed employee self-service. Kenny had run the numbers, and they worked in Ellery's favor. Implementation costs would be offset by savings in manpower, particularly in payroll. Second, shared services. Operating three companies, each with a dedicated HR, IT, and finance department, was wasteful. Centralization, economies of scale—that's how you survive a recession. Another minute; Kenny was drenched. Where the fuck was Donald Lee? Third, he'd be leaving Ellery soon, but admired Rutherford and hoped they could keep in touch. Despite their differences, the CEO and Sarge inspired the same feeling in Kenny: he wanted very much to impress them. Similarly, and more pressing: neither man liked to be kept waiting.

Still holding, Kenny headed back to Rutherford's office. When he got there, he saw that Rosa was gone. *Inside*, Priscilla mouthed, pointing to the door just as—oh thank God—Donald Lee returned on the line. "Hate to ask this, Ken, but I need another minute."

"I'm in a meeting, actually." Kenny wiped his brow. "May I call you back?"

"Just come in Friday. Can you? Listen, I like you, and while I can't make promises, I'll put in a good word—band of brothers and all that. Barry is only here the one day—"

"Friday is great." By the time Kenny opened Rutherford's door, he was panting. "Sorry about that." Afraid to look at Rosa, he studied the floor.

"Kenny, you're all red!" she said.

"My . . . asthma . . ." Sucking in air, he pretended to wheeze. "I'm . . . uh . . . overheated."

Rutherford stood up. "Sorry, guys, but I have another call. Let's meet Friday and finish this."

*Friday?* Wrung out, Kenny wanted to cry. Working was hell.

"I'M HOME!" HE strolled into the kitchen early Thursday evening. "Jeannie?"

Kenny's interview with Barry Hardy was the next morning; he and Janine had plans to eat sushi and prep. He searched the first floor before remembering that she was going out with Les Hough. Come w/us, her text said. We'll prep over dinner. Les can help. xx Kenny liked Les, but play-acting a mock interview with him? Out of the question. No thx. Have fun. xoxo (PS: thank Les for getting me into SCA!)

The Jamison-Vervilles lived on a dead-end street in Short Hills. Kenny's commute was rough—forty-five-minute train to Penn Station, subway to Fourteenth, two-avenue walk—but it made coming home all the sweeter. Their newly built four-story house sat on three acres and backed up onto dense woods. Having grown up in prefab housing on numerous army bases, Kenny still couldn't get over how big it was, or that he owned it. In statistical terms, the property was F-U-C-K-I-N-G M-A-S-S-I-V-E. Three kids, five kids, they'd never run out of space. He treated his home with care, investigating every nook, cranny, squeak, and sigh. He created spreadsheets to track maintenance projects and deciphered the town's garbage pickups (no easy feat, that). "Master of our domain," Janine said, approvingly, when he rewired the parlor bathroom using YouTube and *Home Improvement for Dummies.* "Love a man with secret skills."

The first time Kenny's parents saw the house, his mother, Glenda, had gasped. "It's so grand!" she said, and covered her mouth with both hands, as if witnessing a calamity. His dad agreed. "Lotta house for two people, son." But they were impressed; Kenny saw their reverence as they slid their fingers along the oak banister. Peering into the "children's room," Glenda's eyes glistened; Sarge gave him a thumbs-up. (While Kenny was anxious to kick-start the baby-making project, Janine was dragging her heels. When she got laid off, they discussed it—well, Kenny did—but the subject died. Once he started at SCA, he planned to knock her up, pronto.)

Upstairs, Kenny changed into khakis and tried to coax Dog off the bed. "Come on, girl. We both need exercise." Nestled on Janine's side of the mattress, the furry lump refused to budge, so he went outside alone. A little while later he was on his knees in the dirt, using the last few moments of daylight to shore up beams under the deck. He wished Janine were there to approve his handiwork. "On our first date," Kenny had recounted during his wedding toast, "I told Janine she was the only woman I knew who had beauty, breeding, and—"

"*Big brains*," his best man, Fez, shouted. The reception hall, packed with people, exploded with laughter.

"And yes, Fez, big brains. But she also loved Penn football, *Star Trek*, dogs—"

"And beer!" Janine stood on a chair with her glass raised. "Don't forget beer, baby!"

"Yes—and beer, of course. Do you remember what I said, Jeannie? 'It's like you're the female me.' Well, that didn't sit well with her. 'Let's get one thing straight,' she said. '*You* are the male *me*.' Guess what? She was right. So I stand here today, in front of all of you, and admit that Janine Jamison-Verville, love of my life"—chorus of *awwws*—"is more of a man than I will ever be." The crowd roared. "Hear, hear!"

After his yard work, Kenny spent the rest of the night practicing

responses to mock questions and reading about Barry Hardy's unlikely rise from pot-smoking tennis pro to CEO. Although Janine
wasn't there to assure him, Kenny felt confident. Tomorrow, he
decided, would be a breeze. He waited up for her until midnight,
then went to bed. Where was Janine? She said she'd be home by
nine. Concerned, he texted her several times, but didn't hear back.

"My man," was Janine's wedding toast. "My man." She said other
things, too, but that's what stayed with him, that she had called him
hers.

Minutes, maybe hours later, Kenny felt the mattress dip beside him.

"Hey, baby." Janine's voice, boozy and wet, was in his ear. "Sorry
I'm late."

Surfacing from a sound sleep, Kenny murmured, "What time
is it?"

"After two. Les and I got a bit carried away."

Awake now, he reached for her. Janine tasted like whiskey, smoke,
and something else, something sweet. In the light from the bathroom, he saw her clothes—silk blouse, pants, boots, black cashmere
coat—strewn across the floor. A bra hung off a chair. She wore a
T-shirt and no underwear, and Kenny slid his hands over her ass,
between her thighs, then teased his fingers against the silk folds of
her pussy. "Was it fun?" Her clit was thick, damp; his cock, hugely
erect, sprung from his boxers. Licking her fingers, Janine formed an
O, which she slid up and down his shaft. An animal's growl, a deep
thrum, came from his throat.

"Very, very, very. We started with martinis and then switched to
champagne—"

"So you . . . took the job?" He could barely speak. As Janine
stroked him, his body took over, pulsing and tingling down to his
toes. "Hold on." He gasped, steadied her hand. "Slower . . ."

Janine pulled off her T-shirt. Kenny licked her nipples. "—after
the champagne, Les bought this nasty port. (Oh, Kenny, that's good,

that's good. Keep going.) It tasted like rotten plums, but Les said it cost two-fifty a glass, and UBS was paying, so what the hell? Between us, we drank a thousand dollars of that plum port shit."

"So you did take the job," Kenny repeated, starting on her left nipple.

Janine arched her back. "What job?" Then she whooped. "Hell, yeah, I took it!" She rolled on top of him, spread herself open against the curve of his hip, and then rocked up and down.

"Congratulations, baby." Sleepy, horny, humming with pleasure— Kenny felt enormous, ravenous. "Tomorrow night, Jeannie, we'll celebrate; drink some thousand-dollar plum port."

"Yes, yes," she whispered. "Make me come, baby." Wetness filled his ear again, her tongue, fingers. "I missed you. God, baby, that's good. You ready for tomorrow?"

Starting to spasm, Kenny was about to shoot when he stopped, rolled onto his back, slid her onto his cock, and lost himself in her warm velvet thrusts. "Oh yeah," he said, thrusting deeper, deeper. "I'm so ready."

## 15

Rosa beckoned Kenny into her office. Yesterday, she'd told him she wanted to discuss the upcoming layoffs, so he was surprised to see the new girl in there. "Katherine, could you get me a water?" Rosa asked. "I'm parched." She smacked her lips as if to prove the point.

"Sure, Rosa. Kenny? Water?" Katherine rose from the small conference table.

"Not for me, thanks." Kenny was in a lousy mood. Last Friday he'd kicked ass at SCA, so where was his offer? It was already Wednesday. On top of that, he was annoyed at Janine. "Should we start?" he asked Rosa as soon as they were alone.

"I'd like Katherine to sit in." Rosa patted a stack of printouts. "She'll be right back."

"I thought this meeting was confidential." Kenny checked his screen again. Nothing.

Rosa saw him glance at his phone. "Did your wife get the job? Where was it?"

"UBS—yes, she got it. Thanks for asking."

Rosa was being polite, but Kenny knew she was peeved at him

for calling in sick on Friday. She'd left him a terse voice mail reminding him about their meeting with Rutherford, so he called her back from the men's room at SCA. When she answered, he launched into a pretend coughing fit. Coincidentally, he'd woken up that morning with a stuffed nose and raw throat, so his fake cough turned into a wet, phlegmy hacking that went from bad to really bad. Soon he was wheezing. "*Kenny?*" Rosa had shouted, alarmed. "Are you okay?"

"I'm in the ER. But don't worry, I'll reschedule with Rutherford."

"You're in the ER *now*?" Rosa asked, but instead of replying, Kenny held his phone under the turbojet dryer. Rosa called out, "Kenny? Are you there?" but the dryer was roaring. The last thing he heard before hanging up was Rosa telling him to feel better.

As it turned out, Kenny did not feel better, which made for a shitty weekend. His cold worsened as Friday wore on, and by five o'clock his head was banging. Weak and fading fast after a full day of talking, Kenny was nonetheless excited to celebrate Janine's new job, but she was still recovering from her late night with Les from UBS and already in bed when he got home. On Saturday he woke up feverish, but instead of tending to him, she went shopping with her mother. He felt better on Sunday, so he asked Fez and Hondo to hang out, but neither of them was free, and he dozed on the couch alone with Dog, while Janine attended a baby shower for one of her girlfriends from Penn.

A minute later, Katherine stepped into Rosa's office and handed him a water. "I brought extra," she said, but turned away before he could thank her. Normally Kenny wouldn't care, but today this bothered him. Did the new girl not like him? Maybe she didn't know any black people. At work, he'd met a lot of white people who didn't have black friends. "Well, *you're* my friend," some guy at J&J once said. "We updated a bonus plan together," Kenny had wanted to reply. "That barely makes us colleagues." The presumptuousness of his white coworkers enraged him; that proximity to his blackness entitled them to a status or feeling they hadn't earned. They were so smug, so self-important! While he knew raising the issue would most likely spark a debate he shouldn't have, not in the office, saying nothing (his default position) left him feeling alienated and trapped.

Rosa clapped. "Okay, guys. Payroll, payroll. Let's talk payroll."

Kenny sighed. This was what he meant—one minute Rosa's talking about layoffs, and the next, it's payroll. Not only was she all over the place, but this meeting was confidential and she was letting her secretary sit in. "Rosa, this meeting is about org charts."

"That's right! Org charts, org charts." She grabbed the packets, which she dealt around the table like a Vegas croupier. "So Katherine, here's what you need to know. Rutherford gave Kenny and me an assignment that I thought you could help with—"

She was interrupted by a knock. Leo stuck his head in. "Excuse me, Rosa. I got Brandon Easton a set of board books." Rosa looked confused. "Lorelei's new baby," he added, glancing at Katherine. "You asked me to get her a gift." A look passed between Leo and Katherine, one Kenny didn't understand. He felt left out of something but didn't know what, only that, along with everything else, not knowing pissed him off.

"Thank you, Leo." Rosa waited for him to close the door, but instead of resuming their meeting, she turned to Katherine. "Yes, I do like Lorelei Easton," she said, answering a question no one had asked. "Before she took over Automotive, she was a little mouse, afraid of her own shadow. Still, that was no excuse for how the guys treated her. That happened to me at Sony. Have I told you this story?"

Looking up, Kenny realized she was addressing him. "I don't know; you may have."

"Sony was hard on women. Back then, it was mostly Japanese men at the top, and they were very, very disrespectful. These guys—my coworkers—ignored me when I spoke, 'forgot' to invite me to meetings, hid information. Some were *my* direct reports, if you can believe that! Imagine treating your boss that way! Shameful behavior, worse than junior high. 'No way that Mexican *chica* is gonna run this department,' one guy said. That pissed me off. 'I'm Spanish, you idiot,' I wanted to say. But I didn't. Never give bullies a reason to go after you. The culture was rough—no women, no minorities, no gays—and there I was, a ball-buster from the Bronx. I ask myself how I survived, but I did what I always do: dug in and worked harder than everyone else. I called myself Rosa, never Rosalita—Americanized my name—to cover my bases. At the time, my mother was dying, but I never made excuses. I came in before dawn, left after dark, stayed up all night nursing my mom and then got up and did it again. By year two, I'd exceeded my goals, re-vamped two divisions, and had the place running like . . . like tick-tock. So who had the last laugh? The 'Mexican *chica*' with the night-school degree, the kid who never heard of the Ivy League." She sighed.

An awkward silence followed. While this wasn't the first time Rosa had wandered off the reservation mid-conversation, usually Leo or Lucy was around to ferry her back. But it was just him and the new girl, and Kenny felt out of his depth.

A beat later, as if prodded by an unseen hand, Rosa came to life. "I'm telling you this story, Kenny, because you don't appreciate what's going on here. Rutherford gave you a unique opportunity, and you're squandering it. You didn't feel well last week—okay, we all have our days—but your absence was noted. If it were me, I would've offered to dial in to the meeting. Rutherford would've refused, but the gesture would've gone a long way. I've told you this: to get ahead, you need the CEO on your side—*more than you need me*. I'm imploring you, Kenny, you *must* make this assignment a priority."

"Speaking of which," Katherine said, "can you take us through these packets, Rosa?"

This enraged Kenny: first Rosa calling him out in front of a junior person, then this junior, a *secretary*, taking charge while he sat with his thumb up his ass. Still, he had to marvel at how well Rosa pulled together the threads of her meandering story only to zing him at the end. She was right, though. It had been foolish of him to blow off Rutherford, though once SCA hired him, it wouldn't matter.

"Let's move on." Rosa took a long drink of water, leaving a ring of red lipstick around the mouth of her bottle. Seeing this reminded Kenny of Janine; he hadn't heard from her all day. "I am so distressed about these layoffs, I can't sleep. But as I was lying awake, I came up with a plan to reorganize HR. Right now, we have areas that are understaffed—payroll, operations—so instead of letting people go, let's just reassign these functions."

"Rosa." Kenny was stern. "Rutherford explained his rationale for the layoffs. They're a done deal." His eyes cut toward Katherine. "What about confidentiality?"

"Katherine understands this is confidential." She turned to her. "Rutherford wants to lay off two HR staffers—Rob and Maisie Fresh—but it's a terrible idea for reasons I can't get into."

"That's awful," Katherine said, looking genuinely upset.

Rosa agreed. "Business can be awful, but you have to rise above it; one way is to show your humanity when everyone else's has disappeared." She paused. "I made new org charts, which you'll find in your packets. The biggest change I'm proposing is to have Lucy take over recruiting so Rob can focus on training. Then we could give communications to Marketing. By the way, Lucy is being promoted to number two, which we're announcing soon—"

"*Lucy?*" The idea of Lucy gaining power rattled Kenny. Sure, she was smart, but also a wild card: one night, you're pounding martinis on a booze cruise while she spills her secrets (father, love life, the whole shebang); the next morning, you're a leper. "That's great!" he said with false enthusiasm.

"It is great," Rosa said drily. "We appreciate the endorsement. Anyway, I'd like the two of you to devise a few more scenarios for restructuring HR, with the goal of retaining Rob."

Kenny couldn't believe it. "Rosa, this is a lot of work, and to what end? Rutherford won't change his mind."

Rosa didn't waver. "I suggest you start online. Find out how our competitors are set up. Talk to consultants. Have SHRM pull research on best practices. The answer is out there." She sipped her water. "And guys? Again—discretion, please."

"Got it." Katherine stood up. "Kenny, I'll get going with the online stuff and show you what I find."

"That's great, thanks." Katherine, he knew, was caught in the middle. No need to be a shit to her; she was just a kid. Pretty, too, though not his type. Katherine was scrawny, unlike Janine, whose biceps and triceps were gym toned and rock solid. She was also so pale as to barely register: blond hair, wispy eyebrows. Even Katie's eyes were colorless, a translucent green he could see through.

Leaving Rosa's office, Kenny made the decision to discuss her assignment with Rutherford as soon as possible. The CEO should know what was going on, especially since he'd given Kenny very different instructions. Meanwhile, he sent telepathic messages to SCA and Janine, imploring them to call. Thankfully, someone heard: leaving the gym two hours later, he had a voice mail from the hedge fund's in-house recruiter. "Scarlett Raynes here. Apologies for not returning sooner. Barry's in the Maldives, and Donald has to confer with him before we can proceed. You should hear from us within the week. Again, sorry for the delay. Hang in," she added.

Elated, Kenny texted Janine: SCA called. Offer coming next few days! When she didn't reply, his mood dipped. Up! Down! Up! Down!

She finally checked in an hour later, sounding rushed. "Sorry I didn't call. I've been *insane.* Hair is done. Nails next. I'm *so nervous.* I want this job—I *need* this job—to go well."

Kenny answered in a monotone. "Where've you been? I was sick all weekend, and—"

Janine cut him off. "Are you pouting? Seriously, Kenny? Why do grown men think the damn world stops turning when they get the sniffles? First of all, I saw your text, so don't expect me to join your pity party. Second, my job isn't only important to *me*, it's important to *us*. Do you realize how much money we spend? And third, I may be busy—*my* job starts in *one week*—but I still love you, so don't go falling into some dark hole just because I've been elsewhere."

"I just miss you," Kenny said sheepishly.

"I'm right here; and tonight we'll *celebrate* . . ." She purred like a cat, which made his cock swell. "In the meantime, I want to hear everything the recruiter said, starting with 'Hello' . . ."

Happy to have Janine's attention, he recited Scarlett Rayne's message. Then he told her about Rosa's org-chart project, which she agreed was ridiculous, encouraging him to tell Rutherford. "Kenny, what if Rosa did have a stroke, and what if it left her with a . . . I don't know . . . some mental condition that's impairing her judgment? If you don't say something, he could hold you responsible. Clearly I don't know all the ins and outs, but it sounds like Rosa should step down. There's no shame in getting old, but it's selfish to stay in a job you can't perform when people are lined up behind you—especially in a recession. I don't mean to sound cold, and believe me, I'll be kicking and screaming when it's my time, but I also hope I'll have the good sense to move on without humiliating myself." She paused. "Look, I have to run, but I'll see you tonight. Special menu, so stay tuned." And clicked off with a kiss.

Janine had a point. While Kenny could see why Rosa wanted to save Rob—nice guy, long tenure—he was unmotivated and underperforming. "Rosa," he'd said to his boss earlier, "there are hundreds of Robs out there. Why put yourself on the line when his fate is a foregone conclusion?"

"According to who?" Rosa had snapped. "You? Kenny, there is

so much about Ellery—about the world—you don't know. Nor do you have enough history to appreciate everything Rob has done for our group—including hiring you! So do your work and be grateful you still have a job."

It was only four, but after texting Fez to grab a drink, Kenny shut down his computer and put on his coat. En route to the elevator, he remembered he'd meant to ask Rob about the second payroll clerk they were supposed to be hiring, but when he backtracked, Rob's door was closed.

"Rob's home for a few days," Lucy said, passing by. "Ask Katie for his schedule—or Leo."

"Okay, thanks. Hey, Lucy?" Kenny lowered his voice. "Do you ever think about leaving Ellery? Going somewhere else? Hypothetically?" When Lucy raised an eyebrow, he went on. "Let's say I had an offer from a hedge fund with deep pockets. Let's also say they needed a communications lead. Any of this interest you?"

Lucy smiled. "First I'd like to know who's insane enough to make you an offer."

Something was different about her. It was her eyes, he realized— she wasn't wearing her glasses. Without them her face looked softer, a contrast to her sharp tone. "Seriously, Lucy."

"Seriously, Kenny. And I think it's ironic you may have a new job—hypothetically."

*Ironic?* "Why ironic?"

"No reason. It's just a word." She started to walk away.

"What if it was *a lot* more money?" He paused. "Hypothetically."

"No way," Lucy called over her shoulder. "Hypothetically."

"That's crazy!" he called back. But really, what did he care? From where he stood, Lucy Bender was a waste of brains and talent. Before heading out, he stepped into Leo's office, and was shocked to find Rosa slumped over their colleague's desk as if she'd been shot. What the hell? He crept closer. The woman was napping! Napping! In the middle of the day!

Stepping back, he shook his head. This was *exactly* the kind of bullshit Rutherford should know about. But he could hear the faintest whistle escape from Rosa's lips as she exhaled, and something about the sound prompted pity to surge in his chest. So he lifted Leo's jacket off the hook and draped it, gently, over Rosa's shoulders before closing the door.

See, he told himself. I'm not a total asshole.

"KNOCK-KNOCK." ON FRIDAY, Kenny stood at Rob's door. "Just wanted to talk about the payroll assistant—oh, sorry. I didn't realize you were on the phone."

"We have several candidates," Rob said. "No, Maddy, I'm talking to Kenny. Ken, have a seat." He scribbled notes on a pad. "You called this in? Okay. Love you too."

"Everything okay?" Kenny asked.

"My older girl was sick." Rob let out a ferocious yawn. "Excuse me; it's been intense." He started to tell Kenny about her infection, but Kenny stopped listening. He didn't want to learn anything about Rob's kids, knowing as he did that their dad was getting laid off. When he first heard about Rob, the idea didn't register, not completely. It was like hearing bad news about a guy from school; Kenny felt a twinge of "tough break," then relief to be spared. He felt even less when he updated the org chart. With a click of his mouse, one box merged with another, and eleven years of Rob Hirsch vanished. But now, seeing Rob so frazzled and depleted, Kenny felt sorry for him.

The phone rang. "I apologize, Ken." Rob paused. "No, I can't leave, Maddy. I haven't been here in days." He paused again. "I'll hold. Kenny, this'll just take a second."

Then again, why feel sorry for Rob? He'd made his own choices; he wasn't a victim.

Rob hung up. "As I was saying, Kenny, we have a few candidates, but the pay is too low, so I want to talk to Rosa about retention incentives. Something simple; escalators based on service and goals for data entry—" His phone rang again. "I'll tell you what. Hold on—yes, Maddy, you hold—Kenny, I'll put this in writing. Our Honda just died, and we need a new car, so I'm making a mental note to transfer money . . ."

When he paused, Kenny stood up. "Sounds great, Rob. Don't sweat it."

Out in the hall, Kenny wondered if he should tell Rob he was getting axed. This way he could start reaching out to his contacts, hold off dropping money on a new car. But if Rutherford found out, he'd never trust Kenny again, and Kenny wanted to leave on good terms; who knew how things could end up down the line? Still, he hesitated. In Sarge's world, you never leave any man behind.

"Hey, Rob." Kenny stuck his head back in. "You should hold off on buying a new car."

Still talking to Maddy, Rob stopped mid-sentence. His head swung in Kenny's direction. "Why?" Suddenly, the air in the office felt charged. Seeing the wild look in Rob's eye made Kenny's stomach twist; he scrambled to find a plausible answer.

"Quarterly earnings were just released. The numbers improved, so car prices will shoot up. If you can hold off a little while, until, say, next quarter, you might find a better deal."

Rob nodded slowly, absorbing this. "Kenny said to wait before buying a new car," he told Maddy. "Prices are too high." He thanked the younger man for his advice.

"No problem." Kenny wasn't sure if Rob believed him, but it wasn't his problem. He'd done what he could, given the situation. If Rob were a buddy, Kenny would've told him the truth, but he wasn't. So why risk his reputation for a guy he barely knew?

AFTER CHURCH ON Sunday, Kenny drove to Allentown to see his parents. "Kenny!" his mother, Glenda, said as she gave him a hug. She glanced outside, toward the car. "Where's Janine?"

"Last-minute change. Her mom wanted her to look at a couch."
Kenny turned to Sarge, and the men shook hands. As they settled
in the living room, Glenda ferried out a cheese plate, fresh fruit,
and snack mix. "Look," she told Kenny, raising a Heineken. "Got
it special for you."

"Thanks, Ma, but please sit down. I'm exhausted just watching
you."

Shushing him, she sat down next to her husband on the faux
velvet couch.

At seventy-six, Glenda was a delicate woman, and so slim she
could've slipped through the cushions. Beside her, Sarge, four years
older, but still robust and healthy, rested a protective hand on her
knee.

"What's the occasion?" he asked Kenny, who was helping himself to a cube of Swiss.

"No occasion. Just wanted to check in on you." In fact Kenny
was also here to pick up his old Wharton notebooks, which he
could use for reference when he started at SCA.

"We're doing fine." His father sounded insulted.

Kenny shifted his position. He usually avoided the wingback
chair, which forced him to sit with his back ramrod straight and
shoulders squared off.

"So work's good?" Sarge asked.

He often felt his father expected him to say something of import,
which left him feeling tongue-tied. "Yes," he said finally. "Work's
good."

Sarge and Glenda Verville had tried for years to have children; by
the time Kenny arrived, they were both in their forties. Sarge was
strong and athletic, as well as a bona fide hero, with a Silver Star for
catching mortar fire decades before in Pusan. As a boy, Kenny had
worshipped his father, and Sarge loved Kenny with a warrior's fe-
rociousness. Being a soldier's son, however, wasn't easy. By his eleventh birthday, Kenny had lived in nine different places. While many

of his schoolmates moved just as often, he lacked their intuition for grasping inside jokes and forging alliances, and felt like a perpetual outsider. Thankfully, Kenny had Sarge as a steady companion. They played street hockey on Friday nights and football on Saturdays; both were quick on their feet and able to throw long, elegant passes; they also loved adventure stories, which they read side by side in the living room. But as Kenny got older, his feelings toward his father changed. Other parents joked around with their kids, but Sarge and Glenda were shy and reserved, content to stay home and play cards. To Kenny, their lives were boring and mundane, every day the same as the one before. Though he had birthday cakes, Halloween costumes, and Christmas trees, just like other kids, he still felt unsatisfied. He wanted a bigger, more stirring existence, one filled with the drama and pageantry in his books. Kenny was a gifted student, but inclined toward arrogance; and this concerned Sarge, who felt his son's motivation to be the best could prove harmful. (Even so, when Kenny got the full ride to Wharton, Sarge strutted proudly.) Once he left for school, he saw his parents only for the long breaks, and after graduation, the big holidays. They didn't like Philly—too crowded, too crazy—so they rarely drove in, and he was always studying or working, so he rarely went home. By the time he married Janine, Kenny felt closer to her folks than to his own. Her people wowed him, indulging him with boozy parties and trips to far-flung places. By expanding his horizons, they helped shape his perspective. Wealth, he came to understand, was a means to change the world. Bankers like Fez and his wife were visionaries; they created new markets where none previously existed. They had more money, but were also more deserving; higher risk brought greater reward. Although it only took an hour and change to drive from Allentown to Short Hills, once he and Janine had moved into their new house, Kenny saw his mom and dad less and less; and while he loved them, of course, it seemed the gap between them kept widening.

This afternoon, Kenny didn't have much to say to his parents. He didn't stay long—maybe ninety minutes—but kept wishing Janine were there to carry the conversation. During dinner, when Glenda brought up grandchildren, Kenny held up his hands, as if warding her off. Mostly he sat silently, like a bratty adolescent, and when he did speak, he was short. Sarge was curious about Ellery, and while his questions were innocent—*Busy these days? What projects are you working on? Tell us about Janine's new company*—his tone, like Glenda's, sounded judgmental. As coffee was served, Kenny blurted out, "I may have a new job with a hedge fund. Money's great, and so is the opportunity."

"Well." Sarge folded his wife's hand over his forearm. "You sound fired up."

"Have they offered it yet?" his mother wanted to know.

Kenny shook his head. "But they will. The CFO told me as much."

Sarge considered this. "Maybe you should slow down. Hate to see you disappointed."

*Oh, please.* Kenny had been hearing this his whole life. Suddenly anxious, he jumped up. "I should get on the road. Janine's probably home by now."

Although Sarge frowned, he said nothing. It took him a few beats to stand upright and then a few more to help Glenda. Watching them, Kenny felt guilty. "I don't mean to rush off, Sarge; just wound up. Lots going on." He shook his dad's hand, bent to kiss his mother's cheek, and headed out. He drove home quickly, feeling both relieved and guilty to escape. His parents were so cautious, so fearful of life; God help him if he ended up like them. It was only later, when he was getting ready for bed, that he realized he'd forgotten to look for his notebooks.

## 16

When Kenny was in high school, he found out that Sarge earned thirty-seven thousand a year as an army PX inventory manager. He was aware that this was low, and the number made him uneasy, as if he'd unearthed a shameful family secret. Although he knew his parents weren't wealthy (his mom, a nurse, worked part-time), Sarge's number recast the economics of their situation in harrowing terms. Kenny figured he'd be earning millions by thirty; comparatively, his parents were barely hanging on: thirty-seven grand was as close as you could get to being poor without being poor.

On Tuesday afternoon, Kenny was in Rutherford's office, updating him on the severance packages he and Hal were putting together. Rosa had another meeting, so the two men were alone. Tomorrow marked a week (!) since he'd heard from SCA. He should've gotten an offer by now. On the other hand, hiring decisions always take longer than expected, especially when you're the one waiting. Besides, why would they tell him he'd be hearing about the job "within the week" if an offer wasn't imminent? Companies like SCA never show their cards unless they want you to know their intentions.

"So Kenny, I'm curious," Rutherford said, pausing their brass-tacks discussion. "Why did you choose compensation as a career? Don't most MBAs go to Wall Street these days?"

Despite his agitation over SCA, this thrilled Kenny, to be asked about his personal life by the CEO. "At first, the math interested me, then it was the theory," he began. In fact, it was Sarge's number that drew Kenny to the discipline. He was intrigued by the concept of job valuation; that is, how to measure a job's worth and, by extension, a man's. Was Sarge worth thirty-seven grand in 1992? Was Kenny worth eighty-five in 2010? Was Janine worth a million? Was Fez worth one-point-five? "As an undergrad, I studied how America's job pricing changed from colonial times to the present day through the lens of capitalism, unions, and globalization. I had no idea what I'd do afterward—teach, probably."

"So what happened?" Leaning back, Rutherford rolled up his sleeves.

"My girlfriend, now wife, was getting her MBA and suggested I do the same. She ended up on Wall Street, and I ended up here." He smiled. "I'm a salary man; Janine's the alpha."

"But you like it here?"

Kenny decided not to bring up SCA. With no formal offer (yet!), anything he said would be premature. "Ellery's a great company—strong leadership, solid infrastructure. I mean, there are some redundancies, but those are easy fixes. If we could raise capital, maybe make a few acquisitions, we could increase our market share significantly."

"You interested in moving up the HR ranks?"

"All due respect, I'm not an HR person. I'm a numbers guy, a money man. Comp theory is rooted in higher math, so to my mind, it should be rolled up into Finance instead of HR." If Compensation was an organization's cool, rational masculine head, then HR was its flighty, bleeding feminine heart. At Wharton students mocked HR, the way med students mocked dermatology (zits and

Botox). While it was true that HR had undergone a shift in philosophy and branding (now it was Talent Management, Human Capital,
or some other nonsense name), Kenny would always consider it a
lesser business function.

"Greg Dwyer leads Finance. I can't see him taking over Compensation. He can be"—Rutherford stroked his tie—"*difficult* is a
word that comes to mind."

"I like Greg; he's a smart guy. He can't be any more *difficult* than
Rosa." Stroking his own tie, Kenny smirked. "Right?"

"How so?" Rutherford stood and ambled to his couch. "How is
Rosa difficult?"

The couch easily sat four, but Kenny didn't know if joining him
would be a bad move. However, he did know it was wrong to shit-
talk Rosa behind her back, *and* to her boss. That said, the CEO
had asked him an honest, direct question and therefore deserved
an honest, direct answer. Moreover, Janine was right: Rutherford
should know the truth about Rosa's mental state. "I don't know
what Rosa was like when you first met, nor do I know much about
your relationship—"

"I've known Rosa for decades. I consider her a mentor, personally and professionally."

Then he'll understand that her time has come, Kenny reasoned;
he'll want her to leave of her own volition. "I heard she used to be a
powerhouse, a real maverick. But . . ." Kenny cleared his throat; he
had to get this right. "Sir, I'm concerned Rosa is having cognitive
issues. Of course I'm no doctor, so I can't offer anything but cursory
observations."

Rutherford rolled his hands, as if to say go on.

"She's present in body, but not always in mind. In meetings,
she'll go off on irrelevant tangents or zone out—"

Rutherford cut him off. "I haven't seen this at all; we're frequently
in meetings together."

Kenny backpedaled. "It doesn't happen every day." He assumed

Rutherford had no idea about her erratic judgment or misguided loyalties, which, as Janine pointed out, had real potential to hurt Ellery. "Rosa has lost touch with the business. For instance, I agree with your decision to let Rob Hirsch go; he wasn't performing up to task. But because of Rosa's feelings for him—or her, I don't know . . . *condition*—she can't see that it's better for Ellery, and in the long term for Rob, if he leaves. Instead she has me scrambling to find ways to restructure HR solely to keep him on staff. She asked me to do six or seven permutations! It's a Hail Mary play that's eating up my time and keeping me from truly important initiatives— like the severance packages."

Rutherford snapped a rubber band in his fingers. "How much time are you spending?"

"Twenty-five, thirty hours a week?" Kenny exaggerated. "Her heart is in the right place, but she has no objectivity or boundaries with her staff. HR is pretty chaotic these days."

Rutherford checked his watch. "I have five more minutes." He paused. "So there's no one in HR you feel is a competent manager?"

"Lucy is competent." Kenny chuckled. "Sorry . . . Lucy has a nickname for Rosa. She calls her 'Ozzy.'" Rutherford's lips curved, as if he too had a secret, which Kenny took as a sign to continue. "Like Ozzy Osbourne, the musician with the reality show? He used to be a hard-core rocker, but now he's this oblivious dad. So he wanders around his mansion, bedeviled by simple things, like the TV remote." Kenny cracked up, picturing the singer perplexed by all his devices.

"Actually, the nickname is from the Wizard of Oz." Rutherford was still smiling.

"Oh . . . I . . . didn't realize . . ." Kenny tried to sober up, but he was, literally, bent over, laughing. A minute passed before he realized that Rutherford wasn't laughing with him. Kenny wiped his eyes. "I apologize, sir. Don't know what got into me . . ." He knew it was awful, that he'd burn in hell, but the vision of Ozzy Osbourne's befuddled face *shattered* him. "I'm fine." He gritted his teeth to calm down. "I should probably get going."

"You probably should." Rutherford stood up to usher Kenny out.

Kenny couldn't read Rutherford's expression. "I hope I didn't speak out of turn."

"No problem." The CEO shook his hand. "You've given me quite a bit to think about."

HOURS LATER, KENNY fell asleep watching ESPN in his living room. Jolted awake, he worked the kinks out of his neck. Janine had gone out for dinner, so the coffee table was littered with his empty Heinekens and congealed sweet-and-sour pork. Looking around, Kenny noticed his wife's cashmere coat heaped on the floor, where she must've dumped it when she got home. "Janine?" He called upstairs, but it was silent. That's odd, he thought. Why didn't she tell me she was here? When he picked up the coat, her phone fell out. He noticed a text from Les that referenced him (Is Kenny sleeping? Can I call u?) and his blood froze. What the . . . ? Alarmed, he unlocked the phone (password: LOVEDOG) and scrolled backward in time until he found an earlier exchange between Les and his wife:

> put your money where your mouth is. Come work for me. XOX
> ps—I love your mouth. Have I ever told you that?
> pss—delete this

>> you know where you can put YOUR mouth,
>> ya big dumb bunny
>> xoxo 4ever Jeannie

Thunderstruck, Kenny sat down, still holding the phone. What did this mean; what should he do? He wasn't sure; he didn't know.

*Think*, he told himself. He tried, he tried, but nothing made sense, so he slipped his wife's phone back into her coat, and headed for the stairs.

"You home, sweet Jeannie?"

ON HIS WAY to work the next morning, Kenny retrieved a voice mail message. "Hey, Kenny! Scarlett Raynes. Just wanted to circle back about the comp director spot. Unfortunately, we offered the job to another candidate who accepted this morning, but we'll keep your résumé on file. Thank you so much for your time; sorry it didn't work out. Oh, and by the way: Donald Kwon doesn't go by 'Donald Lee.' Lee is his middle name. I'm afraid my assistant Rory may have confused you. She kept calling him 'Donald Lee' too! Just thought you might want to know in case you cross paths again."

# LUNCH TRUCK

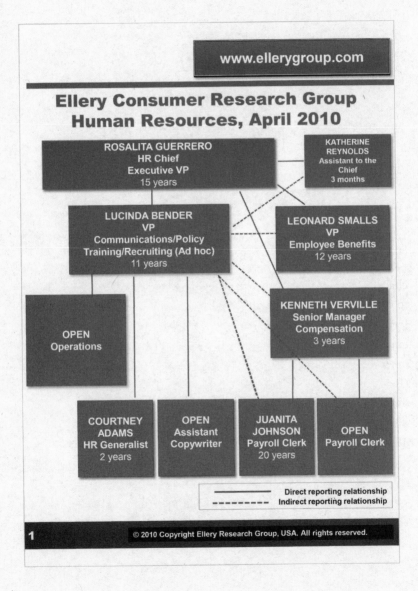

www.ellerygroup.com

# Ellery Consumer Research Group
# Human Resources, April 2010

**ROSALITA GUERRERO**
HR Chief
Executive VP
15 years

**KATHERINE REYNOLDS**
Assistant to the Chief
3 months

**LUCINDA BENDER**
VP
Communications/Policy
Training/Recruiting (Ad hoc)
11 years

**LEONARD SMALLS**
VP
Employee Benefits
12 years

**OPEN**
Operations

**KENNETH VERVILLE**
Senior Manager
Compensation
3 years

**COURTNEY ADAMS**
HR Generalist
2 years

**OPEN**
Assistant
Copywriter

**JUANITA JOHNSON**
Payroll Clerk
20 years

**OPEN**
Payroll Clerk

——————— Direct reporting relationship
- - - - - - - Indirect reporting relationship

## 17

# ROBERT HIRSCH,
# IN TRANSITION

APRIL 2010

When Rob finally realized he was being laid off, he thought of his father. Before retiring, Jerry Hirsch was a hard-charging lawyer with a brutal streak, a natural raconteur who loved to entertain dinner guests with his courtroom shenanigans. To Rob, Jerry was a world-class asshole whose humor came at everyone else's expense. To Jerry, Rob was a sulky teenager who refused to grow up. To the rest of the family, their acidic asides (Jerry) and petulance (Rob) made meals a trial. But two years back, Rob's mother had died unexpectedly, an event that cracked open his father's crusty shell to reveal a soft pink interior. Then the month before, Rob's elder daughter, Alison, got a kidney infection and spent a week in the hospital, with Rob and Maddy trading off nights so someone could stay home with Jessie. Allie recovered, but while she recuperated, Maddy had to fly to San Francisco on gallery business, leaving Rob behind with both girls, a dead Honda Civic, baskets of dirty laundry, and piles of work, all of which (except for the girls) he ignored. Jerry had moved to Cape Cod, and when he suggested he drive down to Brooklyn, Rob reluctantly agreed.

On Jerry's first night in town, they were standing in Rob's

kitchen, making small talk while Rob threw dinner together. Al-though Jerry was sitting at the table, there wasn't much extra space to move around, so Rob felt like his father was on top of him. But just as he was about to ask Jerry if he might be more comfortable in the living room, his father started to speak.

"I wish . . . Rob, I've been thinking . . . hold on a sec—" Jerry peeked around the corner to make sure the girls were out of ear-shot. "Rob, I just want to say that I often wish I'd been less of a prick when you were a kid. Had I been different then, things might be easier for us now." His voice cracked a little at the end, making him sound sheepish and sad.

Peering into the refrigerator, Rob had his back to his father. While gratified by Jerry's words, he was at a loss for his own. "Thank you," he said, focusing on a half-empty jar of Prego sauce. "I wish you had been less of a prick, too." He felt resentful but also wanted to cry, the same way he felt at his mom's funeral when he saw Jerry lean against his litigation partner and collapse into sobs.

Elaine had died from a pulmonary embolism. Though she'd had a knee replacement two months before, it was a routine surgery, so her death came as a shock. After fifty-four years of marriage, it also appeared to have humbled Jerry. "She was the love of my life," he said on his second night in Brooklyn. "I miss her every minute of every day." To which Rob said, "I miss her all the time, too." They reminisced about her, and for a few brief minutes, Rob felt like his father's son, which choked him up all over again. The next day, while Rob was at work, Jerry used his venerable legal skills to stack the dishwasher, vacuum, mop, and wash four loads of laundry. Having never before seen his father do chores, Rob was astonished; it was like seeing a dog drive a car. "My house is so clean you can eat off the floor," his father explained. "Helps pass the time." That night, Jerry taught Allie and Jessie five-card stud, and then they all watched *Titanic*, which the girls had seen nine times, and couldn't believe Jerry hadn't seen once. "Oh my God, Grandpa," nine-year-old Jessie said, climbing over him to grab the DVD. "You'll *die*." Jerry didn't die, but he did blink back tears when the old couple clutched each other as the water roared in. It occurred to Rob, who blinked back a few tears himself, that his father was lonesome, a feeling he'd never associated with the man, largely because he'd never considered Jerry's feelings before. His throat was thick with emotion when he invited his dad to extend his stay for the rest of the week. He wanted to add how grateful he was for Jerry's help. Instead he said, "The kids are so glad you're here," which felt more appropriate—manageable, rather.

Pleased, Jerry continued to cook, clean, and do laundry. When he went into the city to have dinner with Rob's older sister and her family, he encouraged Rob to join him, but Rob declined for reasons he was ashamed to admit. Larissa, a lawyer like Jerry, had done everything right: Wellesley, Columbia Law, lawyer husband, kids at Dalton—the works. While Rob loved her, being with Larissa reminded him of all he'd lost—not just their mom but also the chance to make smarter choices. "Thanks," he said. "Not this trip, though." The next morning, when it was time to head home, neither he nor his dad was ready. "That went too quickly," Jerry said. Standing on the street, he clapped his son on the back. "You're doing great, Rob. For a while there, I wasn't sure you could pull it together. You seemed so rudderless. But look at you! You chose a career and stuck to it. I'm proud of you."

"I *was* rudderless. *You* found my first job; I just showed up. Still, these days I feel lucky to be employed." Rob reached out to shake his father's hand, but Jerry grabbed him in a bear hug. "Keep up the good work!" Jerry's voice was gruff. "Call me." After kissing both girls, he jumped into his car, tooted his horn twice, then zoomed away.

When Rosa called Rob into her office two days later, he was still feeling lucky. So when she said, solemnly, "I'm sorry, Rob. You deserve better," he was drifting a bit, his head up in the clouds.

She paused. "Brace yourself, Robert," she said kindly. "This could hurt."

At which point Rob realized he should probably pay attention.

"Oh," Rosa said sadly. "It's not right." She looked into his eyes, and spoke slowly and clearly, as if he wasn't fluent in her language. "Rob, we're letting you go."

For a second, all the sound drained from the world.

"Rob?"

Blood rushed into his ears. They were letting him *go*? Letting *him* go? Rob heard the words, but they lacked context and floated in the air like dust particles, like dust in the wind. "Dust in the Wind." He liked that song, once. He pictured his mother's face, vivid red lipstick, sunny smile, liquid eyes. He saw his father's shoulders shaking at her funeral, the curl of his hair against a starched white collar. He needed a trim, and now Rob knew why: Elaine wasn't even in the ground yet, but his father was already falling apart. Poor Jerry. Just yesterday, they'd scheduled another visit. This news—that after everything, Rob got himself fired—would crush the man.

"Hold on, Rosa." Rob waved his hands as if clearing away smoke. "You're *firing* me?"

"Don't say 'firing,' no. Let's be precise, Rob. There are legal implications to the words we use; you know that."

Rob's eyes darted around the room. They were alone, which was one reason for his confusion. Separations required an audience: HR rep, supervisor, department head; Legal, too, on occasion. (Last year, when they were processing twenty layoffs a day and tension was high, they stationed a security guard outside the conference room as an added precaution.) Also, Rosa should be following a script with fill-in-the-blank dialogue boxes and contingency wording for every situation. Instead, she kept veering off-message. "It's so warm." She stood up and cracked open her door. "Katherine? Some water, please?" She sat down. "Thirsty, Rob? I'm so dry."

Rob was silent. The only noise in the room was the faint hiss of the radiator.

"Rob, this is a reduction in force, a business decision unrelated to performance. You've been an asset to Ellery, and I'll give you a glowing reference. In fact, we'll have Lucy draft a letter this afternoon. You're not the only one; several other employees will be having this same conversation, three from HR. Of course I shouldn't tell you this, but maybe you already know? We're letting Maisie Fresh go. Also Kenny, though not yet; he still has projects to complete, so we're waiting. To be candid, he was a disappointment; I expected a lot more. I misjudged him, I'm afraid."

"Kenny? *Verville*?" Kenny was a tool, but Rob felt a flash of anger on his behalf. "That's not right!"

Rosa was unmoved. "According to Lucy, he has another job lined up."

Why was she telling him this? Rosa never disclosed confidential details—and certainly not during a separation—yet she continued to list names. "Gregory Dwyer in Finance—he's an asshole, anyway. Good riddance. Anna Fleischman in Legal. I always liked Anna, but apparently I was the only one. Oh, and Roxanne Walker. Her, I'll miss."

It was truly over for him here, Rob realized. Why else would Rosa give up all pretense of decorum? "Does Lucy know?" It sickened him to think that his best friend—yes, that's what she was, he realized—would willingly withhold this information. All these years, he'd also considered Lucy his peer, his equal, which, he saw now, was lunacy. They were never equals. Lucy had been standing on his shoulders from the day she showed up—not that he begrudged her any iota of success. Why would he? How could he? Lucy Bender worked her ass off. In his career, Rob had met lots of women like her: eager to please, happy to help—women who got shit done. (In business as in life, women were far more capable than men. What man could oversee a million-dollar implementation project, change a diaper, sew a SpongeBob costume, and drive carpool—*without complaint*? The gender wars could be summed up in one sentence: "Okay, I'll take it on." Nine times out of ten, this was a preemptive offer made by a woman, for which she expected—and received— nothing in return. "That's okay," Lucy would volunteer, "I'll take it on"—thereby allowing Rob to go home while she and her incomparable work ethic stayed behind until dawn. The tenth time, when Rob would agree to do an assignment, it would be as a favor granted, a debt owed.) Of course this was how his story would end. He was a fool to ever think otherwise. I'll miss her, Rob thought. He and Lucy had spent every weekday together for ten years. Who would he talk to? Who'd make him laugh?

"Lucy knows," he said, this time a statement of fact.

Rosa shook her head. "No one knows. Just the board—and Peter, of course. I told Peter it was a shitty decision, and he agreed. He was furious about it."

"You talked to *Peter*?"

"Peter?" Her forehead furrowed. "No, Peter and I haven't spoken." For a second, her face lit up. "Why, have you heard from him?"

"Rosa, you just said Peter knew." Rob was dizzy and disoriented. The air felt lighter, his breathing shallow. May 1 was two days away, but the temperature outside had dropped. Rosa's office was overheated; under Rob's shirt, sweat leaked from his pores and soaked through the fabric.

"Excuse me." She covered her mouth, embarrassed. "I meant Rutherford."

Though Rob could see Rosa beside him—her honey-colored hair, wide red mouth—her voice was coming from a great remove, as if they weren't just sitting across a table but also divided by glass. The office had taken on a heightened, cinematic quality: this was a scene being staged, and he and Rosa were acting out parts. Is this shock? Am I in shock? Rob touched his chest. Everything worked;

he felt his heart beating, heard his slow, raspy breathing. But why did his hand look so enormous? This is shock, right? Then Rosa started to pace, compounding his discomfort.

"You need to believe one thing, Rob," Rosa insisted. "Rutherford *did not* want to do this. The board forced his hand. You see the numbers. Business is lousy and will be for some time."

"That guy never gave a shit about me; he only cares about the bottom line." Rob stopped, struck by his rancor. "All due respect." Did Leo know? He hoped not. They'd been out to lunch a bunch of times since their brainstorming dinner, and while he didn't think of Leo as a friend, he also didn't want the man's pity. Then again, when had he started caring what Leo Smalls thought of him?

"You've been recruiting a long time, Rob. Since the beginning of your career?"

"Yes, but at Nielsen I focused on training. That's why you hired me, remember? I only took on recruiting because you asked me to."

"Maybe that was a mistake," Rosa admitted.

"It probably was. Training is a better fit for me than recruiting—less paperwork, less phone time, less aggravation. I'm not detail-oriented, as you know. Also, rejecting people takes its toll. I hate this part"—Rob waved at Rosa, then himself. "Layoffs kill me; it's excruciating to watch people leave, even if they're headed to a better place. Sounds like I'm a hospice worker, doesn't it? It's hard to fire coworkers; it makes me feel responsible, or what's the word? Complicit? Still, I can see now"—he waved back and forth again—"it's *a lot* more difficult to be the one getting fired." His laugh sounded fake, but at least he wasn't down on his knees, hugging the floor; at least he was still upright in his chair.

"I know what you mean." Rosa sighed. "Business isn't emotional, but people are, so the lines get blurry; we cross them without meaning to. Rob, I don't want to step over the line, but I feel you might be better served if you shift back to training. You're a personable man. You're also decent, which is a rare quality these days.

Training plays to your strengths; you'll also find more opportunity down the . . . the . . . the whatever, the path." She patted her folders. "We should go through these . . ." But instead of opening one, she sat quietly, staring at him.

"You okay, Rosa?"

"Not really, Rob. I too find these conversations difficult, especially with someone I care about." She squinted, as if trying to recall something. "People react so differently when they're being let go. Some are silent. Others lose their filters and blurt out everything they've been holding back: you're a bitch, you're fat, I always hated you. Once a guy at Sony told me I stank; he was referring to my perfume, but I thought he meant my body. 'You smell like my dead grandma' was what he said. Howard had spent a fortune on a bottle of L'Air du Temps, but I threw it out. Who wants to smell like a dead person? But then the guy remembered he had severance coming, and didn't want to fuck up the money, so he tried to take it back."

Rob couldn't quite follow her logic but laughed anyway. Someday he'd remember this, how instead of making his execution horrible, Rosa had told him a story, offered him dignity.

"You know who aggravates me most, though?" she continued. "The ones who say every day how much they hate this place, but when they get fired, they wail like someone died. I guess someone does die. 'To lose a job is to lose a life'—Leo said that once."

"I do feel like I'm losing my life," Rob said. "This was a life, right? Working here was my life, not my whole life but a large piece of it." Any other time, Rob might have enjoyed this, sitting here with Rosa, musing over the big questions.

She patted her folders again. "We should move on."

The next twenty minutes were a blur of numbers, dates, and details Rob found impossible to absorb, which was odd, given all the times he'd sat on Rosa's side of the table. But the net-net was this: in exchange for two more weeks and his agreement (in writing) to take no legal action, he'd walk away with a decent package. His last day would be May 13. His benefits would end May 31 but he was eligible for COBRA, so he should talk to Maddy and—

Maddy! Icy terror seized him, shrinking his balls. How could he tell her this? She was already so anxious about money. Leaning across the table, he looked Rosa in the eye. "Please don't fire me. I'll buckle down, come in early, stay late—whatever it takes. I'm almost forty-four. Who's gonna hire me? Please don't make me beg, Rosa. Please don't make me beg for my job, please."

"Now listen to me, Rob. You're still young. Second, this isn't the end. Third, I'll go through my Rolodex. So will Leo, Lucy, and Peter."

Her kindness was the only thing keeping Rob from shouting, Shut up, shut up! *Shut the fuck up!* "I need air." He stood up so fast his chair turned over. "Excuse me." He left before Rosa could protest, though in a move he only thought about later, he was careful not to slam the door, as if to demonstrate his professionalism despite his feral state.

Out in the hallway, Leo headed toward him, but Rob didn't stop. He must've looked stricken, because Leo caught his elbow. "You okay?"

What a fucking reversal, Rob thought. Twenty years ago, Leo was the one in the hall, hair matted, face wet. "What's the matter?" someone, not Rob, had asked. "My assignment's over," Leo moaned and continued to moan until a manager led him away. Back then, nothing about the guy made sense—not his crying or his black eyebrows, definitely not his neediness. But in retrospect, now that he knew Leo's dad had been dying, the scene took on tragic dimensions. Rob could see he'd acted deplorably, giving Leo the cold shoulder when he passed by. "I'm sorry, Leo," he said as he speedwalked to the elevator. "I'm really sorry."

Leo trotted beside him. "What happened with Rosa?"

"I'm sorry about your dad. When we were younger, I was a prick.

Maybe if I hadn't been such a prick then, it would be easier now. I don't know. But I'm sorry." He saw that Leo's brow was furrowed in confusion and concern; still, he didn't stop. "I'll call you."

Downstairs, Rob sped along Tenth Avenue. While cold, it was the kind of day he and Evan used to live for: bright sun, clear sky, birds swooping. They'd lock up the office and spend the afternoon at Murphy's, flirting with pretty girls. Scrolling through his Black-Berry, Rob cursed his lot. Here he was, forty-three years old, fired from his job and without a single friend to console him. He spotted Evan's name, which he'd entered into his contacts, believing they might actually see each other again. Of course that never happened.

Fuck it, he thought, and tapped call. Evan shocked him by picking up.

"Hey," Rob blurted out. "It's me. Rob . . . uh . . . Bobby Hirsch. You around? I'd love to see you." He faltered. "If you're free . . . I know it's last-minute. "

There was a long pause.

"We haven't been able to connect, so I thought I'd take a chance . . ."

Another long pause. Rob wanted to die, or at the very least, hang up.

"Sure, Bobby," Evan said finally. And then, as if it had been nine minutes, not nine years, since their last conversation, he told Rob where to find him. "I'll be at the bar. Come down."

IT WAS ROB who had pushed for the business. Back in the late nineties, after almost a decade of eight-hour days in beige-on-beige cubicles, he'd started to feel like a caged animal. Evan, normally game for whatever, was reluctant. "We're two dopes who like to get stoned. What do we know about running a business?" Maddy was similarly skeptical. Allie wasn't even thirteen months old, she'd re-minded Rob. Plus, she was no fan of Evan. "You really want this?" she asked.

"Not just want, Maddy; I need this." Although Rob had graduated from Dartmouth years before, he still hadn't considered his career in any formal way. His degree was in English, he read a lot, he liked travel writing (as a magazine intern, he'd written about a summer vacation in Spain)—but this was the extent of his planning. What were his passions? What did he like to do? Where did he want to be in five years? In ten? He had no idea; he assumed the answers would appear at some point. In the meantime, his dad talked to the head of Legal at Revlon; they had an entry-level spot in HR— recruiting, training, that sort of thing. Sure, it soundly deadly to Rob, but a job was a job until he figured out what came next. A few years later, his boss went to Nielsen; Rob followed, and thus was on a "path." So starting his own business was the first time he'd ever stared his career in the eye and wrestled the fucker to the ground.

In March of 1997, Rob and Evan quit their jobs, combined Rob's meager savings with money from Evan's trust fund, and kicked off Guy Friday, Inc. The pitch: Lifestyle Management for Men of Means. The plan: Hit up their network, especially the cash-rich overworked bankers and lawyers. In theory, Rob and Evan would act as lifestyle curators for busy executives, offering customized advice on everything from business dinners to upscale decor. In reality, they ran errands for Evan's former lacrosse teammates. They picked up dry cleaning, dropped off keys, stood on line at the DMV. Rob, who wasn't cut out for manual labor, never stopped bitching; Evan, who eschewed schedules, missed critical meetings. They bickered as a matter of course. "I've got a kid," Rob said, not just once. "I've got bills. You can't flake out." Evan didn't appreciate Rob using his daughter to guilt him; Rob didn't appreciate Evan's cavalier attitude. Their mutual frustration polluted the air. Minor slipups provoked volcanic reactions. By the one-year mark, they couldn't stand to be in the same room together. It was over; they both felt it. So they went to Murphy's, their favorite bar, talked man-to-man, and elected to put on their wheels and book. (In college there was a kid, a Rollerblader, who said "Guess I'll put on my wheels and book" every time he left the room. Rob and Evan mocked him mercilessly, but the expression endured.)

So it was meaningful, Rob decided, to be seeing Evan today, the very day he lost the very job he started when Guy Friday went south. Equally meaningful: a decade back, all their man-to-mans had taken place at Murphy's, the same place he sat in now, nursing a beer.

The door swung open. Rob turned, but it wasn't Evan. He started to call Maddy then stopped, not ready for the "I've Been Let Go" speech and its sidebar discussion: "Now What?"

Now what?

Twenty minutes later, Rob ordered another beer. Evan was chronically late, and Rob recalled how twitchy this always made him. As he debated leaving, a well-built man glided into the bar. This time it was Evan: same thatch of sandy hair, same proud, athletic strut. He wore a tight T-shirt that showcased his massive arms and broad shoulders. His hair was thinner in front, his jowls fuller; his hooded eyes, once sleepy and suggestive, now narrowed slits under loose skin. But the crooked smile was vintage Evan, that blinding flash still his greatest asset.

"Hey man." The bartender greeted Evan with a raised glass.

Evan held up a hand. "Danny." Spotting Rob, he called out, "Bobby Hirsch! Back in a few." Then he pivoted on his heel to answer his phone. Both men had once carried first-generation clunkers, and seeing Evan's sleek new device reminded Rob that a lot of time had passed.

Too much time, he thought, as the minutes ticked by. This was stupid.

Finally Evan meandered over and slid onto a stool. He ordered a beer, checked Rob's glass, ordered a second, then swiveled around. The two men were finally face-to-face.

"So." Evan's smile was warm, generous. Rob felt himself yielding. "Where were we?"

WE'RE DOING OKAY, Rob thought. It's only been, what? Twenty minutes? Already Evan had leaned over and said, "It's good to see you, Bobby. Wish we hadn't waited so long."

They kept the conversation easy, though not light. Rob talked about his mom dying, his dad's lonely life. "Damn," Evan said, shaking his head over Elaine. "I'm sorry. Your mom was tremendous." They sat quietly, remembering. Evan told Rob about his ex-wife, Gretl, whom he'd married four years before and then divorced six months later. She was young and stunning but—he couldn't believe he was admitting this—a total mystery. "I was so sure I knew *everything* about women, but living with her was nothing like dating her. She was *impossible*." He flashed his famous smile. "Maybe the problem was me." Then he laughed loudly, unconvinced. Rob didn't ask for details; nor did Evan offer any. Apparently they both saw a need for boundaries.

Evan described his girlfriend, Lux, also young, stunning, and a mother with two young sons. She was immersed in the snack-and-juice-box routine; he found this endearing. "Ever think I'd fall in love with a mom?"

"Sure," Rob replied. He studied a woman who was leaning over the bar. Her grin, quick and cunning, reminded him of Lucy's. "Anyone can fall in love with anyone."

Shaking his head, Evan marveled at his own good fortune. "I am head over heels."

To which Rob, feeling drunk, said, "We should go out—you, me, Maddy, and Lux."

Evan gulped his drink. Rob watched his Adam's apple bulge as he swallowed. "Yep. We should. Hey, how's Allie? She's, what? Fourteen?"

"Thirteen. Our younger daughter, Jessie, is nine."

"Two kids! Look at you, big stud." Rob's father had said the same thing: *Look at you!*

They kept talking about people they knew, guys from Dartmouth who made it big, others who flamed out. After they downed another round of beers (Rob's fourth) and two shots of tequila each, Evan told Rob that his father, Victor, was going blind. "Macular degeneration."

Victor Graham was a painter who'd palled around with Jackson Pollock in the 1950s—well known in certain circles, legendary in others. Victor's wild, colorful abstracts fetched high prices, though nowhere near those of his more famous friend's. "I've kept up with your father's career. But didn't hear about his eyes. Christ, Evan, I'm so sorry."

Hunched over, Evan peered into his glass. "I appreciate that. If I seem unresponsive—unreturned calls, canceled plans—it's because I'm preoccupied with him. It's not an excuse; well, maybe it is an excuse. But it's also the truth."

"No, no. I understand." Though the news about Victor was awful, Rob did feel some relief that Evan hadn't kept blowing him off for no reason. "It's also hard to go backward, to see people . . ." He wasn't sure how to finish. "Can I ask you something? About our business." He hesitated. "Do you think it was . . . uh . . . foolish to give it up?" He couldn't bring himself to say "cowardly," which is how he'd felt at the time; that he quit just when it started to get difficult.

"Hell, no. You had a wife and kid. You needed a steady income. Honestly, I can't recall how we split—only that we handled it badly. So for the record, I'm sorry if I was an asshole."

This was a relief, too, that Evan didn't hold him responsible. Rob nodded. "Yeah, me too." He was drunk en route to blasted, and Evan was telling a long, complicated joke that had no punch line, but Rob was already laughing. He was feeling so good that when he remembered he'd lost his job (rather, was in the *process of* losing his job), the idea wasn't so troubling. *I'll just find another one. What's the big deal?*

"I'm glad I contacted you," he told Evan, hoping this fit into the flow of their conversation. "It's great to be hanging out again . . . like this . . . here . . . together."

"My dad is an ox," Evan was saying. "He'll live forever. Two more shots, Danny."

Rob's BlackBerry rang; he ignored it. It was only five, but felt much later inside the dark bar. Checking his phone, he saw that Lucy and Leo had both called. It pained Rob to be leaving Lucy, though they'd barely spent any time together in the last two months—she was working on a project for Rutherford she couldn't talk about, too busy even for a brief constitutional. She'd completely withdrawn, and the abruptness of it stung Rob more than he cared to admit. Impulsively he sent her a text. I miss you xo.

Her reply was quick, as if she was sitting there, waiting. Miss you too. Where R u?

"I should hit the road," he told Evan, sucking back a third shot. It was almost dinnertime; he still had to give Maddy the news. Evan hadn't asked why Rob was free on a Thursday afternoon. Should Rob tell him he was out of work? Hey, he could say, let's resurrect Guy Friday. Chuckling, he pictured Evan's reaction. "Wish I could stay; it was great to catch up."

"MoMA is having a Victor Graham retrospective," Evan said in a beery non sequitur. "Come to the opening, he'd love to see you." Evan gave Rob the date, which Rob keyed, clumsily, into his BlackBerry.

Rob stood up. "Maddy's waiting." His phone jangled. It was Lucy, another text, this one more urgent. Where are you muthafucka? Call me!

"No way, Bobby Hirsch. You can't leave this bar yet; we're just getting started." This time Evan yanked on his sleeve so hard, Rob lost his balance. Luckily, he caught the lip of the bar before smack-ing his face, but the force of Evan's grip stunned him. It reminded him of their roughhousing, which he'd always hated, despite play-ing along. Evan was bigger and stronger; afterward, Rob would be bruised all over and sore for days.

"Stay," Evan commanded, sounding drunker than he had only five minutes before. "Sit with me, drink with me. Oh, shit. You won't *believe* who I ran into—*Daisy Fordham*. You were so hot for her. Tell me, Bobby, please: what did you see in that girl?"

"Daisy Fordham, wow." Rob hadn't thought about Daisy in for-ever. She was a bottom-heavy rich girl with curly hair, whom Rob had worshipped from afar. Not even a kiss passed between them. Evan had slept with Daisy twice, but swore this was before Rob mentioned her.

"You *loved* Daisy," Evan said, which made Rob cringe.

"It was a *crush*."

"Come on, Bobby. Don't sweat it. I'm glad you're happy; your life with Maddy sounds fantastic." Saying this, Evan sounded sin-cere. But then, rolling a shot glass between his palms, he added, "I should confess . . . I fucked her."

Rob's mind reeled. "Maddy?" Evan fucked his *wife*? When?

Watching him scramble, Evan cracked up. "Of course not, you dope." He slapped Rob's cheek. "*Daisy.* I fucked *Daisy Fordham*."

Rob's cheek burned. He hated when Evan did this, wound him up just to see him squirm. Evan hadn't forgotten he'd told Rob about sleeping with Daisy—Christ, he needled Rob about it for years. Evan wanted Rob to think he'd fucked Maddy. He wanted to watch Rob break, even for just a split second, to remind him who was the alpha. "You knew I liked Daisy," Rob said with sudden clarity, "but you slept with her anyway." A long-buried piece of history, yet he couldn't believe how fresh it was, how raw he felt.

"Don't be like that." Yawning, Evan held up two fingers. "An-other round, please."

Rob knew it didn't matter—of course it didn't. Still, he couldn't shake it off. He dug for his wallet. "Not for me, thanks. Gotta go. But Victor's opening is in my phone, so we're set."

"Great; I'll call you." Evan stood up, caught Rob in a hug, squeezed him tight. "You're still a pussy, Bobby," he whispered. "But I miss you."

Rob inhaled Evan's soapy smell, the slightest tang of perspiration. You were my best friend, he thought, wanting to say something to this effect. Instead, he said, "Do that. Call me."

They wouldn't talk again, Rob knew. Evan was the same; maybe he was too. Either way, the rest was different. Besides, Rob had to turn in his BlackBerry, so even if Evan did call, the device would belong to someone else, with any trace of the prior owner stripped clean.

n the morning, Rob had a banging headache and queasy stomach. He was never, ever drinking again. He sat in his kitchen, unsure of his next move. In theory, he should eat breakfast and head to the office. He should meet Rosa so she could finish firing him. He should use his last days at Ellery to organize his network, work the phones, and face the next twenty-odd years of his career. If nothing else, he should address the looming question: Now what?

But Rob didn't place much stock in theoretical pursuits. He was a practical guy who preferred known-knowns, which was why he continued to sit on his ass, suited up in his brown-mouse uniform as per usual, eating Fiber One twigs and trying to appear gainfully employed.

"I'm leaving in five minutes," Maddy called out.

"Right behind you," he replied with forced cheer. "Don't wait for me."

He had three texts and a voice mail from Lucy, two voice mails from Rosa, and two from Leo, all asking where he was, why hadn't he called, and in Rosa's case, what the hell he was thinking. "You can't just walk out! We have legal issues to discuss, such as"—her

voice dropped—"your money." She seemed afraid he was gone for
good, despite knowing full well that no one forfeits severance. At
stake was four months' salary, including unused vacation time (ever
kind-hearted, Rosa had written off the days he lost taking care of
Allie); but to get all this, he had to give them two more weeks of
work. "You're acting like a child, Robert," she added.

Rob scraped the last few twigs with his spoon. Maddy stood
by the door, buttoning her coat. Yesterday, it had been freezing
out; today there was rain. Early spring in New York was always a
kaleidoscope of weather conditions that changed without rhyme or
reason. Luckily, his wife had a coat for all of them: jackets, blazers,
ponchos, slickers, parkas—you name it, she owned it. Today she
wore a lightweight coat—a duster, she called it, a word Rob had
never associated with outerwear. This year, like all years, he wore
his puffy coat until T-shirt season, which Maddy said was nuts. Just
buy a windbreaker or leather jacket, she told him. But Rob was adamant. Why muddy the waters with so many choices? One coat or
no coat was how he rolled.

"Rob? Are you okay?"

He'd been staring into his cereal bowl, probably for too long,
though who could say? Time was elastic, painstakingly slow at one
turn, accelerated the next. Rob found himself losing long stretches
he couldn't recall, but his heart was constantly revving up, like an
engine in overdrive. "You know what the saddest thing in the world
is, Maddy?"

"Poverty? Homelessness? Child abuse?" She picked up the garbage. "I'll take this on my way out. Rob, I really have to go."

"An empty bowl." He held it up, orphan-style. "All gone."

Maddy tucked her keys in her bag. "So what's the deal? You going to work or not?"

"Of course! Why wouldn't I?" Last night after leaving Evan,
Rob had roamed the streets alone, heady with the feeling of release.
What he needed, he decided, was an adventure. Without a job, he

could take off. The world beyond Brooklyn felt untamed and ripe for exploration. But after a few blocks, he had to pee and his neck burned where his bag dug into his skin, so he decided to go exploring tomorrow. Besides, he missed his kids. Once home, he straightened up enough to kiss them hello and good night, told Maddy he was too tired to talk, and then fell into a drunken sleep. He dreamed about Lucy straddling him, with her blouse unbuttoned and tits spilling out. She encouraged Rob to rub his face between them, which he did, gladly, until she pushed him away. "Not you, idiot—Evan." But when he tongued her nipples, he could tell she enjoyed it, which was intoxicating while it was happening but he woke up feeling horrified. And perverted. With a hard-on. What the fuck? He couldn't bear to look at Maddy, so he averted his eyes every time she came near him. Rob assumed they'd have a heart-to-heart over cereal, but bombarded with visions of Lucy's tits, he couldn't bring himself to raise the issue, any issue. "I don't feel like rushing," he said.

"So don't rush, Rob. Oh! My wallet's in my other bag." Exit Maddy, stage right.

Rob was still twitchy, and his head was flooded with worries, not just over rent, but also braces, college, weddings, heart stents, IRA taxes, burial costs. Turned out his casual, laissez-faire attitude hid fears upon fears that were multiplying faster than he could catalog them. Rob's anxiety was so palpable he didn't have the mental bandwidth to wallow in his bad feelings about seeing Evan, though disappointment nagged like an unfinished project. As Rob ran through his family's outstanding payables, he spiraled to that dark place where he was bent over, begging his wealthier sister for help.

Enter Maddy, stage right. "What should we do about the Honda?"

Oh, and a new car. Their ancient Civic was barely running. Maddy had found a 2001 Volvo on Craigslist, but it was five grand minus the trade-in. Last night, Evan mentioned that his girlfriend,

Lux, drove a BMW, a detail that needled Rob. He hated driving—he didn't care about cars—so why did he give a shit about Lux's BMW?

"I like the Volvo," Maddy pressed, "and we have to move fast. Should we buy it?"

Her question was why Rob couldn't talk about his job. While he wouldn't mind his wife's sympathy, telling her would open the floodgates, and he'd be deluged with a hundred more questions just like it—keep HBO? the *Times* delivery? dinners out?—not that his response should be in doubt. Across the board, the answer was no. No car, no way, not now. I'm going down, Maddy! Mayday! Mayday! SOS!

"Rob? The car?"

"I'm thinking." Rising from his seat, he grabbed the Fiber One box.

"What are you doing?" Maddy asked. "*Rob*, it's after nine!"

She kept saying his name, Rob, Rob, Rob, like he was her naughty son, Rob, Rob, Rob, and he snapped, "*What does it look I'm doing?*" and then caught himself. "Sorry." His voice was calm. "I'm having more cereal, Maddy. I haven't taken a shit in two days." He refilled his OBER mug, rubbing the phantom *R* and *T*. The *O* and second *R* were coming off too. Then, as if the thought had just struck, he said, "I like the Volvo, Maddy. It handles well and will last forever. We should buy it." This, he said with finality. "I wonder, though—it's a lousy deal for a nine-year-old car." He sipped his coffee. "You know what? Let's hold off for now. We'll find something better."

"You sure?"

With one hand on the door, the other holding the trash, Maddy was all set to go, but Rob put down his bowl and approached her. As he stared into the brackish ocean of his wife's eyes, he sent her a message: I got fired, Maddy. Who's gonna hire me, with my so-so résumé and cheap shoes? Now what, Maddy? Now what?

"Yes, Maddy," he said quietly. "I'm sure. We'll find a better car."

She nodded, and he suspected she was sending him her own

messages: What is wrong with you? Put your bowl away, wipe down the sink, and get to work. But all she said was, "Call me later." When she walked out, the door slammed behind her.

Alone—finally!—Rob stretched out on the couch and turned on the TV.

DURING ROB'S YEARS of recruiting, candidates of every stripe passed through his door. Most were run-of-the-mill: freshly minted graduates, ambitious middle managers, no-nonsense senior leaders. Others less so: the war hero with an oozing eye wound, the white-collar felon, the former call girl. Still others broke his heart: the eighty-year-old with no savings, the cancer patient desperate for medical benefits. Regardless of their circumstances, they all sat on the other side of Rob's desk, necks scrubbed (or not), suits pressed (or not), nails trimmed (or not), eyes hopeful: Please pick me. Pick me. Please.

Starting out, Rob perceived his job as more of a curiosity than an actual fact. Bursting with youth, smug with lucky breaks, he looked at the human tragedy on parade with a cynical eye. Feeling no commonality with his interviewees, he silently mocked their ill-fitted shirts and bloodstained trousers. Sprayed-on hair and Magic-Markered stilettos. Snake tattoos peeking out of frayed cuffs. Hems patched with duct tape and staples. Pools of sweat. Runny noses. Sneezes and burps. Hiccups and coughs. Misspelled names (their own) on thank-you notes. Once, a female candidate farted. It was innocuous—one brief toot, low and sonorous—but something struck Rob in that off-kilter way, and when his laughter rose up, he couldn't hold back. Jangly with hysteria, he fled the room—still laughing, apologizing. The woman was ideal on paper, references, experience, education all checked out. But in the end, Rob turned her down. It was too much, the thought of passing her in the halls, and him with the way he behaved.

But as he got older, after he had a wife and kids, after his one-shot business tanked and he returned to the nine-to-five grind, Rob realized he was locked into this HR track for, well, for the rest of his working days. His sneers turned to sympathy, then empathy, and by the time he hit his mid-thirties, the candidates had become his lost lambs and he their shepherd. Each soul before him was a father's son, a mother's daughter; and despite the desk that separated them, Rob and his applicants were muddling through together—this moment, this profession, this life. When revenue was high, it was fun to offer jobs, help people follow their bliss. But the economy turned as it does, then turned again; soon, there were too few spots to go around. No, he told most of the people he met. I can't pick you. I'm sorry but . . .

the CEO wants to promote from within
there's no longer a budget for that position
we'll keep your résumé on file, and let you know if something
   opens up.

The one thing he couldn't say—for legal reasons—was the truth: You don't fit in here.

From time to time, Rob tried to inhabit his younger, callous self, but he was now in his forties and far too entrenched. So he went the other way, reveling in his small victories, taking pride in his new hires, inviting Cappy Cuomo over for dinner. But it wasn't enough, and Rob couldn't escape. He'd lie awake, ruminating about the people he'd rejected, his own pathetic fate, and the rounds and rounds of layoffs he was expected to orchestrate. Then one night Maddy asked him, "Rob, do you think you might be in the wrong job? Temperamentally, I mean?"

Actually no, Maddy, he hadn't. Because if he *was* in the wrong job, if he truly had been motoring down the wrong road for the past twenty years, then his whole life was wrong. And then what did he have? Then what, Maddy? He wasn't trained to do anything else.

When he fell into HR, he was too young to know better; now he was too old to start over. Robert Samuel Hirsch was an ocean liner cruising across the water at thirty thousand knots; to change course at this point would take an act of God. You've seen *Titanic*, Maddy, at least three times, probably more—*that's* what could happen.

So here it is, the truth, the whole truth, so help me God: I, Robert Hirsch, hate my job. Rejecting people every day has eaten out my gut, and since I'm predisposed to laziness, I've stopped pushing. I've shrugged my shoulders, dropped the ball, let someone else bear the load. As time goes by, fewer people know I once cared; they see only lethargy, apathy, a marked lack of concern. As a result, opinions are formed, options discussed; final papers drawn up, back-burnered, then drawn up again. Meanwhile, my patience has thinned. Just last month, I interviewed a stay-at-home mom named Martha ("I go by Marty") for an analyst position, who tried to convince me that twelve years of packing lunches and holding bake sales translates to tangible, employable skills. "Being a mom is the hardest job in the world," she said, to which I was dying to reply, *Compared to what? Pediatric neurosurgery? Coal mining? Firefighting? Don't do that, lady. Don't give yourself credit for opting out.*

I had visions of Marty romping through the playground while my beloved wife raced from Jessie's school to the gallery and then back home, where she tutored Allie on Jeffersonian politics and sold a painting worth half a million dollars over the phone. I compared Marty to my sister, a defense attorney who represents the indigent in class action suits while raising three kids. I compared Marty to all the working mothers at Ellery, who choose to juggle work and family while childless supervisors like Rosa forbid them from telecommuting. I wanted to put Marty in her place, to ask a question like "What's the GDP of Laos?" just to see her squirm. But this interview took place last month, when I was safely ensconced in my ergonomic chair on the correct side of the desk, when I still had the luxury of passing judgment on stay-at-home moms with delusions of grandeur. Last month was last month and today is today, and today I am a middle-aged loser about to go on the dole. Today I'm a mope, so today I have compassion. Today I understand how much energy it requires for stay-at-home Marty to shower and dress, to put on her wobbly heels and sit across from a jackass who holds all the power (a jackass, by the way, who can't locate Laos on a map, much less recite its GDP). So if Marty needs to give herself props, to position herself beside surgeons and firefighters, who am I to argue? Who am I, anyway? The hardest job in the world is defined by whoever performs it, and today I have to face my hardest job, which is to hoist myself off the couch, don my puffy coat, and travel into the city so I can get fired.

TWO HOURS LATER Rob's BlackBerry rang, rousing him from his half-awake, half-dreaming state. The ringing stopped and then started again. Although addled, he decided to answer, figuring it must be his assistant following up on all the assignments he'd dumped in her lap over the past few months. "Hey, Courtney," he said, feigning coherence. "What's up?"

"Where are you?" It was Lucy, another accusatory wife, this one with higher voltage, deeper penetration. "Are you coming in?"

Did she know he'd been fired? Rob couldn't tell. He felt guilty, so everyone sounded suspicious or critical. "Of course I'm coming in. Why does everyone keep asking me that?"

"Because it's after eleven. Where are you?"

Rob looked at the TV. *The View* was on. He'd never watched it before, but it seemed imperative that he do so now. The volume was muted, so the hosts (hostesses?) spoke in silence. What grand gestures! Such passion! What are they discussing? Politics? Race relations? He un-muted, but kept it quiet so Lucy couldn't hear. Gwyneth Paltrow. Goop. Goop? Was that English? Maybe French? "I'm out on the street," he said. "Walking around."

Her voice softened. "Are you okay?"

She knew; she had to. "Let's meet at Associated," Rob said. "I need to talk to you."

"What about?"

Maybe she didn't. "I'll tell you when I see you. Let's say two."

She agreed, and they hung up. Rob considered calling Rosa. Instead, he fell back asleep.

AT TWO O'CLOCK, he entered the supermarket. Once again, Maddy had been right about his attire. Rob was drenched in sweat. He took off his puffy coat and knotted the sleeves around his waist; it hung down like a skirt. He looked ridiculous, like a ten-year-old on the playground, but so what? He was ridiculous. Lucy was in the fruit section, studying the apples. Spotting him, she whirled around, her movements loose and floppy, as if she'd lost control over them. "This produce is gross." She held up a bruised apple. "Look! It's mangled, neglected, and lonely."

"It's a piece of fruit, Lucy, not a stray puppy."

Lucy stepped toward him. (Remembering his dream, Rob stepped back.) "Playing hooky?" She polished the apple on her sleeve, pretended to take a bite. "Forbidden fruit, get it?"

Still hung over, he eyed the apple. His stomach was roiling. "Don't feel like working."

When she nodded, Rob realized she had no idea about his layoff. Not to tell her felt weird, and it would feel weirder when he eventually did. On the other hand, he hadn't finished with Rosa, so he wasn't officially off the books. Besides, Lucy didn't need to know all his private business. He was married to Maddy; they were happy together. They had two children. How many times did he have to repeat this?

"You sure you're okay, Rob? You don't seem like yourself." Funny, but Lucy didn't seem like herself either; she kept looking around, as if she were nervous.

"I'm fine." He took her arm. "Come on," he said. "Let's stroll."

They talked as they walked; or rather, Lucy talked and Rob tried to listen. Lucy spoke fast as a rule, and when she was wired, like now, she spewed words so fast he could barely keep up.

"I want to explain why I haven't been around for the past few months," she said.

"I thought you were working on a project for Rutherford."

"I am; I also started seeing someone. He's nice and age-appropriate, which is a pleasant change on both counts." Lucy was wearing high heels (and lipstick, Rob noted), so she was his same height, and they moved through the aisles in tandem, step for step, thigh for thigh. When they reached the pasta section, they sauntered, as if along the promenade, man and mistress, GI and geisha, hooker and john. Why was he thinking this way? Because it was midday and they were AWOL? Because his sporadic boner felt more than friendly? Lucy's dark hair was down; it swept over her eyes, which seemed bigger and bluer. Her face, made up, was lovely.

"His intelligence is impressive because it's unexpected, given his . . . uh . . . work situation."

"Who are you talking about?"

"My boyfriend."

"*Boyfriend*? Since when?" Rob didn't mean to sound harsh, but he was annoyed Lucy had a boyfriend and he was only first hearing about it—jealous too, if he were being honest. "Who is he?"

"It's a funny story. You know him. Well, you don't *know him*, but you've seen him. His name is Manny Flores. He's head of Sanchez Security." She looked up expectantly, but Rob shook his head. "He's one of the security guards," she clarified, glancing away.

"Of your building?" Rob had never been to her apartment.

"*Our* building—the Ellery building." She held out the apple. He shook his head, but she handed it to him anyway. Come to think of it, Leo had mentioned Lucy and a security guard. He relaxed; no way was she serious about this guy. "It's great you're dating, Luce."

"He's very thoughtful, which is a quality I never cared about, but having experienced it, I can't imagine ever dating an asshole again."

"What's so great about being thoughtful? Lots of people are thoughtful." Rob lifted his chin. *I'm* thoughtful, he reminded himself.

"Most people consider it a virtue." Lucy shrugged. "Call me crazy."

"I mean, is he smart? Does he . . . I don't know . . . *stimulate* you?" He shouldn't have used that word. "Hungry?" Rob held out the apple. See? That was thoughtful. But Lucy was walking ahead of him, in the cereal aisle. Behind her, Rob studied the slope of her back, the curve of her ass. What would she do if he lifted her coat and ground against her? Would she ask him to stop? Or arch her body, swivel her hips, flash her perfect tits? When he caught up to her, she was mid-sentence.

". . . then there's my therapist, Dr. Ahmet."

Rob's cock ached. Thankfully, his coat was still wrapped around his waist; the sleeves covered his groin. "You're still going to that guy? The Aesop's-fables nut? I thought you quit."

"I'm working through some issues; these things take time."

"And it has nothing to do with your fear that he won't like you if you leave?"

When Lucy laughed, their eyes met, sparking an electric current that made Rob's whole body hum. He was a live wire, so fucking horny he couldn't see straight. Suddenly he had to tell her. "Lucy, I got fired. Laid off. Whatever—I'm out of a job. Well, I will be . . ."

She lowered her eyes. "I know, Rob. Leo told me. It's why we keep calling you. I—"

"Leo knows?" Rob was horrified. "Does *everyone* know?"

"Of course not. Please, calm down. I'll help you. You have a great résumé; plus you're a recruiter—you know every trick. You'll find something quickly, I'm sure of it."

Rob was done talking about this. "What were you saying? About therapy?"

"It's not important—really, it's not. Let's talk about you. Rob, are you okay? God, I feel so guilty about . . . about everything. I'm so, so sorry, Rob. Whatever you need—"

"Why do *you* feel guilty? It's not about *you*. It's *my* problem and I'm *fine*." Her "so, so sorry" pissed him off. "Finish your fucking story, Luce. Can't we just have a *conversation*?"

"Okay, okay. So I had a revelation about Manny—about men in general. A while ago, Dr. Ahmet said, 'The blind bat sees the sky only when the barn burns down.' The gist, basically, has to do with silver linings, and appreciating beauty in the wake of catastrophe."

He loved her, he did, but why couldn't she speak like a normal person? "Lucy," Rob said wearily and not for the first time, "I have no idea what you're talking about."

"Silver linings in tragedy. Conversely, in every celebration, there's a touch of sadness. Manny is wonderful, but I'm not in love with him. That was my revelation: I don't want to settle, I want to be head-over-heels crazy about someone, and I want that someone to be like, ten times more successful than I am. See? It's stupid and shallow; *I'm* stupid and shallow."

Well, that last bit rules me out, Rob thought resentfully. "Who you love is not stupid, Luce. You're very special, you deserve to be happy." By this point, they were standing so close he could feel her breathing. His need to touch her was crippling him.

"That's nice of you to say, Rob." She studied her hands. "So at the same time I realized Manny wasn't my head-over-heels-guy, Rosa was reading me the riot act. 'You can't be my number two until you get over Rob.' I tried to explain that I didn't love you, but Rosa kept insisting I did. Then, during another session with Dr. Ahmet, I had this major epiphany. I was like, Oh my God, the barn is on fire, and look! There's the moon."

Rob had lost the thread of the story.

"It's a metaphor . . . a figure of, whatever, of speech . . ." She was fumbling, which was odd, to watch Lucy grasping for words. "Rob, I want to tell you something." She rose to her fullest height. "But you have to promise it won't ruin our friendship."

"Ruin our friendship?" This was getting stressful. "Over what?"

Covering her mouth, Lucy spoke through her fingers. "My epiphany was that I loved you, that I was *in love* with you. Did you have any idea? Of course you did. Rosa says it's obvious."

*Rosa?* Rob went cold. "What about Evan? You said you loved him."

"Not love, a crush, a fantasy. But this 'crush' was just a way to be closer to you." Her voice was soft. "I don't know Evan; I know you, Rob. I got confused. I loved you all along—rather, I *did*—but now I'm clear; I worked it all out." She exhaled. "Oh God, that was so hard. But I'm fine; everything is fine. It's such a relief to tell you!"

Now Rob was confused. "It's not a relief to me." On the contrary, he felt like shit. "Here's how I see it: First you tell me you want to date my best friend, then you blow me off for two months, then you tell me you have a new boyfriend, then you tell me, 'Oh, forget him and forget Evan. I loved you, Rob; I loved you the whole time.' Only now you're saying you don't."

Lucy's eyes were shining. "I know, it sounds awful. I'm so sorry, Rob. I've been a lousy friend. Will you forgive me?" She paused. "I'll understand if you can't."

"Of course I can forgive you. But why didn't you tell me how you felt two months ago, instead of cutting me out of your whole fucking life?"

"It wasn't just you, Rob. There were other things going on, too." Lucy shook her head; a tear fell. "But I was afraid if I told you, you'd resent me. I also needed space to figure it out—which I did. But I wouldn't have been able to if we were still on top of each other."

Lucy was fucking with him, Rob could feel it. She never spoke idly; she didn't pick the phrase "on top of each other" at random.

She wanted him to envision her naked and straddling him. Rob stepped toward her. "How could I resent you, Luce? You're my best friend." He was hard as a rock. "Besides, you'll *always* be in love with me." It was a joke, a bad one, but he didn't get how she could love him one minute and then not love him the next. He took another step.

Lucy took two steps back. "Timing is everything, right?" Her laugh was hollow. "Let's chalk it up to a missed opportunity." She sounded miserable. "We should go to the office."

He knew this, but didn't move. "I'm gonna miss you, Lucy; I'm gonna miss you a lot."

"Seriously, Rob. Let's go." Lucy started to turn away, but when she pivoted on her heel, she lost her balance and pitched forward. What could Rob do? He couldn't let her fall. He had to catch her. He had no choice in the matter, no choice but to fold her into his arms and press his mouth against hers, no choice but to surrender to the moment and watch it unfold.

FIFTEEN MINUTES LATER, Rob was on the corner of Eighteenth, across the street from the office. He was on the phone with Leo, who was inside the building, nine flights up.

"Of course you feel shitty," Leo was saying.

"I feel sick." Rob was referring to Lucy—and to his layoff—but mostly to Lucy. "How do I tell Maddy?" He was still holding Lucy's apple, but had no memory of paying for it. He only remembered kissing her, which felt great, really great, ten-years–coming great, but also awful. Their kiss brought instant regret, but he was too full of her to stop, even as he sensed her pulling away, even as he acknowledged his mistake. And it was, he would learn, a terrible mistake. Long after Rob left Ellery, long after he found out how she'd betrayed him (how she'd betrayed all of them), long after they lost touch, Rob's desire for Lucy Bender would haunt him any time he conjured her memory. Overwhelmed, overwrought, he thrust

against her, wishing he was naked, free, and fucking her senseless—
until she recoiled in distress. "Rob, stop—please!" She pushed him
away, and then race-walked out of the market.

"You'll tell Maddy when you're ready," Leo was saying. "In
the meantime, you need to come to the office, finish talking to
Rosa, and sign the papers. In case you're wondering, I only found
out yesterday—at which point I left you, like, fifty messages." He
paused. "Lucy just walked in. I thought you two were together.
Rob, where are you?"

Shielding his eyes, Rob peered up at the ninth-floor HQ, imagining Leo standing at the window, peering down at him. He felt
like a rogue agent being called in from the field by his handler.
Could Leo be trusted?

"I can't tell you where I am; it's classified."

"Rob, please. You're being ridiculous."

Ridiculous, yes. That had been established. "I'm coming in," he
said, resigned to his fate.

Upstairs, Rosa greeted him at the elevator. "Let's go; we have a
lot to cover."

Yesterday's folders sat on her desk. But this time, Rob was
prepared. He had questions needing answers, requests he wanted
granted. Thankfully, Rosa was also prepared—as well as efficient:
she checked off boxes, asked questions of her own.

"Rosa," he asked at one point, "if it's okay with you, I'd like to
work my last two weeks from home. I can't imagine coming here
with, you know, everyone knowing. Do you mind?"

"I'm not a believer in telecommuting, but in this case, no, I don't
mind. Rob?" She paused. "You'll keep your chin up, yes?"

At the end, Rob rose to his feet. "Well, that's it. Guess I'll grab
my things"—after looking around, he picked up a pen—"and, uh . . .
put on my wheels and . . . book. Thank you, Rosa," he added. *See ya
around, Warden.*

Head bent, Rob shuffled down the long, cold cellblock. The

other inmates peered out of their cages to see him off, rattling their bars in a final good-bye. Ignoring them, Rob trudged on. Behind him, an imaginary voice thundered through the concrete corridor. *Hey HO, hey HO. Dead man walking! Dead man walking here!* Rob ached to turn around, to get one last look, but instead he pressed forward, one foot and then another, to face whatever came next.

## 19

# ROSALITA GUERRERO, CHIEF OF HUMAN RESOURCES, EXECUTIVE VICE PRESIDENT

MAY 2010

Rosa was in the tub again, only this time she couldn't get out. Truth is, she'd dozed off. Now the water was cold, and her *People* magazine was on the floor. Idiocy. If she didn't feel so stupid, she'd laugh at her situation.

She laughed anyway.

One, two, three. Up! She tried to hoist herself over the side, but her right arm was still too weak. "Leo!" she called out. "You there?"

No answer.

Leo was home in Brooklyn, she remembered. This was a good thing. Better he shouldn't see her so indisposed. When he was here in February (already three months back!), it was humiliating, the way he'd waited on her. Never in her life did she think she'd allow such closeness with a member of her staff. If there was a word to describe worse than humiliating, worse than shameful, that's how it felt. A part of her had to pretend it wasn't happening; she had to float above herself and watch the proceedings. At the same time, her choices were limited, and he was . . . well, he was Leo. He made it easy to say yes, and in the end they survived. Another lesson learned: never say never. "Always say maybe," she said to Peter.

(Peter, who still hadn't called, whose face, if only in memory, still made her heart flutter.) "Always say maybe. That's my new motto. You on board?"

No answer from Peter either. (Before she was mad, now she was hurt.)

Rosa ran more hot water and reached for her *People*. The text was fuzzy, so she yawned, which made her eyes water. As long as her eyes were moist she could see fine, but when they dried up, she only saw dots. (Funny to be sitting in a tub of water with dry eyes, like being thirsty in a swimming pool.) A similar thing happened to her words, which shriveled on her tongue when her mouth got dry. Dr. Brady said this could happen after the stroke, that Rosa could lose her short-term recall. "Will it come back?" Rosa asked. The idea petrified her. "Maybe," was all the doctor would tell her. Rosa remembered the stroke as a blistering headache, so thick it felt like a presence, so expansive it filled her whole skull. Then after, still- ness. Nothingness. Eventually her body healed, but now her brain had off days, when the spark didn't catch, when she lost words and memories and long stretches of time. Meanwhile, her mind kept churning. Years back, when her nieces and nephews were little, they used to make collages using pictures cut out of magazines: ball gowns, dogs, buildings, apples, tractors, seashells, fairies, anything and everything. They glued the pictures on top of each other, then on top of those, then on top on top, creating a mishmash of faces, places, and things. Rosa's mind was like one of those collages, only when she churned, it wasn't just pictures; she mishmashed ideas, stories, lost memories, movies, books, songs, words, words, words. When she tried to peel off a word, a piece of one stuck to another and they peeled off together. Or one would disappear, except she knew it was there, just below the surface, so she'd work with all her might to grab it. When she got stuck, Dr. Brady told her to count backward from twenty to one.

Be patient, Dr. Brady told her. Stop pushing.

At the moment, Rosa was churning about three things. First, the actress Sandra Bullock. Sandra's husband, it turned out, was a cheat and a liar. Apparently she never saw it coming. The good news was that Sandy was still young and beautiful, with a career and many men yet to meet. Rosa wanted to send her a letter to this effect, and made a mental note to ask Leo for the star's address. I understand, she'd tell her, referring to Peter. I never saw it coming, either.

Rosa's second churn was Rob, whose separation she'd fought, only to lose in the end. He was still getting paid through next week; plus, his severance was fair. But the situation weighed on her like a . . . like a . . . like a thing, like a weight. Some layoffs didn't bother her—i.e., Maisie Fresh Butler, who'd erupted in rage. (After, when Lucy said they should've just posted the news on Maisie's Facebook page [*Dislike!*], Rosa had tried not to laugh.) But watching Rob walk out, head bent like a small boy, made her cry. She was worried for Maddy; such a treasure, that woman! A job loss can destroy a marriage or strengthen it, and while Rosa was optimistic for the Hirsches, who knew what their future held? Losing Rob also made Rosa question herself. She worried that she should've come down harder on him earlier, monitored his deadlines, followed up more aggressively. Should've, would've, could've—every boss's dirty secrets, their private errors in judgment. Maybe she'd give Rob a call, see how he was faring, if he'd heard from Peter. Nice if they could all have lunch, her treat.

Rosa's biggest churn was Rutherford, who had recently asked her to create—and lead—a new mergers and acquisitions committee. It aligned with the strategy work he'd asked for back in November, and there was a financial incentive, but taking it on moved her further away from HR. Rosa wasn't sure; the idea sounded sketchy.

"What should I do?" she asked Howard, who happened to be standing at the door right now, chuckling at her predicament. She knew Howard was here; the bathroom had filled with the sweet pungent smell of his favorite cigar.

"Go limp," he replied. "I'll lift you up."

"Not about the tub, Howard, about Rutherford's M&A committee."

"What do I always say, Rosie? Trust your gut."

This was the problem; her gut was untrustworthy. Since the stroke, she'd become a less confident businessperson. She used to be a pro, able to drill down decisions all the way to the who and what, to the yes or the no—quickly, cleanly, and objectively. But now she got hung up on the why, on motives and emotions, which made everything cloudy. When Rutherford was describing this M&A team, something about his description felt off. His request had other parts—secret parts he didn't mention—and inside those parts was where Rosa got looped.

"This new committee will research companies for Ellery to purchase or merge with," he'd explained. "Growth by acquisition—it's the only way we'll survive."

"We can't afford staff," she pointed out. "How can we afford acquisitions?"

"That's my problem. But I'm talking about partnering with firms in our same situation or distressed assets we can pick up on the cheap. You can handpick your team, take your time, and continue to keep tabs on HR. If anything pans out, you'll get a piece of every deal you find."

"Plus a piece of every other deal," Rosa said. "Regardless of who finds it."

Rutherford laughed. "You never stop, do you?"

There was a catch. Rosa had to appoint a deputy chief, a real number two, and make it official. No more dragging her heels. Another catch—Rutherford wanted it to be Lucy. "You think she's ready?" Rosa asked.

"If you mentor her, yes." Rutherford sighed, not looking her in the eye. "Rosa, HR will always be yours. You'll always be chief. But in October, you'll be sixty-five. At some point, we have to consider what's next. Not now," he added. "I'm not saying now—soon, though."

And there it was, the unsaid parts: *You're done here, my friend; while we appreciate your service, it's time to consider what's next for you—and (more important), what's next for Ellery.* What's next for Rosa was a whole lot of nothing, a lot of sitting around and waiting, a lot of stewing in her own juices. What came after Ellery was a throwaway life.

Rosa never used to think this way, never allowed her feelings to override her sound judgment, but just as it had stolen her words, the stroke had softened her ability to reason. So here's what she needed to know before she decided: One, was Rutherford aware of her stroke? Two, would he do this to a man, put Charles Mayfield out to pasture? Three, could she mentor Lucy without her ego intruding? And four, how would she ever thank Leo for all he had done?

Rosa was still in the tub. She drifted for a few minutes, then decided to wash her hair; sometimes she preferred doing it herself instead of going to the beauty place. As she rinsed out the shampoo, she remembered Delta had never sent her the check. Last month, when she went to the spa, the airline had lost her bag, so she had to buy new clothes and toiletries. She submitted a claim, but they never sent her a refund. That's how they get you. Everyone's too busy to follow up; no one does the extra legwork. Well, Rosalita Guerrero wasn't everyone.

She dialed Leo, careful not to get her phone wet. As it rang, she got angrier and angrier. "Leo!" she was practically shouting. "Leo! What happened to my reimbursement?"

"What reimbursement?" She heard him yawn, which made her yawn, too. "What reimbursement, Rosa?" he asked.

"Delta never reimbursed me for my bags."

"For your spa trip? Rosa, that was last year. And as I recall, they did reimburse you."

"No, Leo, you're wrong. Don't you see? That's how they get you!"

She paused. "Also, please find Sandra Bullock's address. I want to write her a note. She was blindsided, which is funny, since *Blind Side* was the name of her movie. Do you think they called it that on purpose?"

"Actually, you're right, Rosa," Leo was saying. "We never did get your money. Hold on. I'll call Delta and then call you back. Are you having trouble sleeping?"

Rosa checked the time. It was 2:00 a.m.! She'd been in the bathtub for three hours. "I'm fine," she told him quickly. "Sorry to wake you."

"No bother, Rosa. We'll figure it out, and then you can go back to bed."

"I'm right here, kiddo."

She hung up, satisfied that Leo was on the case. She flipped through her magazine, but slower than before. It might take him a while to deal with Delta, and she didn't want to be sitting in this tub with nothing to read. Actually, that was a fifth question, which she'd ask as soon as he called back. Leo, if you were stuck in a bathtub, how would you get out? I don't mean really stuck, she'd say. Just imagine if.

## Part III

# PUNCHING OUT

Ellery Consumer Research Group
Human Resources, May 2010

www.ellerygroup.com

ROSALITA GUERRERO
HR Chief
Executive VP & Special Projects

KATHERINE REYNOLDS
Assistant to the Chief

LUCINDA BENDER
VP
Communications/Policy
Training/Recruiting

LEONARD SMALLS
VP
Employee Benefits

KENNETH VERVILLE
Senior Manager
Compensation/
Operations

COURTNEY ADAMS
Assistant Manager
Training/Recruiting

OPEN
Assistant Manager
Policy
Development

OPEN
Assistant
Copywriter

OPEN
Assistant
Special
Projects

JUANITA JOHNSON
Payroll Clerk

OPEN
Payroll Clerk

——— Direct reporting relationship
- - - - - Indirect reporting relationship

1

# 20

KENNETH VERVILLE,
SENIOR MANAGER,
COMPENSATION & OPERATIONS

MAY 2010

When Kenny was a kid, maybe seven or eight, his father moonlighted a few nights a week at a paper goods factory. Sarge's shift at the army PX was seven to three, and his factory shift was four to midnight, which left no time for dinner. On those nights, Kenny biked to the factory with a hot meal. Once in a while, the shift supervisor let Kenny sit with Sarge in the break room. This thrilled the boy, who was tracking a poster on the wall: 243 Day(s) Since Our Last Lost-Time Accident! (According to Sarge, the same sign hung inside the factory proper, but Kenny wasn't allowed near the lines.) The bosses promised a party when they hit 365, so he was counting the days. True to their word, when the factory went a year with no accidents, there was a celebration (white cake and punch), and Kenny was invited. Six months later, they hit 548 (eighteen months!), and every employee was treated to cake again, along with an extra twenty dollars in that week's paycheck and a blue umbrella with Safety First printed on it in block letters.

Kenny was primed for 730 (two years!), but just before Christmas, the number dropped: 1 Day(s) Since Our Last Lost-Time Accident! Turned out Duane Farmer had caught his hand in the chip feeder two days before. "What a loss," Sarge said, making clicking sounds with his tongue. He was referring to Duane's three fingers, but Kenny thought he meant the 715 days that were suddenly gone. To an eight-year-old boy, the idea of resetting the clock and reworking all those hours seemed impossible, unfair, and filled him with despair, though his dad quit the factory soon after, and it would be years before Kenny thought about lost time again.

KENNY AND JANINE were arguing. They were both cranky lately, so if they weren't shouting, one of them was freezing the other out. Generally, Kenny preferred to shout. Then he knew where he stood—unlike the silent treatment, which left him confused. The other night, for example, after a prickly fight, he found Janine lounging on his side of the bed with Dog. While the sight was unsettling, Kenny felt silly pointing it out. After all, it was only a bed. Still, it needled him to see her lying on his pillow, next to his nightstand, availing herself of his reading materials. "It's obvious you're still mad at me," he said.

"I'm not mad." She spoke out of the side of her mouth, her eyes fixed on (his) *Wired*.

"The garage door broke; it's not a tragedy." Kenny had screwed up the electric eye again, but instead of calling a guy like he promised, he'd made it worse by trying to fix it himself. Okay, he'd failed. Did that warrant her behaving like such a baby?

"I'm tired." Her words were terse, cold. "My new job—which if you recall, I only started *three weeks ago*—is killing me." Then she turned off his light and curled up with her baby-dog, as if everything were normal. Kenny did the same, but he felt disoriented stretched out on her side. He could barely see the TV, and the heating vent roared in his ear, so he tossed and turned for hours. The next morning, Janine didn't mention their sleeping arrangements, but he could sense hostility, like fumes, rising off her body.

At the moment, they were fighting about food. "You promised,

Kenny! You said you'd make dinner. Stop making promises you can't keep." Having beaten him home from the office, Janine had already changed into a long lavender sweater over lavender pants. Unbuttoned, the sweater flapped behind her like royal robes as she stomped through the kitchen.

While Kenny understood the implications of "making promises," he chose to focus on making dinner. "I had to work late, Janine." (This wasn't true—Kenny had stopped for a beer in the city with Fez—but whatever.) "Why does that piss you off? I have a job too."

"You want to know why I'm pissed? Because you can't be bothered to make dinner or call the garage guy or do your other chores. Because the second I went back to work, you stopped pulling your weight." Pivoting in disgust, she headed for the stairs.

Kenny watched her go. Janine was always bitchy when she started a new job, as if the only way to handle the unfamiliar testosterone on the trading desk was to take it out on him. Sure, he had sympathy for her; all day, she heard her male colleagues threaten to "fuck that bitch in the ass," "that bitch" being any female in the room (including her). But if she'd always been competitive, Wall Street had made her ruthless. She used to fight on Kenny's behalf; now he was her adversary. If he was tired, she was exhausted. If he was hungry, she was starving. She stacked the dishwasher better than he did, her sense of direction was keener, and she could've fixed the garage door with her eyes closed.

Knowing that this was how she blew off steam, Kenny usually let her rail, but sometimes he got fed up and fought back. Fighting used to feel good, like fucking, though these days it was a poor substitute because nothing between them was ever resolved. And tonight Janine happened to be right: Kenny wasn't doing his chores. Still, he refused to give in. What he wanted was for her to admit she was fucking Les Hough. For the past month, it had taken all Kenny's restraint not to hold up her phone and shout, "Look what I found!"

Here was the thing, though: confronting Janine would be "going nuclear," as Fez, no stranger to marital woes himself, might say. Before this Les Hough business, Kenny believed his and Janine's core values (work, family, fidelity) were in sync and unyielding, but now everything felt open to debate. While one affair shouldn't be enough to bring them down, Kenny worried it might.

Here was the other thing: Kenny's golden glow had faded. The SCA Capital offer had fallen through, his job search was stalled, and instead of caring for Janine, Dog, their house, or himself, he was phoning it in at Ellery and licking his wounds at the bar while his chores piled up. So he didn't feel strong enough to go toe-to-toe with Les Hough, who, in addition to being Janine's boss, was very, very white and very, very rich, far richer than Kenny.

Upstairs, Janine was playing with Dog. He could hear her ask the dog questions, then make doglike responses. She was so light and playful, so loving. Why Dog? Why Les Hough? Why not him? Other men competed with kids for their wives; Kenny had to compete with other men—and a pet—while remaining childless.

"Jeannie?" He grabbed a bottle of wine, two glasses, and a box of Triscuits and trotted upstairs, where he stripped to his boxers, climbed into bed, shooed away the dog, and wrapped his wife in his arms. Until today (May 21, 2010), it had been 1,481 days since their most recent fight. Sure, they bickered, but in the whole of their relationship, they only had two blowups on record: the first in 1999, the second in 2006. They were still young in 1999, so it was easy to recover, but 2006 was a different story. They had history; more was at stake. One night a minor dispute ramped up too quickly; words like *character*, *work ethic*, and *values* were tossed out—hard words to yank back. In the end, Janine stormed off to her parents' in Saddle River. Is this it? Kenny wondered. Are we done? Distraught, he called her the next day, and Janine came home. But the ensuing months were dicey. Faced with the threat of another breakdown, they tiptoed around; it took weeks to get back on track. No way Kenny wanted to go through that again. Which is why, rather than ask about Les Hough, all he said was, "Let's not fight." Better to keep the clock ticking, add one more day to their long-running tally. Anything else would cost too much, and after 1,481 days of relative ease, Kenny was afraid to risk it. "I'm sorry for everything, Jeannie."

"Me, too." Sighing, she burrowed against his chest. "I'm sorry, too."

They had sex, but it was quick, and when they finished, Kenny felt lonelier than ever. "Jeannie?" he whispered, but she was already asleep.

THE FOLLOWING MONDAY, Kenny was in his office when Rosa called. "We're making a change," she said. "Wait there." Then she hung up. No hello, no how are you, no nothing.

Kenny didn't care. He didn't care about anything: working out, finding another job, or doing the stupid job he had. Over the weekend, he'd lost his grip on another rung of the mental-health ladder and slipped deeper into the black maw of depression. Now all he could do was sit at his desk, log on to Facebook, and check Janine's feed for any sign of Les Hough.

Rosa wasn't the only one treating him like shit. The rest of the department was too, which he figured was related to his talk with Rutherford last month. It pissed Kenny off that when the CEO asked for his honest assessment of the group, instead of respecting that another professional was speaking to him man-to-man, he'd turned around and told Rosa everything. Or so it seemed; Kenny had to piece all this together because people would barely acknowledge him—including Rutherford, who refused to return his calls. That one chat had triggered a streak of bad luck. The Les Hough business had driven a wedge into his marriage. Then SCA rejected him. Then he got iced by the whole office. Kenny was still spinning from all the injustice.

He heard Rosa shuffling down the hall. When she pulled on his door, it swung open too fast; she lost her footing, but quickly righted herself. "Kenny! I told you to get this fixed. You know what a lawsuit could cost us?"

He focused on his computer screen. "I thought we were hiring someone to do that."

Lucy strolled in and sat down next to Rosa. "What did you say? I missed that."

"I said I thought we were hiring a facilities guy." Lucy was always around lately, like she was checking up on him. Had Rutherford said something to her, too?

"Sit up, Kenny." Lucy spoke quietly. "Look at us, not your screen." She crossed her legs. "Put down your phone. Come on, you're at work. Act like it."

Resentful of her tone, but unnerved by her new look, Kenny complied. Gone was the sloppy woman wearing clunky glasses. In her place was a sleek executive whose steel-blue eyes cut through him. When combined with a form-fitting black dress, sheer stockings, silver jewelry, and sky-high heels, the overall effect was chilling. Now *this*, he thought, was a woman he could see on Wall Street. Rosa, on the other hand, looked exhausted and messy. Her jacket was frayed, her pantyhose had a run in the knee, and her eyes were washed out, with dark circles underneath.

"On the phone you mentioned a change," he asked her. "Did you mean for me?"

"Peter is gone," Rosa replied, her voice loud and shaky, as if she was first hearing the news and reeling from shock. "He is not coming back."

"Peter's *been* gone," Kenny said. "Candidates have been in and out. What's the holdup?"

"Your buddy Rutherford decided not to spend the money." Lucy raised her eyebrows. "He wants to tap existing resources, and your name came up."

"I'm not fixing broken doors, if that's what you're getting at."

Rosa butted in. "We'll give you twenty hours of Katherine's time to help you—"

"Wait, wait, wait. Are you seriously asking *me* to take on facilities?" He had an MBA from Wharton; did they really want him plunging toilets?

Lucy shook her head. "We're not asking. Rosa and Leo have been overseeing operations since December. They don't have the time anymore. You do."

"We have checklists for everything," Rosa said. "Talk to Leo if you have . . . have . . ." She squinted, as if trying to see the word in the air.

"Questions?" Kenny filled in.

"I'm right here!" Leo stuck his head in the door.

"Leo!" Rosa whirled around. "Are you spying? You're always creeping up behind me."

"Of course not. I was passing by and heard my name. Oh, sorry, Lucy, I didn't realize you'd be here. Are you supposed to be?"

"Yes, Leo, of course. Check the schedule."

"So where's Katie?" Leo asked, glancing into the hall.

"Not here, obviously, but she's not supposed to be. *I'm* here. *Check the schedule*, Leo."

"What schedule?" Rosa asked Kenny. "Do you know what she's talking about?"

Kenny had no idea. Leo and Lucy were acting out some absurd comedy of errors that didn't include him. Fuck this place. He should quit—once again they were asking him to take on projects beyond the scope of his job. But if he quit, what would he tell prospective employers? What would he tell Janine? Most important, with no job, he'd be dependent on his wife, and Les Hough, that fucker, would seem even more godlike. "If I take operations, will I get a pay bump?"

"Don't be greedy," Rosa said. "No one likes a greedy person, especially when he shows up to work unshaven and disheveled. You used to wear a suit every day. What happened?"

"I'm having troubles at home," he said, trying to elicit compassion.

"Please." Lucy's irritation was palpable. "Stop acting like a teenager. This is a *business*. Rosa is your *boss*. Seriously: *get it together*." But then her tone shifted; her voice lost its edge. "Look," she said, smoothing her dress with the flat of her hand. "I realize we sprung this on you without warning. So if it's not what you want, we'll understand."

"Thank you." Relieved, Kenny's own voice faltered. "I appreciate that." Because Lucy had been so cold to him—they all had—her offer felt like a small kindness.

Standing now, she turned to go. "Let us know what you want to do. And of course, if you decide to move on, there'll be no hard feelings."

Startled, Kenny raised his hand. "Wait—if I don't do facilities, I won't have a job?" He pictured Rob Hirsch sitting in some dirty unemployment office; less than a month gone, and already forgotten. Kenny wondered if he'd bought a new car—probably not, he figured.

Dismayed, Rosa shook her head. "We're a team; we're supposed to work together. But you don't do your fair share. When you take more than you're willing to give, it never works out in your favor. Trust me. I know from experience: the organization always wins."

"I need a decision by Friday," Lucy said. Resting a manicured hand on Rosa's arm, she guided her out. Neither woman said good-bye.

Alone, Kenny scrolled through job sites. He was stuck. Any-where else, he could take his case to HR, but Rosa was chief, and Lucy was de facto chief. Again, he thought of Rutherford. What had Kenny told him that was so terrible? That firing Rob was smart? That Rosa might have cognitive issues? That Lucy had given Rosa a nickname? All of this was true! Plus, Kenny was entitled to know why operations had been thrust on him. So he left the CEO a fifth message, and this time the big man called back.

"Son." Rutherford's twang was on full display. "You need to go through the proper channels with this kind of issue. As your super-visor, Rosa Guerrero is empowered by me to make decisions for HR, so please direct any and all questions to her."

THAT NIGHT JANINE was out with a friend (which Kenny figured meant fucking Les Hough) so he was alone, eating wings and watch-ing ESPN, when his mother called. "Hey, Ma," he said, happy to hear her voice. "Sorry I've been MIA. Work is insane."

"Kenny, I'm calling because your father had a fender bender. Don't worry, he's fine, although"—Glenda chuckled—"his pride is bruised."

Kenny was startled. "But he's okay? When was this?"

"He's okay, but the car's totaled. It happened a week ago, but it's not the first time—"

"*A week ago?*" While it was true that Kenny hadn't called in a while, he was their only son. He shouldn't be hearing this kind of news a week later! "Where's Sarge now? And what do you mean, it's not the first time? He's had other accidents?"

"Your dad is sleeping, but if you call tomorrow, he'll be thrilled. And yes, he has clipped the car before. It may be his depth percep-tion, so we're getting his eyes checked."

Sarge was sleeping? It was only eight. "I'll call him tomorrow," Kenny promised. "Please tell him that, okay? Love you, Ma." When he was a boy, Glenda used to call him her "only only," which had made him cringe; now he missed it. He said good night to his mother and went up to bed. It was still early, but he was tired of waiting around for Janine.

TWO DAYS LATER, Kenny marched to Rosa's office, determined to reason with her. It had been hard enough admitting to Fez that the SCA spot fell through. How could he say, Oh, guess what? I'm overseeing facilities now; how's that for a career move?

Rosa's door was closed, so Kenny stood in the hall, debating whether to leave a note.

"She's out," Katherine called from her cubicle. "Perhaps I can help you?"

"I'll call her later, thanks." Despite the fact that they were working together on two separate projects, Katherine was stiff and formal in his presence. Kenny found this upsetting. Even the secretary hated him! He wanted to strike up a conversation, but all he knew was that she lived in Queens, this was her first office job, and she came in crazy early. But she seemed smart, and, judging from her speed and accuracy entering payroll data, industrious. She was also the only one in their department who'd look at him. "So Katherine, how are you doing?" He stepped inside her cube, then backed out of it awkwardly, not wanting to impinge on her space. "What do you think of Ellery? Are we meeting your expectations, and all that?"

"It's great, I love it. I'm learning so much." She started to put her earbuds back in, but Kenny motioned for her to wait and then leaned over to whisper a secret.

"Some friendly advice?" Unsure where to put his hands, he gripped her nameplate. "You can do better than Ellery; the company's dying. You'll make lots more money somewhere else."

She didn't reply. Kenny was sure she'd start typing, but she only looked at her hands. "I like it here. Everyone is really nice. It's a hundred times better than my last job."

"Which was what?"

"Working at my uncle's ice cream shop in Corona. I don't have my degree, so all I can do is fast food or retail. I went to Baruch for two years," she added quickly, "but my mom got sick, and I took time off to take care of her. I planned to go back, but she didn't get better, and after she"—Katherine blinked a few times—"after she died, I didn't have the money. So I'm grateful that Rosa hired me. To be honest, I'm more worried about her being happy with me than the other way around.

"It's why I get here so early," she continued. "To practice Excel and PowerPoint. Kenny, I felt *so bad* when we did those spreadsheets; I could tell you were frustrated with my questions. But you were *so nice* and *so patient*." Her pale cheeks reddened. "I'm getting better. Next time we work together, I'll be a pro!"

"No, no, you were great." Guilt rose in his stomach. "I should've realized you might have trouble; I could've shown you shortcuts." She was just a kid! This was her first real job! At his first job, his supervisor had hovered over him for two months! "It was wrong not to spend more time with you; I'm sorry I left you to fend for yourself."

"I was embarrassed, I guess. Rosa goes on and on about how smart you are, and all your degrees, and I didn't want you to think I was too inexperienced to be here."

"Katherine, I'd never think that. And as you probably know, I'm on Rosa's shit list at the moment, so I can't imagine her saying anything positive about me."

"Oh God, that's not true. She tells me *all the time* to finish school. 'Look at Kenny' "—Katherine mimicked Rosa's earnest tone—" 'He's got a big job, and he's still in his thirties!' "

Hearing this shocked Kenny. Rosa praised him? She thought he had a big job? "I'm sorry about your mom, Katherine. If my mother had gotten sick, I like to believe I would've dropped out of school, but I don't think that's true." He coughed, and his eyes watered.

Of course it wasn't true. Case in point: Sarge had been in a car accident, and Kenny still wasn't sure how it happened because he was too wrapped up in his own stupid life to find out. Yesterday, when he called to check in, Sarge had stonewalled him, so the two men sat without speaking much, the line crackling between them. "Bad connection," Kenny said eventually. "It is," Sarge agreed. Listening to his dad's heavy breathing, he thought of their long-ago football games, the strength of Sarge's body as he went out for a pass. "I got it!" he'd shout, already jumping. In those days, seeing his father leap into the air was like catching a glimpse of God: back arched, head up, arms spread like wings. Remembering this, Kenny felt a pang of remorse. Maybe he and Sarge didn't talk like other fathers and sons, but there had been real tenderness between them, once. Shutting his eyes, he breathed along with Sarge over the wire, imagining their chests rising and falling in unison as if they shared one set of lungs, a single beating heart.

"I'm sorry about your mom," he repeated. He felt sad for Katherine and doubly sad for himself, for his marriage, for Sarge. And yet, if anyone asked, he couldn't say how his life had come undone, and so quickly. "I'm not close with my folks. We used to be, though." This choked him up. The tears were in his throat, tightening his Adam's apple. He swallowed them. Jesus, he told himself. Get a grip.

"You'd help them if they needed you. People surprise themselves when someone they love gets sick. Besides, they're your parents. I couldn't imagine anyone else taking care of my mom." She paused. "Hey, do you mind calling me Katie? Rosa says Katherine is more professional, but I can't get used to it."

This girl had him all wrong. He was not a good man, a man who'd make sacrifices for someone else, even his parents. Rather, he was brusque and selfish. A prick, basically. "You can call me Kenny. I mean, you should continue to . . . um . . . call me . . . Kenny." His cheeks burned.

Katie nodded. Then she put in her earbuds and returned to her computer. Kenny didn't want to stop talking, but had nothing more to offer, so he patted her nameplate and walked off. En route to his office, it occurred to him that operations might not be so terrible. If I take it, he thought, I can keep my job and stay here awhile. Then maybe Janine won't be so angry. Maybe, too, I can get her to love me again.

He turned around. He wanted to tell Katie he could help her with Excel, but she was already bent over her keyboard, her fingers flying. Watching her golden head bob up and down, he caught the beat of her music, and for one brief, flickering moment, Kenny Verville—V as in Victory—could almost recall how it felt to be happy.

THAT NIGHT, TO Kenny's relief, he and Janine rediscovered each other. She took the first step, but he made an effort, too. He picked up sushi and set the table with daisies, cloth napkins, and their wedding china. During dinner, he focused on her—UBS, friends, parents—and steered clear of any relationship talk. After, they sat on the deck in their matching coats, and he told her about the operations job. "It's more responsibility. It will help the department. I want to contribute something of value, Jeannie; I want to make a lasting impression. At the moment, it seems Ellery is the only place where I can do that, so I may as well give it a try."

After his conversation with Katie, it had occurred to Kenny that his life with Janine was centered around accumulation, consumption, and not much else. They spent entire weekends driving from Bed, Bath & Beyond to Home Depot and then to Costco, where they bought pallets of meat lasagna, sixty-count egg rolls, and four pounds of butter—food they'd never eat, not in several lifetimes. He wanted to ask her why they did this, where they were headed. What about kids? Did she still want kids? They used to talk about having a litter of children and taking them to visit Penn and Disneyland. What happened to that idea? Or their plans to drive cross-country? Should he suggest they rent a Winnebago and see the Grand Canyon? (Probably not.) But here was the real question: If Janine was still sleeping with Les Hough, what did a grand house or his-and-hers coats or any of their plans for the future matter?

"So don't worry about me," Kenny told her. "I don't need SCA— or any hedge fund; I'm okay where I am. And then maybe we can, I don't know, take a trip, have a baby . . ."

For some reason, this made Janine cry. "Oh, Kenny. I'm so sorry."

Seeing her tears made Kenny well up too. He didn't cry, but the threat existed. "What's wrong? You can tell me." He braced himself for her confession, but all she said was, "I just need time." Leaning over, Kenny kissed her. "Take however long you need," he said, pleased they had a plan. Though it was chilly, they had sex outside, right on the deck chairs, which wasn't completely satisfying but felt like a good start.

STANDING OUTSIDE LUCY'S office, Kenny breathed deeply to steady his nerves. Now that he and Janine had made up, he was ready to course-correct everything else. While he'd rather talk to Rosa, these days she was never without an entourage, so it was impossible to get her alone. He had with him a five-point plan for the rest of his life:

MILESTONE ONE: Fix job situation (including redeeming self in Rutherford's eyes)

MILESTONE TWO: Continue to work on marriage

MILESTONE THREE: Have child or two (with Janine)

MILESTONE FOUR: Look after Sarge and Mom, as needed

MILESTONE FIVE: Retire

Lucy was on a call, but beckoned him in. "I'm almost done. No, Mom, I'm talking to someone else"—she covered the phone— "Have a seat."

Kenny looked around. On Lucy's wall, there was a poster of a kitten clinging to a pull-up bar under the words HANG IN THERE, BABY. Pointing to it, he smiled.

Lucy gave him a thumbs-up. "Just get Willa *What to Expect* and sign the card from me—and no, I don't want a shearling vest. . . . *Thanks, but I said no.* . . . Love you too, but I'm hanging up." Lucy looked at him. "Sorry. My sister is pregnant, and my mother is wandering around Costco."

"Congratulations!" Kenny offered.

"Thanks! Congrats to me, the spinster aunt." She rolled her eyes. "So what's up?"

"I've thought about your proposition, and I accept. I'm ready to take on operations."

"Really?" Lucy leaned back. "Well, that's a surprise."

How should he interpret this? A good surprise, he hoped? "I'm totally committed. I can also mentor Katie, who I recently found out has a few knowledge gaps."

"You do realize Katie's been here four months?" Lucy stopped. "Kenny, I'm thrilled!" She stopped again. "Did that sound sincere? As a manager, I should express enthusiasm even when I'm on the fence. And to be frank, Kenny, I'm on the fence about you. In fact, you're being put on a performance improvement plan, also known as a PIP."

Struck by her bluntness, he faltered. "Why? I mean, I know *why*, but I'm determined to turn things around. I'm taking my new assignment very seriously. I'll work my ass off, Lucy."

"I want to believe that, but here's the deal: starting next week, Rosa will be leading a strategy team focused on growth—mergers, acquisitions, that kind of thing. She'll continue to keep an eye on HR as far as big picture, but I'll be overseeing our day-to-day business."

Though he'd known this was coming, hearing it worried him. "Great! Congratulations!"

"Now who sounds insincere?" She smiled. "Regardless, I am

listening to you. You say you're committed, and that you're taking this assignment seriously, but your track record is lousy. Kenny, you've been a disappointment to Rosa. It's not your work product as much as your attitude; you never stop telling us, in one way or another, you're too good for us. Did you hear that? *You have a bad attitude. You're a disappointment.* Having worked for several women over the years, I've noticed that as a gender, we're very observant and fully attuned to our colleagues' feelings, but we are *abysmal* at confrontation. Truth is, I rarely have this issue working for men. There are other issues, of course, but not that one." She paused. "So."

"So." Kenny's heart beat faster. "What's next?"

"Great question! Well, the big news is that I'll be your boss! Fun, right? I envision lots of changes. We need rigor, Kenny, rigor and discipline. So as deputy chief, I plan to institute weekly one-on-ones, clearly defined roles, aggressive but measurable targets, and so on. I also want to take on longer-term projects, like infrastructure, employee self-service—"

"ESS was my idea—"

"Yes, Kenny, I know. You have excellent ideas. You could also be a highly competent manager. However, in the spirit of new beginnings, I have to say that you're arrogant, combative, and display no generosity of spirit. Too direct? Possibly, but I'm in a bind. I have more work than I do time, and I need a rock-solid steady Eddie to oversee comp *and* operations so I can focus on larger issues. I want you to dig deep and ask yourself if this is truly where you want to be. Can you see yourself at Ellery five, ten years down the line? This isn't a joke, Kenny; I want you to ask yourself why you're the right fit. Tell me, please: What is the Kenny Verville value proposition?"

Kenny understood: Buck up or else. "You're right, Lucy. I've been arrogant and ungenerous. I have not been a team player. My behavior is unacceptable. I'm sorry. When I look in the mirror, I'm not happy with the person I see." Holding her gaze, he sent telepathic messages, *Please, Lucy, don't give up on me. Please, please.* "But my situation has changed. *I've* changed. I want to stay and take on operations. I *need* this job. I'm committed." *Please.* He cleared his throat. "I promise."

She studied him then made a V sign. "Scout's honor?"

Kenny mirrored her V with his own. "Cross my heart, hope to die."

"Good." She sat up straight. "The first thing you should do is schedule time with Leo; he's our operations expert. At the moment, we have two pressing issues: the Atlanta lease, which is up for renewal, and Rutherford's town hall in July. Leo will tell you about the lease, but as far as the town hall, you'll have to find the space, negotiate a deal, confirm equipment, oversee setup, test acoustics, order snacks. Last year, we had people fill out a questionnaire—which you also have to coordinate—and they complained they couldn't see the presenters, so this year, Rutherford wants a riser or stage. You'll have to figure that out . . ."

As Lucy listed everything he had to do, Kenny took feverish notes. He was better at lofty concepts than granular details, but it didn't matter. He had to follow her instructions down to the letter—or else. Don't fuck up, he scribbled. Do. Not. Fuck. This. Up.

"The trick is to get organized," Lucy said in summation. "Anything else?"

"I have a question, but it's off-topic."

She rolled her hands, telling him to keep going. It was a gesture he'd seen Rutherford use many times, which suggested she was closer to their CEO than she let on.

"So, remember a few months ago, when I mentioned a hypothetical new job? I was curious why you called it 'ironic.'"

Lucy didn't miss a beat. "Kenny, you were about to get fired."

"Are you sure?"

"I'm your manager. Of course I'm sure. We were waiting for you to finish the layoffs, and then . . ." She turned up her palms. "So it was *ironic* you found another job right when you needed one. But Rosa believes in second chances, so despite your past infractions, she thinks you're worth saving. You know the business, you know Ellery—now you'll learn all about operations. Plus, replacing Peter is very expensive, but with you, we get two managers for the price of one."

Kenny flinched.

Seeing this, Lucy warmed. "Sorry, that was harsh. Sometimes I speak without thinking first. I definitely have to work on that. Rosa has the manager thing down, but there's a fine line between oversight and power. Speaking of power players, how's your wife?"

"She's okay." Lucy could be pretty funny sometimes, Kenny thought, recalling the booze cruise they'd gone on two years earlier. They'd gotten trashed and laughed a lot, mostly about the stupid shit people did at work, like leaving copies of their biometric screening results in the printer. Lucy also opened up a little. When he mentioned Sarge, she said he was lucky his father was still alive; her own left when she was six. "Growing up, I was jealous of girls whose fathers taught them how to ride a bike; that felt like the ultimate dad experience, and I'd missed out. It's probably why I'm such a bitter shrew—because I had to learn everything on my own."

"Actually," Kenny added, honestly, in the spirit of new beginnings, "the last few months have been rough. Janine and I haven't been getting along. She's busy with her new job, and I'm . . . well, you know how I am."

Lucy sighed. "Relationships are difficult."

She had a nice face, Kenny decided. Smart idea to get rid of those clunky glasses. "We've been together since college. That should count for something, right?"

"You'd think." Lucy glanced out her window. Sunlight cast shadows across her face, made her blue eyes gleam like jewels. "Let's hope your problems don't impact your performance. But truthfully, Kenny? I'm, like, the last person you should be asking about love."

KENNY'S MOTHER CALLED a few nights later. "How are you?" she asked.

He glanced at his watch. Jeanie would be home any minute. "Great, Ma. Everything's great." Circling the table, he set down plates. Dog scampered between his legs. Kenny was trying to re-create last Wednesday night, substituting home-cooked chicken for takeout sushi and adding candles. "In fact"—he pulled back the blinds to search the street—"I'm making a romantic dinner for us." A spray of headlights flashed in his eyes. "She's home!" he called to Dog, who started to bark. But instead of turning into the driveway, the car sped off. Kenny and Dog looked at each other, dejected.

"We'd love to see you." His mother's voice was pressing; she mentioned Sarge, who was doing better, but still a bit shaky. "He misses you; we both do."

Kenny pictured his father, younger, stronger, rocketing into the sky. A man with the grace of a superhero, faster than a speeding bullet, mighty enough to defy gravity. "I miss you guys too, Ma. I'll come this weekend, I promise."

It was almost seven. The chicken was cold and starting to congeal, so he stuck it in the microwave. The cooker hummed, and as the bird rotated, Kenny's stomach growled. As hungry as he was, though, he wanted to wait for Janine; he wanted to talk as they ate. It was time to come clean, so he sent her a text.

I know about Les Hough but I forgive you. Hope you get home soon so we can talk. Xo

An hour later, the chicken smell lingered as Kenny continued to wait. He had so much to say. First, he no longer cared about

Les Hough; he was tired of hauling that weight. Second, the other night, when he'd told her about the operations assignment, he hadn't clarified that it was a last-chance opportunity. Third, he was worried about his parents, especially Sarge. Finally, they belonged together; they were a family: Kenny, Jeannie, Dog. But in an unexpected twist, Janine never came home, so Kenny didn't get the chance to say any of this, or that he loved her, which to him, was most important of all.

LATER THAT NIGHT, his phone dinged with a text from Janine.

> I need time; I'll be with my folks

Was this it? Were they done? In the past, there were arguments, recriminations, tearful ultimatums. None of it had mattered, though, not to Kenny, who believed he and Janine were forever. But now it seemed they were over, if only because the ending had come without fanfare. No yelling, no slammed doors; just one simple text, and then silence. The next morning, when he called Janine and got no reply, Kenny had visions of racing to UBS and clocking Les Hough. Instead, he went to the office. When he got home, his wife's clothes were gone, and so was Dog, which raised a question he hadn't considered: Could seven years of marriage, one mammoth house, one spoiled pooch, and countless his-and-hers gifts all be negated with twenty-seven characters?

The next three weeks were hard, but Kenny had been agonizing over Les Hough for so long, it was almost a relief to let go. Janine had left, and for once, he didn't chase her. At first, when he opened her closet and saw all the empty hangers, he had to lie down, but as time passed, he began to feel lighter, as if one hundred and forty pounds of frustration and regret had been hoisted off his shoulders. Though Janine sent brief replies to his texts, she didn't return his calls, so Kenny stopped checking his phone. He went out with Fez, and when he spilled the whole story, Fez listened and offered sympathy. While the experience felt new and weird, it didn't feel bad, which, in a way, Kenny could say about everything. He felt weird living alone, weird not having a dog, weird not having someone say "Good job!" when he stained the back deck, weird deciding what to eat for dinner. Not a bad weird, just a weird that required getting used to. Meanwhile, the one constant, the only constant, was Ellery, so that's what Kenny did every day: he went to work.

SUDDENLY IT WAS June, and Kenny was cranking out projects like a well-oiled machine. Between the Atlanta lease, Rutherford's town hall, the cracked ceiling in Leo's office, the scorched floor by the copier, and the mailroom guys (allegedly) trafficking Ecstasy, he was barely treading water. And these were only his top five tasks—the operations checklist had thirty more. Plus, he had to research executive pay plans, and according to Lucy, Rutherford wanted to discuss ESS, which he should consider a positive sign. In the halls, the big man offered him a jocular "Hey-o," but Kenny understood there would be no more private chats. Not that he had time. Now that he was overseeing operations, he got in early, skipped the gym, and ate lunch over his keyboard. But the work kept coming in, and Lucy was on his back to get it done. No one had ever ridden him this hard, not even Rosa.

Thank God for Katie.

"I'm here," she said. It was 7:00 a.m. on Wednesday, the third week in June, and they were alone. (Well, Leo was there too, bitching about all the goddamn early birds.)

"Katie!" Kenny gestured to a stack of folders. "Make this all go away, please." He gave her a toothy smile, like a cartoon dog, not caring how dopey he looked. He and Katie had been working side by side for more than a month, and every day, in every way, she saved his ass. Her hidden genius was organization. In addition to color-coding the operations checklist, she created a binder for each project, developed timelines and budgets, and then color-coded those. She could locate any document, hard copy or digital. Finally—and this had less to do with saving his ass than restoring his faith—she was nice to him. Yesterday, he showed up bleary-eyed and exhausted. "Rough night," he told her. "I didn't fall asleep until two." Whereas Janine would've trumped him with her own worse experience—her night was *excruciating*, she didn't sleep *at all*—Katie furrowed her brow. "Sorry to hear that. What's on your mind?"

"What can I do for you?" she asked now, pen poised over a legal pad.

He showed her the Atlanta office lease. "We have to renegotiate this, but the terms are too high. I'll probably have to fly down." He paused. "Hey, you ever been to the South?"

Katie's eyes widened. "Seriously? I'd *love* to go!"

"Oh, wait, Katie . . ." Kenny hadn't meant to imply he could bring her along. But when a lock of hair fell across her cheek, he had the sudden, impulsive desire to brush it away. "I don't see why not," he said, at the same time thinking, Are you out of your mind?

"Really? No way!"

Her enthusiasm reminded him she was just a kid. He was feeling fraternal, he decided, brotherly, the way he'd feel toward any girl twelve years younger. But when she leaned in for a hug, he panicked, afraid she might kiss him.

Two hours later, they were in the conference room, waiting for the managers' meeting to start. Usually they sat together, but today Kenny had opted for the seat next to Leo. Katie sent him a text.

Why r u so far away?

Kenny gathered up his computer, iPhone, BlackBerry, files, legal pad, pens, pencils, water, coffee, and keycard, and moved to the seat on her left.

Hello!

Kenny beamed. He turned to see Rosa walk in, with Lucy and Courtney, Rob's former assistant. Rosa and Lucy were behind closed doors all the time now, so Kenny rarely saw either of them. Today Rosa wore a brown knit suit, her hair was neatly coiffed, and she seemed more alert than she had in a long time. She sat down at the head of the table. Lucy was on her left, dressed in a white blouse with French cuffs and a black skirt. As they waited for everyone to assemble, Lucy scanned the room with a critical eye. "Before we start," she said, "I asked Rosa to update us on her new committee. Also, going forward Courtney will be attending these meetings, which are no longer limited to senior staff. So Courtney"—Lucy waved like a game show host—"welcome."

Courtney gave Lucy a mock salute, drawing chuckles all around.

"I'll be coming, too!" Everyone turned to Juanita, a fine-boned woman with a shock of white hair who'd been processing payroll nearly as long as Kenny had been alive. "I'm on the team!"

"That's right." Lucy nodded. "We're including all of HR. . . . So, Rosa, why don't you go first? Then we'll have manager updates, review our financials, and close with this week's case study."

As she spoke, Kenny studied Courtney. Tall and lanky, with ropy brown hair that swished like a horse's tail, she was the same age as Katie, but not nearly as pretty. Catching his eye, Katie waved, and Kenny pictured her lying naked beside him. While this was not a brotherly thought, the more he tried not to see her, the more open and yielding she looked. Sweating, he slid a binder on his lap—ATLANTA LEASE RENEGOTIATION—while conjuring up sad images to get rid of his boner: earthquake footage from Haiti, Iraqi children with no arms, puppies in captivity, the way his mom lost her jaw when she took out her teeth.

"As you know," he heard Rosa say, "I'm working with Rutherford on a committee that will research undervalued companies to purchase. We met for the first time last week—"

"Actually it was last month, Rosa," Lucy cut in. "Our first meeting was in May."

Rosa scowled. "Not only are you interrupting me, but you're wrong. We met last week."

"You know what, Rosa?" Kenny double-checked his calendar. Now that he was refocused on the discussion, his erection was gone. "Lucy's right. Your meeting was in May, because that's when the board approved the 401(k) match."

"No." She was firm. "I need everyone to stop correcting me. It was last goddamn week!"

Thumbs working, Lucy checked her BlackBerry. "Oh, you're right; it *was* last week." She glanced up. "Rosa, I apologize. I was mistaken."

This confused Kenny. Lucy never relented, even when she was wrong—and this time she wasn't. But Rosa looked so sure of herself, he kept his mouth shut.

"That's all I'm authorized to say about the committee," Rosa went on. "We met last week, and our important work continues. Kenny, operations. What's doing with the town hall?"

"We're right on target, Rosa," he said proudly. "We've narrowed down our choices to three sites, including the Hyatt." He held up a binder—TOWN HALL, JULY 13, 2010—as if introducing it into evidence. "We'll tour them all next week, and have a decision by Thursday."

Rosa clapped. "Excellent work! What about Atlanta? Lease signed?"

"Massey won't budge. Looks like I have to fly to Atlanta—"

Suddenly Rosa snapped. "That's *bullshit. Bull. Shit.*"

Stunned, Kenny backpedaled. "I don't have to go. Millie can ride with the broker and send pictures of alternate buildings. But flights to Atlanta are cheap, in case that's your concern."

But Rosa was fixated on the lease, not the trip. "How many times did we talk about this?"

"You and I never discussed the lease, Rosa."

"That is *bullshit*." Leaning forward, she stuck out a finger. "I told you *nine months ago* this would happen. I said if you waited too long, Massey would screw us—now look. It's *June*, and the lease expires in *July*. We don't have time to find new space, oversee a build-out, and orchestrate a move, which means we'll be on the hook for two offices. The same thing happened in 2004. Massey had us over a barrel then, too! Dammit, Peter, why don't you listen to me?"

The conference room was silent.

Kenny felt attacked. "That's not fair," he started to say, but stopped. Something was wrong. Although Rosa was coiled like a wire, her eyes were vacant, as if the life behind them had been extinguished. Kenny turned to Katie. *What should I do?* But she was watching Lucy.

"Rosa," Lucy said, jumping in, "let's move on, why don't we?"

"This is *my* meeting, Lucy. I still work here. Correct me all you want, my dear, but you can't push me out yet." She returned to Kenny. "Why did you let this go on so long? Why didn't you call him when I asked?"

She has no idea who I am, Kenny realized. She thinks I'm Peter Dreyfus. A month before, he would've sneered at this, but a month before he'd been a prick. Now he felt a hitch in his chest, the shift of hard edges crumble and give way. "You're right." Rosa wasn't some foolish old goat screwing up names. She was a sixty-four-year-old woman, still young by most measures, whose brain was failing. "I'm sorry; I'll fix this."

"What happened?" she asked, puckering her lips, as if tasting something sour.

"I'm stupid sometimes." Kenny didn't have to fudge the truth to say this. He'd lost his wife, lost his dog, almost lost his job. He was stupid, period.

When Rosa lifted her chin, the recessed lights bleached her face with the cruelty of an interrogation. Seeing every wrinkle exposed, every fine line laid bare, Kenny understood how bad off she was.

Was she scared? He thought of Sarge, the tough motherfucker, whose doctor advised he stop driving: his vision was bad and unlikely to improve. When Kenny asked him about this, Sarge had grunted, "Overreacting." But maybe, deep down, Sarge was scared, too. Maybe he was thinking, First my keys, then my home, then what? The old guy must be terrified. "I'm sorry, Rosa," Kenny repeated; he was referring to everything—the lies he'd told, the work he'd blown off, all the ways he was a jackass. "I am very, very sorry."

Rosa held his gaze. "We'll see," she told him.

After the meeting, Lucy pulled Kenny into her office and closed the door. He worried he'd done something (else) wrong, but she only wanted to confirm what he already suspected. Four months back, Rosa had suffered a stroke. Since then, her mental functioning had rapidly deteriorated; she was as bad off as he'd thought. "But so we're clear," Lucy said, "Rosa is the only reason you're still around. She fought for you."

Hearing this, Kenny's throat tightened. "Have you told Rutherford?"

"No, although he probably knows something's up." She shrugged. "Maybe he does, maybe he doesn't. Either way, he hasn't said anything to me so it's business as usual. Rosa's behavior is unpredictable. When she's addled—like today—we hunker down in her office or leave the building. You must've noticed she's rarely around and when she is here, she's never alone. Right after the stroke, Leo, Katie, and I took over her job, the department—everything. It seemed impossible at first, but it's surprisingly easy to push your weight around. People are so afraid of losing their jobs, they do whatever you say if you sound authoritative. Plus, Leo knows a guy in IT who gave all of us access to Rosa's desktop; he also put a delay on her e-mails, so we can intercept them, coming and going. Katie answers her phone; Leo and I triage her work—reports, P&Ls,

correspondence—and attend all her meetings. Luckily, Rutherford has her on this acquisitions committee; I'm on it too. Rosa says I'm still 'training' to be chief, so she and I are together all day. The woman never leaves my side."

Kenny was skeptical. "You really think you can pull this off?"

"We've *been* pulling it off. It's been *four months* already! You had no idea—and you're *in* our department! Our goal is to keep this up through the summer, until September, when Rosa becomes eligible for her full pension. We thought about asking Rutherford to pay her out early, but he's legally bound to the rules of the plan; plus, if he knew why, he'd have to tell the board, and who knows what they'd do. Hopefully, in another three months the markets will stabilize, she'll see some traction in her 401(k), and she can retire on her own terms. For now, we're just taking it one day at a time."

"What can I do?"

"Work autonomously. Come to me with questions. Stay away from Rutherford. The idea is to protect Rosa at all costs. You think you can do that?"

Kenny didn't blink. For once, he was on the inside. "Yeah, I can. Absolutely."

AT NOON ON Monday, Kenny and Katie were reviewing the revised lease. On Friday, when Massey wouldn't budge on the terms, Kenny flew down (alone) to try to convince him. Though Kenny was skeptical that he could change Massey's mind, in the end the guy capitulated, which thrilled Rosa. Kenny felt heroic on the plane back to Newark, and for the rest of the weekend, he had the exhilarating sensation that his life was starting over.

He and Janine were in contact, though only by text, which made her feel more like a pen pal than an estranged wife. While it was nice to be in touch, thinking about her didn't flatten him like it once did, maybe because she seemed far away. They kept their messages transactional, focusing on the house, finances, and Dog, so on Saturday, he was surprised when she wrote:

> I didn't sleep with Les; I wanted to but didn't. He flirted with me. I got caught up in the attention and flirted back, but that was it. I swear.

> I don't believe u. I want to but I don't.

Janine didn't reply that night or on Sunday. Like everything else, that she might never come home was a weird concept, but not catastrophic. Meanwhile, Kenny looked forward to Monday, when he could go back to work. Used to be his job, any job, was a stepping stone to some undefined future, but Ellery was no longer a means to an end. Sure, overseeing operations was less intellectual labor than analyzing Maslow's theory of needs, but it was no less honest. Or difficult. Or satisfying. Kenny loved having tactile, solvable problems, and every time he ticked off an actionable task, he felt a physical rush:

Atlanta lease—done
Town hall—in progress
Leo's ceiling—done
Scorched floor—done
Ecstasy ring—false alarm

Now, too, his work had meaning. People depended on him; there were real-life consequences when he flaked out. He also got to see Katie, who was putting away the Atlanta lease into the binder marked ATLANTA LEASE RENEGOTIATION.

"You did a great job with Massey," she repeated, and then laughed at his expression. "Am I *embarrassing* you, Kenny? Are you feeling *self-conscious*?" She punched him with fondness—no, more than fondness, with affection. Katie-and-Kenny were a thing, just like Lucy-and-Rob used to be, like Lucy-and-Leo were now, with inside jokes and a private language. "Let's talk town hall." Flipping open the binder marked TOWN HALL, JULY 13, 2010, she pulled out pictures of hotel banquet rooms. "The Hyatt has the best deal, even if we have to build a riser. The Sheraton and the Marriott are both too expensive."

If they got married, Kenny thought, this is what house-hunting would be like. They'd have a color-coded binder—KATIE-AND-KENNY: FIRST HOME—filled with pictures, owner disclosures, and financial statements. House hunting with Katie would be different than it was with Janine. Back then, Janine had led the charge, deciding which town, how many bedrooms, hardwood or carpeting, paint or wallpaper. Trailing behind, Kenny indicated yes or no, less to offer his opinion than to ratify her choices. Janine-and-Kenny were queen and servant, but Katie-and-Kenny would be partners. Would Katie want kids? If so, how many? Four? Five? He wanted five. It was a lot, but they'd make it work. KATIE-AND-KENNY: CHILDREN.

"Kenny?" He glanced up to see Katie studying him. "Clearly, you're distracted," she said. "So let me follow up with the hotels." Walking out, she turned to give him her brightest can-do smile, and when she mouthed *I've got this*, Kenny's heart split wide open.

Ten minutes later, he was alone in the men's room, jerking off. He wanted to touch her so badly he couldn't focus, couldn't function, without relief. He came hard, with a groan. Released, he pulled up his pants, washed his hands, and returned to his desk, where he powered through his checklists for the rest of the afternoon. Don't fuck up, he told himself, wanting and not wanting to do his work, wanting and not wanting to think about Katie.

Do. Not. Fuck. This. Up.

Katie came back at six. "Oh my God!" Papers covered Kenny's desk. Half a burrito from lunch sat on a greasy wrapper. A comp textbook was facedown on the floor. "What happened?"

"I've been busy, busy, busy." He checked his watch. "Go home! It's late."

"I can stay; I want to stay." This time she was the one who blushed.

Their eyes met, and Kenny felt heat rise between them. (Well, he hoped it was heat; he hadn't been close to a woman other than Janine in years.) "My one-on-one with Lucy is tomorrow," he said, redirecting his attention. "I could use help pulling together a status report."

For the next half hour, they went over Kenny's projects until he suggested they take a break and order dinner. But when he picked up his desk phone, there was no dial tone. "Hello?"

A voice murmured in his ear. "Hey, baby." It was Janine. Her voice, husky and familiar, made his mouth dry up.

"The phone didn't ring!" Kenny was perplexed. "I picked it up, and you were there."

"That's a sign," Janine said, chuckling. "It means we're still connected—which is good because I'm calling to see if we could talk." She paused. "I'm downstairs."

"You're *here*?" Startled, his voice rose so high, he sounded like a crow. *Here? Here?* "It's Janine," he told Katie. "She's here!"

"Let's finish tomorrow." Katie stood up. "You said yourself it's late."

"Kenny?" Janine asked. "You there? I just need five minutes. Please?"

"But I'm starving; you must be too. Janine wants to talk, but it won't take long."

"Who are you talking to, Kenny? I'm sorry to be interrupting, but I—"

"Janine, I'll call the front desk to buzz you in. Take the elevator to nine." He hung up. "She'll only stay five minutes. I like you, Katie," he blurted out. "Please don't go."

"I like you too, Kenny; I mean I like you as a . . . you know . . . as a coworker . . ."

He dialed security, happy to hear that Katie liked him. As he said, he liked her very much as an employee, a person, and, sure, as a woman. Hustling down the hall to meet Janine, he called out, "I'll be right back!" He felt okay; rather, he felt fine. It was good Janine was here. They could talk, finalize details, and then she'd leave. But when she stepped off the elevator, and he got a whiff of her sweet perfume, his heart did a rat-a-tat-tat and his breath came in gasps. How should he greet her? Hugging seemed too little, kissing too much. He stuck out his hand.

"Hello," he said as if they were at the UN and she was a visiting dignitary.

Janine put her arms around him. "Hey, you look positively edible."

It was odd to see her in the reception area, odder still to feel her breasts, which she pressed against him (deliberately, he decided). Even so, she looked good enough to eat, or whatever she just said. She wore a light, filmy summer sweater that hung down to her knees over her navy Armani wrap dress, which pulled in all the right places and showed a hint of gorgeous cleavage. As he led her through the empty halls, she looked around, curious. "What a quirky place!" she said, and he remembered she'd never been here before.

Kenny stopped. "This is me." Up until now, this exact moment, he was feeling okay—fine, rather. His work situation was much improved. He was half of Katie-and-Kenny. His coworkers didn't despise him. But as his (ex? former? estranged?) wife stood outside his cube-with-walls and pulled on the makeshift door he'd jerry-rigged himself, Kenny's confidence flagged. He saw Ellery through her eyes: particleboard walls, cheap construction, scuffed floors. For all its "quirky" charm, this place was a slum compared to the marble, steel, glass, and chrome of UBS, and he was little more than a glorified janitor who also processed spreadsheets.

Inside, Katie stood where he left her. Although he'd asked her to stay, seeing her here was unsettling. "Janine, this is Katherine Reynolds, my colleague. Katie, this is Janine, my uh, my Janine."

When Katie gushed, "I've heard *so much* about you," Kenny was reminded of her youth. In low heels and an ill-fitted suit, she looked like someone's kid sister, though definitely not Janine's, who stood two heads taller in pointy stilettos. Wrapped in her royal robes, Queen Janine was tall, dark, and regal. She dwarfed Katie, not just with her height but also with her bearing.

"I've heard a lot about you as well," Queen Janine said coolly.

"*When?*" Kenny's rancor surprised him. "You left a month ago; I didn't know her then."

"Oh my gosh!" Behind him, Katie was giddy. "I *just* realized your coats *match*." She pointed to the picture of them wearing their Christmas-babies coats. "That's *so cute*." Kenny couldn't tell if she was being sincere. And what had she meant before, when she said she liked him as a coworker? Just a coworker?

"They were presents. Every year my folks give us his-and-hers gifts." Janine gave Kenny a smile. "It's a tradition; Kenny and I have the same birthday."

Why was she acting so proprietary? *She* left *him*, didn't she? "We share a birth *month*, Janine, not *day*." Seeing the picture, Kenny was struck by how clownish they looked. In his memory of that coat, it was heavy and constricting, like shouldering a bear's pelt.

He turned to Katie. "It's late. You worked hard today; go home. But take a cab and save the receipt—I'll expense it."

Katie looked relieved. "Janine, it was nice to meet you."

Murmuring a similar sentiment, Janine walked the younger woman out, as if this were her office. She tried shutting the door, but it wouldn't align with the wall, so she whirled around, her filmy sweater rising, like a parachute. "Kenny, I didn't mean to barge in . . ." Her voice was shaky, and he realized that despite her proud bearing, she was nervous. She thrust her hands forward, palms up, as if making an offering. "Let's start over. Hi Kenny, it's good to see you. I'm here to say I'm sorry. I shouldn't have left the way I did. It was wrong, and I apologize."

"So why did you?" Watching Janine try to relax, Kenny felt himself softening.

"Lots of reasons. I needed time to think, mostly. We'd been drifting apart for a while. I kept hoping we'd find our way back; instead we continued to fight. Things were miserable, but we couldn't seem to help each other."

"Was it really that bad? I mean, I know it's been rough with our jobs—"

"I've felt disconnected from you for the past year or so. Then Les and I started to get closer, and it scared me. Why did I need his attention? Why did I feel starved for—"

"Sex?" Kenny could barely say the word. "We have a great sex life, Janine. We fucked every day, practically."

"Not sex. Intimacy, closeness. I thought if we paused for a minute, I could figure out what I need—"

"But you never *said* anything. You just *left*."

"*Of course I did*. You don't hear me. For a long time, I've been telling you I'm only thirty-three; I'm not ready for kids. But you kept pushing. You wouldn't relent, and by the end, I felt so trapped, all I could think to do was run. But it helped, Kenny; this past month has been enlightening. You and I have been together since college, and we still love each other, so maybe we can figure out how things went sideways. Maybe we can go for counseling, find our way back together, and then move forward . . ."

Kenny started to panic. It was too much, the idea of rehashing their marriage, revisiting every single you-did-this and you-did-that. "Janine," he started to say, when she cut him off.

"I don't want to throw out all those years. I can't start over with someone new."

"But maybe we're better off." Saying this, Kenny realized it was true. "My priorities have changed; *I've* changed. All I care about is keeping my job—*this* job. I need to start looking after my father. He had a car accident; he needs my help, and I want to give it to him. I want to"—he mumbled here—"be a good person."

"Oh my God, is Sarge okay?"

"They won't tell me the details. I'm the man's only son, and I've been a rotten one." This too was true. Kenny felt ashamed, the kind of bone-deep shame that was indelible, that would mark him for life. "Who else does he have if not me?" His voice splintered, but he refused to break down in front of Janine.

"Baby, listen. We'll take him to my dad's doctor; he's at NewYork–Presbyterian. Sarge and Glenda can stay at my parents' house. My dad can drive all of us into the city together. His car is a boat."

Admittedly, Janine's voice was soothing and her offer generous. Kenny might've been lulled into agreeing. But he was distracted by how focused she was on all that was hers—*her* father's doctor, *her* parents' house. He remembered their wedding, her toast. "My man, my man." As hard as he tried, he couldn't recall the rest of her speech—not a single word—except that, like everything else, he belonged to her.

He could see she was trying, and if he were anyone else—rather, the man he used to be—this would thrill him. "See, Janine. That's the thing. I want to take care of Sarge myself."

"*Yourself?* What does that even mean, Kenny? What can you do?"

"I don't know, but I want to find out. Janine, you and I were never people who'd quit school to care for our folks, but we should be. That's the kind of son, the kind of man, I want to be. It's the kind of man I want my son to be. I have to go," he said abruptly, the shock of understanding jerking him awake. "I have to go now."

So he left her, his wife, standing in her regal robes inside his silly little cubicle, calling out, "Kenny? Where are you going? You can't just leave me here!" He raced into the elevator, down to the first floor, and across the street to Hertz, where he presented his Amex, grabbed a set of keys, and drove home, to Allentown, to his parents. It was almost eight, but if he sped like a demon, he could make it there by nine thirty. Any later, and he'd scare them. Along the way, Kenny prepared his speech, the one that explained who he was and how he became this way. "I'm sorry," he'd tell them. "I'm so sorry."

See, here's the thing: three weeks before, when Janine walked out, Kenny had felt like he was starting over, and he *was* starting over, except he didn't go back far enough. To move forward, he had to return to the very beginning. He had to reset the clock at zero and rework all those lost hours, only slower this time and more dil-igently, so that every moment of every day counted for something, so that in the end, his life would add value. Now too he had to pay closer attention. What did it mean? What did it all mean? There was only one true way to read the signs, and to do this, Kenny had to strip himself down, open himself up, and wait for the universe to reveal itself. Which is why, when a wide-eyed Sarge and a worried Glenda met their only only in the foyer, Kenny's speech was forgot-ten, why his throat closed up and his knees buckled, why he fell into his mighty father's arms and started, finally, to cry.

## 21

# LEONARD SMALLS,
## VICE PRESIDENT,
### EMPLOYEE BENEFITS

LATE JUNE 2010

Leo felt great. Well, not great, but good, good enough. Work was hectic but manageable, and Rosa was holding steady. Plus, he'd lost weight, which made him eager to dress his less-tubby body. Overall, a solid B, despite the humidity. Summer, Leo's worst time of year, had rolled in with a vengeance, and outside it was swamp city. He spread out a napkin, slipped his tie into his shirt, and opened a Light & Fit yogurt. Now that Kenny had experienced some sort of spiritual awakening and arrived before eight thirty *every goddamn morning*, Leo was back in his secret lair up the eleventh floor, where he could eat his gruel in peace.

As Leo swallowed, he wistfully recalled his morning muffins, his cranberry nut, golden raisin, raspberry crumble, and lemon tart—each one, like the sex-rampant bath houses on the West Side Highway, a delight of the past. Good-*bye* glory holes! Good-*bye* lemon tarts! Leo Smalls had binged on his last empty calorie, a decision he made after his first dinner with Rob in March, three months back. That night, the two men forged what had become a genuine friendship. (*Was becoming*, Leo revised; don't jinx it.) By offering his Authentic Self, Leo had revealed his vulnerability, to which

Rob responded in kind. Exhibit A: Who did Rob call when he got laid off? Exhibit B: Who invited Leo to dinner with his family? It was a beautiful thing, this give and take. Whatever Leo offered Rob—anecdotes, insights, advice—was one more sliver of self he was learning to appreciate. Authenticity was hard work, as was feeling good, but one step led to another, and now Leo was up and running—walking briskly, rather.

Same with his size. One morning Leo scrutinized his naked reflection. The sight was heinous. "Leonard Smalls," he said, gently but firmly. "You're unhappy because you're fat, and you're fat because you're unhappy. This must stop." But instead of announcing a new diet on Facebook, he kept his mouth shut. He stopped with the self-pitying and carb-loading—no more French fries, no more mocha Frappuccinos—and slowly, but incredibly, the weight fell off. Now his clothes were looser, he had more energy, and he felt better, which, in turn, made him feel more principled and fulfilled by all his life choices. According to Dr. Saul, he was shedding his exterior to reveal his true self, which pleased Leo immensely. Therapists had a way of making his life feel scripted and thematic, like he was the star of an action-packed feature film instead of an ordinary fool bumbling through random events.

"Hey Leo!" It was Lucy, shouting from the far end of the floor. "Do you have any jelly?"

He pretended not to hear her.

"LEO! Come on, I know you're there."

"Lucy, this is my private time; please act like I'm not here."

A few weeks before, with help from Manny in security and Kenny in operations (ha!), Lucy had smuggled a desk, lamp, credenza, and bonsai plant up to eleven, where she fashioned her own separate workstation. Then Kenny built two high-walled cubicles—one for her at the north end of the floor, the other for Leo at the south—effectively creating dueling enemy camps in a deserted war zone. The cubes had no ceilings, the floor no rugs, and their every move echoed through the raw space, so Leo could hear the scrape of Lucy's chair and then her heels tap-tap-tapping as she got closer.

Appearing in his doorway, she held out a muffin. "Please, sir, may I have some more?"

Like Kenny, Lucy was a newly minted early bird. After Rosa's stroke in February, she'd started coming in at eight thirty, but her morning madness had really kicked into high gear (*seven thirty on some days!*) at the end of April, when Rob was laid off. Though Rob's exit had been depressing for all of them, Leo figured Lucy would take it hardest; he kept waiting for the *Anna Karenina* aftermath, where she dragged herself through the halls in open mourning. Instead, she took the whole thing in stride. Honestly, from one day to the next, Lucy seemed to lose all interest in Rob, as if he hadn't just left the company but fallen off the earth. While Leo found this curious (how do you walk away from a ten-year relationship, even if it only existed at work?), he was too busy to care. Besides, Rob's layoff turned out to be a bonanza of friendship for him, and he now had both Rob and Lucy clamoring for his time and attention.

To be clear: Leo was thrilled to be closer to Lucy. Not only were they taking care of Rosa together, they were co-running the department. Even so, her co-opting of his eleventh-floor safe haven annoyed him very (very) much. While he didn't mind offering sanctuary, too many undesirables had breached the border. Katie came first, followed by Kenny, who was clearly in love with her. Then Courtney. By the time Manny appeared, hauling up a leather sofa (per Lucy), Leo was fuming. Equally egregious was Lucy's disregard for the concept of "quiet mornings." She'd already interrupted him three times with bullshit requests—first a pen, then a notepad, and now condiments.

Sighing, he handed her a jar of orange marmalade.

"That's all you have?" She wrinkled her nose. "No one likes orange."

"Lucy, you're taking advantage of me, and I don't like it. You need to stop right now."

She smiled. "Oh my God, you're so bossy! Now that you're skinny, I guess you don't have to take shit from anyone." She broke off a piece of muffin. "Even me."

He snorted. "Oh please; I'm hardly skinny." But inside he was glowing. *Skinny me! Skinny me!* "Lucy, you are such a manipulator."

"The master," she agreed. "So let's get to work. Right now, our biggest issue vis-à-vis Rosa is the town hall, which is less than a month away." She chewed thoughtfully. "Can I just say what a great job Kenny is doing? Shocking, right? How that turned out?" Kenny was spending a few weeks with his parents—his father had been in a car accident—but he'd been getting all his work done remotely, which impressed Lucy to no end. (Unlike Rosa, she encouraged telecommuting.)

"Shocking, yes." Given that Kenny had treated Leo like a second-class citizen for years, it would be disingenuous for him to say that he was as enthralled by Kenny's new attitude as Lucy. Even so, she'd described how broken up Kenny was about his dad, and Leo hated to see anyone in psychic pain.

His phone rang, and he saw it was Rob, but didn't pick up, despite a twinge of guilt. The past two months had been painful for his friend, first Rob's unceremonious firing, now his fruitless job search. Leo spent a lot of time talking him off the ledge.

Lucy sighed. "Answer your phone! I know it's Rob. You don't have to sneak around."

"I'm not. But I feel funny talking to him in front of you."

"I'm giving you permission! Whatever, Leo. We have to focus. Rosa will be here any minute." Lucy hiked herself onto his desk. "So I'll lead the town hall run-through. We can repurpose last year's deck, but—you'll hate this—Rutherford wants Rosa to present and then stick around afterward for an impromptu board meeting. You think she's up for that?"

"For what? Giving a speech or meeting with the board?"

"Either. Both. Confining herself to name, rank, and serial number should she fall behind enemy lines."

"Hard to say. Every day is different." Leo scrolled through his e-mails, skimming some, deleting others. Again his phone rang; again, he ignored it. "What does Rutherford want her to talk about?" Christ, he felt overwhelmed, and it was only eight thirty in the morning.

Still perched on his desk, Lucy bounced her leg. "HR bullshit, Ellery's future, nothing crazy. Just ten minutes, Leo; not a big deal."

"Then why can't you do it? You're deputy. Stop kicking my desk, Lucy."

"All the department heads will be there; she can't be the only one who begs off. It's not my decision, it's Rutherford's. He's adamant that she address the troops."

This pissed Leo off. Rosa would pull herself together—she always did—but it would exhaust her, and in turn exhaust him. "Rutherford is *such* an asshole." Lucy was still banging his desk. The sound was driving him mad. "*Enough* with the *kicking.* What is with you?"

She threw up her hands, elated. "*I have so much work.* I haven't felt this motivated in *years!*"

Leo had a lot of work, too, but unlike Lucy he was drowning. It was too much—doing his job, caring for Rosa, counseling Rob. These days, Rosa was so unpredictable, someone—him, Lucy, Katie, now Kenny and Courtney—had to be with her all the time. (To coordinate this, Katie tacked up color-coded charts, like battle plans, detailing Rosa's work and home schedules.)

To be clear: Lucy was very effective as a troop leader. Like Rosa, she made smart decisions quickly and delegated fairly. But she was more devious than Rosa and had no compunction about exploiting her colleagues' misfortune. It was her idea, for instance, to have Kenny take over Peter's job once his secret talks with Rutherford came to light. Everyone else had wanted him gone, including Rosa, but Lucy suggested instead they give him an ultimatum. While this turned out to be the right call, she couldn't have foreseen that his marriage would implode or that he'd get a crush on Katie, both of which compelled him to work longer and harder—and finish projects for which Lucy could claim credit.

In sum: Leo was impressed with Lucy's upward mobility—her appearance alone was fabulous (Good-*bye*, Red Lobster uniform)—but she was no Rosa.

Case in point: because Lucy was so overloaded, mistakes had been made. They frequently bungled the schedule, and for all their Stasi-like oversight, Rosa was constantly wandering off, jeopardizing the whole operation. But the most egregious fuckup was Rob's layoff. Had Lucy been aware of Rutherford's plan, she could've stopped it. (Lucy disagreed; she said the CEO's decision was final.) Even so, Leo would never forgive Rutherford for letting Rob go; he was only just beginning to forgive Kenny for knowing beforehand and not telling anyone.

Lucy was studying the scheduling charts. "The old girl's busy today." Behind her, Leo was also studying the charts. Rosa had an M&A committee meeting at nine and two conference calls. Then she had a blowout at one and a dentist appointment at three. "Very," he agreed.

A WEEK LATER Leo had lunch plans with Rob, but when he got to the diner, Rob wasn't there. Then a fat guy waved to him from a booth in the back. "Leo! I'm here."

Leo couldn't believe it! Rob looked *awful*, unshaven and unkempt. His beard had grown wild and threaded with gray. He had dark circles under his eyes, and his face was puffy.

"I didn't recognize you," Leo said as he sat down.

"I know, I look like shit. I feel like shit, too. I'm tired and fat and I hate myself."

The former, inauthentic Leo would've said, "Welcome to my

world," but these days he was only a little fat and didn't hate himself. Instead, he nodded sympathetically and proceeded to scan the menu. Although he always ordered the same meal—egg whites, no potatoes, sliced tomatoes, dry toast—he liked to peruse the deliciousness he was forgoing: greasy fries, vanilla shakes, moist muffins—corn, bran, diner blues, and *oh!* double chocolate-chip.

Rob was asking about Lucy. "Have you spoken to her?"

"Of course. I speak to her every day."

"About me, I mean?"

"No, not about you." The problem with dieting, Leo decided, was that now he was more obsessed with food than ever.

"Really?" Rob looked at him in disbelief. "Never?"

"I lost another two pounds," Leo said, changing the subject.

"You don't look any different from the last time I saw you."

"I haven't been this thin *in years*. How can you have a wife and two daughters and not know that when I say 'I lost two pounds,' you're supposed to say 'You're wasting away'?"

"You look very thin," Rob said unconvincingly.

Rob signaled to the waiter as he passed. "I'll have a BLT and fries. No mayo, please, and a Diet Coke."

The waiter turned to Leo, who looked up and gave Thomas (per his nametag) a once-over. If Thomas were ten years younger and had a little less paunch, he'd be a dead-ringer for Hector, his dark, broody ex. Patting his own (decreasing) paunch, Leo ordered his usual, thanked Thomas, and returned to Rob. "How do you feel?"

"Totally and completely discouraged, like I'll never find another job."

"Rob, you *just* left. Two months is *nothing*. In this economy, it takes thirteen months on average to find a job. For most people, it's like sixteen." Having made up this statistic, Leo wasn't sure if thirteen months sounded too short or too long; he just wanted Rob to relax.

"I know, *I know*. But it's so *demoralizing*. You know what frustrates me most? I was finally getting ahead—not rich or well off, but I was able to put a little money away. I didn't feel clenched all the time. Then BAM! The bottom drops out. Now my life feels amorphous—there's no center, no framework to hold it together. Every morning I get up and face a long stretch of empty hours that I have to fill. But with what? Leo, it's a mess. I'm a mess."

It was unfair. It was scary. But Leo didn't know what else to say except, "You'll find something. I have faith in you." Rob's situation sounded so different, so distant from his own. Leo knew he was tempting fate to think this—the bottom could drop out for him, too—but it felt like there was a vast gulf between being employed and not. At the moment, he was standing on one side; Rob, all the way on the other.

Their food came, but Rob picked at his sandwich. "I don't get it. I went to a good college, I got a job. Maybe I'm not the most ambitious guy, but I showed up every day. I lived modestly, no fancy vacations or expensive cars. But none of this matters; it's like the past twenty years were a complete waste, and I'm starting over from square one."

"But you're not, Rob. You have experience, intellectual capital, maturity."

"To what end? What's the point? You go to school, get a job and then what? You die? There has to be more. Leo, I didn't plan to be a recruiter or trainer; I didn't plan to be anything. I'm an HR guy because I made no effort to be anything else; I just fell into the river and let the current take me. What kind of career is that?"

Leo swallowed a bite of his eggs. Random events had landed him in HR too, but he always figured this was normal. Didn't most people, most middle-road joes, cobble together a career? Growing up, Leo's only goal was to get out of Florida. He came to New York to do something creative. Although he didn't have any unique talents, he figured, how hard could it be to get a job as a magazine editor? Pretty fucking hard, it turned out, so he ended up temping. Then his parents died, one after the other. Leo plunged into a depression and drifted from job to job. At one point, he read benefits administration was a growing field, so he got his master's in public policy and ended up at Pfizer. Then he met Rosa at a conference, and they hit it off. When she offered him a job, he said yes. Nothing about Ellery was appealing—it was small, disorganized, and he didn't quite grasp what they did—but he decided to stay for a while and then move on. The next thing he knew, it was twelve years later.

"What do you want to do?" he asked Rob. "Forget money, experience, all of that. If you could have any job in the world, what would it be?"

"I'm married with two kids. Who gives a shit what I want? I have to make money." He was leaning forward because Thomas the waiter was hovering, as if waiting to interrupt.

"Can I help you?" Leo asked.

Thomas flashed a conspiratorial smile. "I hate to butt in, but are you guys together?"

Rob snapped, "Of course we're together. Do you see anyone else at the table?"

"Rob," Leo said gently. "He's asking if we're a couple."

Leo turned to tell him no, but Rob cut him off. "Of course we're not *together*." He flashed his wedding band. "I'm *married*. I have a *wife*. I have *kids*. I'm not *gay*." He spat the word *gay*, which made Leo flinch.

Backing away, Thomas raised his hands, don't-shoot-me style. "Okay, buddy. I get it. You're not *gay*. But there's a photographer outside from the *Times* doing a story on gay relationships; he's taking pictures of random couples, so I thought if you *were* together, you might get in the paper. Trust me: I am *not* asking *you* out." He stalked off, muttering "Asshole!" loud enough for them to hear.

"*I'm* the asshole?" Rob was incredulous. "How am I the asshole? He was the rude one!"

"Are you kidding?" Leo was equally incredulous. "He was

friendly. *You* were *rude*. *You* were the *asshole*. You *went off* on him because he suggested you might be gay. That is fucked up, Rob. It's the kind of attitude that can ruin people's lives."

"Come on, Leo." Rob chuckled nervously. "Don't you think you're overreacting?"

This enraged Leo. "No, Rob. I'm *not* overreacting. I'm educating you about the world beyond your privileged hetero existence. You're a white man with a wife. Your life is *acceptable*. You don't have to hide in the shadows or pretend to be something you're not."

"I know that, Leo. I'm—"

"*You don't know shit, Rob.* You're totally blind to what goes on around you."

Rob took umbrage. "I think I'm aware of people's differences—more so than most men."

"Really? If you're so *fucking* aware, then how could you work with Peter Dreyfus for eleven years and not know he was a closet case?"

"*Peter Dreyfus?* What's he got to do with this?"

"Peter Dreyfus was a victim of the attitude you just revealed—that it's *horrifying* to be gay. Do you know why he stole, Rob? Because he made a pass at . . ."—Leo fumbled—"another employee, but was so afraid of being found out, he let himself get caught. Think about it. He'd rather have people believe he's a *criminal* than be outed as gay; he'd rather *be* a criminal than admit he likes men." (Leo didn't know if this was true. Yes, Peter tried to kiss him; yes, he did steal, but these facts may not have been linked. Even so, it felt true.)

Rob snorted. "That's bullshit. Peter had a sick mother and too much of his money tied up in real estate. It's 2010; the stigma of being gay in business is over."

"You know this how? Because you're such an integral part of gay culture? Because of all your work as a homosexual activist?" Leo was so furious he could barely breathe. "Peter was a solid corporate citizen for twenty years. One day, he skims off tens of thousands of dollars, and doesn't even bother to cover his tracks. How does this make any sense?"

"Did Peter make a pass at you?" Rob asked quietly. "Is that what's bothering you?"

"No, Rob, what's bothering me is that you're being *obnoxious*, and if you're so mortified that some waiter thinks you're gay, then we can't be friends. *I'm gay, Rob.* I am a gay man, and your behavior offends *me*. *You* offend *me*." He meant this; he couldn't have even one inauthentic person in his life. "And you ruined my lunch."

Rob tugged at his T-shirt as if the collar was choking him. "I'm sorry, Leo." His voice had a pained, reedy quality. "I was out of line." He spoke stiffly, like he wanted to say more, but they finished their meal in silence. And when Leo checked his phone—two texts from Katie, three from Lucy, and a call from Rosa that he returned, right at the table—Rob didn't say a word. Nor did Leo protest when Rob paid for both meals and left Thomas a fifty on a thirty-dollar tab.

Outside, Rob apologized again. "I am sorry, Leo. I've been wrapped up in myself for months, and I'm all over the place—but that's no excuse for being an ass." He paused. "I don't care if the guy thought we were together. It just came out that way."

"I accept your apology." Leo was still smarting but wanted to give Rob a pass; he was his friend, after all. "Everyone says—and does—stupid things. God knows I do."

To which Rob replied, "We kissed. Lucy and me."

This got Leo's attention. "Really? When?"

"The day I got fired. She told me she loved me—*was* in love with me; well, *used to be* in love—then I kissed her. She pushed me away, and we haven't spoken since."

"That's it? One kiss?"

"It was a *very* forceful kiss." Rob grimaced. "I can't stop thinking about her."

Leo considered this. Of course, he thought. No wonder why

Lucy was avoiding Rob; the whole thing was probably too awkward to deal with. "I'm surprised it didn't happen sooner, frankly. You're human, she's human. Let it go, Rob. Let her go."

They were on the sidewalk. Down the street—just like the waiter said—a guy in a fedora was snapping pictures of gay couples. Some held hands, others made dopey faces. Watching them, Leo felt sad for Lucy, sad for himself. Why was it so hard for them to meet nice, available guys? Leo was so preoccupied, he didn't notice Thomas rushing out of the diner.

"I'm glad I caught you!" he told Leo, and then glanced at Rob. "I know, I know, this is *totally beyond creepy*, but what can I tell you? I'm *gay*." And he thrust a note into Leo's hand.

> *Dear nice friend of rude customer,*
> *Hearing you take down your lunch companion was so inspirational!*
> *(I know it wasn't a date because HE IS NOT GAY!) But I*
> *am GAY and on behalf of ME and GAY MEN in and out of*
> *CORPORATE AMERICA, I salute you. Fight the power!*
>> *Your comrade-in-arms and loyal server,*
> > *Thomas Lange Xavier*
> > *PS: You have a great body. You're totally wasting away, so stop*
> > *dieting NOW.*
> > *PPS: Waiters hear EVERYTHING.*
> > *PPSS: Drop me a line, tlx@verizon.net*

ROSA WASN'T SLEEPING. All week she complained to Leo that a strange smell in her bedroom was keeping her up. "It's thick and heavy, like my old apartment in the Bronx when the neighbors cooked soup, only it's not soup; it's damp and dirty." She was also paranoid, and "churned" (her word) with anxiety. "Lucy is listening to my calls; yours, too, I bet."

Leo was firm. "Lucy would never do that."

"You're a sweet kid, but a naive person. You don't know Lucy."

Leo had no idea what, if anything, had happened between Rosa and Lucy, though this concerned him too, that he'd been neglecting the department. He still called Rosa twice a day, and he was on top of her schedule; but he was distracted, and not because of work or Rosa or Rob or Lucy, or any of the other baby chicks whose lives he mother-goosed. Leo had a new friend. *Leo Smalls was in lust. Leo Smalls was in*—Wait, wait. WAIT!—*Leo liked a guy who seemed to like him back.* So Rosa was definitely on Leo's mind, but Thomas Lange Xavier was too. Since meeting Thomas ten days before, Leo had been late to meetings, unable to follow simple conversations, and rarely showed up at his desk before nine, much to Lucy's annoyance.

He and Thomas had yet to go on an official date, because Leo was too busy, but they spoke a lot—like, *a lot*—on the phone. Thomas was a freelance web designer (*ding!*) who waited tables for extra cash (*ding!*). He was forty-four (*ding!*), single (*ding!*), and "tired of all the bullshit games" (*ding! ding! ding!*). But this was the best part: he thought Leo was cute (*ding* times infinity!). "I never approach customers, even the handsome ones," he admitted. "But when I overheard you and your friend, you sounded so smart and sane, I had to meet you. So I made up that story about the *Times*—I had no idea who that guy in the hat was, or why he was taking pictures!"

So yes, Leo was distracted, but he was also concerned about Rosa, which is why he'd trudged into the city today, a Saturday, to make sure there wasn't a dead mouse, or worse, in her walls. It was the second week of July, and brutally hot; if an animal had died in her walls, the smell must be unbearable.

Leo stepped into Rosa's lobby, and the doorman waved him up, but when he got off the elevator, Rosa refused to let him into her apartment. Door cracked, she spoke to him over the chain. "What are you doing here?" She was annoyed. "My family's visiting from upstate. Besides, it's Saturday. Boundaries, Leo."

"I left you a message."

"I know, and I called you back, saying not to come."

A man called out behind her. "Who's there, Rosalita?" It was Nando, her brother.

"Open the door or close it," her sister, Marcy, chimed in. "You're letting out all the cool air." Leo heard Marcy's shoes clip-clop across the floor. "Who's there?" She tried to peer around Rosa. A large woman, she towered over her sister, but Rosa wouldn't move.

"Hi Marcy! It's Leo Smalls, from Ellery. I was in the neighborhood."

"Rosalita! What's wrong with you?" Pushing past Rosa, Marcy unchained the door and ushered him inside. "Leo; it's so nice to see you again." She gave him a hug.

Thanks to Rosa's generosity, Marcy had enormous breasts (implants) and va-va-voom hips (lipo), which she showed off in a cropped sweater, tight jeans, and slide-on mules. She was the antithesis of Rosa, who looked ready to lead a budget meeting at home in a tailored blouse and pressed slacks, a strand of pearls around her neck.

Leo returned Marcy's warm welcome. Although they'd crossed paths only briefly when Rosa was in the hospital, Marcy had explained how difficult it was for her to get to Manhattan, while thanking him profusely for his help. (Nando, by contrast, pretended Leo was invisible.) At the time Leo had judged them harshly for abandoning their sister, but Rosa kept insisting she was fine, so maybe Marcy simply chose to believe her. Every family has its own unique crazy, and it's easy to judge when you're on the outside looking in.

"Nando! Look who's here. It's Leo, from Rosa's job, remember? We met at Lenox Hill."

"You sound like a horse in those shoes," Rosa snapped, stepping aside to let Leo pass.

Ignoring her, Marcy led him to the dining room, where it was blessedly cool. Nando sat at the table, which was piled with bagels, spreads, fruit, juice, and coffee. "Leo, we're having a late lunch. Please join us. Nando and I are only here until tomorrow, and Rosa ordered way too much food."

Like Marcy, Nando wore several gold chains, but instead of jeans, he was dressed in a tracksuit and Nikes. He was a round man with an egg-shaped forehead and loose jowls that quivered as he swallowed a heaping forkful of coleslaw. "Long time no see," he said, but he didn't look up, nor did he shake Leo's hand.

"Thanks, Marcy, but I can't stay long." While Leo didn't like Nando, out of respect for Rosa, he wanted to be polite. "I'm just here to check on the smell."

Nando raised his face from his food. "What smell?"

"Rosa said there's a smell in her bedroom. I thought maybe a mouse died in the wall."

"Why didn't you tell me, Rosalita?" Nando's voice was accusatory.

"There was nothing to tell. I had the exterminator come, but he didn't find anything."

From the way Rosa averted her eyes, Leo knew this wasn't true. "You know what? I'll check it now, just to be sure." Although Rosa glared at him, he strolled into her bedroom, which he circled a few times, sniffing the air. Everything was in order, so he returned to the dining room. "Seems okay," he said. "Guess I'll head out. Nice to see you, Marcy. You too, Nando."

Rosa followed him into the hallway. "Thank you for coming, Leo. I'm sorry I was rude."

"No problem." The elevator arrived and he stepped inside. "I'll see you Monday?"

"Leo, wait." Lurching forward, she grabbed his arm. "I have something to tell you. But please don't tell them. Please, Leo; Leo, I have to be able to trust you."

"What's going on, Rosa?" he asked nervously.

She glanced behind her. "Leo"—her voice dropped—"I can smell ghosts in the walls."

"Rosa, what—" But she'd already moved back inside and shut the door. Immediately, Leo picked up the phone and dialed Lucy. "We have a situation," he said.

LEO WAS STUNNED. A well-built man wearing aviator sunglasses, faded Levi's that hugged his ass, and a crisp white shirt strolled into the diner. *No way.* He remembered Thomas as handsome, but didn't realize he was so . . . *holy shit.*

"Am I late?" Thomas pointed to Leo's empty water glass.

"I was a little early." Leo had arrived *almost an hour before.* Outside, it was blisteringly hot, so he gave himself extra time to cool off. Still, he could feel his eczema flaring up. Soon his back would be a mess of angry sores. "Actually, I was *very* early."

"That's okay." Thomas's smile was like a flash of white light. "I circled the block three times." He slid into his seat and put his hands on the table. "So. Here we are. Finally."

Despite his attempt to appear calm, Leo blurted out, "Do I look different than you remember?"

Thomas gave him a once-over. "You're even hotter. Definitely. Much skinnier, too."

Leo smiled shyly. "It's only been three weeks. I'm not *much* skinnier."

"*I know.* I keep asking myself, 'Could he really lose that much in only three weeks?'"

"Now you're making fun of me."

"Now I'm flirting." He lowered his voice. "I want to kiss you, but we barely said hello."

Maybe this won't be so bad, Leo decided.

Twenty minutes later, Thomas was explaining why, like Leo, he was eating egg whites and dry toast. "Turning forty ruined me. I played sports all my life, so I never had to think about food. But a few years ago, my metabolism changed, and the next thing I know, I'm a big fat fuck. So I went to Weight Watchers—it's the new AA for middle-aged men. 'My name is Thomas, and I'm a fatty.' This tastes like fucking sandpaper," he added, holding up his toast. "I'd give my left nut for a blueberry muffin."

"Me, too!" Leo was breathless. Everything about Thomas wowed him: the crescent-shaped birthmark along his jaw, the way he squinted while he listened, his disarmingly frank manner. He was very physical, tapping Leo's arm or hand to stress a point. Leo had a tendency to stiffen when people touched him, but with Thomas, it felt (almost) natural.

"Hey," Thomas asked. "Did you ever call Rosa's neurologist? How's she doing?"

This touched Leo, Thomas asking about Rosa. Leo realized he hadn't thought about her in how long? Fifteen minutes? "I didn't call, but I have been watching her more closely. She's been fine. I mean, she *seems* fine, although it's hard to get perspective—"

"Because you're too close to her?"

"I don't think we're *too* close. I meant because I see her every day, so I'm used to her behavior—rather, it doesn't faze me. I mean, the ghosts-in-the-wall thing shook me up, but Rosa has insomnia. As soon as she took Ambien, she slept through the night, and felt much better." He paused. On the phone, Thomas had seemed to understand his and Rosa's relationship; now he sounded judgmental. "Rosa isn't just my boss. She's like my family."

"No, I get it, Leo. I really do."

A waiter was clearing their plates, so the words hung in the air like toxic mist, but by the time the check was dropped off and a credit card procured ("Let me," Leo insisted), Thomas had moved on. "This was fun!" He stood up. "Well, thanks for lunch—"

"Wait," Leo said anxiously. "You seem mad. Did I say something wrong?"

"Listen, Leo." Thomas sat back down. "I really like you, but I don't think I can date another workaholic. I told you my last boyfriend was an oncologist, right? Morgan was a saint—a decent, caring man—but there are very few happy endings in his line of work. It's a grueling profession, and he got too tangled up in his patients, but I couldn't complain about it—ever. If he missed my birthday dinner, it was because he was comforting a thirty-year-old mother dying of breast cancer. Trust me, Leo. You can't get angry at a saint. Back then I was at an ad agency, and also married to my job, which is probably why we lasted so long. But a few years ago, I realized I was lonely and unhappy, so I quit my job, went freelance, and Morgan and I split up."

"But I'm not married to my job," Leo said. "It's just a way to make money. When Rosa retires, I don't have to stay at Ellery; I'm just not sure what to do next." Christ, he sounded immature. At forty-three, his dad had a family and was more than halfway through his career.

"That's good to hear—not that you don't know what to do, but that you're available. I was afraid you were one of these go-go-go types. Still, you should find work that you love. You give a lot to your job; you should get a lot back." Thomas paused. "You like to give, don't you?" He gave Leo a sly grin, and when Leo nodded, Thomas leaned across the table and kissed him on the mouth. "This is gonna be so great," he said. "Just watch."

## 22

A week later, after months of meetings, phone calls, and Rosa-triage, the all-employee town hall had finally arrived. It started at eight thirty, so Leo and Lucy met for coffee, hailed a cab, and swung by Rosa's building at seven. But when they pulled up to the curb, Rosa told them she preferred to walk. "The hotel is a few blocks away." She knocked on the driver's window to hand him her credit card. "We could all use the exercise."

"Speak for yourself," Lucy said, still in the cab. "We have a lot of gear."

Leo was sweating in his suit. "It's too hot." He also had a nagging hangover. The night before, he'd met Thomas for a drink, which turned into three (each), and the next thing he knew, they were making out like teenagers. Knowing he had to be up at five, Leo went home alone, and now he was wired, cranky, and still horny as hell. "I vote we ride."

"Stop whining, both of you," Rosa said, already halfway down the street. "Let's go."

The good news: Rosa was in excellent form. She wore a new St. John in a tomato-red color that matched her lipstick, and her hair and makeup were flawless. As they trooped to the hotel with their bags, she reviewed the agenda and assigned last-minute tasks, all the while on the phone with Katie.

Leo was trying to text as he walked, but he kept stumbling.

"Are you texting your new boyfriend?" Rosa asked coyly, watching him.

"Who told you I have a boyfriend?"

"I have eyes, Leo, first of all. I see everything. Second, you've had your head in the clouds for weeks. And third, why shouldn't you have a boyfriend?"

"I haven't been in the clouds; I've been here and focused."

"Oh, Leo, please. I don't want you *here* and *focused*. I want you to have *a life*. Oh! There's the hotel!" Rosa sped up. "Come along, come along. We have a lot to do!"

Leo glanced at Lucy. "She seems fine, right? Maybe we worry too much."

"Fake it till you feel it. Isn't that what she always says?"

"You think Rosa's faking it?"

"I was referring to myself."

Katie stood outside the hotel, clipboard in hand. "Over here!" She waved.

Seeing her, Rosa lit up. "Good morning!" She looked around. "Where's Kenny?"

"Oh, he's been here for hours; right now he's with the events manager."

"Terrific! Let's find him and see what's what." Rosa crossed the lobby, flanked by Lucy and Katie. Behind them, Leo noted how put-together they looked, even Katie, who wore a slim-fitting gray suit, silk blouse, and heels. So far, Lucy's influence on her had been strikingly positive, which Leo found reassuring. To his mind, it could've gone either way.

When they stepped into the banquet room, Kenny leaped to grab their gear as he filled Rosa in on last-minute details, including the

10 percent discount on the food and drinks he'd managed to negotiate. Looking around, Leo could see that Kenny had done well co-
ordinating the space and acoustics. The room had thirty-five round
tables, each with ten seats, to accommodate everyone in the New
York office. Along the walls, a buffet offered bagels, muffins, fruit,
and coffee. At the front, a makeshift stage rose four feet off the
ground, and a lectern and chairs were set up for department heads
and board members, who had started trickling in. By this point,
Rosa was front and center, shaking hands. In her bright St. John,
she added a punch of color to the crowd of mostly middle-aged men
in drab suits and ties. Rutherford had been pleased with her presentation during last Friday's run-through, so Leo felt optimistic—and
relieved—about today.

His phone dinged with a text from Rob, wishing him good luck.
(After Leo's out-and-proud speech last month, he was sure Rob
would ditch him, but in fact, their argument drew them closer. Now
they spoke every day.)

Twenty minutes later, the town hall was under way.

So far so good, Leo thought as Rosa stepped toward the lectern.
Seated directly in front of the stage, the HR team had a perfect
view. Not that it mattered—he was texting with Thomas.

Gorgeous day. Let's be 2gether NOW NOW NOW

        V tempting but at town hall then full day of work

No more work, want 2 take train 2 Coney Island, soak in sun, study
locals & each other

        UGH. Coney Island=Yard Time @ prison
        Dirty sand, toxic water, people fighting 4 space

It's Tues morning, beach will be empty . . .

Up on the riser, Rosa thanked Rutherford for his introduction and then turned to the audience. "Good morning. I'm so pleased to be here. I've been asked to present HR's current initiatives and say a few words about each of our projects for 2010. Boy, we have a lot going on! So . . ."

At which point, heads bent over devices and side conversations resumed.

. . . blue sky, hot sun, lapping waves, ME, ME, ME . . .

For the next ten minutes, Leo texted with Thomas, tried to focus on Rosa, and then texted Thomas some more. The start of an affair was by far the best part, particularly since Leo's track record with men wasn't great. Over the years he'd had a series of boyfriends, but except for Horatio, none of his relationships lasted more than nine months. He worried this might happen with Thomas. They'd date for a while, fuck their brains out, and then what? They'd fall in love, move in together. Then one of them would cheat. Or need more time than the other could give. Or work too much. Or work too little. Then the other would bolt. *Whoa*, Leo thought. *Slow down.* This always happened, too: he got ahead of himself, envisioning the end before things even started.

Rosa's voice deepened. "And now, I have an important announcement."

Lucy looked up. "What kind of announcement? Katie, what is Rosa announcing?" She nudged him. "Leo, pay attention! Rosa is going rogue."

Say yes, say yes, say yes!

"When I first came to Ellery, HR was just a handful of clerical workers and one facilities manager. But Rutherford had a vision, which he hired me to execute, and now, sixteen years later, I'm proud to report that our department is more robust and responsive than even he imagined. As a strategic business unit, HR develops programs that will help drive Ellery's growth, efficiency, and profitability through the next decade and beyond. HR recruits the highest-performing talent; offers comprehensive and affordable benefits to you and your families; and provides training opportunities so that each of you can flourish professionally."

Closing his eyes, Leo envisioned hot sun, sandy beaches, iced coffee, Thomas. Focus on the now, he told himself. Stay in the moment. Don't ruin this.

"Ellery depends on you, and you depend on Human Resources. So let's give a round of applause to the HR team. Guys! Stand up, please: Lucy Bender, Leo Smalls, Kenny Verville, Courtney Adams, Juanita Johnson, and Katherine Reynolds. Leo! Lucy! Come on, everyone up, up. On your feet."

Leo opened his eyes. Was she serious? "Lucy, was this part of the speech you wrote?"

"What do you think?" But she stood up and waved. "I want to die," she said through a clenched smile.

". . . which is why," Rosa went on, "I want to announce—"

LEO? Where R U?

"—my retirement, effective this December. In the coming months, I'll transition—"

"Her retirement?" Lucy asked, turning to Leo. "*Since when?* Did you know about this?"

Up on the stage, Rosa Guerrero was giving the speech of her life. First, she backtracked, describing her early years and what corporate life was like for women and minorities. "I was a second-class citizen. If my coworkers didn't ignore me, they cut me off or spoke over me. I had to fight every day to be heard. We've made some progress, but still have a long way to go. So I implore you to reach out to coworkers who don't look or sound like you—reach out and truly listen to them. Our industry is becoming more diverse every day; Ellery must be equally diverse, not just to keep pace, but to thrive in the twenty-first century." Then she talked about employees she'd mentored in her career, using words like *investment*, *loyalty*, and *sacrifice*, and explaining why it was vital to contribute to a greater good. "I started working when I was eighteen. I'm sixty-four now, so that's forty-six years. *Forty-six years*. In business, we're not supposed to discuss age, but I'll tell you one thing: forty-six years is a *very long time*. I'll tell you another thing: it wasn't always easy. But even on my most challenging days, I felt something: exhaustion, pride, joy, sometimes sadness. Mostly, I felt strong for having survived. Which is probably the greatest lesson of all my years in business: a working life doesn't just keep you solvent, it defines you, shapes your character, reveals what you're made of. Work was where I found my best self, and even after forty-six years, there's no place in the world I'd rather be." Finally, Rosa expressed her love for Ellery, and thanked Rutherford and the board for their ongoing support. She especially wanted to thank her staff, each of whom reflected a part of her legacy.

Holding the microphone, Rosa glided across the stage like a beloved politician. She looked so fluid, so polished in her red suit, she was the picture of lucidity and control. But hours later, people would recall how, when the shimmering lights overhead caught her eye, she stumbled in her sensible pumps and skidded forward, then flew off the riser and into the air. She was so graceful, some thought it was part of her speech, even as her legs came out from under and her head smacked the floor. A half beat, a pause, then all hell broke loose.

# 23

## ROSALITA GUERRERO,
## CHIEF OF HUMAN RESOURCES,
## EXECUTIVE VICE PRESIDENT

JULY 2010

She missed Peter; it was true. He used to bring her gifts from the road: sweet Georgia peaches ("a sweet peach for a sweet peach"), chewy peanut brittle, a snow globe from Raleigh. Little treats that made her day. Peter was a giving man, a loving man, which is why his behavior continued to baffle her. How does a person show up with a perfect piece of fruit one day and embezzle the next? How did that make sense?

Rosa never did find out if they caught the kid in the hoodie, the one who stole all the iMacs. She bet he was still at large. A scam like that took forethought; the kid probably plotted for months. Peter, by contrast, sat at his desk and wrote himself checks. The clumsiest robbery on record, but he almost pulled it off, so shame on her for being blind. On the other hand, he'd never given her any reason to doubt him, so of course she trusted him. She trusted him so much she doubted herself, despite the black-and-white proof in her hand.

Rosa was in her office. Someone had switched out her chair; this new one was too low and gave her a backache. Every time she shifted, searing pain radiated up and down her spine. *Radiate* was a ten-dollar word. She'd forgotten that expression, "ten-dollar words."

It came from grammar school, from Mrs. Hutch in fourth grade who gave her *Weekly Readers*, which Rosa had devoured. She still read the paper every day, but whether or not this habit started with the *Weekly Reader*, who knew. Analyzing too deeply was borrowing trouble. Teasing the devil, her mother would say when Rosa asked too many unanswerable questions. In business you have to focus on the whos, whats, whens, and hows; you can't get bogged down with the whys. And the pain did radiate, which was the best way to describe the burning that fanned up and out, across her back, like rays of the sun. It hurt too much to sit up and type, so she hunched over and hand-wrote a note.

"Lucy." She spoke aloud as she scribbled. "I want the engagement survey. I realize there were mitigating circumstances, but I'm losing patience." What else? "Thank you," she added.

Despite this business with the survey, Lucy was turning out to be a superb number two. One day she'd make a fine chief. Now, though, her tongue was still too sharp, and she was overly concerned with the whys. But Lucy was smart, so the whys were in her nature, and Rosa could see she was trying to change. Eventually she'd soften up, and the world would be hers to run as she pleased. This, Rosa knew because in her first big job, she'd been a bitch on wheels until she realized she didn't have to be nasty for people to do as she asked. Kindness, she learned, went a whole lot farther. Lucy was just unhappy at the moment, which is a rite of passage for some businesswomen of a certain age. They hit their forties and suddenly realize they've spent too many lonely years waiting for a man to appear and their real lives to start, when all along, something *was* happening, these *were* their real lives. Waiting is itself a choice, and when you're a woman, it's the choice to put work before family.

Rosa understood Lucy's predicament all too well; she went through this herself before she met Howard. She woke up one day too old to do anything except tend to her career. Men no longer saw her as female, children (her own) were out of the question. It was painful, yes, but it passed, and afterward she was content with her lot. Nor did she regret not having kids; her life was rich and full. Funny, then, that she met her husband only after she gave up on love. The world was a mysterious, enchanted place, which Rosa was reminded of first when Katherine showed up at Ellery hours after helping her at Starbucks, and second when Kenny grew up right before her eyes. That's what made Rosa a great chief. She saw the man Kenny could be, and voilà, he emerged. This is what she wanted for all her people—Leo, Lucy, Katherine, even Rob, even Peter—to dig deep and find their best, most true selves. For some, it would happen at Ellery; for others it would take moving on, though this was the beauty of a corporate career: every new job is another chance to reinvent yourself. The key is to be the same person at home and at work. This doesn't mean bleeding your personal problems all over your desk—no one cares about your bunions or your kid's solo in *Hairspray*—but your core self should appear in both worlds. And for what it's worth, Lucy looked outstanding these days, so at least she could play the part. As chief, you learn that how you feel is less important than how your staff and your board believe you feel, so your job is to convince them you have it all covered. Fake it till you feel it. This, too, Rosa knew from experience.

"Lucy," she continued, "you have until Friday the . . ."—What was the date? Rosa glanced at her watch, but her arm was bare. The town hall had been on Tuesday, two days back, July the . . . the what? She couldn't remember—" . . . until this Friday to give me the survey. Period."

Rosa's door was open, and she could hear a woman's heels click like knitting needles as she strode down the hall. Rosa was attuned to the sound of women's shoes, an unconscious habit she picked up as a child. Her mother, Anita, had no arches in her feet and always wore a wedge, day and night, for support. As soon as Anita came home, she took off her street shoes and slipped on an ancient pair of mules, which she clomped around in all evening. Lying in bed, half-asleep and half-awake, Rosa was comforted by the dusty *clip-clop, clip-clop* of her mother's feet as she moved through their apartment, tidying up the kitchen and shutting off the lights.

Rosa tried raising her left arm, but it too was sore. She lifted her right one (her stroke arm), and that seemed okay, but it was hard to tell since most of the feeling was gone. Once upon a time, she had been a hearty woman, strong and busty. But lately she felt frail; she also had no appetite. All her St. Johns hung like drapes, which was why she'd bought the new red one. (It wasn't because of her retirement announcement; that was a coincidence.) Plus, she planned to consult after she retired, so she'd still need her St. Johns. What else would she do? Sit alone and watch TV? Knit booties for the grandchildren she didn't have?

"Lucy, please see me if you have questions. Period. Thank you (again). Best, Rosa." She couldn't push send, so she placed the note in her out-box. "Send," she said anyway.

Swiveling around, she called out, "Leo!" and was startled to see him slumped in a chair, next to her desk. "Oh my God! You look terrible." He was rumpled and unshaven, as if he hadn't slept for days. "How long have you been sitting there?"

Blinking, he rubbed his eyes. "I was here most of the night."

"Are you *insane*?" Even so, she was proud to hear this, her loyal footman pulling an all-nighter. "Go home and get some sleep." She heard her bossy tone. *Fetch the car, James. I have a board meeting at noon.* "I'm not kidding, Leo."

"I'm fine." He yawned. "I'm more concerned with how you are."

How was she? How was she? It was nice that he cared, but honestly, she felt fine. Well, her back was stiff and hurt like hell—because of the new chair, she assumed—and her mouth was dry, her right side felt bruised, and she couldn't lift her left arm. "I'm okay," she told him.

"What about your head?"

Now that he mentioned it, her head was killing her. "I do have a headache. There's Tylenol in my bag. Also? I wouldn't mind a Starbucks."

She started to stand up, but Leo leaped out of his chair. "Don't move! Stay right there. I'll get whatever you need. By the way, your sister stopped by. She's in town."

"Marcy came here? Really?"

"I know! I couldn't believe it either, but she's in the city and staying at your place." Leo stretched his arms and legs and then checked his phone. "I'll be right back, so please try and relax."

"Coffee with milk—whole milk, please," she said, waiting for him to chide her about the whatever, the whatchamacallit, the points. "A doughnut, too. And I'll just *relax* here until you get back." She chuckled. *Relax*—what a cockamamy thing for him to say. As if she could ever relax with people racing down the halls, her BlackBerry pinging, her phone ringing, ringing, ringing with requests for payroll clerks, extra time off, permission to work from home. The Wizard of Oz, Lucy used to call her, Ozzy when she felt generous. Lucy figured she didn't know about the nickname, but of course she did. (And for the record? Rosa *loved* the name Ozzy. It was a compliment, after all.) Rosa was HR chief. She knew everything: Leo had an eleventh-floor hideaway; Lucy went out with the security guard but broke it off; Kenny no longer loved his wife but couldn't tell her. They all had their secrets, which she accepted. This was a business, not group therapy. It was the thievery, the lying, she couldn't abide.

She heard Leo talking out in the hall. He was supposed to be at Starbucks. Instead he was chatting with a woman Rosa couldn't see, though it sounded like Lucy.

Annoyed, she called out, "I thought you were getting coffee."

"I am," he called back. "Rosa's head is bothering her," she heard him tell Lucy. "She asked for Tylenol, but maybe she should get something stronger."

Why was he telling Lucy about her head? "Leo, please tell Lucy to come in, and bring Katherine with her. I'm retiring in December; we have lots to cover before then!"

"Katie isn't here," Leo told her, still out in the hall. "She'll stop by this afternoon."

"Oh, that's right—*Katherine* is at the dentist." Rosa had no idea where the girl was, but didn't want to admit this to Leo. And why did he still call her Katie, after so long?

It was getting hard to keep things straight, probably because she'd been so tired. She never slept anymore, but she didn't want to admit this either. After work, she went home, ate dinner, watched TV, read a book, called Leo to say good night, and then lay in bed, wide-eyed, until daybreak. Same thing had happened when she went through menopause. She'd stay up, drenched in sweat, seized with terror and then sorrow, begging for sleep. Every night she was haunted; and every morning, she'd go to the office and try to function. Now she was haunted by the smell in her walls—that crazy smell was ruining her life!

"Her head is bothering her," she heard Leo repeat. She wished he'd stop. No one cared!

An older woman stepped into her office. She had hair like steel wool and arms that swung like scissors. "How are you feeling today?" the woman asked.

Rosa didn't like the way this stranger waltzed in without knocking. When Rosa fired Peter, she'd also fired Spring Cleaners. Kenny hired this new service, but clearly he forgot to explain how things worked around here; or, if he did, no one took note.

"I heard your head hurt," the cleaning woman said.

Again, with the head? "I'm fine, I'm fine, I'm fine." But Rosa was starting to panic. Something wasn't right. She looked around. Wait, wait, wait. Wait just one minute.

Leo rushed in. "Rosa! Why are you shouting? She's only taking your pulse."

"Just your pulse, dear," Steel Wool said, with false cheer.

"Oh, I know that, Leo," Rosa replied, keeping her mind clear and her face blank. "Of course I know."

STARTLED, ROSA WOKE up. She looked around, hazy and disjointed. Next to her bed, Leo was sitting in a chair, working on his laptop. He didn't realize she was awake, so she closed her eyes, pretending to doze. She'd been in the hospital four days, though it felt more like five minutes, probably because they were giving her Ambien, and she was finally sleeping. Also, the place smelled of piss and bleach, which made her gag but didn't keep her up during the night. The sleep had been refreshing, but she felt like a prisoner, and she wanted to go home. Apparently, she was in good shape. Her only external injuries were a sprained shoulder and a tender spine; and her scans showed superficial bruising, along with a minor hematoma. Her doctors said they just wanted to "observe" her, but no matter how often she asked, or how politely, no one would give her a release date; they wouldn't even offer a timeline.

According to Leo, she fell during her town hall presentation and was brought here in a—what's the word? In a something. Rosa was surprised when he said this. No, surprised wasn't right. She was astounded. That really happened? To her? She remembered giving her speech, but after that, there was dark space, as if someone had taken a marker to her niece's art collage and blacked out the pictures. She wore her tomato-red St. John, brand-new from Bloomingdale's, and her patent leather Ferragamos, which Katherine had warned were too slippery. Rosa loved them and refused to budge, but in the end, the kid was right. Leo said she tripped on those godforsaken shoes and toppled off the stage. Rosa was so humiliated she wanted to die; she'd made a fool of herself in front of the whole company. "You brought down the house," he kept saying, as if that mattered. Why would she care about her fucking speech when people saw her flailing around like a demented old lady? Rosa couldn't bear to look at him, at any of them, that's how mortified she was. And

in the past few days, everyone from Ellery had called and her favorites had stopped by, so she was forced to make polite chatter,
knowing what they were thinking: *Thank God she's retiring. Rosa
Guerrero can't even make it through a ten-minute town hall. Good riddance
to that dried-up bag of bones.* Well, no more! Yesterday, when the staff
neurologist Dr. Somebody stopped by at the crack of dawn, she had
demanded her release. The doctor had hedged. "Rosa, while you
certainly *could* leave—"

"My name is Rosalita Luz Esperanza Guerrero," she said proudly.
"I don't call you Mike or Paul or Gregory, and you shouldn't call
me Rosa."

"Of course, Mrs. Guerrero, of course." He buried his nose in her
chart. "We recommend that you stay. The hematoma is resolving
quite nicely, but we want to monitor you for another twenty-four
hours, at a minimum. So let's see how today goes and talk again
tomorrow."

His tone had infuriated her. She was a grown woman who ran
her own department in a multimillion-dollar research conglomer-
ate, yet he was talking to her like she was a fucking fourth-grader.
"That sounds ridiculous," she'd snapped, which she regretted.
"You're a patronizing jerk," she added, another regret. But rage sat
like sour milk in her mouth, and she had to spit it out. Even so, a
foolish move. She'd gone through this before, first with the TIA
and then the stroke; to win her freedom, she had to play along.
Her own neurologist agreed. Dr. Brady had moved downtown but
called Dr. Somebody later that morning. In her medical opinion,
she said, Rosa should not be treated as an inpatient; an extended
hospital stay could impede her recovery, possibly even make her
worse. "One more day," she promised Rosa. "Sit tight." Well, one
more day was one more day, and Rosa wasn't going to spend it lying
down. So she had Leo go to her house and pick up her clothes and
makeup kit, shoes, jewelry, and hair products. Then she got out of

bed, got dressed, and sat upright in a chair like a goddamn executive
VP and chief of HR.

"Oh," Leo said. "You're up."

"I've been up." Speaking of Leo, why was he always hovering?
He kept eyeing her like a security guard. She hadn't even showered
yet! "You spend too much time here," she snapped.

"I'm worried about you, Rosa, that's all." He looked wounded.

"I'm a grown woman, and you're a grown man. You should be
with your boyfriend, not watching me rot in this jail cell."

"Stop bringing up Thomas, Rosa. I told you: *he's not my boyfriend*."

"Did you have a fight?"

"No, Rosa. We didn't have a fight."

"So why aren't you with him? I never see you texting him anymore."

"I only met him a month ago. It's too soon to spend every waking
moment together. Besides, I don't know if I even want a relationship
right now." Grabbing his bag, he stood up. "I'll call you later."

Rosa didn't like his answers. He wasn't telling the truth about his
boyfriend, and she didn't know why. He looks like a husk of a person, she thought. Like a scarecrow missing its stuffing. "You're too
skinny," she shouted, but he was already out the door, so she called
and left a message on his voice mail. "I'm sorry, Leo. Please forgive
me; I'm just so frustrated." She gulped down tears. "You're like a
son to me. How can I repay you for all you do? Thank God you're in
my life, kiddo." She hung up before she could tease the devil again.

Finally, Rosa took her shower and started her morning, even
though it was eleven o'clock and the day was half over. This, she
thought with dread, is what retirement will be like. I'll be a throwaway person with a throwaway life, sleeping till lunch and then
lazing till dinner. No way, José. Instead, she styled her hair, applied
her makeup, and sat upright wearing her new lemon St. John and
diamond-stud earrings. She looked dynamite.

Standing at the door, Howard chuckled. "You stuck again, Rosie?"

"Nothing I can't fix," she told him.

She called Katherine to request her Day-Timer and files, and before the girl could ask if working was allowed, Rosa told her she was going home the next day. "So I really need to know what's going on in the office." To Rosa's delight, Katherine showed up a half hour later, holding a bouquet of flowers. Such a nice kid! What a superb hire! "Hello! Come in, please." Sitting in her chair, Rosa beamed. Katherine beamed back. "I'm so happy to see you, Rosa!"

Now Rosa's day could really start.

Katherine stayed a long time. They reviewed all Rosa's projects, which made her feel good, like she was up and running again, and when the kid had to go, Rosa tried not to act glum. "I'll be here when you're discharged," Katherine promised. "I'll help get you home."

"Oh, that's not necessary," Rosa replied, but inside she was thrilled. She loved when the kid came over and they ate snacks and talked about life. "Even so, if you insist, I won't say no."

A few hours later, Rosa was still upright in her chair, despite her throbbing back. Shifting her weight the slightest inch made her gasp in pain. But anyone who saw her would immediately know she was a fully functioning adult who had her faculties intact and wouldn't fall off a stage during a presentation—if indeed that's what happened. Given all she knew about her staff's tendency to skirt the truth, Rosa had her doubts. What if they'd only told her she fell so they could lock her up in here? For what reason, she couldn't fathom, but maybe it had to do with Lucy not wanting to wait four months to be chief. Lucy was a conniver, anyone could see that. But why would Leo agree to go along with it? This was the puzzle piece Rosa couldn't find.

"Don't you look nice, dear." Another nurse walked in—again, without knocking. This one was round, dark, and sweet-natured, but also an imbecile. "Oh! Such pretty lipstick. But it's smeared on your cheek. Should I find you a mirror?"

Rosa pretended not to hear. She could fix her own fucking face, thank you. Her phone rang. It was Leo. "Where are you?" she asked.

"On my way. I'll be there by six so we can eat dinner together. How are you?"

"Much better, Leo, so call your boyfriend and have dinner with him. You don't have to spend all your time together, but at least give him a chance. Life is too short. Trust me, kiddo."

Leo didn't say anything.

"Leo?" His silence sounded mad. "You've been here every single day. I want you to have fun. I don't mind eating alone tonight."

"I'll be there at six." Leo clicked off, leaving Rosa bewildered. Did he think she didn't know about the boyfriend? What was his name? Thomas? Of course she knew. She had eyes and ears everywhere. And FYI: she'd only gone up to Leo's hideaway on eleven because she was curious. Call it a gut instinct, which turned out to be right because that's where she found the charts. At first she wasn't sure what she was looking at, but when she realized, she was shocked. It was *her schedule*! Not just her work schedule, her personal appointments too, *hanging on the wall for the whole world to see*. There was also a binder, with her name on it: ROSA SCHEDULES, 2010, which she knew Katherine had made.

That was the moment she knew she had to go.

"I'd rather be a throwaway person than a burden," she'd told Rutherford. "Are you aware they have a top-secret office where they plan out my days?" The CEO had looked at her for a long time and then paused, as if he was about to say something important, but in the end he played dumb. What do you mean, a top-secret office? he asked. In this building?

Rosa didn't believe him. They all lied, every single one of them. Even Peter.

"How dare you!" is what she should've said to her staff when she found the charts.

Oh, oh, oh, she was churning now, kicking herself for all the things she didn't say, all the ways she'd gotten it wrong. She never used to be this way. In the past, she decided, acted, and moved on—that's what it takes to be chief. A chief can't afford to dwell on her mistakes. Some refused to admit they made mistakes, and Rosa considered them inferior. If you didn't make mistakes, how did you learn? Most were white men, which was racist and sexist, but go ahead, sue her; it happened to be true.

Staying in this hospital was rough, but Rosa was also worried about going back home. What if she continued to have smells in her walls? How would she sleep? In the beginning, the smells were foods from her childhood—spicy noodle soup, sizzling peppers and onions, hot beans and rice. They were delicious, but so strong they filled up her nose and dripped down her throat. Soon, they were less like food and more like animal. When she told Leo about the smells, she wanted him to imagine a small and tame creature, a mouse or a cat; she couldn't admit that they were, in all likelihood, horse. Imagine what he'd say! "This is a luxury building, Rosa! You can't have a horse in your walls. Maybe a mink or a fox, something to make into a coat, but not a wild stallion." Leo would laugh her right out of town. In his defense, he did come by to check, except Marcy and Nando were visiting that day, discussing her will. She didn't want to tell Nando about the smell, but once Leo brought it up, Nando wouldn't let go. "Could be a problem in the air conditioning," Nando, the know-it-all, had said. "When did you last have the ducts cleaned?"

"Ducks?"

"Ducts."

"What a strange word. Are you sure that's right?" Rosa had picked up the phone.

Nando got suspicious. "Who are you calling, Rosalita?"

Rosa loved her little brother, but bitchiness was in his nature, and that's all she had to say on *that* subject, now and forever. "I'm calling my friend Lucy. She knows words."

"Hang up. I'll call the exterminator." So he called the exterminator, who found nothing. "No smell," Nando gloated when the guy left. "No smell; it's all in your head, maybe?"

Rosa wanted to remind him that she distinctly told him *not* to call the exterminator, first because she'd already done so, and second because the smell *only* came at *night*. Instead, she kept her lips zipped. Nando liked to tell her what to do, and occasionally she complied, but mostly she said okay and then did as she pleased. Still, three facts: she had a smell; it kept her up at night; and she had no one to tell except Peter. Well, four facts: Peter, her best friend, was gone.

She should've said, "I won't say anything about the money, Peter. I will zip my lip and spare us both. Just tell me the reason, and I'll make it go away."

She should've said, "I love you, Peter Dreyfus, and I believe you love me too."

## 24

The next day Rosa was awake at five thirty. Up and at 'em, her mother used to say. She showered and dressed, put on her face, styled her hair, packed her bag, and sat in her chair, ready to go. But then the goddamn doctors came by and said another goddamn day. She was crushed. All she wanted to know was why. "What's the point?" she asked Dr. Somebody.

"We'd like to see the bruising disappear." One more day, they promised, which Rosa told Marcy when she stopped by at ten. Nando didn't come, which made the visit better; on her own, her sister was a lovely person. "When you get out," Marcy said, "I'm gonna help you. I promise you, Rosalita. I'll make sure you have everything you need. It won't be like last time."

This delighted Rosa. "I know you're busy, so I appreciate that. You're my sister, and sisters are forever. I'd like to say brothers are forever, but I don't like how Nando behaves with Leo. Leo is my friend and a coworker. Nando is disrespectful."

"Nando is a fool. Remember when he drove Mr. Sousa's car? He confused the gas and the brake? He drove too far into the garage and smacked the wall!" Marcy's laughter rang out.

Rosa shrieked. "They had to call an engineer!"

"He tilted the whole house!"

Soon they were laughing so hard they were weeping, and when Marcy left, they hugged and kissed good-bye with love. At noon, Lucy and Katherine stopped by. Rosa wanted to ask about Leo's mood—if he seemed mad at her, for instance—but got distracted when Lucy mentioned they were having problems with employee self-service. "Oh!" Rosa loved a challenge. "This same thing happened at Sony. Let's conference in Kenny."

Lucy glanced at Katherine but then said okay and punched in Kenny's number. "We'll make this quick. You're supposed to be resting."

"I rest all goddamn day, Lucy," Rosa told her.

Lucy looked smart in a crisp white blouse and brown slacks, which she said were Theory, a brand Rosa didn't know. She wore a long silver necklace and matching hoop earrings, and after Rosa noted how pretty they were, Lucy tried to give her the set as a gift, which of course Rosa wouldn't accept. Then, when Katherine offered to get everyone Starbucks, Lucy handed her a twenty and told her to keep the change. These small, spontaneous gestures demonstrated to Rosa that Lucy had it in her to be a superb chief. It's also why, when Kenny sheepishly admitted he'd underestimated the number of vendor interfaces, Rosa felt it was okay to step in on his behalf.

"Kenny!" Lucy snapped. "You have to think everything through! Now we have to backtrack, which will throw off our timeline. What am I supposed to tell Rutherford?"

"Don't let her get away with that," Rosa chimed in. "Remember, you went to Wharton; she only went to Cornell." Though she pretended to joke, she was deadly serious. She wanted Kenny to understand that, one, he was just as smart as Lucy; two, he shouldn't let her steamroll him or take a tone during a meeting; three, if he wanted to parade his bona fides, it was better to do so with humor; and four, just because Rosalita Guererro fell off a stage and hit her head didn't mean she couldn't remember where her staff went to college.

So Rosa was thrilled (and relieved) when Lucy took her joke in stride. "Very funny, Rosa; all I know is Cornell kicked Penn's ass in football."

"No way, Lucy!" Kenny came back roaring. "Your defensive line sucks!"

Inside, Rosa was elated. You still got it, Rosie, she told herself.

Later, as Lucy and Katherine were leaving, she debated whether or not to confess she'd found their charts. While Rosa didn't mind reprimanding Lucy, she didn't want Katherine to feel guilty. They'd done the right thing, even if, to Rosa, it felt wrong. Nor could she blame them for keeping tabs on her; yes, they'd betrayed her, but it was in service to the greater good. Had she been in their shoes, forced to weigh the success of the department against one old lady's ego, she would've nudged the old lady aside. But it hurt to *be* that old lady, especially since in her mind, she was still a young maverick. *I can do this!* she ached to shout. *I'm still here!*

Leo came by at six fifteen, and as soon as she saw him, she snapped, "Why aren't you with Thomas?" She didn't mean to sound harsh, but she couldn't stop churning over those damn charts. Once she was back in the office, they'd see how healthy she was. Maybe then they'd stop following her around like she was on some kind of terrorist watch list.

"Because I wanted to surprise you with a special dinner." He held up a bag.

Rosa pursed her lips. "Not hungry." Smelling the food, she reconsidered. "What is it?"

Leo smiled. "Cheeseburgers, extra pickles, french fries, and coke, real Coke, not diet."

Suddenly she was starving; she was so hungry she could eat a—

"Leo, this looks so good!" The burgers were rare inside and burned out, with melted cheese and grilled onions, and when she took her first bite, the taste was so meaty, she groaned. The fries were crisp and salty, the ketchup cold and sweet, and the icy Coke full of bubbles. "This is so so so delicious." She licked her lips. "I could kiss you, kiddo!"

Leo took a deep breath. "Rosa, I know you found the schedules. I'm very sorry I didn't tell you about them. I speak for all of us when I say we were only trying to look out for you."

"I would prefer not to discuss this, Leo." How did he know? It had to be Rutherford. Goddamn that man! She couldn't trust any of them.

"Can I at least tell you why?"

"I don't care why, Leo. Why doesn't help me; why only complicates matters of business. I care about the who, what, when, and how. As an executive, those are my concerns."

"That's a smart philosophy. But I'll tell you anyway; you don't have to listen . . . okay, so . . . so after your stroke, there were times when you seemed . . . confused. We felt we had to intervene, to protect your pension and make sure you had the best medical benefits until you were ready to retire, so that's why . . . we . . . did it . . ." Leo faltered. "But it was wrong to go behind your back, and for that, I am truly sorry."

Rosa didn't want to talk; she just wanted to enjoy her cheeseburger. "Don't apologize, Leo. You did it for the good of the department. I understand that."

"No, Rosa. We did it for *you*. We care about *you*. You're our mentor and our friend. We wanted to make sure you could retire in your own time and on your own terms."

As Rosa's eyes grew misty, she cursed her soft heart. "I know you care, Leo. Please." One tear spilled, and then another. "Please, Leo.

I can't discuss this. My burger is so luscious, and I'd like to finish—"
She broke off because she was crying, and she couldn't cry, not in
front of her staff, not even in front of Leo.

"We don't ever have to talk about it again. I just wanted to say
I'm sorry."

They ate together. The silence was comfortable and familiar, and
Rosa regretted all her bad thoughts. "I know it annoys you when
I bring up your boyfriend. But you were so happy, I don't get why
you're not with him. I realize you're scared, but you have to risk
it." And then, just as these words came out of her mouth, a heavily
bearded Rob Hirsch appeared at her door.

Seeing him, Rosa did a double take. Rob Hirsch? Hadn't she
fired him? Why was he here?

"Knock-knock." Rob stepped into the room. "Am I interrupting?" A dark-haired man was with him. Although he was unfamiliar to Rosa, from the way Leo's face bloomed like a flower, she
knew, instantly, this had to be Thomas.

"Oh my God," Leo said. He looked from Rob to Thomas. "What
are you doing here?" He ran his hand through his hair. "Rosa, this
is Thomas. Thomas, this is Rosa." Leo's voice was shaky. "Really
guys, what's going on?" He turned to Rosa. "I have no idea why
they're here."

"It was his idea." Thomas pointed to Rob. "He showed up at
the restaurant, and asked if I wanted to take a ride uptown. I was
finished with my shift . . ." He shrugged.

Leo looked at Rob, wide-eyed. "You did this?"

"Robert Hirsch!" Rosa blurted out. "You're a mensch! An absolute mensch. What a rascal you are. But I love you!"

"You're not mad?" Rob asked Leo. "You said you're too busy for
a relationship, that it was too soon, but—"

"Mad?" Rosa interrupted. "How could he be mad? Look at how
happy you made him!" Leo's face, bathed in the early evening light,

had taken on a golden glow. Rosa was bursting. The world was an enchanted place. And this . . . this moment, this miraculous, was proof. It wasn't only Thomas and Leo dazzling her. From what she could see, Leo and Rob had found each other, too. Oddball pairs. If not for Ellery, these oddball pairs wouldn't exist, so thank God for Ellery. She couldn't wait to go back.

## 25

The smell was here, in the hospital. Rosa pressed her face against the pillow, but couldn't escape it. Wild pony was everywhere: heavy, musky, barnyard. She should alert someone, but the doctors were releasing her tomorrow—they promised, hand to God—and telling them would throw a wrench in her plans. Not because a horse in the walls was implausible—horses ran free, they could be anywhere—but because raising the issue could backfire. Over the years, Rosa had learned that in any given situation, people could absorb only three, maybe four ideas at one time; any more was overload. So her doctors had to consider her physical state (greatly improved), mental acuity (sharp), whether she could resume her normal activities (absolutely), and her looks (gorgeous). (In her thoughts, Rosie was a funny woman.) To bring up the horse was to divert their attention to a fifth issue, which could derail them—an issue, by the way, that didn't concern her health. True, a conscientious citizen would tell them about the horse, and possibly save another patient from insomnia, but Rosa kept her mouth shut. Here, now, she had to save herself.

She heard voices in the hall, but no one she recognized. After six days, she'd gotten to know the staff, and they weren't as dumb or rude as she thought. The problem, she realized, was that they kept forgetting she was an executive. They confused her with the other patients, many of whom were elderly and feeble, so they talked to her as if she was elderly and feeble too. There was one unfortunate incident when an aide gave her a pair of cranberry-colored scrubs to sleep in. They were so comfortable she wanted to write a thank-you note, but when no one could find pen or paper, she got angry. Very. The hospital staff didn't realize that being sick didn't mean you stopped being chief or CEO or the crown prince of Siam. To them, you were a problem to solve: a bone to set, a virus to eradicate (good word), symptoms to treat. Mostly, you were sleeping in a bed they needed for someone else. Also, treating her like a demented old lady helped them maintain a professional distance. Rosa understood this. As chief, every Ellery employee was her problem to solve, so she had to move them along, one after another, while making sure she didn't get overly involved in their issues—too much emotion, and she'd drown.

Outside her room, a woman passed by. Rosa could tell it was a woman from the *clip, clip, clip* of her pumps. The men wore dress shoes that squeaked or clogs that shuffled, but women had more variety. They wore heels and flats, sneakers and sandals. They clicked and squeaked, shuffled and clomped. The only thing they didn't do was *clip-clop, clip-clop* like her mother's wedges. Every morning Anita dressed for work in a straight skirt and fitted jacket, underwear, slip, girdle, bra, garters, heels, earrings, watch, necklace, hat, and gloves. She also wore pricey silk stockings that she took off at night, rinsed out in the sink, and hung over the tub. In the bathroom, all the dry pairs would beckon to Rosa, *Touch me, touch me.* Rosa was Mrs. Hutch's pet, the *Weekly Reader* champ, but she couldn't resist those stockings. She rubbed them between her fingers, held them against her cheek, let the silky softness drape over her face.

"Rosa?" It was Leo, he was in her room.

Frightened, she sat up. "What are you doing here?"

"You have a visitor. But he wanted to ask if it was okay before he came in."

"It's the middle of the night, Leo. This is not a good time to see people from work."

"It's the afternoon, Rosa."

When she looked around, she saw that yes, it was daylight. "Oh, I know that, Leo," she said, embarrassed. She was losing track of time. This worried her, as did a moment yesterday, when the round nurse wished for windows that opened to "breathe air into this place," and Rosa saw the walls start to sway, inhaling and exhaling like a person.

Leo was talking about the special guest. "Rosa, he came all the way from New Jersey."

This got her attention. "New Jersey?" Part of her was hopeful, another part was afraid to hope. "Give me a minute to freshen up." She applied a fresh coat of Chanel Rouge Noir and adjusted her St. John. A minute later, she heard a deep voice say, "Rosa?"

She was right! Her old friend Peter stood at the door. He looked shabby and forlorn, but his thick mane of silver hair was still glorious, simply glorious. "May I join you?" he asked politely. He held lilies, her favorite, and she nodded, beckoning to him.

Sitting down, Peter folded his hands in his lap and waited for Rosa to speak. She thanked him for coming. "A sweet peach for a sweet peach, I remember that."

"I'm sorry, Rosa," was his response. "I showed extremely poor judgment. I don't know what I was thinking . . . I was . . ."

Rosa watched his throat move as he searched for his words; he swallowed with difficulty, like a boy choking down an orange wedge. She held up her hand. She didn't want to discuss this. He'd stolen. He'd lied. He'd likely done other things too. But she'd been chief a long time. She'd seen it all. People step out of character, compelled by forces they can't see or explain. But sometimes there are no whys for the ways we behave; our impulses override our good sense. We are all each of us flawed beings; we deserve a day in court, a bit of kindness, a second chance.

"I accept your apology," Rosa said. "But I'd rather hear about Arthur's son, the little one who can download iTunes. How's he doing?"

That's where they started, with Peter's great-nephew, and they moved to books and movies, the TV shows they both loved, her family and his, until eventually, inevitably, they returned to work. Peter had been hired by a builder in Parsippany, so the commute was easy, and he saw his mother every day. Rosa was retiring in December, could he believe it? They reminisced about Howard, how they missed him, all the good times they'd had, so many laughs. Did she ever wish she could be her younger self, do it all again? Hard to say, really. What about him? Did he? Sometimes he did, Rosa. Although there were a few things he'd probably do differently, given the opportunity.

Near the end of his visit, Peter took Rosa's hand and squeezed it, and Rosa felt warmth spread through her old bones. "I missed you, Peter," she said.

"I missed you too, Rosa," Peter said in his courtly way. "I missed you quite a bit."

"We had fun, didn't we?"

They sure did. Oh boy, they had fun.

THE ART COLLAGE was peeling away, one picture and then another. Memories were twisting and turning, stories losing their beginning and end, bleeding together in flashes, like a continuous dream. Rosie moved fluidly through time and space, recalling people she knew, places she'd been. Stunning, the whole of it.

The hospital was quiet. She couldn't find a comfortable sleeping position; her neck was stiff, and pain radiated along her spine. Even in her agony, she remembered *radiate*. A good sign. Unfortunately, the horse was here. As soon as she heard the *clip-clop* of its hooves, the room filled with the earthy smell of animal hair and warm dirt, dry hay and moist leather. It was like sleeping in a barn, which was ironic because any time they left doors open, her mother would shout, "You live in a barn?" and invariably Marcy or Nando would moo and whinny. Yes, they'd shout back, they lived in a barn. Moo on you.

"Are you all right, dear?" the round nurse asked. "You called."

"I need to use the ladies' room, please."

"Here, let me help." The nurse grabbed Rosie's arm and steadied her as she shuffled along the slippery floor. Everyone was sleeping except her mom. Rosie heard the *clip-clop* of Anita's wedges as she moved through the kitchen and hall, shutting off the lights along the way.

"Mommy?" Anita didn't answer. She must've gone to bed. So Rosie made her way to the bathroom quietly. In the living room, above the fireplace that didn't work, a painting of the Holy Family hung on the wall, and on the mantel, there was a statue of the Blessed Mother and a picture of Julio wearing his junior high graduation gown. Anita trusted Rosalita most, but it was Julio she loved best, probably because all her kids could grow up, but Julio would stay forever in eighth grade.

Rosa made it to the bathroom without incident. Inside, she thanked the round nurse for her help. "I can take over from here."

"Are you sure?"

"Yes, dear. I'm sure." Afraid she sounded sarcastic, Rosa said it again with extra-special pleasantness. No one should ever accuse Rosalita Luz Esperanza Guerrero of being impolite.

Inside the bathroom, her mother's stockings draped over the railing like eight loose arms suspended from the ceiling. Fluttering above her, they called, "Hey, Rosie." *Hey, Rosie.* She looked up. "Howard?" *Fetch the car, Rosie.*

"Rosalita! Those are clean! Don't touch."

"I won't," Rosie yelled back, a good girl, the teacher's pet.

"Are you okay in there, dear?"

The light passing through the pearled material made the stockings glow. They were so shimmery she gasped. She couldn't resist. She crept closer, stood on her toes, and then plunged her face into the long silky arms, just as the brightness overhead burst in her eyes.

"I'm fine, dear," Rosa called out, feeling the silk sweep her cheeks as she rocked slowly, back and forth, in ecstasy.

## 26

## LUCINDA BENDER,
## CHIEF OF HUMAN RESOURCES,
## SENIOR VICE PRESIDENT

AUGUST 2010

Lucy had started on the first annual engagement survey the day she walked through Ellery's doors, eleven years before. It was one of those projects that got delayed, reconceived, put off, and then abandoned entirely, only to be resurrected last November when Rosa told her to rip off the Band-Aid and get it done once and for all.

The goal of the survey was to measure prevailing employee attitudes toward the mission, benefits, pay, leadership, and other factors related to the overall experience of working at Ellery. In 1999, to encourage participation, HR had planned to raffle off a Sony Walkman. Lucy figured the entire project—survey, focus groups, preliminary findings, detailed analysis, executive summary, and PowerPoint—would take six months from start to finish.

The project kicked off on January 4, 1999. Rosa, thrilled to have a communicator on staff, assigned the survey to Lucy on Monday morning. By Monday afternoon, Lucy had created fifty questions, which Rosa felt was too many, so Lucy whittled them down to twenty. Six months later, Rosa, Rutherford, and Legal finally agreed on how the questions should be worded. The plan was to distribute the survey in July, but Ellery had recently acquired a company in Raleigh, and Lucy was asked to hold off until the sale closed.

The first annual engagement survey was set to go out in January of 2000 (raffle prize: Sony MiniDisc Walkman), but after careful consideration, Rosa decided she didn't want to survey employees at this juncture since Raleigh's pay and benefits were richer than New York's, especially after adjusting for cost of living. She told Lucy to draft fifteen questions—no more—and hold them until the two locations were aligned. That same afternoon, Lucy designed a streamlined survey, which she held on to for the next four years.

The first annual engagement survey was set to go out in January of 2004 (raffle prize: 4G iPod with color screen), but the more Rosa thought about it, the more inclined she was to go with the longer version, and told Lucy to return to the original fifty questions. It had been five years since those questions were drafted, so Lucy spent four hours updating them and seven months getting them approved. This new survey was set to go out in July, but Ellery had recently closed on a company in Atlanta, and Rutherford wanted to include the new employees' opinions. Lucy redesigned the questions to reflect Atlanta's benefits, which differed from NY/Raleigh. By the time Rosa and Rutherford signed off on the new questions (fuck Legal; they take too long), the board had approved two policy modifications: (i) office hours increased, from 9:00–5:00 to 9:00–5:30; and (ii) medical contributions increased 36 percent, owing to the prior year's claims experience. Together, these changes had a negative effect on morale, so Rosa told Lucy not to send out the survey until the collective mood improved. By May of 2005 (sixteen months later), Lucy was sick of waiting, fed up with Ellery, and disgusted with her life choices. She reread *Being and Nothingness*, then informed Rosa she was distributing the survey the following morning, morale be damned. However, that night, in a rare moment of self-disclosure (after many glasses of merlot), Rosa told Lucy about her TIA. Shaken, Lucy deferred to Rosa's better judgment and held off distribution.[21]

The first annual engagement survey was set to go out in January of 2006 (raffle prize: 2G iPod mini). Then Lucy's mother got cancer. Luckily, Lucy was emotionally prepared (re: footnote 21), and signed on as Valerie's caregiver. Though she offered to distribute the survey (always a team player!), Rosa said to wait until Valerie finished chemo. By June, Ellery's benefit plans were chiseled again, which meant Lucy had to retweak the questions. Regrettably, she was still using the original 2003 template, which had long before become corrupted, so she asked Horatio in IT for help. Unbeknown to Lucy, Horatio in IT was sleeping with Leo in HR, and she happened to breeze into Horatio's cubicle just as he was breaking up with Leo. Leo begged Horatio to reconsider,[22] but Horatio stuck to his guns. "We're done, and that's final."[23] The moment was awkward for everyone, and while it shouldn't have had any impact on the survey, distribution was delayed. Meanwhile, Leo was upset about the breakup, and spent several afternoons with Lucy complaining how *rude* and *unfeeling* Horatio was to dump him at *work* and how he'd *never* do that to *anyone*. He also said he didn't want the survey going out during Open Enrollment. Coincidentally, Rutherford announced they were acquiring two companies, one in Charlotte, the other in Louisville, and to please hold off on distribution.

The first annual engagement survey was set to go out in February

[21] The evening was a turning point for Lucy. Afterward, she spent several sessions discussing Rosa with Dr. Ahmet, who offered only conventional metaphors: circles of life, seasons of time, sands through hourglasses, tidal pulls. Lucy couldn't imagine Ellery without Rosa, and from then on was less contrary to and judgmental of her—and, also, of her mother. Instead, she tried to appreciate their maturity and wisdom as she accepted their vulnerability.

[22] This being the moment that compelled Leo to seek out Dr. Saul and begin forging his Authentic Self.

[23] Horatio and Leo would continue to have sex on and off for several years after this ostensible final pronouncement.

of 2007 (raffle prize: 3G nano with video), but Charlotte fell through and Louisville took longer than expected, so Lucy had to wait. This was okay because in June, Leo sent out a series of e-mails announcing Ellery's new wellness initiative, and staff complained (via e-mail) that HR sent out way too many e-mails (not just about wellness, fatness, "Knowing Your Numbers"—about everything). In the meantime, Lucy redrafted questions to reflect three separate benefits and pay programs: (i) NY/Raleigh; (ii) Atlanta; and (iii) Louisville.

The first annual engagement survey was set to go out in January of 2008 (raffle prize: 5G nano with video camera, FM radio, and pedometer). However, on January 4, the board voted for Atlanta and Louisville to adopt New York's benefits and policies, so Lucy had to redesign the questions. By April, Louisville was off, but Rutherford said to go ahead with the original survey. (Which original survey? Lucy wasn't sure.) Rosa disagreed. Their debate was prolonged because the CEO took his three daughters to Vietnam and was off the grid until the end of June.[24, 25] By the time they compromised on twenty-five questions and Lucy redrafted them, the market crashed and layoffs were underway. Rosa said, "Better to wait."

Between September of 2008 and November of 2009, the economy was in free fall, so the first annual engagement survey was the last thing on anyone's mind.

In November of 2009, the final layoffs were over (or so they were told), and the first annual survey was resurrected. Rosa and Rutherford agreed on everything: fifty questions, focus groups in all facilities, senior leader interviews, a raffle for an iPhone, and dinner at

---

[24] A surprising development. Three girls?

[25] Rutherford's girls lived with their mothers (the CEO's first and third ex-wives) in Richmond and Los Angeles, respectively, and had only recently started spending time with him. That he had three ex-wives and three children scattered across the country only enhanced his appeal for Lucy, an issue she plans to explore with Dr. Ahmet.

Mia Dona. But then Lucy got distracted by monumental life events and blew off the survey.

Baking under the hot sun, heels sinking into the soft grass, Lucy felt her eyes burn with tears. More than a decade earlier, Rosa had tasked her with a simple project that should've taken six months, tops. Yet despite knowing the importance of this project, Lucy had failed to attack it with her usual fervor, and now Rosa would never see the fruits of their labor.

You deserved better, Rosa, she thought.[26, 27, 28]

Her phone vibrated. It was her mother. "Where . . . are . . . you?" Valerie was panting, hard.

Where was she? Lucy looked around. The cemetery grounds, somewhere up in the Bronx, were lush and green with rolling hills, fields of flowers, and headstones from here to eternity. It was an interesting vista, one she would've enjoyed but for the sound of her mother gasping for breath. "Mom! I can't talk. Where are you?"

". . . Elliptical . . . three . . . miles . . . Oh! . . . Oswald's funeral . . . I forgot."

"Her name was Rosa," Lucy said bitterly, which wasn't fair because Valerie was merely parroting back Lucy's own words.[29] Still, show some respect, for God's sake. She hung up.

Show some respect: Rosalita Guerrero, HR chief, executive VP, was dead.

---

[26] In Lucy's defense, she *had* attacked the engagement survey feverishly for the first ten years. However, as these words apply to the period between December 2009 and September 2010, then yes, her attention was elsewhere.

[27] Lucy has since reordered her priorities and recommitted herself to the successful execution of this critical project.

[28] At the moment, however, she's in mourning.

[29] At some point in the past seven months, Lucy stopped calling Rosa "Ozzy." It wasn't a conscious decision, but one she may not have noticed if her mother hadn't said it. But to hear "Oswald" from Valerie, especially in the middle of Rosa's funeral, felt horribly inappropriate.

THE FUNERAL WOULD'VE been lovely, but it was the first week in August and sweltering. Rosa hated the heat. This, Lucy learned during her interview in 1998. "I do poorly in summer," Rosa had told her. Turned out she also hated the cold, so she did poorly in winter, too. Peter Dreyfus was forever in her office, adjusting the thermostat. Today's heat and ungodly humidity would've made Rosa very unhappy. Then again, she'd be alive.

Rivulets of perspiration ran down Lucy's back, soaking her black linen suit. Her phone vibrated in her pocket, but she ignored it, figuring it was the least she could do.

So, the weather was ghastly. The flowers were wilting. People were overheated, pink-cheeked, and moaning. The priest was a stranger and unnervingly childlike, with doughy hands and cherubic face. (They tried to get Father Joseph from Rosa's Bronx parish, but he was ninety years old and suffered from vertigo, so they brought in a much-younger substitute, who, while not without compassion, had never met Rosa and spoke without feeling.) And Nando, that cocksucker, was in Vegas because he had a nonrefundable flight there he refused to forfeit.[30]

But other than that, Lucy decided, shielding her eyes as she scanned the hordes of well-dressed mourners gathered around Rosa's grave site, the turnout was a triumph. Except for Nando, Rosa's entire clan was here: Marcy, the nieces and nephews, extended cousins, and people from her old neighborhood she considered family. Doormen and porters from her current building showed up to pay their respects (Rosa was a big tipper), as did coworkers from all her previous jobs. It would've pleased Rosa greatly to see the size of this latter group, and despite knowing none of them, Lucy personally

---

[30] Nando also pleaded poverty re: Rosa's funeral expenses. "I'll get lucky at the tables," he told Lucy, who, along with Leo and Rutherford, paid for the arrangements.

thanked each one for attending. One decrepit man wearing an old-timey suit, pocket watch, and spats pumped Lucy's hand with a gusto that surprised her. ("Al Moscowitz," he rasped. "Rosie's mentor.") But the biggest group, by far, was from Ellery. Rutherford had hired a coach bus, and the entire New York office hitched a ride. Some knew Rosa well, others only in passing, some just wanted the morning off. Whatever the reason, employees were everywhere on the grass, like sheep in mourning clothes. Board members in somber suits clustered together, anxious to move the sadness along. Business units found each other, as did the mailroom guys, maintenance men, and building employees. Sanchez wasn't here, which was fine. Lucy lacked the wherewithal to make polite chitchat; it was all she could do to avoid Rob, who stood in the back, looking lost in a rumpled suit. Among the other no-shows: Peter Dreyfus and Leo's boyfriend, Thomas.

As the odd young priest started his homily, Lucy continued to sweat from her scalp, which dribbled into her eyes. With her frizzy halo of hair and mascara-streaked cheeks, she probably resembled Alice Cooper circa 1973, a look inconsistent with her newly minted status as chief. Stupidly, she'd deferred to Leo on all funeral matters and now she could kill him for insisting people speak at the graveyard, amid nature, instead of inside the air-conditioned church. Nor would he let Lucy help. From the moment Rosa tumbled at the Hilton until half an hour earlier, Leo had been the lone show-runner. In the hospital, he conferred with her doctors and fetched her Starbucks. Then, after she died, he made plans with Marcy and the odious Nando; coordinated with the undertakers; and met with Rosa's lawyers, financial advisors, and condo board. Lucy kept expecting him to fall apart—especially when Marcy called to say that Rosa'd had an aneurism during the night and expired instantly—but he was remarkably stoic. Even so, she feared a storm was brewing down under.

Now Leo stood beside her, red-faced and dripping. She squeezed his hand. "You good?"

"I just can't believe she's really dead." He squeezed hers back. "You?"

"I can't either; it all feels surreal. But you put together a beautiful funeral." Was this proper etiquette? Lucy wasn't sure; she should've googled it. "Rosa would've been pleased."

They both glanced at her casket. A color photo of Rosa from one of Ellery's earliest annual reports was perched on top. Marcy had given Leo candid shots,[31] but he went with the professional pose. In it, Rosa wore pearls and red lipstick, eyes bright behind thick glasses.

After the homily, Lucy took the opportunity to s-l-o-w-l-y turn her head and check out Rob. At first glance, she saw tears, but when he mopped his neck, she realized it was sweat. If they were still speaking, she would've told him his wool suit was too heavy for this heat. In fact, she was surprised Maddy didn't suggest an alternative, but given his startlingly distended belly, maybe nothing else fit. Lucy felt sympathetic; Rob must hate himself for getting so plump. They hadn't talked in almost four months—not since he kissed her. Earlier, they'd exchanged cordial hellos, which would probably be the extent of their conversation for a while, maybe forever, given their newly divergent lives. Though Lucy preferred not to admit it, this was a relief.

Directly behind Lucy, Kenny was standing tall, eyes forward, jaw set. He'd been so helpful this past week, taking on Leo's work to keep the department running smoothly.[32] Beside him, Katie cried noisily. She and Rosa had grown very close. Lucy suspected Katie was also feeling the loss of her mother all over again, which made

[31] Remarkable how you can spend eight hours a day with your coworkers yet have very few pictures of them. (Remarkable, that is, if you're over thirty and didn't grow up documenting your every waking moment.)

[32] This supported Lucy's theory that Kenny would make an ideal number two. She just had to keep him out of Janine's clutches. Determined to win him back, Janine had launched a full frontal assault for his affection, but Lucy was equally determined to keep him focused and on task. *Victori spolia!*

her feel like crying, too, since she'd just hung up on Valerie (Really, though. Was it too much to ask that she step *off* the elliptical before dialing?), but she fought against her tears. As Katie's mentor, it was her duty to stay strong. Mentoring Katie was helping Lucy find her best self, which required, among other skills, reconsidering her long-held idea that sincerity was synonymous with weakness. Lucy was working hard to be earnest, which felt more revealing, but also more human. "It's better to be kind than to be right," Rosa liked to say. While Lucy didn't buy this completely, she was willing to give it a go.

Seeing her glance his way, Rutherford nodded. He was standing with the board, looking presidential in a trim gray suit, shiny wingtips, and dark aviators. His clothes were pressed, his hair immaculate—the guy barely broke a sweat. His only concession to the ungodly heat was a few beads of wetness above his upper lip.

*You are too perfect, Mr. Beaumont,* Lucy told him silently, nodding back.

Unbeknown to anyone, over the past seven months Lucy and Rutherford had forged a silent partnership. Since last January, they'd been spending evenings together, working on a hush-hush plan to reconceive Ellery as a profitable business. A shrewd man, the CEO was in fact more self-aware than Lucy originally thought.[33] In their first meeting, he explained that the only way to save Ellery was to strip the company down to its studs and rebuild from the bottom up, essentially creating a new organization. "I'm tired of helming a battered ship. I can't spend the rest of my career watching it sink." Then he asked Lucy to help him shape Ellery's future by "throwing some ideas at the wall and seeing what sticks."[34] "Throwing some

---

[33] *Three* ex-wives?

[34] While Lucy was intrigued and flattered by Rutherford's offer—his maritime metaphor about the battered ship notwithstanding—his use of the hackneyed "throw some ideas" expression made her want to rip out his tongue.

ideas," Lucy learned, meant sitting in his office after hours while he expounded on complex business theories. At first, her lack of facility with numbers slowed them down; she often had to interrupt his "spitballing" and "blue-skying"[35] so he could walk her through basic corporate finance. But once she figured out the mechanics and math, the rest was a breeze. They needed board approval and large infusions of cash, so her next task was to produce a PowerPoint deck (her forte) they could copresent. In the meantime, she was studying C-suite management journals to prepare herself for an executive role in the new company.[36, 37] HR chief, Rutherford made clear, was just a starting point for her, careerwise.

"At this time," Lucy heard the doughy priest say, "I call on several people to offer a few words. Rutherford Beaumont will be speaking first. Rutherford, will you step up, please?"

Lucy had agreed to say a few words, but only if she could go last. While this was a coveted spot, she feared she might cry, and needed to be able to hustle off to the ladies' room to compose herself. When he heard this, Rutherford had balked. "It's perfectly appropriate to cry."

"You're a man. You can take off your pants and speak in your boxers. This is my first week as chief. Better I keep my clothing on."

Rutherford could be a hard-ass, but did have moments of kindness, or maybe he was a kind man who had moments of hardness. Either way, he did right by Lucy. During their working sessions, he spoke lovingly of his third ex-wife—he spoke lovingly of all his ex-wives, even the horsey girl from Virginia who ran off with a

---

[35] Ibid and Ibid.

[36] Thus far, her reading indicated that management consultants—Bain, McKinsey, BCG, Accenture—are con men who sell fake words, invented theories, and sham philosophies for millions of dollars.

[37] Re: footnote 36: in her humble layman's opinion.

jockey.[38] Naturally, any time he mentioned his ex-wives, daughters, colleagues, or any other female in the United States and abroad, Lucy felt a stab of jealousy.[39] Now, as she listened to him describe Rosa's integrity, loyalty, and humanity, it occurred to her that Rutherford was one of the few men—business or civilian—she hadn't manipulated into making a pass at her, thus compromising their respective positions, or at the very least making it unpleasant to sit in a meeting together. This, she realized, was an unlikely success story, one she must share soon with Dr. Ahmet.

Lucy held many ideas about sexual dynamics in the workplace. When she was younger, a good-natured, raring-to-go ingenue with firmer tits, she had no inkling of her carnal powers or how to wield them. Indeed, had she been more conniving, she could've had her middle-and upper-age managers falling all over themselves to approve raises, promotions—anything she wanted. But the idea of using her body as currency had never appealed to her at all. Ironically, now that she was in full command of her sexuality, she was too old and invisible to be desired, either by her same-age peers or younger subordinates. While the old-olds showed interest, their greatly diminished authority (like her looks) would yield nothing. At the moment, however, she was poised for an executive-level career; she couldn't afford to ignore anything.[40]

Rutherford's comments were having an emotional effect on the crowd. Lucy heard sniffling from all sectors. "Losing Rosa is a tremendous blow," he concluded. "Her impact on this organization

---

[38] Apparently this was a thing in certain parts of the US—well-heeled debs running off with trainers, jockeys, groomers, etc., to the consternation of their cuckolded husbands and rich families.

[39] Including, to her infinite shame, a member of the cleaning staff who stepped into the CEO's office and asked if she could vacuum around his desk, and to whom he offered a beatific "Of course, my dear."

[40] Some things, in fact, she actively planned to change. See footnotes 11 and 12.

is immeasurable. Without her contributions, Ellery as we know it wouldn't exist today. Her influence is in every aspect of our business. 'It's all connected,' she used to tell me. 'And it all flows through HR—our policies, people, personality, and perception. HR is a warm, beating heart that pumps blood into the organization; HR gives Ellery life.' But I believe it was Rosa who connected us all. Rosa was our warm, beating heart. Rosa gave us life."

So dreamy, Lucy thought.

Next up were select executives, including the assbag Chuckles Mayfield, who banged on about his devastating loss. Lucy found this curious, given how lousily Chuckles had treated Rosa while she was alive.[41]

A gaggle of young women stood in the back. Lucy didn't know any of them personally, but saw them around the office. Or maybe it was different women. (At twenty-five, twenty-six, they all looked alike.) She had only distaste for these girls, who showed no deference to the proceedings as they chattered like magpies and flipped their hair. Compounding their abominable behavior was their abominable clothing. Lucy came up during the worst period of women's business attire, the era of flesh-colored pantyhose, floppy bow blouses, frilly dresses, Colonel Sanders neckties, and bulbous white sneakers, like moon shoes, for office commuting. While she wasn't hoping for a return to polyester, these girls wore flimsy skirts, sleeveless tees, and the sin of sins—*flip-flops*. Today they wore black skirts and shirts, *but they still wore flip-flops on their feet*! To a *funeral*!

For the record: Lucy hadn't gotten rid of Maisie Fresh Butler only because she lacked personal boundaries, basic skills, and common sense. She also came to work in a dress that looked like a dress but was actually a *beach cover-up*! During lunch, Maisie went to her gym's

---

[41] Lucy had every intention of making the life of Chuckles (who, by the way, had recently hired his own son as a "special consultant") a living hell. There was no level to which she wouldn't stoop to avenge her mentor and friend. Brace yourself, Chuckles: there's a new bitch in town.

rooftop pool, took a swim, and then returned to her desk *still wearing a wet bikini!*[42] Lucy knew this because years before, she'd done the same thing. Which is what these dumb girls with their instant-access lives didn't realize: Lucy Bender was fully versed in office hijinks. She, too, used to messenger house keys to friends a block away, Xerox pictures of her ass, and read *People* at her desk, inside a folder marked "Important!" Since she'd already done it all, little could shock her. In sum: when she was fighting the Man, these antics had made her laugh; now that she *was* the Man, they were unacceptable.

Hearing Chuckles call her name, Lucy felt a flash of panic. But she squared her shoulders, stepped up to the podium, and cleared her throat. "What can I say about Rosa Guerrero?"

HOW COULD LUCY sum up the whole of Rosa's corporate life? How could she sum up anyone's life? She admired her? Respected her? Loved her—or was love too much? Was it possible to love someone who indirectly paid your mortgage?

Over the years, Lucy had served a panoply of bosses: Pol Pot, Buzz Aldrin (lost in space), the Invisible Man, Smelly Cat, Chang aka Eng (aka Siamese Twin), Stone Cold Fox,[43] Topper, Dr. Zaius, and Captain Chaos. Some she revered, others she tolerated, most she couldn't bear. As a manager, Rosa often blurred the lines between boss/mentor/colleague/confidante. Coming from banking, Lucy

[42] And yet Maisie Fresh had beaten them all at their own game. Lucy recently read in the *Wall Street Journal* (of all places) that Maisie Fresh had just outed herself as the author of an anonymous blog on LinkedIn (of all places), where she'd been chronicling her daily life as an HR wage slave for the past eighteen months. But it wasn't the blog that chapped Lucy's ass; it was the soon-to-be published *book*. Somehow Maisie had turned her 500-word posts into an *actual hardcover novel*. (Lucy had no idea the kid could read a whole book, much less write one.)

[43] An adoring, high-powered boss, the Fox still worked at JPMorgan Chase, overseeing global employee development, and still owed Lucy a favor, which she'd recently called in.

wasn't used to intimacy at work.[44] At the same time, she liked Rosa too much to maintain a professional distance, which made it hard to admit that after her TIA and subsequent stroke, Rosa had never been the same.

Her phone vibrated. It had to be her mother. *Oh, Mom.* That Lucy knew she'd have to go through this again, and soon, made today's awfulness worse. Maybe not next year, maybe not in five years, but eventually, inevitably, she'd stand on this dais in a tasteful black suit and eulogize Valerie. Then, in time, some as-yet-unnamed individual (a man, hopefully) would stand up and eulogize her.

What could Lucy say about Rosa that didn't sound saccharine or trite? She was like a sane mother, fierce big sister, wise aunt. She showed me how to be an adult. She taught me not to fear my future. She was everything I aspired to be. All of this was true, more or less, so that's what she said, more or less. "Recently, Rosa was training me to take over for her. What a gift this was, to work so closely together. I knew it was difficult for her to hand over the reins to me, a younger, lesser person, just as it will be difficult for each of you, when the end comes, to accept that your career is over. Yet Rosa never let her ego get in the way of a job well done, even if it required, as in this case, relinquishing the job to someone else. I will never forget Rosa Guerrero. She was my boss and mentor but also my friend. She compelled me to dig deep and find my best self, to be kind more often than right. I will never be one-tenth of the woman she was, but I will spend the rest of my days trying." Then she lifted her head, acknowledged her fellow mourners, and stepped down to assume her new role as chief.

HOURS LATER, LUCY was back at work; the office was deserted.

After the funeral, as people were leaving, she asked Leo about his

---

[44] Unless it involved sex, though to call those encounters "intimate" was a stretch.

plans. There was a one o'clock showing of *Eat, Pray, Love*, he said. It promised air conditioning, popcorn, and solitude.

"You sure you want to be alone?"

"Lucy, please. You *don't* have to worry about me." Leo gave her a smile, but his eyes were bloodshot and glistening; under his ruddy sunburn, his skin had broken out. Having gotten thin (too thin, in her estimation), he looked fragile and—God, she hated to think this—old. He hadn't seen Dr. Saul in six months. Should she encourage him to go back? Or would this be overstepping, now that he reported to her? So many questions, so little time, no manual.

The funeral had depleted her, too. There was only one place she wanted to be. So after saying good-bye to Leo (and Rosa), Lucy took the subway down to Ellery, where she swept through the turnstiles while ignoring the reception desk (unnecessary since the Asian guy,[45] and not Manny, was on duty). Up on nine, she passed through the glass doors, headed to her office, plopped down in her clunky chair, and let out a deep, grateful sigh.

For the past decade, Lucy's office had been her refuge. She loved her cheap faux-wood desk and particleboard credenza. She loved her flimsy bookshelves. She especially loved her HANG IN THERE, BABY poster, circa mid-seventies.[46] Rutherford was insisting she move into Rosa's office, but Lucy didn't want to. Not only did appropriating the larger office feel disrespectful, she found its spaciousness daunting. For the whole of her career, she'd been a backroom worker, content to toil unobserved in her closet-size cave. Better to turn Rosa's office into a small conference room.

---

[45] His name, she learned from Manny, was Gerald Leong. He had a BA in economics from Baruch and was headed to law school in the fall, part-time. Married with one child, Gerald lived in Queens, where he enjoyed Mexican food, mid-twentieth century jazz, and restoring vintage cars.

[46] The poster was meant to be an ironic statement about the subjugation of women in patriarchal institutions. Not one of her coworkers got the joke—most figured she just loved cats.

Although it embarrassed her to admit this, Lucy's decision to gun for number two wasn't only rooted in a desire for money and status, or a celestial call to lead, which were the reasons she gave Rutherford and, eventually, the board. The other catalyst was the sickening jealousy she felt upon finding out (from her mother, on yet another Costco run) that her sister, Willa, was pregnant.[47] Before Willa's news, Lucy had awaited her big break (and/or perfect man) in a largely reactive stance. True, she'd "tossed her hat into the ring" when Peter Dreyfus was fired last December, but she wasn't really hell-bent on being Rosa's number two; after all, that job sounded a lot like the one she already had.[48] A month later, however, the W Incident occurred, and Lucy suddenly realized that *time was running out* and *she didn't have a plan.* Should she stay at Ellery? Go somewhere else? Rejoin Match.com? Change careers? Write a novel? Frantic, she googled sperm banks, Single Mothers by Choice, executive recruiters, the Peace Corps, Middle-Aged Matchmakers, and Teach for America. (Also: the Hemlock Society, forever Plan B.) Fingers flying, eyes on the screen, Lucy kept asking, *How did this happen? How the fuck did this happen?* How did her not-very-nice, nor-very-pretty sister, who boasted a third banker husband, a place in Manhattan, *and* a house in the country, also get a baby? How was this fair? All Lucy had was nothing: a worthless apartment in a building that smelled of herring and curried rice, a mid-level job at stupid-ass Ellery, birthday thirty-nine on the horizon (*next up: forty!*), and shameful crushes on unavailable men. She didn't even have a dishwasher.

Rattled as never before, Lucy knew that Dr. Ahmet was the only

[47] A moment so powerfully fraught it was like a dirty bomb detonated in Lucy's brain, shattering all capacity for rational thought. Hereafter, this announcement, made on January 20, 2010, is referred to as "The W Incident."

[48] Should anyone doubt the veracity of this statement, Lucy would quickly point out that if she *were* going to recommend herself for a promotion, would she really say something as trite as "I'd like to toss my hat in the ring" in  a roomful of colleagues? *Please.*

person she could discuss this with—anyone else would call her a selfish, jealous beast. So she scheduled an emergency session, during which she tried to reach into her corroded black heart and pull out a shard of decency. It wasn't easy. When Dr. Ahmet heard her grievances (her sister was pregnant! she had no one! she was so bloated!), he became deadly serious.

"Lucinda, consider the snake that swallows its own tail and still remains hungry."

"*What. The. Fuck. Does. That. Mean?*" Biting off each word, Lucy wanted to shake the man until his eyes fell out. "*I. Am. In. Crisis. Here.*"

Dr. Ahmet pursed his lips. He was not happy with her. "Once more again, this time with slowness. 'Consider the snake that swallows its own tail and still remains hungry.'"

Then it hit her: she was eating herself alive. Yes, she was petty. Yes, she was sinfully jealous. But she could remain forever empty—hungry, as it were—or take action. "I get it!" she yelped, and then raced to the office, where she proceeded to reboot her life on all fronts. So, three weeks later, when Rosa had her stroke in February, Lucy's Lifestyle Upgrade™ was already in full swing. She exchanged her glasses for contacts, colored her hair, and applied a full face of makeup each morning, including dreaded mascara. She bought new suits. Got collagen and Botox injections (don't judge). Wore shoes with high heels and complicated straps. She strategized with Rutherford in secret, said yes to a date with Sanchez, interviewed at Nielsen (just to be sure), and schemed with Leo to protect Rosa's job, knowing in the end it would eventually be hers.

(Included in all this progress was one area she was still figuring out: men. Last fall, Lucy was fixated on Rob's ex-friend Evan, but after her painful New Year's Eve, she was ready to admit he was only a fantasy. Dr. Ahmet agreed. "So tell me, Lucinda," he'd asked. "What is it about the idea of this Evan you like so well?"

"He seemed perfect: he's my age, educated, literate, cares about people, pro-monogamy." He had also, from what she recalled, said something wildly erotic about her mouth.

Dr. Ahmet raised his brow. "Sounds exactly like someone else we know, does he not?"

When Lucy realized whom he meant, the blood drained from her head. "Oh my God." She felt woozy. "How dumb can a person be?" All this time it was *Rob*? She was an *idiot*.[49]

Suddenly, Rob was no longer Rob. Well, he was still *Rob* but an updated, enhanced model: Rob 2.0. The next day, she and Rob strolled to Associated. It was the same walk they always took, same route, same banter. Same puffy coat, same knit hat. But this time it felt different. Rob's shoulders were broader; she saw a boyish glint in his eye; he seemed taller, somehow. Still, he had a family; they were colleagues. To confess her feelings would ruin a decade of friendship, so she kept her mouth shut. *Thank God! Thank God, thank God!* A week later, the W Incident occurred, kicking off Lucy's Lifestyle Upgrade™. Three weeks after that, Rosa had her stroke. So from February through April, Lucy saw very little of Rob. This wasn't just because she was avoiding him—though she was; she was also preoccupied with Rosa and Rutherford. In fact, when Rob was laid off, she realized they hadn't had a real conversation in months. To rectify this—and aware the layoff would shatter his ego—Lucy tracked him down and agreed to meet at Associated. But as soon as he showed up, she knew it was a mistake. Not only was Rob a disheveled mess, in his addled state he'd decided *he* was attracted to *her*. Look, Lucy was the *last* person to pass judgment on someone in the throes of a sexual delusion, but seeing Rob like

---

[49] In fairness, Lucy's feelings for Evan and Rob were more complex than this conversation might suggest. For years, she had dismissed Rosa's claim that she was in love with Rob. She also took umbrage every time Dr. Ahmet referred to "this Evan" as her "fantasy man." Yet they were both right: Lucy didn't love Evan—she loved *the idea of* Evan. (Point, Dr. Ahmet.) And she did love Rob. (Point, Rosa.) In the end, however, all of this became moot.

this confirmed for her a simple, sad truth: any desire she'd felt for him was gone. Now she pitied her friend, especially as he lunged forward and tried to kiss her. It was all too awkward, and because of this—and other reasons—she hadn't spoken to him since.)

IT WAS ALMOST five when Rutherford called. "Did you review the July numbers?"

Lucy was still at her desk. "I did."

"Excellent. By the way, Luce. You did good today." He paused. "I miss her already."

Last January, at the kickoff of her Lifestyle Upgrade™, Lucy read an article in *More*[50] that listed tips for career advancement. One was to schedule a frank discussion with the highest-ranking person she could safely approach. Another was to state, specifically, what she wanted; she had to be direct—like a man, like Jamie Dimon. So Lucy asked the CEO for a meeting, and once they were settled, rather than dick around with vague questions (à la "If you were me what would you do?"), she reached between her legs and grabbed her big balls. "Rutherford," she began. "Thank you for meeting to talk about my future. If you'll turn to page one of your PowerPoint, I've created a chart that tracks my progress over the past decade. As you can see, I've brought a lot to Ellery. I'll go through each bullet in depth, but first I'd—"

Bemused, Rutherford smiled. "Lucy—"

"—like to ask you a question: what do you foresee for me here going forward?"[51]

"Lucy, let's dispense with the PowerPoint." He was still smiling. "I'm delighted you called; your timing is very fortuitous." The CEO picked up a paper clip and began to untwist it.

---

[50] Gift subscription from her mother.

[51] The subtext: her future at Ellery was bound to Rosa's; one could thrive only at the expense of another. What did this mean for her, long-term?

So far, so good, she thought.

"I've been watching you for years. You're smart, well educated, articulate; you do bring a great deal to Ellery. But I believe you can make an even more impactful contribution." He leaned back, his chair squeaking. "Recently, Rosa and I discussed the prospect of my mentoring you, teaching you the business beyond HR. Of course, this is contingent on your interest, so I'd like to hear what you're thinking. Feel free to speak candidly," he added. "We're off the record."

He'd been watching her? For years? Lucy didn't know whether to feel flattered or terrified. "I like it here," she said, aware that he expected honesty, but only up to a point.[52]

"Good to hear. So tell me, what do you want?"

"I *want* . . ." She tried out the word. "I *want* a challenge. I *want* to excel. I *want* to make a lot of money." She also wanted wage equality; recognition for all women, regardless of their age or station; and permanent funding for Planned Parenthood—but one thing at a time.

"But you'd stay? If the situation was right?" Rutherford was sizing her up, which she knew because she was sizing him up, too. "Sure," she said. "If the situation was right."

Thus, their secret partnership was formed. A month later Rosa had her stroke, and Lucy was faced with a heart-versus-head decision. While telling Rutherford felt like a betrayal to Leo and Katie (and Rosa), she also felt she had no choice. Despite what she'd said, they couldn't protect Rosa without involving Rutherford. So after seeing her in the hospital, Lucy cabbed back to Ellery and went directly to the CEO's office.

---

[52] Regrettably, it had taken her many years and much anguish to understand that in business there was no such thing as "off the record." Indeed, as a junior employee, she spent countless afternoons in a postdiscussion frenzy, trying to recall, recalibrate, and recant all the unvarnished truths she'd offered to leadership in the spirit of "honesty."

"How is she?" Rutherford asked.

"Worse than you can imagine." Like seeing a statue topple, she thought.

The news shattered him. For a horrible second, Lucy feared he might cry. "She'll recover," he said. "She's a fighter. But I have to reduce her load, which means—"

Feeling jumpy, Lucy cut him off. "We should restructure HR, move people around."

Rutherford considered this. Like her, he was restless. "Okay, let's play this through. Tell me what you'd do. Assume everyone is up for grabs. Here's what I envision: in the short term, you become deputy, work closely with Rosa, and then take over as chief when she retires."

"And in the long term?" Lucy raised an eyebrow. "You'll replace me with someone younger and hotter?" Although she laughed, it wasn't a joke, exactly.

"I see you in a lucrative executive role, as yet undefined—but the sky's the limit."

That phrase! Lucy blanched.

From that day forward, Lucy kept Rutherford informed about day-to-day life in HR. Soon the CEO would know everything: all the ways they covered for Rosa, their eleventh-floor hideaway, the scheduling charts. He, in turn, told Lucy what was going on at the executive level: how Chuckles Mayfield was trying to force Rosa out, his own ideas for a fake "research" assignment to keep her distracted and Chuckles at bay,[53] why he'd do anything, even risk his reputation, to protect his mentor and dear friend. "If not for Rosa," he explained. "I wouldn't be where I am." All of this came later, though. Back in February, Rutherford was only interested in how Lucy would shift staff around to help Rosa out.

---

[53] Eventually this became the Mergers and Acquisitions Committee, which was really just Rutherford, Lucy, and Rosa sitting in a conference room, talking about plans that would never happen.

So she told him. "Fire Maisie. Give operations to Kenny—or tell him to take a hike. Hire more assistants—young, cheap, hungry—to burn through the grunt work. Give Leo a raise."

Standing at his desk, Rutherford flipped through some papers. "What about Rob Hirsch?" He said this casually, but Lucy sensed backdoor conversations to which she hadn't been party.

What about Rob Hirsch? "You just want my opinion, right? Nothing I say is definitive?" Her pulse raced, foot bounced. "And should anyone ask, the idea came from you?"

Rutherford assured her of this.

"Rob Hirsch is burned out, unmotivated, and we can get two juniors for what we pay him. Even better, we can groom Courtney Adams to do his job, and hire another associate to support me."[54]

Lucy couldn't work with Rob anymore—and it wasn't just because of their complicated relationship. To be chief, she had to do it right, which meant surrounding herself with staff she could depend on, people who realized success meant sacrifice. Rob was dead weight—not just on the department, also on her. If she let him hold her back, professionally or personally, she might pass up, or fuck up, this opportunity, which had the potential to sustain her all the way through retirement; she'd never forgive herself. Rob also needed to move on. If he stayed at Ellery, he'd be stuck on the middle rung of a rickety ladder for the rest of his career.

"This is just talk?" she'd asked Rutherford six months back.

"Of course," the CEO replied. "We're just talking."

Her voice deepened. "Cut him loose."

---

[54] This is how the feminist revolution would begin. She'd promote hardworking, overlooked women, train them to assert themselves, and show them how to run a business with their heads as well as their hearts.

## 27

Lucy hated getting up early, but since February she'd been clocking in by seven thirty. This was due partly to Rosa and partly to her workload, but it was also because she was avoiding Manny Flores (Sanchez Security). In hindsight, she'd acted hastily vis-à-vis romantic liaisons in the weeks following the W Incident. Not that she regretted dating Manny; on the contrary, she was very fond of him. But she could also see how someone else might accuse her of using him as a human tow line to pull her out of the emotional wreckage wrought by her sister's pregnancy.

Lucy and Manny's connection had begun last September—almost a year before—when her keycard started malfunctioning. It would work fine for a week, then suddenly her access to the elevators would be cut off. Each time this happened, the Asian guy had to buzz her in, and she'd trudge down to the basement, where Manny would reprogram the settings. This went on for months, so by March, when she was crazy busy with Rosa, not being able to race through the turnstiles was a real issue. Fed up, Lucy marched down to security, intent on giving Manny, the building owner, and Mayor Bloomberg a piece of her mind. But when she presented her case,

Sanchez admitted shyly, slyly, that the problem had nothing at all to do with the card. "I'm sorry, miss," he said, clearly conflicted about his brazen behavior. "I've tampered with your ID."

"What?" Lucy didn't understand. "Why?"

"Because I wanted to see you. I thought we might have coffee."

"Coffee?" A beat, a turn of the gears, a click, and then . . . "*Oh.*" She felt herself blush. "I see."

"So, would you like to . . . do that?" Sanchez was blushing, too.

At first Lucy said no. How could she? Way too weird. Then she said yes. Because why not? He was nice, he was handsome. Then she said no; she wasn't a snob, but she was a VP and he worked security, what would they talk about? Finally, she offered a vague "Sure, some time." Then Leo got involved. Convinced she and Manny were a match, he reminded her that Willa was having a baby. "She's younger than you, right?" The next day, Lucy put on her tightest dress and highest heels, applied red, red lipstick, and rode downstairs. "I can't believe it," she said, leaning over Manny's desk. "You went to so much trouble just to talk to me."

"You are a very beautiful woman," he said.

At which point she noticed his dark eyes and long lashes. Manny, she decided, was sexy in the rough-and-tumble way of long nights on the road, battered guitar cases, Spanish love songs, and dangerous men with gentle hands. Nor, it turned out, was he a workaday guard; he was the head of Sanchez Security with a BA from St. John's. He was charming, polite, curious about her; and if, at thirty-two, he was a bit young, he made up in enthusiasm what he lacked in maturity. Plus, he owned a Jeep, a Vespa, and a Bosch dishwasher, which was more than she could say for herself. During their handful of dates—which included whipping through the backstreets of Red Hook on the Vespa in the cold, an exhilarating late-night rendezvous she wouldn't soon forget—Lucy maintained a silent monologue. Would Don (Willa's third husband) reprogram her keycard so he could meet her? Would Reggie (Willa's second husband) buy her fingerless gloves? Would Dylan (Willa's first husband) plan a date, text to confirm, show up on time, and kiss her with abandon underneath the Brooklyn Bridge?

No, no, and no, she admitted, lying against Manny's hairy chest. Those guys, all rich, were asshole workaholics. Still, Lucy sensed something missing with Manny—heat, va-va-voom, she didn't know what to call it. Even worse—God, this killed her—he believed she was racist. Her! The girl who, at eight years old, had collected money for migrant farm workers! *Racist?*

"What do you have against Asians?" Manny had asked on their second date.

They were at a bar near his house in Sheepshead Bay. They'd just finished their freezing Vespa excursion, and Lucy's ears were numb and still ringing. Sure she'd misheard, she asked him to repeat his question.

"Why don't you like Asians?" Manny looked her dead in the eye. "We've only gone out twice, but you already mentioned your old boss, Chinese Shame, and the other one. Chang? Eng? Plus, you keep calling my coworker 'the Asian guy.' Why not 'the tall guy' or 'the guy with the birthmark'? Or Gerald—which is his name, by the way. Gerald Leong."

Lucy's face burned. "I didn't mean anything." She wanted to disappear—no, die, that would've been better. "I'm so sorry." Do not, she warned herself, *do not*, bring up the Cesar Chavez fund raiser from third grade.

"Not to make a big thing," he continued, "but I'd feel bad if you called me 'the Spic.'" He cracked a grin. "I don't call you 'the Hot White Girl Whose Keycard I Fucked With.'"

Though this didn't reassure Lucy, she understood what he was saying. In fact, Manny shifted her perspective—not a lot, not about everything—but enough to make her think twice about Gerald the next time she passed him in reception. Still, as much as she liked Manny (and she did, very much), and as good as he was to her (far more than she merited), Lucy didn't love him the way she wished she did, the way he deserved. Deep down, she also felt ashamed of her racism (bias, whatever), ashamed he'd seen it. But rather than act honorably, and explain all this, she cut him off. To wit: when he asked about their future, she resorted, disgracefully, to corporate-speak. "We have different goals, Manny. I don't see us growing together long-term."

"You are so hard," Manny told her.

And she knew it was true.

ON MONDAY MORNING, Lucy heard the muffled ringing of her Black-Berry. She scrambled to find it, but her desk was in shambles. Files, proposals, reports, bills, and other detritus littered one end to the other. Was there no bottom? Her phone! Spying the caller, she did a double take. It was Rob. She put it down and then picked it up, but of course by then he was gone.

His message was excruciating. "Rob here." He coughed. "The funeral on Friday was nice. Well, not nice, God no, I didn't mean nice, I meant it was nice to see you." More coughing. "So listen . . . I uh . . . got a call from someone you may know. Sally Rakoff at JPMorgan? She's the HR division head, who reports to the global director (so many departments over there!). She saw my résumé on-line and asked me in. Well, a recruiter asked, but Sally and I have a phone thing. So I'm hoping you can give me insight into her . . . into her, into her whatever. Thanks."

It took Lucy a minute to compose herself. Then, when she dialed back his new number, she froze. "Hello?" Rob asked. "Lucy?"

She opened her mouth, but no sound came out.

"Lucy?"

"I'm here," she choked out. "It's me; I got your message."

"Oh, hey. . . . Thanks for returning my call. So I was wondering if you knew Sally Rakoff. Oh! And congratulations on your pro-motion. It must feel good to be chief."

"It would, if not for the way it came about."

"You mean Rosa?"

What else could she mean? A beat of quiet, and then she plunged ahead. "Yes, I know Sally. She took my job when I left." (*So* I left, Lucy corrected herself. Sally *stole* my job, *so* I was forced to leave.) "Will you be reporting to her?"

"Not directly. She'll be a few people above me. They're creating a new talent development program, and need someone to oversee it. I'm interviewing for that job."

As Rob talked, Lucy cleaned off her desk (the madness!) and checked her e-mail. She didn't need to hear the details of Rob's interview because she was the one who'd set it up. Sally Rakoff was a sociopath, but she reported to the Stone Cold Fox,[55] whom Lucy had called a month earlier to ask if he could help Rob. At most she'd expected a referral; that the Fox came through with an actual position endeared him to her all over again.

"Great idea to move into training," she said when Rob finished. "It suits you."

"Not really." He laughed. "But out of all the jobs I've had, it's the one I hated least."

"I'm sure you'll do well. When's the interview?"

"Two weeks." He cleared his throat. "Hey, is Leo in? I've been trying to reach him"

Lucy shook her head and then realized he couldn't see her. "Not yet. But I'll have him call you. And Rob?" She sighed. "We miss you; it's not the same here without you."

THE NEXT MORNING, halfway through her first official staff meeting, she received a text from Rob.

Need help! Leo in trouble! Come to his apartment?

[55] Refer to footnotes 3, 4, and 43.

When she looked up, she saw everyone waiting. "Excuse me." She texted Rob back.

Leo called out sick for the past two days.

I'm in a meeting. Can it wait?

Rosa warned her it would be like this, jumping from one crisis to another for ten hours a day. "Forget planning, forget agendas. Forget all of it. The job is a constant fire drill." While Lucy did get a brief taste as number two, Rosa had acted as a stopgap. Now there was nothing behind her but wide-open space and a long, dark fall.

Leo is depressed. Won't get out of bed.

Lucy stared at Rob's text. What would Jamie Dimon do? Would he leave his staff meeting? Would he go to an employee's house? Fuck that. What would Rosa do?

Sorry, can't get away. I'll come after work.

Hours later, she was squinting at the building numbers on Smith Street and deciding on a game plan. Discuss their relationship? (No.) Bring up the kiss? (God, no.) What if he kissed her again? (Rebuff.) Thus, prepared for anything, she hiked up Leo's stoop, but when she stepped into the apartment, Rob barely glanced at her. Instead, he offered a quick hello and then ushered her to the bedroom, where Leo lay on his mattress and stared at the wall. The place was a disaster: dirty clothing strewn over furniture, piles of newspapers, cartons of half-eaten takeout. The air stank of unwashed socks and fried rice.

"Hey Leo," she said softly. "How are you?" He didn't answer, so she turned to Rob. "How long has he been this way?"

"Since the funeral."

"Where's Thomas?"

"The Virgin Islands," Leo said bitterly, his voice thick with tears. He rolled over to face her. "On vacation. Couldn't be bothered to cancel his plans—"

"You told him to go!" Rob cut in. "The vacation had been planned for months. You told him not to miss it. You said you'd be fine without him!"

"He's forty-four. He should know what's appropriate behavior. But whatever, I don't care. You said it yourself, Rob: there is no point to anything. All we do is live and then die."

Lucy looked at Rob. "You said that? When?"

"Right after he got laid off," Leo said. "He was totally despondent."

His tone was accusatory. Lucy wondered if he knew that Rob's layoff was her doing. Either way, she was accountable, a concept that left her queasy. Rosa had said to expect this, too. "The job makes you feel powerful and powerless at the same time. People will hate you." And sometimes, Lucy thought, they'll be justified.

Leo started to cry. "I don't know what to do with myself."

Her throat closed. "Leo, I understand you feel lost with Rosa gone. You miss her—we all do. But you need to see Dr. Saul. He's a professional; he can help you get through this."

Leo scoffed. "This isn't about Rosa. *This is about my life.*"

"Your life is in transition," Rob said. "A lot of things are changing, you're in a new relationship, you're sad about Rosa." He was using a therapeutic tone Lucy had never heard before, not in the entire decade she'd known him. Was this Leo's influence, or was Rob in therapy too?

"Should we order dinner?" she asked. "I'm happy to stick around."

Leo said he wasn't hungry. "I appreciate you coming, but I just want to be alone. I had no idea Rob called you."

"She's your boss," Rob said. "She should know what's going on."

Turning to Lucy, he told her Leo needed a few days off. "Just to get himself together."

"I'm also his friend, Rob." She didn't like being relegated to the sidelines. (She was here, wasn't she?) "Of course, Leo, take all the time you need." (Although she probably shouldn't have said this.) She bent down to pat his shoulder. "Call me, please."

"I'll walk you out," Rob said.

Steering her into the hallway, he moved with crisp efficiency, as if he had a host of people waiting in the wings. All day Lucy had wondered what it would feel like to see him. Now, trailing behind him, she knew: it felt like bad timing, missed chances, impossible scenarios, and a long story ending. "I'm glad you called." She didn't want to talk to his back, but the hallway was too narrow for her to squeeze beside him. "I wish there was something else I could do."

"That you came is a lot."

They reached the front door. She wished they had more time—so much to say!—but he ushered her out. "Luce?" He touched her shoulder, gently. "I want to be friends." He spoke atonally and quickly, as if he'd rehearsed this in front of a mirror.

"I want to be friends, too, Rob," she said, though this wasn't exactly true anymore. "Everyone misses you at work." This, on the other hand, was very true.

"We'll talk soon," they both said, offering air kisses and corporate hugs.[56] "I'll call you."

"I DID THE right thing," Lucy told Dr. Ahmet the next day. "With Rob *and* Rutherford." She sat up straight, anticipating the therapist's approval. When he didn't respond, Lucy prompted him. "I think my actions reflect a lot of *progress*. I'm replacing bad habits with new behaviors."

---

[56] To hug corporate-style, create a circle with your arms around a colleague's shoulders. Lean forward. Do not touch torsos. Do not touch necks or faces. No body part except upper arms should make contact.

Still nothing.

Did he not hear her? "Particularly with Rutherford. Because of *my* work with *you*, I can see that flirting with my boss is self-destructive." She tilted her head expectantly. Funny how Dr. Ahmet had to be silent and withholding for her to care what he thought.

When he finally responded, he was uncharacteristically sharp. "You are the mighty lion, Lucinda, who has no pride."

This sent Lucy reeling. "Excuse me?" He sounded so critical! Lucy's leg bounced so frantically she would soon achieve liftoff. Rearranging herself only got the other leg going.

"Lucinda, I must tell you this once and for the end. You are traveling the wrong way. The source of love is not found atop the mountain; it is *inside* the mountain, it is *of* the mountain, it is the *mountain itself.* You climb and climb, yet you remain alone and"—Lucy couldn't make out the next word. It sounded like *perverted*, but that had to be wrong. What therapist would call his patient a pervert? "This is difficult for the both of us."

"Why is it difficult for you?"

"The bird soars only when she leaves the nest. This I would like to see."

Lucy panicked. Was he breaking up with her? Oh, how the tables had turned! All this time, she'd believed she could see him as long as she wanted, that he'd continue to offer soothing if convoluted aphorisms until . . . well, until she died, basically. "You want me to leave your nest?" she asked quietly.

Perhaps sensing her distress, Dr. Ahmet shifted to a more melodic register. "Not my nest, Lucinda. Listen to me: None of these men interest you. Not the EMT or the Recruiter-slash-Trainer or your CEO. They are all one and the same. I did have hopes for the Doorman—"

"Manny? He works in security; he's not a doorman."

"Be that as it may, he is a possibility for later, not a *poss-i-bil-i-ty* for now. For now, you must understand who all these men represent.

Consider this with your big brains. Who are you always the most wanting of? Who are you always never speaking about but always bereft of?"

Lucy had no idea, though this could've been a result of his poor grammar. (What she wouldn't give to whip out paper and pencil and diagram his sentences.)

"The father is the son of the man, Lucinda. You are of the mountain; the mountain is inside you. You cannot fly free unless you release yourself."

"The mountain is my father?" Now she was annoyed. "All my problems go back to him? That is so fucking reductive!"

"I did not say *all* your problems come from the Deadbeat, but you must explore those that do. Lucinda, you listen, but do not *listen*. There is a difference, no? I think again of the goat, not up on the mountain but down in the valley. Which is why we must speak of your grief over the Deadbeat's long absence. We must also speak of your grief over your Wizard, who has passed on. We can no longer dwell always on the sisters who compete for the mother's love. One of the sisters is to be a mother herself. And perhaps she has never competed; perhaps it was only you. Your behaviors, when appropriate, are not always kind, and when kind, not always appropriate."

Lucy's face reddened. She knew this, of course she did; she should be helping Willa choose a crib, not ignoring her calls. The idea of her little sister having a little baby filled Lucy with unexpected warmth. She loved Willa deeply; she'd love Willa's baby, her niece, just as much. She made a note to call Willa and tell her this. Maybe she'd also call her mother; it would make the old bird happy to hear from her. "It's so ironic." Shamed, Lucy wanted to cry.

"What is ironic?"

"What does 'ironic' mean? Is that what you're asking?"

Dr. Ahmet shook his head. "You forget that I too am a man of fine education. I know what 'ironic' means. I meant what is the situation that is of irony?"

"I didn't mean to offend you."

"I am not offended, Lucinda, though you can be offensive, yes. (I refer to what you told me about your Security Man and his Asian friend, how he called out your prejudices.) But this is another defense we can speak of later; for now we must focus. What is ironic?"

"I've been thinking about quitting therapy."

"Since when?"

"Since our second session." Admitting this (finally!), Lucy felt liberated.

"That was five and a half years ago, Lucinda."

"Please don't take it personally, Dr. Ahmet. It's not you. I don't listen, which is obvious, given that it's years later and I'm still doing the same stupid shit. But maybe I've been in therapy too long. Maybe I'm just immune to the process."

"I disagree. You have made several changes. You are Chief. You did not chase the Recruiter-slash-Trainer or the CEO. You broke it off with the Security Man for sensible reasons. You will be, I suspect, a wondrous leader. Yet your heart still aches."

"So I shouldn't quit? I mean, I really don't want to."

He shrugged. "I do not know what to tell you, Lucinda. As I have said, I am not the kind of doctor with the answers. I am the doctor who can only pose the questions."

Surprisingly, Lucy was calm. Her foot, she noticed, no longer bounced. All these years, she'd been waiting for one grand epiphany that would assuage her mental turbulence, but maybe this— confidence in her job, faith in her loopy therapist, a plan to come back—was as good as it got. Christ, who knew that therapy—sitting in a chair and talking about herself—could be so demanding? Luckily, Lucy Bender never shied away from hard work.

"I think we're done," she said, using her newfound earnestness. "But I'll be back next week. And Dr. Ahmet? It might take awhile to sort out this 'father of the man' thing. You know that, right? You won't give up on me?"

"I won't give up," he assured her. "And do not worry. Time flies like an arrow."

"Fruit flies like a banana," she shot back.

It took him a second. Then a tiny laugh escaped his lips. "You made a joke!"

Smiling, Lucy gathered up her things.

"Fruit flies like a banana." The good doctor was still chuckling as she saw herself out.

## 28

ROBERT HIRSCH,
CANDIDATE FOR DIRECTOR OF TRAINING,
JPMORGAN CHASE

AUGUST 2010

Rob could tell Leo felt a lot better. Although still sad—grief is a process, he kept reminding Rob—he was definitely out of the woods. "Don't worry," Leo said. "I'm seeing Dr. Saul tomorrow, and then once a week for the foreseeable future."

Riffling through a tie display, Rob was relieved to hear this. It was Thursday morning, and they were in the Men's Wearhouse near Wall Street, trying to find a suit for his interview. JPMorgan was his first real lead since he lost his job three months back, and Rob was determined to make the most of it.

"I told Lucy I'd be back in the office on Monday. Also"—Leo turned his head, suddenly bashful—"Thomas is home. He only went on vacation because I insisted—he really didn't want to miss Rosa's funeral. So, uh, yeah. You were right."

Rob held up a red tie embossed with silver banjos. "Too much?"

Leo covered his eyes. "Ugly, cheap, dated, and what's with the pattern?"

"Not for you. Is it too much for me?"

"Oh . . . for you, it's fine." Plopping into a chair, Leo sighed. "I hate Men's Wearhouse."

For someone who supposedly felt better, Rob thought, Leo was very cranky. "This interview is important, none of my suits fit, and this place is affordable." He held up a second tie, this one solid navy. "This one?"

"Better." Leo pulled out his phone. "Rule of thumb: patterns on ties are a *shonda*. Second rule: one high-quality suit beats five shitty ones." Head bent, he was texting. "Third: let's go to Barneys."

"Do you even know what a *shonda* is? I'm Jewish, you're not."

"A shame upon your people." Leo smiled. "Thomas says Men's Wearhouse is fine, and don't let my snobbery influence you." He offered Rob his phone. "Wanna see his text?"

"Just tell him I say hi." Scanning the ties, Rob felt a wave of panic; why were there so many choices? He looked for a salesman. "Little help, please?" Rob thought shopping with Leo would solve all his problems; instead he was chasing after a skinny man with a yellow tape measure looped around his neck like reins. "I'll be right with you," the man said, turning back to a beefy guy appraising himself in the mirror.

The store was crowded for a Thursday morning. Why weren't all these people at work? Probably because of the two-for-one sale. *Two for one!* Rob still couldn't get over it.

"Thanks again, Rob," Leo was saying. "Like I said, you were right about Thomas. Sorry I was so difficult."

"No apology necessary." While rarely right about anything, Rob had been spot-on about Thomas. Still, he felt no need to say "I told you so." It was enough to see Leo back on his feet. Inconsolable after Rosa's funeral, Leo had lain in bed for four days with a worried Rob by his side. Then he stopped answering his phone, and Rob spent another stressful few days hunting him down. Leo wasn't Rob's only problem, by the way. Maddy, feeling the pressure of his unemployment, kept suggesting ways to reduce their expenses, but they were mostly his pleasures (cable TV, video games, booze), as if to punish him for losing his job. Similarly, Allie was sick of seeing his face. ("So, Dad, don't you have, like, anywhere to *go*?") But Rob's biggest ass-pain, by far, was his father. Concerned about his son, Jerry drove down from the Cape to lend moral support, which in his mind meant asking questions. So all weekend, Jerry interrogated him: "Did you call my buddy Stan? Did you call Mom's friend Terry? Did you call your sister? Should I reach out to my old team? Seriously, why didn't you call Larissa?" Between Leo's hysteria and Jerry's pushiness, Rob wanted to throttle them both.

*Men*, he thought now. *Such drama queens.* Heaped on the checkout counter were two suits, six shirts, four ties, two belts, two packs of socks, two sports jackets, and two raincoats.

"That's quite a haul," Leo said, handing the guy his credit card. When Rob protested, he insisted. "This is my birthday present to you." Rob was turning forty-four next week, the day after his interview.

"Thanks, Leo." Rob didn't want to argue, particularly since they'd just spent the past three days together. Seeing his friend so miserable had stirred something in Rob. Refusing to let Leo wallow, he'd gotten him up, showered, and out of the house every morning. As it happened, wandering around town like tourists was relaxing for both of them. They rode the train out to Coney Island (Leo complaining the whole time), strolled through the Met (Rob bought postcards for the kids, a mug for Maddy), and ate hot dogs on the steps of the New York Public Library. Rob was living off severance, so while he wasn't feeling the money crunch yet, he knew it was coming.

"Christ, it's hot," he said as they left the store. Both men broke into a sweat.

"Let's go to a movie," Leo suggested.

"Can't. The kids have a half day at camp, and I promised them an outing this afternoon. We're going to Prospect Park or Jones Beach. You can come with us if you want."

"I'd rather set myself on fire—which may happen if I don't go inside." Shielding his eyes from the sun, Leo mopped his face. "What about this weekend? Maybe a double date?"

They were almost at the subway. "I'll ask Maddy." She and Leo had a mutual admiration society, for which Rob was grateful. Since his layoff, her admiration for him had taken a beating, so Leo's presence in his life boosted his standing at home. "Thanks again for the clothes, Leo." Rob paused. "Hey, did you tell Lucy about grad school yet?"

"I'm waiting until I'm back in the office. I think it's a face-to-face talk."

Recently, Leo had told Rob that he needed a career change. Apparently Rosa had been pestering him for years to make a long-term plan, but it wasn't until she died that he felt motivated to act. After much discussion, he decided on a second master's, this one in social work with an emphasis on elder care. He'd applied for January admission at Hofstra, which meant he'd have to leave Ellery or reduce his hours, which was fine with him; he was sick and tired of the corporate grind. More important, the current had carried him long enough. "Seems pathetic to begin a brand-new career in my forties, but what's the alternative? Reporting to Lucy until I retire? At least this way, I'm choosing a direction." Hearing this, Rob felt envious. He was starting over, too, but it was hardly his choice; unlike Leo, he remained in the river, being ferried along with no say and no idea where he'd end up.

Rob shifted the Men's Wearhouse bags into his left hand. He was looking forward to his second shower of the day. "Lucy will support your decision," he said, believing this to be true. "She wants the best for you."

Leo corrected him. "Lucy wants what's best for Lucy. She's a hustler. How do you think she became chief?"

"It's not like she wasn't qualified, Leo. Even if Rosa hadn't . . . um . . ."—mindful of his friend's feelings, Rob hesitated—"gotten sick, Lucy would've taken over eventually."

"Not for years. Rosa wanted Peter to be number two, and when he left, Lucy saw an opening. Don't kid yourself, Rob. She's manipulative. It was her idea—You know what? Forget it. It's not important. You said she's barely crossed your mind lately."

"She hasn't," Rob lied, his curiosity piqued. As Leo took out his MetroCard, Rob grabbed his arm. "How is Lucy manipulative? Finish your sentence. What was Lucy's idea?"

"If I tell you this, Rob, you can't unknow it."

"Now you have to tell me." A rare breeze wafted through the heavy air. Turning his head, Rob stopped to drink it in. "Tell me, Leo."

"According to Rosa, Lucy was having secret meetings with Rutherford about the HR department. In fact this last restructuring— her promotion, Kenny taking on operations, layoffs, all of it—was her idea, not his."

Hearing this, Rob's stomach dropped. "It was *Lucy's* idea to get rid of me?" He didn't believe it. "How did Rosa find out she was working with Rutherford?"

Leo shrugged. "No clue."

"So it may not be true." In the hospital Rosa had been confused and paranoid; she barely made sense. She'd probably concocted stories about all of them; Leo was too close to know.

"It may not be. Either way, it's business, Rob; you can't take it personally."

"Lucy *got me fired*, Leo. *Of course* I can take it personally." Rob's cheeks burned with the sting of a slap. "Why am I only just hearing this now?"

"I knew it would hurt you if I said anything. You have very naive ideas about the kind of person Lucy is. She does whatever it takes to get what she wants."

"You *just said* it may not be true. Make up your mind." Rob didn't know what to think. Lucy *loved* him; she was *in love* with him, she said so herself. (She had also said these feelings were gone. Rob couldn't understand how you could just unlove someone, but when he saw her at Leo's apartment last week, she'd been distant and chilly.) It made sense, didn't it? That Lucy was underhanded? That she'd set him up? This scared Rob: If all these years he'd been wrong about her, what else had he missed? How stupid was he, really? "I don't believe Lucy would do that," he said emphatically.

"Believe what you want." Leo had already swiped his Metro-Card and was standing on the opposite side of the turnstile. "I'm just relieved she's out of your life."

OCCASIONALLY, AFTER ROB hung out with Leo, he'd think about Evan. He never made it to Victor's opening, though he googled it, and he saw a candid shot of his friend (ex-friend, rather) holding his aged father's arm. Sometimes, too, he got the urge to speak to Evan. Once or twice, he went so far as to compose an e-mail (Hey Evan, been thinking about you) but never sent it. In his mind, their bar outing had taken on the glow of magic hour: two best buddies, shooting the shit, howling like maniacs. Still, he knew there was no going back, not to Evan, not to Lucy. You can't fall in love like a kid when you're a fully grown man. That whirlwind sweep of *now it's gonna be different, now it's gonna change* never pans out the way you expect. Nine times out of ten, it ends abruptly, like a punch in the face. How can someone occupy your every waking thought for years and years, and then vanish in the mist? Rob didn't know; they just do. He sees this with his kids. *Daddy, daddy, daddy*, they say, *Sasha is my best friend. I love her so much*. Take it down a notch, girls, he warns. But still, they get carried away; still, they feel their feelings. And years from now, they'll think of Sasha with fondness, with memories tinged only barely with truth because they won't remember their friend, they'll only recall the sweeping, the *daddy, daddy, daddy* that spun them around and around.

"BUT DADDY, YOU *promised*." A few hours later, Rob's ten-year-old daughter was whining, while he lay on the couch, trying to ignore her. "You *said* you'd take us on an outing."

Jessie was a tall kid, with dark hair and olive skin that tanned golden brown, a near-perfect blend of her parents. Fortunately for her, she had less him and more Maddy. Sinking into the overstuffed club chair, she propped up her sneakers on the coffee table. From his position, Rob could see their bottoms, which were god-awful filthy. Had she walked through tar? If Maddy were here, no way this would be happening, not the nasty sneakers on the furniture, or the whining, or the cherry Popsicle dripping off her fingers. But Maddy was at work, so Rob was on duty. He wouldn't mind a Popsicle himself, actually.

"The beach is too far, Jess. It's already two thirty; the day is almost over. Why don't you and Allie go to the park?"

"Because you *said* we'd do something *together*. That means *you too*." Frustrated, she waved her hands, and Rob studied her chipped red polish and, on her wrist, a frayed purple bracelet and the gluey remains of a stick-on tattoo. Christ, I love this kid, he thought.

"I don't want to go out," her older sister, Allie, said. Unlike Jessie, Allie was built like a peasant, short and stocky; sadly for her, more him than Maddy. "Stop whining, Jessie," she added in a tone so reminiscent of her mother that Rob had to smile. "You're being a baby."

"But he *said* we'd go somewhere fun. And now we're just sitting here, doing nothing."

Jessie was right, but Rob had offered to go on an outing at ten o'clock last night, when he was half-asleep and cocooned in his air-conditioned bed. At that time, Prospect Park was a cool meadow with enormous shade trees, where he could ogle wealthy women with long, tender legs. Now, in the light of day, it was a sun-scorched desert, a Mad Max apocalypse, where they'd hike up dusty mesas and bake on a burned-out playground. "Okay, okay." Rob forced himself up, off the old, dilapidated couch where the soggy cushions had formed to the shape of his body. He loved his couch, and leaving it was like bidding farewell to his only true friend. "We'll go to the park. I'm a man of my word."

Leaping out of her chair, Jessie hugged him. "I love you!" she squealed, which made Rob want to burst. But he was no idiot. This was only temporary, so he had to make hay while the sun shone. In a few years she'd be as old as Allie, and then no one would be laughing—unless it was at him, and cruelly.

Standing by her side, Allie didn't look five years older than Jess. She was only two inches taller, with zero boobs, whereas her younger sister was unusually developed for just-turned-ten. Rob knew Alison's flat chest bothered her, but only because Maddy had told him so. There were limits to what his girls shared, even with Maddy; they mostly "swallowed their feelings" (an expression Rob recently learned). When he was growing up, everyone "swallowed their feelings," so it surprised him how well informed Maddy was about the kids' interior lives; to his mind, parents and children were better off ignorant of each other's despair.

"It's like a hundred degrees out," Allie said. "Why can't I just stay here?"

Why couldn't she stay here? Why couldn't he? Why couldn't they all grab handfuls of snacks, blast the air, and check in with their friends on TV? "We had plans for an outing, dear daughter," Rob said. "Find your hat, put on sunscreen, and let's go."

Allie stalked off, stringy ponytail swaying; Jessie was behind her, a bounce in her step.

Rob sighed. In the past three months, Allie had grown sick of him. His dad jokes were lame, his observations uninteresting; his very existence, it seemed, pissed her off. It occurred to him that she'd probably been sick of him for years; he'd only started noticing these past three months. Before that, he was gainfully employed, and didn't have time to notice—or care, frankly—if his kid considered him a capital-L Loser.

When Allie returned, he pulled her aside. "We'll go for an hour, tops."

No eye roll this time, just a heavy sigh. "Whatever."

"Whatever yourself," he said, with bite. Then relented. "After, we'll go to Louie G's for ice cream."

Since he'd been fired, Rob's home life had undergone a dramatic shift. The first couple of weeks were rough; he had no idea how to organize his time or where to park himself. Everything felt out of sync. His family rushed off while he idled at the table (or, more accurately, in bed). His internal clock was calibrated in hour-long intervals (9:30–10:30 staff meeting, 12:00–1:00 lunch, 3:00–4:00 constitutional with Lucy), so he found the long stretches of unbridled time disconcerting. Still, his intentions were pure—each night, he created a to-do list and call sheet for the next day, set his alarm for six thirty, and only allowed himself one hour (or two) of TV— but by his third week he was sleeping till eleven, eating Hefty Man brunches (eggs, bacon, pancakes, the works), and punching out by three. (He was also jerking off, frequently.) As a result, he and Maddy argued, mostly about his lethargy and lack of "proactive plan" (her words), after which he'd burrow under the covers, where waves of depression acted like a narcotic. Leo was a big help, though; he nagged Rob, relentlessly, about scheduling his days. So by Rob's second month post-Ellery, he had a routine. He got up (relatively) early, jerked off, ate Fiber One twigs with fruit, and embarked on at least four solid hours of job search. Then he ate lunch and (sometimes) jerked off. In the afternoon, he hung out with the girls after school. They did homework, which he checked with Talmudic concentration, ran errands (groceries, hardware store, dry cleaners), went somewhere fun (museums, movies), and made dinner. By the end of June, the girls were out of school and in day camp, so their moods were much improved. Rob still hadn't found a job, but he was in a better mood too. The house was running smoothly. He felt closer to his kids, Maddy was happier, and he didn't want to throw up every time he remembered he was out of work. In fact, if not for his money anxiety, Rob didn't mind being laid off, not completely. It was nice to enjoy breakfast with his family, eat lunch in front of the

TV, and stroll through the neighborhood. It was fun to jerk off while he had the place to himself. It was a gift to spend hours with Jessie and Allie (eye rolls notwithstanding), learn their habits, get to know them as people. Granted, the shadow of despair clouded his vision. But once he'd accepted its presence, the feeling became so familiar as to be comforting, like a dark mole that he studied every day but was likely benign.

And then, at the end of July, a visit to Lenox Hill Hospital had altered Rob's worldview. (He disliked the expression "game-changer" but there it was.) When he stepped into Rosa's room, his senses went into overdrive. He was assaulted by the smell of disinfectant, boiled food, and something else—old age, maybe, or sickness. Down the hall, he heard moaning. Then a tray fell to the floor with a bang, and Rob felt shaken awake. Recently he'd told someone, Leo probably, that he considered dying in the office the worst way to go, as if other ways would be somehow pleasant. But looking at the ghost of Rosa Guerrero and thinking of his mother, Rob suddenly remembered a critical fact about death: there is no good way to die when you're not ready. Losing a job wasn't losing a life. Losing a life was losing a life. Losing a job was a setback, a wrinkle, and it behooved him to get up off his fat ass and find a new one—fast. He was still alive, wasn't he? Wasn't he?

He felt Jessie tug at his T-shirt. "Daddy, I am *so, so, so, so, so* hot." She'd given up on this outing sooner than expected—fifteen minutes in, by his count. This time he had no problem saying "I told you so, Little Buffalo," ruffling her hair to make it funny; well, he tried to ruffle her hair, but it was stuck to her head. "Didn't I tell you it would be hot? Let's go." He glanced at Allie, who approved. "We'll get ice cream."

As they left the park, they passed a teenage girl who looked to be Allie's age. She was in the family way, having swallowed, along with her feelings, a baby the size of a beach ball. *That,* he told Allie silently, *is what's called a cautionary tale.* He often talked to Allie in his mind, imparting fatherly wisdom, to which she listened with keen interest and admiration. In response, she told him she loved him, that he was the best dad in the whole world.

"Wow," Allie said a few beats later. "That pregnant girl was so young!"

And her skirt was so short! And why can't you wear a T-shirt over your bra top? Why must we all see your underwear? "I know," was all Rob said. "Too young to be a mother."

"Allie, can you imagine being a teen mom?" This was from Jessie.

"Don't even say that, Jess." Allie crossed her arms in front of her chest, as if warding off an unwanted advance. "A baby is the last thing I need. Besides"—she tweaked her sister's hair—"I still have you to take care of."

"I just turned ten," Jessie said, but without conviction. She loved when Allie coddled her.

Listening to them, Rob beamed. *Maybe I'm not such a bad father.* Now that he had time to take inventory from a 360-degree perspective, he found himself questioning his competence. According to Leo, he was a superstar, particularly compared to Leo's dad, but Rob wasn't so sure. First of all, Leo's father didn't set the bar that high; and second, Leo had a habit of making astute observations about the girls that never occurred to Rob—not just deep shit, but gimmes even an idiot could pick up. A few weeks back, for instance, Leo was over for dinner. When the girls were out of earshot, Leo remarked on how well they got along, despite their age difference.

"Funny, too, how they switch back and forth; one minute Allie's in charge, next minute it's Jessie. Girls are so interesting. They function on many levels, a lot more levels than boys."

Maddy agreed. "But most people aren't insightful enough to see that."

This had concerned Rob. *Like me?* he'd wondered. *Am I not insightful enough?* He knew he had a tendency to miss nuance. But was this an everyman thing, or a Rob thing?

"Hey Allie," he said now, licking his chocolate cone. "If you ever want to talk about anything . . . your friends, boys, your life . . . I'm here, you know."

Her vanilla cone was dripping; Rob handed her a napkin. "I know, Dad; but I'm okay," she said, a reply for which (despite everything) he felt relieved.

LATE THAT NIGHT, he and Maddy were in bed, naked. In general, their sex life hadn't suffered since Rob lost his job. But now he couldn't get hard. This had never happened to him. Well, except for last fall (when he was also preoccupied with Lucy), which made it twice in less than a year. Christ, he felt shitty about himself.

Lying beside him, Maddy patted his hand. "You're going through a lot, Robby—looking for a new job, worrying about me and the kids, missing your friends—"

"I see Leo all the time."

"I meant Lucy. Have you heard from her?"

"Not since May." Rob felt a pang. "I called her about JPMorgan, but that's it."

"Well, that *sucks*." Sitting up, Maddy switched on the light. "You were friends for ten years!"

Rob thought about their kiss. "Lucy and I were work friends, not life friends."

"Leo was your work friend, and now he's your life friend." Maddy shook her head. "*You* got laid off, not Lucy. In fact, she got promoted! Calling you is the decent thing to do. You know what? Fuck her. You have Leo. You'll get another job. You'll make more friends."

It touched Rob to see Maddy so protective. "You're right, I do miss her, and it is shitty she didn't call. But . . ." He closed his eyes. "Leo told me she was working in secret with Rutherford to reorganize our department; that, basically, she orchestrated my layoff."

"Rob! That's awful. Why didn't you tell me?"

"I only just found out." Rob rolled onto his back. "I also don't want to believe it. God, I feel so stupid." He stared at the ceiling. "Maddy, do you think I'm unperceptive?"

"Because you didn't know Lucy was a snake? God, no. I found her self-absorbed and ambitious, but it never occurred to me that she could be so deceitful. It's unconscionable."

"No, it's business, and I was barely hanging on. I'm not defending her, but I was in a hole and couldn't dig myself out. Anyway, I don't just mean Lucy. I feel like I'm constantly missing things about people—Allie and Jessie, for instance, like I'm oblivious to their complexities; I don't see beneath the surface. I feel like you know them better than I do. Even Leo understands them in ways I don't. And I worry that this is because I lack insight."

"I understand the girls because I am a girl. Leo is extra empathic, which is why he's such a good friend. We live on different frequencies; it's not only about insight." She paused. "I'm really sorry about Lucy. That's just shitty."

"Very shitty." Leaning over Maddy, Rob shut off her light. "You should go to sleep. You have to get up early. I love you a lot, and feel lucky to be married to you."

"I love you, too," she replied. They kissed good night and drifted off. "I wish I had a job," Rob said eventually, but Maddy was already sleeping.

TWO DAYS LATER, on Saturday, Rob and Leo went to see the movie *Inception*. Maddy had taken the kids to the beach, and Thomas had a shift at the diner, so it was just the two of them.

"Rosa's lawyer called," Rob told Leo as they inched toward the box office. "He asked me to come to his office, something about her will. He was very cryptic." They paid for tickets, then went to the concession stand, where he ordered popcorn. "One with butter, one without—actually, no butter on either—and two Diet Cokes." He turned to Leo. "I've lost seven pounds already. My new suit is already a little baggy."

"Are you seriously telling me about your weight?" Leo said. "Please stop . . . Anyway, the lawyer called me, too. He wouldn't tell me anything over the phone, either. I'm seeing him Wednesday. Why don't you see him the same day? We'll go out for lunch after."

"Can't Wednesday. My interview with JPMorgan's at noon."

They made their way into the packed theater. Rob found seats, but when he sat down, Leo gave him a funny look. "Move your bag." Leo waved at the empty seat between them, where Rob had tossed his backpack. "Someone will have to sit there."

Rob was puzzled. Why did Leo care? "If someone comes, I'll move my bag."

When the lights dimmed, Leo was still annoyed. No one tried to claim the empty seat, but for the next two hours, Rob could feel him fidgeting; he also kept sighing loudly, as if making sure Rob knew he was pissed off. Soon Rob was pissed off, too. Leo was distracting him, which made it hard to follow the movie. True, *Inception* had a lot of freaky shit going on, so he probably would've missed most of it anyway, but still. Why didn't Leo just admit something was bothering him? How was sulking being an Authentic Person?

"Everything okay?" Rob whispered at one point.

"Everything's *fine,* Rob."

Clearly everything was not fine, but this wasn't Rob's fault. He had been overly solicitous of Leo all afternoon. Being an Authentic and/or Perceptive Person, frankly, was fucking exhausting. By the time the movie ended, Rob was miserable.

"Do you want to grab dinner?" he asked, trying to act chirpy but sounding false.

"I'll pass." Leo averted his eyes. "I have a lot to do tonight."

"Leo, did I offend—"

Leo blew up. "Yes, Rob! You did."

"I don't mean to sound stupid, but I'm drawing a blank here."

This made Leo angrier. "Your backpack? The extra seat?"

Rob shrugged.

"You never sit next to me! The last time you didn't, I was like 'Okay, the theater is empty,' but this time the place was *packed*. So the *only reason* you'd force me to sit *two seats away* is so people won't think we're a gay couple. It's *exactly* like the time we met Thomas!"

"Leo, that is not true." Was it true? Rob didn't think so; he and Evan had always left a seat in the middle. If someone asked to sit down, they moved over. Until this moment, Rob had never given it a second thought. But was Leo right? Was he a homophobe? "Leo, I promise I didn't put a seat between us because I'm afraid what people will think. I always put my bag on the seat, which we can both agree is rude, but not a hate crime."

"You *always* put your bag on the seat? Even when you're with Maddy—or Jessie and Allie?" Leo shook his head. "I can't see it, Rob. Sorry."

"I think you're"—Rob was about to say "overreacting," but that never went well. And it was true he always sat next to Maddy and the kids. But if it was just Evan or another guy, they usually left a seat in the middle. "Leo, I'm totally fine with you being gay—"

"Well, good for you, Rob. Aren't you evolved!"

"Don't be nasty, Leo. I'm not making excuses. I know I'm a caveman when it comes to gay men—gay people, gay whatever, in-dividuals. But I haven't spent much time thinking about the issue. I didn't have gay friends—not because I rejected the idea, because I traveled in different circles. Regardless, my best friend is gay, so I have to rethink my behavior. You've had decades to consider every aspect of your gayness. I've had a few months."

"I feel like that's just an excuse, Rob."

"Well, it's not. What about respecting my Authentic Self? I'm trying to be honest, but you're not giving me a chance. When we were growing up, being gay was forbidden. I never hugged my male friends. We used words like 'retard,' 'spaz,' and 'faggot.' They were an integral part of my vocabulary—a reflexive part—like 'idiot,' 'fool,' 'doofus,' 'nerd,' and 'geek.' 'Retard' and 'fag' were no more insulting than 'geek' and 'doofus'; they were all equally insulting, but also words I used all the time. I understand now that these words are offensive, I also get why. Leo, let me repeat. *I understand that 'faggot' is an offensive word.* But I have to train myself to think and act differently. I never thought an extra seat means I'm homophobic, but maybe it does. Maybe I have all kinds of deep-rooted prejudices. I'm not evolved, but I'm evolving. I know 'midget' is offensive—they're 'little people'—but I only just learned that 'Eskimo' is too. The proper term is 'Inuit.' I'm college educated, I read the paper, I'm in *HR*! But Leo, I'm willing to change. It just might take awhile, and I might not get everything right. I am doing my best, though."

"Okay," Leo said, calmer now. "I understand what you're saying."

"Your friendship is important to me." Embarrassed, Rob studied his hands. "When I was first laid off—Christ, Leo, you saved me, mostly from myself. You've helped me be a better father, maybe a better husband, definitely a better man. But it would also be nice if you gave me the benefit of the doubt. You can't keep looking for ways I'm insulting you, because I'm not; I'm just a stupid schmuck. There's no malice behind what I say or do; and frankly, I think I've proven this, several times."

Leo's face reddened. "You brought Thomas to the hospital. If you hadn't, we might not be together."

"I wouldn't go that far." Rob glanced at his watch. He was hungry. He wanted to sit in air conditioning and eat a side of beef. He wanted to be with his family. "Why don't you come for dinner? Maddy and the kids will be there."

Leo's "sure" was automatic. Then he paused. "How could you not know about the Inuit? I love you, Rob; I do, but sometimes you're an idiot."

## 29

When people learned Rob was an in-house recruiter, they often asked for job-hunting tips. Regardless of their age, gender, income, or industry, he'd always said the same thing: it was all about connections. Over time, Rob's advice changed. Now it was 2010, and there was an Internet with supersonic search engines. Networking alone wasn't enough. These days, it was a numbers game: cast the widest net to get the most bites. So when Rob left Ellery, he started fishing. He called people he hadn't seen in ten, fifteen, twenty years. Then he hit the web. He posted his résumé on Monster and fifty similar sites, joined LinkedIn and Facebook (ugh). Filled out online applications for jobs that likely didn't exist. Chased after twenty-four-year-old hiring managers, who surely shredded his résumé as soon as they hung up. He called his sister, Larissa, who was warm, gracious, and thrilled to help. "I'll do whatever I can, Rob." She invited his family to her home in Woodstock so all the cousins could hang out. "I miss you," she said, which made him realize he missed her too. Why had he doubted her? What the hell was his problem?

Encouraged, Rob widened his circle. He dipped his toe in the

PTA(!). Joined the Neighborhood Watch. He engaged anyone, everyone. One day he spied his former colleague Gus "Cappy" Cuomo schlepping through the streets, wearing sloppy cargo shorts and a frayed boonie hat. Rob's first instinct was to flee, but instead he trotted up to Cappy and tapped his shoulder. His ex-coworker turned, Rob stared into Cappy's eyes, and there it was: the burned-out zombie gaze of the unemployed. So he extended his hand, told Cappy the latest, and invited him for a drink. "I'm in touch with people," he said. "Call me." Though Cappy gave him a nod, Rob could see the guy was clearly on the ropes, waiting—hoping—for the final wallop. "Call me, Gus, or I'll call you. I'm serious. I *will* follow up." For all he knew, six months from now, he would be Gus. Anyone could. Falling off the grid is an incremental process. First shaving goes, then suits then ties then Dockers then soft sweats then pants with seams. Nothing is unusual when the scale is small; you accept the unacceptable bit by bit, you unwind and unwind until you're unwound, and then one day you're broken.

So with all this activity, all this goodwill, when Sally Rakoff contacted him, Rob was feeling confident. He'd put in the hours, made the calls, reached out to people he barely remembered who barely remembered him. He'd endured humiliation, rejection, and abject stupidity that bordered on spitefulness ("You graduated in *1988*? Before *computers*?"). But it was worth it. JPMorgan Chase had an actual position in an actual department. "Overseeing corporate training and development," Sally had said on the phone. "HR material—discrimination classes, conflict of interest—and some subject matter. Our classes are mostly online, but a few are in person. You'll have your own staff, three full-time and a paid summer intern."

"My own staff?" Rob didn't mean to sound surprised.

"Yes," Sally said. "Is that a problem?"

That Rob found Sally Rakoff terse and full of herself was inconsequential. (When he mentioned Lucy, Sally was cold to the point of brittle. "I don't remember much about Lucy," she said dismissively. "We worked together ages ago.") But Sally was only his first hurdle, a phone screening. His next hurdle—today!—was an in-person interview with Tessa Phillips, the team lead; if that went well, another in-person meeting with the unit head. Sally had called Tessa "a real pro," which Rob saw as a positive sign. Plus, the money was right, the benefits decent. The stars, it appeared, were finally aligned.

That morning Rob got up at eight, shaved, showered, donned his new suit, and strutted into the kitchen like the cock of the walk. The kids had already left for camp, but Maddy had a doctor's appointment in the neighborhood, so she was working from home. She didn't have to say a word; when she looked up, he saw it in her face.

"Wow!" Maddy exclaimed. "You look great!" to which Rob responded by voguing for the invisible paparazzi. She clapped with enthusiasm. "But isn't the interview at noon?"

"I have to run a few errands first." Rob poured himself Fiber One and coffee, then joined Maddy at the table. "I want to head in early; feel like a real commuter." He traced the letters of his OBER mug, which he'd soon have to call his BE mug.

Before leaving the house, Rob grabbed his new trench coat. It was double-breasted with wide lapels and cool secret spy pockets. Wearing it, Rob felt like James Bond, that is, if James Bond was an unemployed Jew living in an overpriced walk-up with a wife and two kids.

"Why are you wearing that coat?" Maddy asked. "It's ninety degrees out."

"Rain," Rob replied, squinting up.

SO AGAIN, MADDY was right. Rob didn't need the coat, which he was forced to tote around town like a body bag. The sun, high and hot overhead, baked his scalp, so he spent most of the morning hunkered down in Starbucks. Along with the heat, the crowded trains, crowded sidewalks, and crowded crowds conspired to dampen his spirits, but he drank water and read over his notes. His phone rang. It was Leo. "Rob . . . you won't believe . . . Rosa . . . made me . . ."

"What?" Rob shouted, but when Leo repeated himself, he still couldn't understand, so he stepped outside, into the wall of heat. "Start again; take it slow."

"I just met with Rosa's lawyer! She made me the executor of her will. Apparently, Nando tried to push her to change it, but she refused. She stood up to that asshole!" Leo started to cry.

"What's wrong?" Were these happy tears or sad tears?

"I miss her, I miss Rosa. But I'm proud she took on Nando; it must've been so hard."

"I'm sure it was—Leo, I don't mean to cut you off, but I'm standing on the street, and I have to prepare for my interview."

Leo's next sentence came out in a rush. "Rob, Rosa left you twenty thousand dollars."

"Ha ha. Funny. I have to go. It's ten thousand degrees out; I'm sweating my balls off."

"Really, Rob. Rosa left you money in her will. Twenty grand."

"Why would she leave me money?" Despite the heat, Rob was shaking. Twenty thousand dollars? *Jesus Christ*. He imagined Maddy's smile when he told her the news. "That makes no sense."

"She said you and Maddy should put the money toward an apartment."

"My *own* apartment?" Now Rob was the one crying. "Are you serious?" Happy tears, definitely. What a world, he thought. What a world.

AN HOUR LATER, Rob's good luck had turned. As he sat across from Tessa Phillips, VP of professional development, his suit was again drenched, only this time it was flop sweat. The most important interview of his career, and Rob was choking.

"So Rob, what do you bring to JPMorgan Chase?" Tessa asked.

Rob wasn't prepared, not for this. Tessa was thirty-one, with silky blond hair that fell to her shoulders. Her crimson lipstick was tasteful but sexy as hell, as were the black glasses she put on to read. She wore a navy suit, crisp blouse, and shiny high heels with red soles. She was warm, professional, generous of spirit, and seemed interested in what Rob had to say. ("No," she told him. "I didn't cross paths with Lucy, though I've heard great things about her.") But he was off his game. All she wanted was breezy conversation, and Rob had prepared for a dissertation defense. He'd studied corporate training psychology and tactical applications. He could spout statistics, run scenarios, and devise creative solutions. Thanks to Kenny Verville, he had anecdotal background on the bank, as well as street gossip; thanks to Facebook's lack of security controls, he knew more about Tessa Phillips than he probably should. Rob was primed for battle—ready to stroll in, open his spy coat, whip out his guns, and shoot up the room.

"Rob?"

"Oh, sorry. What was your question?"

Tessa blinked, her eyes glazed over. The interview, Rob knew, was done.

"What do you bring to JPMorgan?" Her welcoming lilt was replaced with a dial tone.

"I have years of experience working in the training arena, a solid record of success, and a strong work ethic." Rob hated himself for this answer, which sounded like he'd memorized his résumé. He hated his cheap suit and sunburned head. He hated his raincoat, which hung off his chair like the shorn pelt of a bear. Mostly, he hated that at forty-four fucking years old (tomorrow!), he was being forced to go through this fucking exercise in order to feed his fucking family. Where was the justice? Where the fuck was the justice?

"Great," Tessa said, with the enthusiasm of an undertaker, which was fitting because Rob wanted to be buried alive.

The problem, he decided, was her youth. That she was pretty

didn't matter. Or smart (MBA, U of Chicago, BS, U of Chicago). Or female. He'd worked for great-looking, genius women before—his boss at Revlon, with her melon-size breasts and Harvard pedigree, had fueled many a midnight fantasy. But he had too many years on Tessa Phillips. Tomorrow Rob would be closer to forty-five than forty; soon he'd be fifty, then fifty-five, then sixty. At thirty-one, Tessa Phillips was a generation younger. His elder daughter was almost fourteen. Tessa Phillips was one whole Allie his junior. The math was crippling.

Tessa was scanning his résumé, feigning interest. "Why do you want to move into training when you've spent so much time in recruiting?"

Another gimme. "I like working with people, younger people especially. I like giving back, helping them do their jobs better and shape their careers."

"Well, some of our employees are considerably older. Recently, we've acquired several companies, so we do a lot of reeducation. You'll have lots of trainees in their forties and fifties."

"I like working with old people too," Rob said. "*Older* people, I mean."

Tessa glanced at the clock.

*Help!* Rob screamed. *SOS!*

They volleyed, and things picked up. Rob recounted stories of HR insanity, which made Tessa laugh. He shared a colorful anecdote about a senior executive, a notorious bully, making sure to include the dramatic pauses and kooky inflections that always got laughs at dinner parties. "Our training involved videotaped role-playing. Of course the guy balked—he canceled three times—but when we finally got him in front of the camera, his inner thespian emerged. He forgot he was being taped, and launched into a cyclonic tantrum. To the guy's credit, when he saw himself on film, he felt badly. 'I had no idea,' he kept saying."

Tessa seemed impressed. "You have a nice way," she said,

disarming Rob with her candor. "I bet people enjoy having you as their supervisor. You're very approachable and warm. We need someone like you in our group. Everyone is so anxious these days."

Turning red, Rob mumbled, "Thanks." Hearing the praise—which he liked very much—he remembered Rosa. Earlier Leo had mentioned that Rob wasn't the only Ellery employee to benefit from Rosa's largesse. Breaking all rules of confidentially, Leo told him that he'd also inherited cash, as had Kenny and Peter Dreyfus. "Just a token amount." For Katie, Rosa set up a college fund. "Lucy got nothing," he added. "In case you were wondering."

But Rob had been focused on Peter Dreyfus. "That criminal?" he squawked.

"She loved him," Leo said simply. Everything else—her apartment, furniture, investment funds—went to Marcy, Nando, her nieces and nephews. "Despite her fears, she didn't end up broke." Neither will I, Rob thought. Thanks to Rosa.

"My sister oversees a hundred people," Tessa was saying.

"She works in banking, too?"

Tessa nodded. "At Goldman. Her management style is brutal, which I think is cultural. Chase isn't as rough—at least not our group. We believe in nurturing younger staff, not beating them up. On the other hand, she's an investment banker; I'm in training, so it's different."

Hirsch couldn't be sure, but he thought he sensed layers of conflict baked into Tessa's comments. "Is your sister older or younger?"

"Older. Older and bossy." Tessa smiled. "But, you know . . . sisters."

"I have two daughters, and it's like kabuki theater watching them interact. Girls are so complex." He made a leap—an iffy one, but already flailing, he had little to lose. "I spend a lot of time helping them with their homework, and I've noticed they both learn very differently. Allie, the older one, is self-motivated and likes to solve problems on her own, whereas her sister prefers a group setting where she can listen to ideas and talk them through. So if I were to develop a training philosophy and strategy—which is the first thing I'd do—I'd consider all the different ways people can approach the same material."

"Interesting," Tessa said. "We do some variations on our curriculum, but not much."

"Well, at least we have a starting point." Rob was revving up. He could turn this interview around; it didn't happen often, but it wasn't impossible. He recalled Rosa's advice, all the hours she'd spent with him. Get it together, she'd say. Come on, Robert. Dig deep. Find your best self. "Tessa, I hope I didn't seem distracted before." On one hand, he knew pointing out his poor performance ran counter to every interview rule ever espoused. On the other, he wanted to win—he *needed* to win—but on his own terms. Turned out, Rob Hirsch had an Authentic Self, too. "But on my way here, I got news about my former boss. Rosa Guerrero? Ellery's HR chief?"

Tessa shook her head. She didn't know Rosa.

"Rosa died recently, and apparently there was infighting over her will. The story did have a happy ending, but it was upsetting all the same. Rosa was a mentor and a friend. She changed my life." Rob stopped. It occurred to him that this was true: Rosa had changed his life in ways he was only first beginning to see. During his layoff, one of the last things she'd said was, "Rob, you'll do great things in the future, you just won't do them here." At the time, he'd bridled at what he thought was a snarky insult, but in fact she was being earnest and encouraging. Not everyone, Rob told himself, is out to get you.

"How so?" Tessa asked.

"Rosa convinced me to focus on training. She said I understand and encourage without being pushy." Rob flashed a killer smile. "That's only half-true. I do push—and hard—when I have to." He was raring to go. "So Tessa, you mentioned recent mergers. I assume you're referring to Bear Stearns and Washington Mutual. I'm interested in how we're integrating these employees; which on-boarding platforms are in place; where we might need to supplement. Can you walk me through everything you're doing, starting with timing?"

"Sure!" Tessa's face was a wide-open book.

Rob was in. He felt it in his bones.

IT WAS THREE o'clock and still blazing outside when Rob emerged from the subway like a drawing of evolution, only backward. Instead of the fish-amphibian-ape-caveman-salesman motif, he came out fully dressed and stripped naked. Up on the street, he shed his raincoat, jacket, tie, and shirt, all of which he stuffed into a Duane Reade bag. By the time he reached his block, he was down to a discolored undershirt.

Rob picked up his pace. Maddy would be home from the doctor, and he couldn't wait to share his good news. Tessa had invited him back! They needed someone as soon as possible. "We're prepared to make a deal quickly," she said just as he was leaving. "I'm positive everyone will like you as much as I do. Plus, you come highly recommended."

He had a job! Holy Christ, he had a job! Rob knew it was risky thinking this way. With nothing in writing, a deal isn't a deal; it's a hope, a wish, a dream as yet unfulfilled. But he could hedge later. Right now, he wanted to envision himself gainfully employed, with a salary, benefits, keycard, and staff—a staff!—all his own.

Could this be true? Could it really be happening? No way, no fucking way.

But look at him—look at Rob Hirsch, the way he races up his front stoop. Look at him reach the top step and turn his key in the lock. Look how he rises up, up, up the stairs to the third floor, where Maddy, his better half, is waiting inside. Rob knocks on the door to let her know he's home. "I'm coming in!" he calls out. "Get ready." And still he is rising, light as a feather, stiff as a board; still he can feel his future unfurling before him like a long red carpet laid out in his honor. Look at Rob, look at him, swollen with joy, flush with good fortune, a man among men, and rising, still rising.

# EPILOGUE

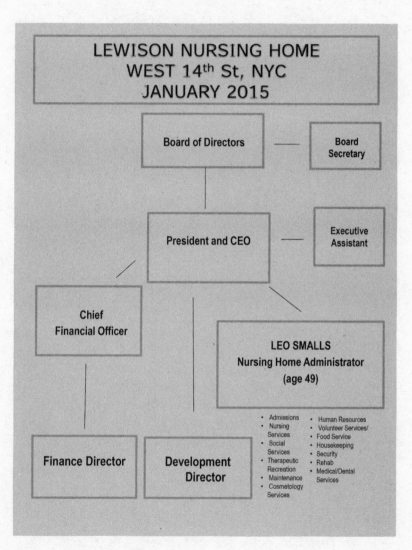

LEWISON NURSING HOME
WEST 14th St, NYC
JANUARY 2015

Board of Directors

Board Secretary

President and CEO

Executive Assistant

Chief Financial Officer

LEO SMALLS
Nursing Home Administrator
(age 49)

Finance Director

Development Director

- Admissions
- Nursing Services
- Social Services
- Therapeutic Recreation
- Maintenance
- Cosmetology Services

- Human Resources
- Volunteer Services/
- Food Service
- Housekeeping
- Security
- Rehab
- Medical/Dental Services

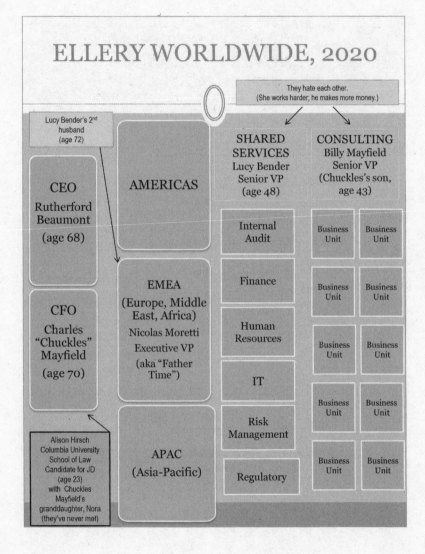

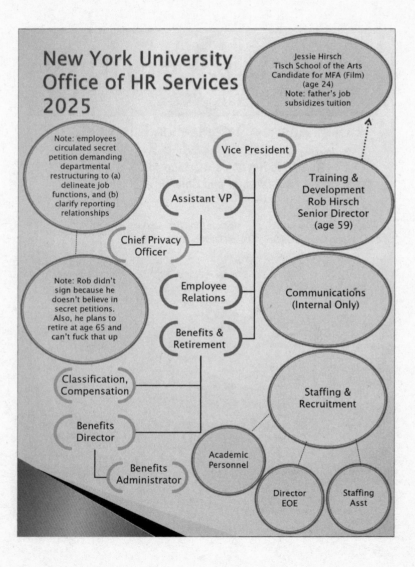

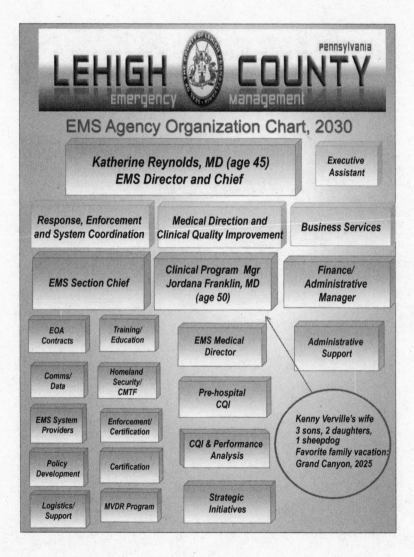

# LEHIGH ☩ COUNTY
### pennsylvania
### EMERGENCY management

## EMS Agency Organization Chart, 2030

**Katherine Reynolds, MD (age 45)**
**EMS Director and Chief**

Executive Assistant

Response, Enforcement and System Coordination

Medical Direction and Clinical Quality Improvement

Business Services

EMS Section Chief

Clinical Program Mgr Jordana Franklin, MD (age 50)

Finance/ Administrative Manager

EOA Contracts

Training/ Education

EMS Medical Director

Administrative Support

Comms/ Data

Homeland Security/ CMTF

Pre-hospital CQI

EMS System Providers

Enforcement/ Certification

CQI & Performance Analysis

Kenny Verville's wife
3 sons, 2 daughters, 1 sheepdog
Favorite family vacation: Grand Canyon, 2025

Policy Development

Certification

Logistics/ Support

MVDR Program

Strategic Initiatives

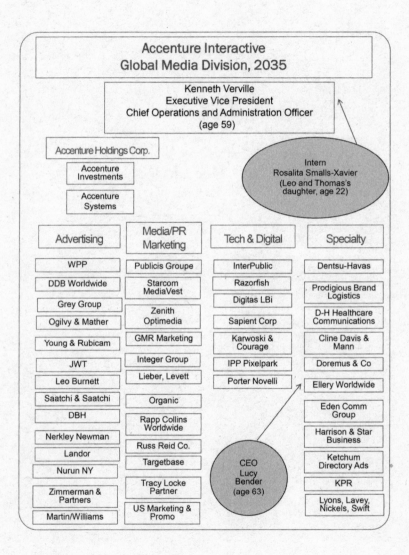

# ACKNOWLEDGMENTS

BY 2008, my career as a writer had hit the skids. I hadn't sold a book in eight years, my second novel tanked, and my third was rejected by twenty-five publishers. Desperate and disillusioned, I called Jen Gates[57,58] and presented my case for quitting—not writing, necessarily, but publishing—along with the seeds of an idea for a literary novel about work. I mentioned the idea only in passing; at that point, I didn't just lack the skill set for such an ambitious project but men dominated the niche and my books[59] skewed female. Plus, my track record was dismal. Plus, I'd just quit.

While I rattled on, Jen mostly listened. Finally she said, "Oh, you could definitely write that book." She said a lot of other things, too—wise, measured, thoughtful things about what it would take,

[57] While this makes it seem like no big deal to pick up the phone and start wailing to a brilliant, high-powered literary agent, Jen coedited my first novel, *Hunger Point*, so I'd known her a long time. In 1997, she left HarperCollins and joined ZSH Literary (now Aevitas), where she became the rock star she is today.

[58] What? You thought I was done with the footnotes? They're my favorite part of the book!

[59] Funny/sad family sagas.

not just about the art but about the commerce. "It won't happen overnight," she made clear. Even so, a corporate novel wasn't out of the question. On the contrary, she was taking the idea—she was taking me, the broken writer, washed up at age forty-five—seriously. "Let's focus on the book you're writing now,"[60] she advised. "And then, in a couple of years, we can turn our attention to the next one."

Never gonna happen, I remember thinking.

———

DEEP GRATITUDE AND big love to:

Jen Gates and Aevitas Creative Management, especially Esmond Harmsworth, Todd Schuster, Lane Zachary and Allison Warren.

Emily Griffin and Harper/HarperCollins, especially Tracy Locke, Jo O'Neill, Nikki Baldauf, Stephanie Cooper, Frank Albanese, Jonathan Burnham, Kate McCune, Sara Nelson, Tina Andreadis, Amber Oliver, Lillie Walsh, Janice Suguitan, Kate Walker, Carolyn Zimatore, Peter London, Virginia Stanley, Leslie Greenfield, Miranda Ottewell, and everyone who worked so hard in support of this book.

Nicole Dewey[61] and her partners at Shreve Williams PR.

Special thanks to Jane Rosenman who, upon finishing an early draft, said, "It's good, but where's all the stuff about HR?" thus helping me elevate this manuscript from a typical, run-of-the-mill novel to a cultural phenomenon.[62]

Todd Lane for all the laughs especially when everything went sideways.

Aon Consulting, Deloitte, and the Segal Group, especially my

———

[60] *I Couldn't Love You More*, which sold in 2010 to Grand Central Publishing, where I met the equally brilliant, generous, creative, hard-working, and all-around-amazing Emily Griffin.

[61] Nicole's reputation preceded her. Everyone I asked told me she was one of the savviest, smartest, and biggest-hearted publicists in the business. So of course I was skeptical; no one's that good, right? Uh, wrong. She's all that and more.

[62] Someone had to be brave enough to say it.

bosses and their bosses who encouraged me when it would've been easier to do otherwise: David Blumenstein, Randy Carter, Patrick Donohue, and Jen Schuster.

Drs. Nan Jones and Karen Hopenwasser for saving my life and then saving me.

The Writers Room in New York City, Virginia Center for the Creative Arts.

My beloved work-friends and life-friends for their careful reading, enthusiasm and shrewd counsel: Ann Bauer, Karen Bergreen, Laura Cochran, Marcy Dermansky, Robert Ellis, Emily Listfield, Colleen Magee, Jeff Masarek, Erin Naumann, Victoria Skurnick, Lynn Schnurnberger, Diane Swisher, Nick Tarrant, Ettore Toppi, Lily Vakili, Laura Zigman.

Naomi Medoff, Lewis Medoff, Kim Worth, Mara Medoff, Joy Dawson, Steve Nakata, Patrick Butler.

Keith Dawson, for illuminating my world every day, in every way.

Sarah Dawson, Liv Dawson, Mollie Dawson: the reason, the reason, the reason.

## About the author

## About the book

## Read on

Insights,
Interviews
& More...

# Meet Jillian Medoff

© Nina Subin

JILLIAN MEDOFF is the author of the national bestseller *I Couldn't Love You More*, as well as the novels *Good Girls Gone Bad* and *Hunger Point*. A former fellow at MacDowell, Blue Mountain Center, Virginia Center for the Creative Arts, and Fundación Valparaíso, she has an MFA from NYU. In addition to writing fiction, Jillian has a long career in management consulting and is currently a senior consultant at the Segal Group where she advises clients on all aspects of the employee experience. ∾

# Reading Group Guide

Discussion Questions
for *This Could Hurt*

1.  One could say that *This Could Hurt*
    is a novel with five protagonists.
    How does the author distinguish the
    five characters from one another?
    Was there a character you related to
    more or cared about the most?

2.  What did you make of Rosa and
    Rob's misunderstanding over the
    loan? Have you ever had a
    misunderstanding like that at work?
    How did it get cleared up?

3.  The epigraph from Miss Manners
    says, "Employees are not to be treated
    the same as family." But clearly in
    *This Could Hurt* it happens. What are
    some examples of personal
    relationships and familial roles that
    the different characters play?

4.  Which of the friendships in the book
    grow closer over time? In the case of
    Lucy and Rob, do you think their
    friendship was doomed from the
    start? How do the characters'
    relationships outside the office grow
    and change?

5.  How does this novel relate to the
    Me Too movement? Does Peter's
    behavior toward Leo constitute
    sexual harassment? Should Leo
    have told Rosa about it? ▶

6. How does Ellery generally treat its employees? How does it treat an employee going through a rough patch in his or her personal life? Do you think this fictional company is kinder or harsher than most workplaces that you've been in?

7. Were you surprised when members of Rosa's staff tried to protect her job when her health faltered? Would that ever happen where you work?

8. Is Lucy's power play justified? Do you think that it is viewed more harshly by Rob by virtue of her being a woman? Have you noticed differences between female and male bosses in your own work experience?

9. How does Medoff use typical elements of corporate communications (i.e., organizational charts, footnotes, etc.) to deepen the story and drive the narrative forward? What about at the very end of the book? What does the story of the engagement survey say about the ways in which corporations operate?

10. How does Kenny's father's job serve as a contrast to the work that these employees do at Ellery? Do you sense a divide between manual labor and military work and the kind of desk jobs that the Ellery employees do?

11. What was your impression of human resources as a field before reading

*This Could Hurt*? Did it change after you finished the book?

12. Have you ever read another book set in a workplace? What similarities did it share with *This Could Hurt*? How did it differ? ✑

# I Refuse to Be the Office Mom

*"I Refuse to be the Office Mom" originally published in* Lenny Letter *on January 23, 2018. Republished with permission from the author.*

I refuse to be the office Den Mother. True, I'm perfectly suited for the position: middle-aged, middle manager, generally forgiving, with a deep understanding of my business (corporate communications). Also true: I'm a mother in real life. But of all the roles I've played in my career—and after several decades in management consulting, there've been several—Den Mother would be the absolute worst.

The requirements for Den Mother are surprisingly steep: maturity (though not necessarily age; I'm fifty-four, which is more typical, but I've seen women as young as twenty-three get saddled with the position), a take-charge attitude, a willingness to arrive early and stay late, and the ability to get shit done with no complaint. (Den Mothers often double as Martyrs; more vocal female employees are generally ignored, or scoffed at, then ignored, or sent on long business trips and ignored from afar.) And yet, despite the high bar for entry, a Den Mother's work is demeaning and her rewards are meager.

If I agreed to be Den Mother, along with performing my own job, I would be expected to clean up everyone else's messes—in the communal kitchen, on the shared-file drive, with pissed-off clients—while teaching my adult colleagues the difference between right and wrong. ("Bob, we don't clip our toenails at our desks. The office is a public space." "Sally? Sally? Sally! Put down your phone. We're in a meeting.") I'm supposed to be the older, frumpy, shapeless, sexless female who always has a stapler, never raises her voice, and pesters the team to submit their expenses. But I won't do it. Yes, I'm a feminist. Yes, sexual harassment disgusts me. But I am too fucking busy to be the in-house cop. *You're grown-ups*, I find myself shouting (silently). *You should know how to act.*

It wasn't always this way. When I was first starting out, raring to go, eager to please, and thrilled to have a job, I was grateful to play the Dutiful Daughter. I love my father—I love men in general— so when my (mostly male, mostly older) bosses offered insight and guidance, I accepted their help with grace and humility. Same with female managers— over the years, I've had a series of women mentors whom I have admired and emulated and whose advice I still seek. The Dutiful Daughter was a youthful phase, and, like youth, it ended quickly, with a bittersweet sting.

By my late twenties/early thirties, I was evolving into the Ingénue. Smart, savvy, and indefatigable, I was happy to flirt and to feign delight when more ▸

senior men (and occasionally women) showed interest in my work—and in me. Sure, there were inappropriate overtures and questionable behavior, but that's a different conversation. Single, childless, and ambitious as hell, I lived fearlessly, saying, "yes, yes, yes, I'd *love* to," whether it was a swanky client dinner or a last-minute trip overseas. I understood my role and kept myself in check, especially when things crossed the line. (The Ingénue is alluring because she's unattainable.) As long as she's got looks, moxie, energy to burn, and nothing to lose, the Ingénue dazzles. But the clock is always ticking, and the party eventually ends.

By thirty-seven, the fun was winding down; exhaustion had settled in. I was pregnant, married with two stepdaughters, and still—always—working. Forty came, then forty-five, and suddenly I was the Beck-and-Call Girl who never said no. "Thank God for you," my manager used to say. Then she'd pause. "Hey, do you mind taking over Entropy for Mike?" *Did I mind?* Of course not! Beck-and-Call Girls live to serve; we love being *productive*, feeling *important*, knowing we're *vital to the operation*. Beck-and-Call Girl was a great role—at first. I made lots of money, was promoted several times, and if my coworkers found me bossy and overbearing, what did I care? In addition to kids, I had a second career as a novelist, so being bossy enabled me to triage my clients, my family, and my books.

But there were downsides. In business, success begets success, and work begets work, which means the more I did for Mike, Mark, Susan, and Celeste (and my kids and my husband), the less each one of them did for themselves. Along with turning in lousy first drafts, they skipped meetings and missed deadlines, knowing I'd pick up the slack. So, I might've been thriving and flush, but I was also overworked, overwrought, and desperate for sleep. Beck-and-Call Girl was burning out.

Now, at fifty-four, Den Mother beckons. These days I'm wedged between the executives and the junior staff. (Likewise, my kids are older, but my parents are, too.) Demands come from all directions. Some tasks I despise but they're part of my job; I do them to stay employed: teaching associates how to answer the phone, reminding consultants to track their billable hours, nudging my boss to approve vendor bills.

It's the other tasks I can't abide, the ones I'm obliged to do simply because I'm a premenopausal female and (ostensibly) nonthreatening. I don't know exactly when I crossed into Den Mother territory, but here are actual sentences I've said to my coworkers in recent months: ▶

### I Refuse to be the Office Mom *(continued)*

- *No, you can't bring your dog to the office; there are liability issues.*

- *Please walk faster; we're going to be late.*

- *Why do you keep arguing? Just do as I ask; we'll discuss my reasons after the call.*

- *I don't know why Lauren doesn't like you; maybe it's because you're mean to her.*

It's not just trivial stuff, either. Now that the #MeToo movement is picking off predatory employees and has HR departments scrambling for cover, who do you think is expected to police bad behavior in the office day to day? That's right—the Den Mothers; women of a certain age who, having survived our own #MeToo moments, are no longer taking any shit. We're the ones expected to censor, interrupt, and confront offenders. ("Uh, Bob? Whipping out your penis during a performance review is inappropriate.")

No. Just no. I won't do it. I won't be a Den Mother. Instead, I'm paid to be a boss, so I act like one. This means I . . .

- Delegate: Team members are employees, not children; they're getting paid, too.

- Give clear instructions, including deadlines, when assigning projects, so there's no ambiguity in what I expect.

- Confront problems and enforce consequences.

- Lead by example: Meet my deadlines, hit my sales targets, track my hours, and submit my expenses. This way, my solid performance eclipses my gender.

- Maintain boundaries: I only discuss my age, weight, pap-smear results, and Botox when I'm with other women of a certain age.

And you know what, younger colleagues? You shouldn't be a Den Mother either. Not now, not ever. One thing I've learned in all my years of working (and mothering) is that people will step up when called upon. So the next time you're thrust into a thankless role, follow my lead: Shake your head, move aside, let someone else bear the load. What happens next will amaze you. ⌒⥈

"A WORKPLACE SAGA WITH HEART." —NPR.ORG

"Periodically a writer captures the pattern of comedy and tragedy that peppers office life like alternating colors of carpet squares. . . . As smart as Medoff's critique of corporate inanity is, it's tempered by compassion for these people, who are ultimately tender with each other, too. . . . Medoff finds plenty of hurt—but strains of hope, too."
—RON CHARLES, *WASHINGTON POST*

"This smart, jaunty novel takes the lid off a small company's faltering human resources department to reveal intrigue and backstabbing that only intensify when the boss gets sick. But, as Medoff deftly reminds us, decency can find a way of surfacing even among the filing cabinets." —*PEOPLE*

"This bighearted dramedy of manners stars Rosa, one of the most intriguing characters ever to walk the halls of an HR department, and her supporting cast of flawed but devoted employees."
—*O, THE OPRAH MAGAZINE*

"A refreshingly authentic portrait of corporate America and the varied souls that dream, conspire, flounder, and triumph there. . . . A very enjoyable book." —JOSHUA FERRIS

"An incredibly funny, incredibly human book. And it is, I think, maybe the best book I've ever read about what work means, about how to do it better, about how to manage people, about how to be a good colleague, about the intrapersonal relationships of an office. . . . I haven't read something with as much pleasure in six months."
—DAVID PLOTZ, *SLATE*'S *POLITICAL GABFEST*